PRAISE FOR THE WRITING OF ROBERT SILVERBERG

"*Nightwings* is Robert Silverberg at the top of his form, and when Silverberg is at the top of his form, no one is better. A haunting, evocative look at a crumbling Earth of the far future and a human race struggling to survive amidst the ruins, full of memorable characters and images that will linger in the memory, this is one of the enduring classic[...]   [...]tin

"What wonders and adventures[...]   [...]P. OF —Ursula K. Le Guin

"No matter if Silverberg is dealing with material that is practically straight fiction, or going way into the future . . . his is the hand of a master of his craft and imagination." —*Los Angeles Times*

"When one contemplates Robert Silverberg it can only be with awe. In terms of excellence he has few peers, if any." —*Locus*

"The John Updike of science fiction."
—*The New York Times Book Review*

"In the field of science fiction, Silverberg occupies a place in the highest echelon. His work is distinguished by elegance of style, intellectual precision, and far-reaching imagination."
—Jack Vance

"One of the very best." —*Publishers Weekly*

"Robert Silverberg is our best . . . Time and time again he has expanded the parameters of science fiction."
—*The Magazine of Fantasy and Science Fiction*

"He is a master." —Robert Jordan

AT
WINTER'S END

AT
WINTER'S END

The New Springtime, Volume 1

ROBERT SILVERBERG

OPEN ROAD

INTEGRATED MEDIA

NEW YORK

Cover design by Kelly Parr

ISBN 978-1-4804-4850-6

This edition published in 2013 by Open Road Integrated Media, Inc.
345 Hudson Street
New York, NY 10014
www.openroadmedia.com

AT
WINTER'S END

An axe-age, a sword-age, shields shall be sundered;
A wind-age, a wolf-age, ere the world falls.
The sun turns black, Earth sinks in the sea,
The hot stars down from heaven are whirled;
Fierce grows the steam and the life-feeding flame
Till fire leaps high about heaven itself.

—ELDER EDDA

Everyone on earth for a million years or more had known that the death-stars were coming, that the Great World was doomed. One could not deny that; one could not hide from that. They had come before and surely they would come again, for their time was immutable, every twenty-six million years, and their time had come 'round once more. One by one they would crash down terribly from the skies, falling without mercy for thousands or even hundreds of thousands of years, bringing fire, darkness, dust, smoke, cold, and death: an endless winter of sorrows. Each of the peoples of Earth addressed its fate in its own fashion, for genetics is destiny—even, in a strange way, for life-forms that have no genes. The vegetals and the sapphire-eyes people knew that they would not survive, and they made their preparations accordingly. The mechanicals knew that they could survive if they cared to, but they did not care to. The sea-

lords understood that their day was done and they accepted that. The hjjk-folk, who never yielded any advantage willingly, expected to come through the cataclysm unharmed, and set about making certain of that.

And the humans—the humans—

1

The Hymn of the New Springtime

It was a day like no day that had ever been in all the memory
of the People. Sometimes half a year or more might go by in
the cocoon where the first members of Koshmar's little band had
taken refuge against the Long Winter seven hundred centuries
ago, and there would be not one single event worthy of entering in
the chronicles. But that morning there were three extraordinary
happenings within the span of an hour, and after that hour life
would never again be the same for Koshmar and her tribe.

First came the discovery that a ponderous phalanx of ice-eaters
was approaching the cocoon from below, out of the icy depths of
the world.

It was Thaggoran the chronicler who came upon them. He was
the tribe's old man: it was his title as well as his condition. He had
lived far longer than any of the others. As keeper of the chronicles
it was his privilege to live until he died. Thaggoran's back was

bowed, his chest was sunken and hollow, his eyes were forever reddened at the rims and brimming with fluid, his fur was white and grizzled with age. Yet there was vigor in him and much force. Thaggoran lived daily in contact with the epochs gone by, and it was that, he believed, which sustained and preserved him: that knowledge of the past cycles of the world, that connection with the greatness that had flourished in the bygone days of warmth.

For weeks Thaggoran had been wandering in the ancient passageways below the tribal cocoon. Shinestones were what he sought, precious gems of high splendor, useful in the craft of divination. The subterranean passageways in which he prowled had been carved by his remote ancestors, burrowing this way and that through the living rock with infinitely patient labor, when they first had come here to hide from the exploding stars and black rains that destroyed the Great World. No one in the past ten thousand years had found a shinestone in them. But Thaggoran had dreamed three times this year that he would add a new one to the tribe's little store of them. He knew and valued the power of dreams. And so he went prowling in the depths almost every day.

He moved now through the deepest and coldest tunnel of all, the one called Mother of Frost. As he crept cautiously on hands and knees in the darkness, searching with his second sight for the shinestones that he hoped were embedded in the walls of the passageway somewhere close ahead, he felt a sudden strange tingling and trembling, a feathery twitching and throbbing. The sensation ran through the entire length of his sensing-organ, from the place at the base of his spine where it sprouted from his body all the way out to its tip. It was the sensation that came from living creatures very near at hand.

Swept by alarm, he halted at once and held himself utterly still. Yes. He felt a clear emanation of life nearby: something huge turning and turning below him, like a thick sluggish auger drilling through stone. Something alive, here in these cold lightless depths, roaming the mountain's bleak dark heart.

"Yissou!" he muttered, and made the sign of the Protector. "Emakkis!" he whispered, and made the sign of the Provider. "Dawinno! Friit!"

In awe and fear Thaggoran put his cheek to the tunnel's rough stone floor. He pressed the pads of his fingers against the chilly rock. He aimed his second sight outward and downward. He swept his sensing-organ from side to side in a wide arc.

Stronger sensations, undeniable and incontrovertible, came flooding in. He shivered. Nervously he fingered the ancient amulet dangling on a cord about his throat.

A living thing, yes. Dull-witted, practically mindless, but definitely alive, throbbing with hot intense vitality. And not at all far away. It was separated from him, Thaggoran perceived, by nothing more than a layer of rock a single arm's-length wide. Gradually its image took form for him: an immense limbless thick-bodied creature standing on its tail within a vertical tunnel scarcely broader than itself. Great black bristles thicker than a man's arm ran the length of its meaty body, and deep red craters in its pale flesh radiated powerful blasts of nauseating stench. It was moving up through the mountain with inexorable determination, cutting a path for itself with its broad stubby boulderlike teeth: gnawing on rock, digesting it, excreting it as moist sand at the far end of a massive fleshy body thirty man-lengths long.

Nor was it the only one of its kind making the ascent. From the right and the left now Thaggoran pulled in other heavy pulsing emanations. There were three of the great beasts, five, maybe a dozen of them. Each was confined in its own narrow tunnel, each embarked upon an unhurried journey upward.

Ice-eaters, Thaggoran thought. Yissou! Was it possible?

Shaken, astounded, he crouched motionless, listening to the pounding of the huge animals' souls.

Yes, he was certain of it now: surely these were ice-eaters moving about. He had never seen one—no one alive had ever seen an ice-eater—but he carried a clear image of them in his mind. The oldest pages of the tribal chronicles told of them: vast creatures that the gods had called into being in the first days of the Long Winter, when the less hardy denizens of the Great World were perishing of the darkness and the cold. The ice-eaters made their homes in the black deep places of the earth, and needed neither air nor light nor warmth. Indeed they shunned such things as if they were poisons. And the prophets had said that a time would come at winter's end when the ice-eaters would begin to rise toward the surface, until at last they emerged into the bright light of day to meet their doom.

Now, it seemed, the ice-eaters had commenced their climb. Was the endless winter at last reaching its end, then?

Perhaps these ice-eaters merely were confused. The chronicles testified that there had been plenty of false omens before this. Thaggoran knew the texts well: the Book of the Unhappy Dawn, the Book of the Cold Awakening, the Book of the Wrongful Glow.

But it made little difference whether this was the true omen of spring or merely another in the long skein of tantalizing disappointments. One thing was sure: the People would have to abandon their cocoon and go forth into the strangeness and mystery of the open world.

For the fullness of the catastrophe was at once apparent to Thaggoran. His years of roving these dark abandoned passageways had inscribed an indelible map of their intricate patterns in lines of brilliant scarlet on his mind. The upward route of these vast indifferent monsters drilling slowly through earth and rock would in time carry them crashing through the heart of the dwelling-chamber where the People had lived so many thousands of years. There could be no doubt of that. The worms would be coming up right below the place of the altarstone. And the tribe was no more capable of halting them in their blind ascent than it would be of trapping an onrushing death-star in a net of woven grass.

Far above the cavern where Thaggoran knelt eavesdropping on the ice-eaters, Torlyri the offering-woman, who was the twining-partner of Koshmar the chieftain, was at that moment nearing the exit hatch of the cocoon. It was the moment of sunrise, when Torlyri went forth to make the daily offering to the Five Heavenly Ones.

Tall, gentle Torlyri was renowned for her great beauty and sweetness of soul. Her fur was a lustrous black, banded with two astonishing bright spirals of white that ran the whole length of her body. Powerful muscles rippled beneath her skin. Her eyes were soft and dark, her smile was warm and easy. Everyone in the tribe loved Torlyri. From childhood on she had been marked for distinction: a true leader, one to whom others might turn at any time for counsel and support. But for the mildness of her spirit, she might well have become chieftain herself, and not Koshmar; but beauty and strength alone are insufficient. A chieftain must not be mild.

So it was to Koshmar and not Torlyri that they had come, on that day, nine years earlier, when the old chieftain Thekmur had reached the limit-age. "This is my death-day," sinewy little Thekmur had announced to Koshmar. "And so this is your crowning-day," said Thaggoran. Thus Koshmar was made chieftain, as it had been agreed five years before that. For Torlyri a different destiny had been decreed. When, not long afterward, it was the time of Gonnari the offering-woman to pass through the hatch as Thekmur had, Thaggoran and Koshmar came to Torlyri to place the offering-bowl in her hands. Then Koshmar and Torlyri embraced, with warm tears in their eyes, and went before the tribe to accept the election; and a little later that day they celebrated their double accession more privately, with laughter and love, in one of the twining-chambers.

"Now it is our time to rule," Koshmar told her that day. "Yes," Torlyri said. "At last, our time is here." But she knew the truth, which was that now it was Koshmar's time to rule, and Torlyri's time to serve. Yet were they not both servants of the People, chieftain as well as offering-woman?

Each morning for the past nine years Torlyri had made the same journey, when the silent signal came through the eye of the hatch to tell her that the sun had entered the sky: out of the cocoon by the sky-side, up and up through the interior of the cliff along the winding maze of steep narrow corridors that led toward the crest, and at last to the flat area at the top, the Place of Going Out, where she would perform the rite that was her most important responsibility to the People.

There, each morning, Torlyri unfastened the exit hatch and stepped across the threshold, cautiously passing a little way into the outer world. Most members of the tribe crossed that threshold only three times in their lives: on their naming-day, their twining-day, and their death-day. The chieftain saw the outer world a fourth time, on her crowning-day. But Torlyri had the privilege and the burden of entering the outer world each morning of her life. Even she was permitted to go only as far as the offering-stone of pink granite flecked with sparkling flakes of fire, six paces beyond the gate. Upon that holy stone she would place her offering-bowl, containing some little things of the inner world, a few glowberries or some yellow strands of wall-thatching or a bit of charred meat; and then she would empty yesterday's bowl of its offerings and gather something of the outer world to take within, a handful of earth, a scattering of pebbles, half a dozen blades of redgrass. That daily interchange was essential to the well-being of the tribe. What it said to the gods each day was: *We have not forgotten that we are of the world and we are in the world, even though we must live apart from it at this time. Someday we will come forth again and dwell upon the world that you have made for us, and this is the token of our pledge.*

Arriving now at the Place of Going Out, Torlyri set down her offering-bowl and gripped the handwheel that opened the hatch. It was no trifling thing to turn that great shining wheel, but it moved easily under her hands. Torlyri was proud of her strength. Neither Koshmar nor any man of the tribe, not even mighty Harruel, the biggest and strongest of the warriors, could equal her at arm-standing, at kick-wrestling, at cavern-soaring.

The gate opened. Torlyri stepped through. The keen, sharp air of morning stung her nostrils.

The sun was just coming up. Its chilly red glow filled the eastern sky, and the swirling dust motes that danced on the frosty air seemed to flare and blaze with an inner flame. Beyond the ledge on which she stood, Torlyri saw the broad, swift river far below, gleaming with the same crimson stain of morning light.

Once that great river had been known as the Hallimalla by those who lived along its banks, and before that it had been called the Sipsimutta, and at an even earlier time its name was the Mississippi. Torlyri knew nothing of any of that. To her, the river was simply the river. All those other names were forgotten now, and had been for hundreds of thousands of years. There had been hard times upon the earth since the coming of the Long Winter. The Great World itself was lost; why then should its names have survived? A few had, but only a few. The river was nameless now.

The cocoon in which the sixty members of Koshmar's tribe had spent all their lives—and where their ancestors had huddled since time out of mind, waiting out the unending darkness and chill that the falling death-stars had brought—was a snug cozy burrow hollowed out of the side of a lofty bluff rising high above that mighty river. At first, so the chronicles declared, those people who had survived the early days of black rains and frightful cold had been content to live in mere caves, eating roots and nuts and catching such meat-creatures as they could. Then the winter had deepened and the plants and wild animals vanished from the world. Had human ingenuity ever faced a greater challenge? But the cocoon was the answer: the self-sufficient buried enclosure, dug into hillsides and cliffs well above any likely snow line. Small groups of people, their numbers strictly controlled by breeding regulations, occupied the cocoon's insulated chambers. Clusters of luminescent glowberries afforded light; intricate ventilation shafts provided fresh air; water was pumped up from underground streams. Crops and livestock, having been elegantly adapted to life under artificial illumination by means of magical skills now forgotten, were raised in surrounding chambers. The cocoons were little island-worlds entirely complete in themselves, each as isolated as though it were bound on a solitary voyage across the deep night of space. And in them the survivors of the world's great calamity waited out the time, by centuries and tens of centuries, until the day when the gods would grow weary of hurling death-stars from the sky.

Torlyri went to the offering-stone, set down her bowl, looked in each of the Five Sacred Directions, spoke in turn the Five Names.

"Yissou," she said. "Protector.

"Emakkis. Provider.

"Friit. Healer.

"Dawinno. Destroyer.

"Mueri. Consoler."

Her voice chimed and echoed in the stillness. As she picked up yesterday's bowl to empty it, she looked past the rim of the ledge and downward toward the river. Along that bare steep slope, where only gnarled and twisted little woody shrubs could grow, brittle whitened bones lay scattered and tumbled everywhere like twigs idly strewn. The bones of Gonnari were there, and of Thekmur, and of Thrask, who had been chronicler before Thaggoran. Torlyri's mother's bones lay in those scattered drifts, and her father's, and those of their fathers and mothers. All those who had ever left the hatch had perished here, on this plunging hillside, struck down by the angry kiss of the winter air.

Torlyri wondered how long they lived, those who came forth from the cocoon when their appointed death-day at last arrived. An hour? A day? How far were they able to roam before they were felled? Most, Torlyri expected, simply sat and waited for the end to come to them. But had any of them, overtaken by desperate curiosity in the last hours of their lives, tried to strike out into the world beyond the ledge? To the river, say? Had anyone actually lasted long enough to make it down to the river's edge?

She wondered what it might be like to clamber down the side of the cliff and touch the tips of her fingers to that mysterious potent current.

It would burn like fire, Torlyri thought. But it would be cool fire, a purifying fire. She imagined herself wading out into the dark river, knee-deep, thigh-deep, belly-deep, feeling the cold blaze of the water swirling up over her loins and her sensing-organ. She saw herself then setting out through the turbulent flow, toward the other bank that was so far away she could barely make it out— walking through the water, or perhaps atop it as legend said the water-strider folk did, walking on and on toward the sunrise land, never once to see the cocoon again—

Torlyri smiled. What foolishness it was to indulge in these fantasies!

And what treason to the tribe it would be, if the offering-woman herself were to take advantage of her hatch-freedom and desert the cocoon! But she felt a strange pleasure in pretending that she might someday do such a thing. One could at least dream of it. Almost everyone, Torlyri suspected, now and then looked with longing toward the outer world and had a moment's dream of escaping into it, though surely few would admit to that. She had heard that there were those over the centuries who, growing weary of cocoon life, actually had slipped through the hatch and down to the river and into the wild lands beyond—not expelled from the cocoon as one was on one's death-day, but voluntary sojourners, setting forth into that frigid unknowability of their own will simply to discover what it was like. Had anyone in truth ever chosen such a desperate course? So it was said; but if it had happened, it had not been in the lifetime of anyone now living. Of course those who might have gone forth in that way could never have returned to tell the tale; they would have died almost at once in that harsh world out there. To go outside was madness, she thought. But a tempting madness.

Torlyri knelt to collect what she needed for the inward offering.

Then out of the corner of her eye she caught a flash of movement. She whirled, startled, turning back toward the hatch just in time to see the small slight figure of a boy dart through it and race across the ledge to the rim.

Torlyri reacted without thinking. The boy had already begun scrambling over the side of the ledge; but she pivoted, moved to her left, grabbed at him fiercely, managed to catch him by one heel before he disappeared. He yowled and kicked, but she held him fast, hauling him up, throwing him down onto the ledge beside her.

His eyes were wide with fright, but there was boldness and bright audacity in them too. He was looking past her, trying to get a glimpse of the hills and the river. Torlyri stood poised over him, half expecting him to make another desperate lunge around her.

"Hresh," she said. "Of course. Hresh. Who else but you would try something like this?"

He was eight, Minbain's boy, wild and headstrong all his life. Hresh-full-of-questions, they called him, bubbling as he was with unlawful curiosity. He was small, slender, almost frail, a wriggling little rope of a boy, with a ghostly face, triangular and sharply tapering from a wide brow, and huge dark eyes mysteriously flecked with scarlet specks. Everyone said of him that he had been born for trouble. But this was no trifling scrape he had gotten himself into now.

Torlyri shook her head sadly. "Have you gone crazy? What did you think you were doing?"

Softly he said, "I only wanted to see what's out here, Torlyri! The sky. The river. Everything."

"You would have seen all that on your naming-day."

He shrugged. "But that's a whole year away! I couldn't wait that long."

"The law is the law, Hresh. We all obey, for the good of all. Are you above the law?"

Sullenly he said, "I only wanted to see. Just for a single day, Torlyri!"

"Do you know what happens to those who break the law?"

Frowning, Hresh said, "Not really. But it's something bad, isn't it? What will you do to me?"

"Me? Nothing. It's up to Koshmar."

"Then what will *she* do to me?"

"Anything. I don't know. People have been put to death for doing what you tried to do."

"*Death?*"

"Expelled from the cocoon. That's certain death. No human could last out there alone for very long. Look there, boy."

She pointed down the slope, at the field of bleached bones.

"What are those?" Hresh asked at once.

Torlyri touched his thin arm, pressing against the bone within. "Skeletons. There's one inside you. You'll leave your bones on that hill if you go outside. Everyone does."

"Everyone who's ever gone outside?"

"They all lie right there, Hresh. Like pieces of old wood tossed about by the winter storms."

He trembled. "There aren't enough of them," he said with sudden defiance. "All those years and years and years of death-days—the whole hill ought to be covered with bones, deeper than I am high."

Despite herself Torlyri felt a grin coming on, and looked away a moment. There was no one else like this child, was there? "The bones don't last, Hresh. Fifty, a hundred years, perhaps, and then they turn to dust. Those you see are just the ones who have been cast out most recently."

Hresh considered that a moment.

In a hushed voice he said, "Would they do that to *me*?"

"Everything is in Koshmar's hands."

There was a sudden flash of panic in the boy's strange eyes. "But you won't tell her, will you? Will you, Torlyri?" His expression grew guileful. "You don't have to say anything, do you? You almost didn't notice me, after all. Another moment and I'd have been past you and over the edge, and I would have just stayed out till tomorrow morning, and nobody would have been the wiser. I mean, it isn't as though I *hurt* anybody. I only wanted to see the river."

She sighed. His frightened, beseeching look was hard to resist. And, truly, what harm had he done? He hadn't managed to get more than ten paces outside. She could understand his yearning to discover what lay beyond the walls of the cocoon: that boiling curiosity, that horde of unanswered questions that must rage in him all the time. She had felt something of that herself, though her spirit, she knew, had little of the fire that must possess this troubled boy. But the law was the law, and he had broken it. She could ignore that only at the peril of her own soul.

"Please, Torlyri, please—"

She shook her head. Without taking her eyes from the boy, she scooped together what she needed for the inward offering. She glanced once more in each of the Five Sacred Directions. She spoke the Five Names. Then she turned to the boy and indicated with a brusque gesture that he was to precede her through the hatch. He looked terrified. Gently Torlyri said, "I have no choice, Hresh. I have to take you to Koshmar."

*   *   *

Long ago, someone had mounted a narrow strip of glossy black stone at eye level along the central chamber's rear wall. No one knew why it had been put there originally, but over the years it had come to be sacred to the memory of the tribe's departed chieftains. Koshmar made a point of brushing her fingertips across it and quickly whispering the names of the six who had ruled most recently before her, whenever she felt apprehensive over the future of the People. It was her quick way of invoking the power of her predecessors' spirits, asking them to enter into her and guide her to do the right thing. Somehow calling upon them seemed more immediate, more useful, than to call upon the Five Heavenly Ones. She had invented the little rite herself.

Lately Koshmar had begun touching the strip of black stone every day, and then two or three times each day, while saying the names:

—*Thekmur Nialli Sismoil Yanla Vork Lirridon*—

She was having premonitions: of what, she could not say, but she felt that some great transformation must be descending upon the world, and that she would stand soon in need of much guidance. The stone was comforting in such moments.

Koshmar wondered if her successor too would observe this custom of touching the stone when her soul was troubled. It was almost time, Koshmar knew, to begin thinking of a successor. She would be thirty this year. Five years more and she would reach the limit-age. Her death-day would come, as it had come for Thekmur and Nialli and Sismoil and all the rest, and they would take her to the exit hatch and send her outside to perish in the cold. It was the way, unalterable, unanswerable: the cocoon was finite, food was limited, one must make room for those who are to come.

She closed her eyes and put her fingers to the black stone and stood quietly, a husky, broad-shouldered, keen-eyed woman at the height of her strength and power, praying for help.

Thekmur Nialli Sismoil Yanla—

Torlyri burst into the chamber just then, dragging Minbain's unruly brat Hresh, the one who was forever sneaking around poking his nose into this place and that one where he had no business. The boy was howling and squirming and frantically writhing in Torlyri's grasp. His eyes were wild and shining with fear, as though he had just seen a death-star plummeting down toward the roof of the cocoon.

Koshmar, startled, swung around to face them. In her irritation her thick grayish-brown fur rose like a cloak about her, so that she seemed to swell to half again her true size.

"What's this? What has he done now?"

"I went outside to make the offering," Torlyri began, "and an instant later out of the corner of my eye I caught sight of—"

Thaggoran entered the chamber at that moment. To Koshmar's amazement he looked nearly as wild-eyed as Hresh. He was waving his arms and sensing-organ around in a peculiar crazed way, and his voice came in such a thick blurting rush that Koshmar could make out mere fragments of what he was trying to tell her.

"Ice-eaters—the cocoon—right underneath, coming straight up—it's the truth, Koshmar, it's the prophecy—"

And all the while Hresh continued to whimper and yowl, and soft-voiced Torlyri went steadily on with her story.

"One at a time!" Koshmar cried. "I can't hear anything that anybody's saying!" She glared at the withered old chronicler, white-furred with age and bowed as though weighed down by the precious deep knowledge of the past that he alone carried. She had never seen him looking so deranged. "Ice-eaters, Thaggoran? Did you say ice-eaters?"

Thaggoran was trembling. He muttered something murky and faint that was drowned out by Hresh's panicky outcries. Koshmar looked angrily toward her twining-partner and snapped, "Torlyri, why *is* that child in here?"

"I've been trying to tell you. I caught him trying to slip through the hatch."

"What?"

"I only wanted to see the river!" Hresh howled. "Just for a little while!"

"You know the law, Hresh?"

"It was just for a little while!"

Koshmar sighed. "How old is he, Torlyri?"

"Eight, I think."

"Then he knows the law. All right, let him see the river. Take him upstairs and put him outside."

Shock registered on Torlyri's gentle face. Tears glistened in her eyes. Hresh began to scream and howl again, even louder. But Koshmar had had enough of him. The boy had long been a nuisance, and the law was clear. To the hatch with him, and good riddance. She made an impatient sweeping gesture of dismissal and swung back to face Thaggoran.

"All right. Now: what's this about ice-eaters?"

In a shaky voice the chronicler launched a bewildering tale, raggedly told and difficult to follow, something about searching for shinestones in the Mother of Frost, and picking up a sense of something alive nearby, something big, moving in the rock, something digging a tunnel. "I made contact," Thaggoran said, "and I touched the mind of an ice-eater—I mean, one can't really speak of ice-eaters having *minds,* but in a manner of speaking they do, and what I felt was—"

Koshmar scowled. "How far away from you was it?"

"Not far at all. And there were others. Perhaps a dozen, all told, close at hand. Koshmar, do you know what this means? It must be the end of winter! The prophets have written, 'When the ice-eaters begin to rise—'"

"I know what the prophets have written," Koshmar said sharply. "These things are coming right up under the dwelling-chamber, you say? Are you sure?"

Thaggoran nodded. "They'll smash right through the floor. I don't know how soon—it could be a week from now, or a month, or maybe six months—but beyond any doubt they're heading straight for us. And they're enormous, Koshmar." He stretched his arms out as far as they could reach. "They're this wide around— maybe even bigger—"

"Gods spare us," Torlyri murmured. And from the boy Hresh came short sharp panting sounds of astonishment.

Koshmar whirled, exasperated. "Are you two still here? I told you to take him to the hatch, Torlyri! The law is clear. Venture outside the cocoon without lawful leaving-right, and you are for-bidden to enter it again. I tell you one last time, Torlyri: take him to the hatch."

"But he didn't really leave the cocoon," said Torlyri quietly. "He stepped out just a little way, and—"

"No! No more disobedience! Say the words over him and cast him out, Torlyri!" Once again she turned to Thaggoran. "Come with me, old man. Show me your ice-eaters. We'll be waiting for them with our hatchets when they break through. Big as they are, we'll cut them to pieces as they rise, a slice and a slice and a slice, and then—"

She cut herself short as suddenly a strange hoarse sound, a rasping strangled gurgling sound, came from the far side of the chamber:

"*Aaoouuuaaah!*"

It went on and on, and then it died away into an astounded silence.

"Yissou and Mueri! What was that?" Koshmar muttered, amazed.

It was a sound such as she had never heard before. An iceworm, perhaps, stirring and yawning just below as it made ready to smash through the wall of the chamber? Bewildered, she stared into the dimness. But all was still. Everything seemed to be as it should be. There was the tabernacle, there was the casket in which the book of the chronicles was kept, there was the Wonderstone in its niche and all the old shinestones around it, there was the cradle where Ryyig Dream-Dreamer slept his eternal sleep—

"*Aaoouuuaaah!*" Again.

"It's Ryyig!" Torlyri exclaimed. "He's waking up!"

"Gods!" cried Koshmar. "He is! He is!"

Indeed so. Koshmar felt awe flooding her spirit, making her legs go weak. Overwhelmed by sudden vertigo, she had to grasp the wall, leaning against the strip of black stone and whispering again and again, *Thekmur Nialli Sismoil, Thekmur Nialli Sismoil.* The Dream-Dreamer was sitting bolt upright—when had that ever happened before?—and his eyes were open—no one in the memory of the tribe had ever seen the eyes of Ryyig Dream-Dreamer—and he was crying out, he who had never been known to make any sound more vehement than a snore. His hands raked the air, his lips moved. He seemed to be trying to speak.

"*Aaoouuuaaah!*" cried Ryyig Dream-Dreamer a third time.

Then he closed his eyes and sank back into his unending dream.

In the high-roofed, brightly lit growing-chamber, warm and humid, the women were at work plucking the unwanted flowers from the greenleaf plants and pruning the tendrils of the velvet-berry vines. It was quiet work, steady and pleasant.

Minbain straightened abruptly and peered around, frowning, holding her head to one side at a steep angle.

"Is something wrong?" Galihine asked.

"Didn't you hear anything?"

"Me? Not a thing."

"A peculiar sound," said Minbain. She looked from one woman to the other, to Boldirinthe, to Sinistine, to Cheysz, to Galihine again. "Like a groan, it was."

"Harruel, snorting in his sleep," Sinistine suggested.

"Koshmar and Torlyri, having a good twine," said Boldirinthe.

They laughed. Minbain tightened her lips. She was older than the rest of them, and at the best of times she felt distant from them. It was because she had once been a breeder-woman, and after the death of her mate Samnibolon she had become a worker-woman. That was an uncommon thing to do. She suspected that they thought she was strange. Perhaps they believed that the mother of a strange child like Hresh must herself be a little odd. But what did they understand of such things? Not one of the women in the room with her had ever been mated at all, nor borne a child, nor did they know what it was to raise one.

"There," Minbain said. "There it goes again! You didn't hear it?"

"Harruel, definitely," said Sinistine. "He's dreaming of coupling with you, Minbain."

Boldirinthe giggled. "Now there's a match! Minbain and Har-ruel! Oh, I envy you, Minbain! Think of how he'll grab you and push you down, and how—"

"Hssh!" Minbain cried. She snatched up her basket of green-leaf blossoms and hurled it at Boldirinthe, who managed barely to deflect it with her elbow. It bounced upward and away, turn-ing upside down, and a mass of the sticky yellow blossoms came tumbling from it, scattering over Sinistine and Cheysz. The women stared. Such a show of temper was a rarity indeed. "Why did you do that?" Cheysz asked. She was a small, sweet-souled woman and she seemed altogether astounded by Minbain's angry outburst. "Look, they're stuck to me all over," Cheysz said, and seemed almost ready to burst into tears. Indeed, the pale chartreuse blossoms, rich with their thick shining nectar, were clinging to her fur in clusters and patches, giving her a bizarre mottled look. Sinistine too was covered with the things, and as she tried to pull one away the fur began to come with it, making her howl with pain. Her pale blue eyes glinted icily with wrath, and, seizing a stout black velvetberry tendril that was lying at her feet, she advanced toward Minbain, wielding it as she would a whip.

"Stop it!" Galihine shouted. "Have you all gone crazy?"

"Listen," said Minbain. "There's that sound once more."

They all fell silent.

"I heard it this time," said Cheysz.

"Me too," said Sinistine, staring in wonder. She tossed the velvetberry tendril aside. "Like a groan, yes. Just as you said, Min-bain."

"What could it have been?" Boldirinthe asked.

"Perhaps it's some god walking around just outside the hatch," Minbain said. "Emakkis, looking for a lost sheep, maybe. Or

Dawinno trying to clear his nose." She shrugged. "Strange. Very strange. We should remember to tell Thaggoran about it." Then she turned to Cheysz, smiling apologetically. "Here. Let me help you get those things out of your fur."

Ryyig had been awake only a moment; the whole thing had come and gone so swiftly that even those who had witnessed it could not fully believe they had seen what they had seen and heard what they had heard. And now the Dream-Dreamer was lost once more in his mysteries, eyes shut, breast rising and falling so slowly that he seemed almost to be carved of stone. But his crying out was significant enough, coming so soon after Thaggoran's discovery of the ascent of the ice-eaters. These were omens. These were definite harbingers.

To Koshmar they were signs that the new springtime of the world was nearly at hand. Perhaps the time had not yet arrived, but surely it was coming.

Even before this day of strange events, Koshmar had felt changes beginning to develop in the rhythm of the tribe's life. Everyone had. There had been a stirring in the cocoon, a ferment of the spirits, a sense of new beginnings about to unfold. The old patterns, which had held for thousands upon thousands of years, were breaking up.

Sleep-times had been the first thing to change. Minbain had remarked on that. "I never seem to sleep any more," she said, and her friend Galihine had nodded, saying, "Nor I. But I'm not tired. Why is that?" It had been the custom among the people of the cocoon to spend more of their time asleep than awake, lying coiled together by twos and threes in intricate furry tangles, lost in hazy dream-fables. No longer. Now everyone seemed strangely alert, restless, active, troubled by the need to fill the extra hours of the day.

The young ones were the worst. "These children!" the gruff warrior Konya had grumbled. "If they're going to be wild like this, we should put them to military drills!" Indeed they were shattering the tranquillity of the cocoon with their frenzies, Koshmar thought, especially strange little Hresh and lovely sad-eyed Taniane and that brawny, deep-chested Orbin and even plump clumsy Haniman. Young ones were supposed to be lively, but no one could remember anything like the maniacal energy that those four displayed: dancing maddeningly in circles for hour after hour, singing and chanting long skeins of nonsense, clambering hand over hand up the shaggy walls of the cocoon and swinging from the ceiling. Only last week, when Koshmar had been trying to celebrate the rite of Lord Fanigole's Day, they had had to be ordered into silence, and even then they had been slow to obey. Hresh trying to get outside this morning—it was all part of the same wildness.

Then the breeding pairs had caught the fever, Nittin and Nettin, Jalmud and Valmud, Preyne and Threyne. Plainly enough, all three pairs had accomplished their season's work—there was no question of it, you could see their swelling bellies—and yet there they were, coupling zealously the whole day long anyway as though someone might accuse them of defaulting on their duty.

And at last the older members of the tribe had been infected by the new restlessness: Thaggoran sniffing around the old deep tunnels for shinestones, burly red-bearded Harruel climbing the walls like a boy, Konya flexing his muscles and pacing back and forth. Koshmar felt it herself. It was like an itch deep down, beneath her fur, beneath the skin itself. Even the iceeaters were rising. Great changes were coming. Why else would

Ryyig Dream-Dreamer have awakened this morning, even for a moment, and cried out that way?

"Koshmar?" Thaggoran said finally, when they had all been silent a long while.

She shook her head. "Let me be."

"You said you wanted to go to the ice-eaters, Koshmar."

"Not now. If he's awakening, I have to stay by him."

"Can it be?" Torlyri asked. "Awakening now, do you think?"

"How would I know? You heard what I heard, Torlyri." Koshmar realized that the boy Hresh was still in the room, silent now, motionless, frozen with awe. She glowered at him. Then her eyes went to Torlyri's, and she saw the soft pleading there.

Torlyri made the sign of Mueri at her, gentle Mueri, Mueri the Mother, Mueri the Consoler, Mueri the goddess to whom Torlyri was particularly consecrated.

"All right," Koshmar said at last, with a sigh of acquiescence. "I pardon him, yes. We can't cast anyone out on the day the Dream-Dreamer awakens, I suppose. But get him out of here this minute. And make sure he knows that if he misbehaves again I'll—I'll— oh, get him out of here, Torlyri! Now!"

In the chamber of the warriors Staip paused in his drills and looked up, frowning.

"Did you hear something just then?"

"I hear the sound of shirking," Harruel grunted.

Staip let the insult pass. Harruel was big and dangerous; one did not challenge him lightly. "An outcry of some sort," he said. "Very like a howl of pain."

"Drill now. Talk later," said Harruel.

Staip turned to Konya. "You heard it?"

"I was at my task," Konya said quietly. "My attention was where it belonged."

"As was mine," Staip retorted, with some heat. "But I heard a terrible cry. Twice. Perhaps three times. Something may be happening out there. What do you think? Konya? Harruel?"

"I heard nothing," Harruel said. He was at the Wheel of Dawinno, rolling the great heavy spool around and around. Konya held the spindles of the Loom of Emakkis. Staip had been doing his turn on Yissou's Ladder. They were the three senior warriors of the tribe, strong and somber men, and this was how they burned off their surging energies each day, day after day, in the long sweet isolation of the cocoon.

Staip stared bleakly at them. He saw the mockery in their eyes, and it maddened him. He had been working just as hard at his drills as they. If they hadn't heard those three frightful screams, what fault was it of his? They had no right to jeer at him. He felt anger rising. There was a pounding in his chest. So proud of their diligent drilling, they were. Calling him a shirker, accusing him of letting his attention wander—

Was it his imagination, he wondered, or had they both been aiming little jabs at him for some weeks now? They had said things which he had let slide by, but now, as he thought it over, it seemed to him that in many ways they had been telling him that he was lazy, that he was stupid, that he was slow.

Life was more difficult these days. There was a new mood to everyone: keener, more alert, more prickly, everyone on edge. Staip had found it hard to sleep of late; so, apparently, had the others. There was more bickering than before. Tempers flared easily.

But still—these insults—they had no right—

His anger overflowed and he stepped toward them, intent on a challenge. He started toward Konya, and was already beginning to go into kick-wrestling stance when he checked himself and swung away. He and Konya were about an even match. There would be no satisfaction in that. Harruel was the one he would fight. Great towering arrogant Harruel, the top man of all—yes, yes, that was the way! Knock *him* down and they'd all understand that Staip was no one to trifle with! "Come on," he said, glaring up at Harruel and balancing in the posture known as the Double Assault. "Wrestle with me, Harruel!"

Harruel seemed unperturbed. "What's the matter with you, Staip?" he asked calmly.

"You know what the matter is. Come. Now. Fight me."

"We have our drills to do. I have the Ladder yet to go, and the Loom, and then an hour of leaps and bends—"

"Are you afraid of me?"

"You must be out of your mind."

"You've insulted me. Fight me. Your drills can wait."

"The drills are our sacred duty, Staip. We are warriors."

"Warriors? For what war do you prepare yourself, Harruel? If you call yourself a warrior, fight me. Fight me or by Dawinno I'll knock you down whether you take the stance or not!"

Harruel sighed. "Drills first. We can fight afterward."

"By Dawinno—" Staip said thickly.

There was a sound behind him. Into the chamber of warriors came Lakkamai, a wiry dark-furred man with an austere, remote manner, who was given to uttering few words. Silently Lakkamai walked past them and took his seat at the Five Gods, most taxing of all the drilling devices they used. Then, as if noticing for the first time the tensions in the chamber, he looked up and said, "What are you two doing?"

"He said he heard a strange sound," Harruel replied. "Like a cry of pain, he said, repeated two or three times."

"And so you are going to fight?"

"He called me a shirker," Staip said. "And there were other insults."

"All right, Staip," Harruel said. "Come. If you need a beating, I'll give you one, and a good one. Come, and let's get it over with."

"Fools," Lakkamai said under his breath, and thrust his arms into the coils of the Five Gods.

Staip advanced toward Harruel again. Then he paused, abashed, wondering why he was doing this. Lakkamai's cool disdain had sent all the rage whistling from his inflamed spirit as though from a punctured air-bladder. Harruel seemed puzzled too, and they looked at each other, baffled. After a moment Harruel turned as though nothing had happened, and returned to his drill. Staip stared, wondering if he should go through with the challenge all the same, but the impulse had passed. Lamely he went back to his own drill. From the far side of the room came the sounds of Konya hard at work once more on the Loom.

For a long while the four men went at their drills, none of them saying a word. Staip still felt a dull angry throbbing in his forehead. He was not sure whether he had won or lost in his interchange with Harruel, but it had not left him with any sense of triumph. To ease his soul he worked with triple ferocity at the drilling machines. He had spent his whole life at these machines, training his body, tuning his muscles, for it was a warrior's duty to make himself strong, no matter how peaceful the life of the cocoon might be, and peaceful it always was. A time would come, so it was said, when the People must leave the cocoon for the world outside; and when that time came, the warriors needed to be strong.

After a very long while Lakkamai said, in response to no one's query, "That sound Staip heard was the Dream-Dreamer. He is waking up, so I hear."

"*What?*" Konya cried.

"You see?" Staip said. "You see?"

And Harruel, jumping down from Yissou's Ladder, rushed forward in amazement, demanding to know more. But Lakkamai merely shrugged and went on with his drill.

All day long Koshmar stood beside the Dream-Dreamer's cradle, watching his eyes moving beneath his pale pink lids. How long, she wondered, had he slept like this? A hundred years? A thousand? According to the tradition of the tribe he had closed his eyes on the first day of the world's long winter and he would not open them again until winter's end; and it had been prophesied that the winter would last seven hundred thousand years.

Seven hundred thousand years! Had the Dream-Dreamer slept that long, then?

So it was asserted. It might even be so.

And all that time, while he slept, his dreaming mind had roved the heavens, seeking out the blazing death-stars that journeyed toward the earth trailing rivers of light and observing them through all their long trajectories; and he would sleep on and on and on, so it was said, until the last of those frightful stars had fallen from the sky and the world had grown warm again and it had become safe for human folk to come forth from their cocoons. Now he had opened his eyes, though only for a moment, and had begun to speak, or at least to make the attempt to speak. What else could he have been doing, if not proclaiming the end of winter? That strangled gurgling sound: surely it heralded the coming of the new age. Torlyri had heard it, and Thaggoran, and Hresh, and Koshmar herself. But could that grotesque sound be trusted? Was this really winter's end? So the omens portended. There was the evidence of the ice-eaters; there was the evidence of the odd restlessness that had afflicted the tribe. Now this. Ah, let it be so, Koshmar prayed. Yissou, let it happen in my time! Let me be the one to lead the people forth into sunlight!

Koshmar peered around warily. It was forbidden to disturb Ryyig Dream-Dreamer in any way. But many things that had been forbidden seemed permissible now. She was alone in the chamber. Gently she put her hand to the Dream-Dreamer's bare shoulder. How strange his skin felt! Like an old worn piece of leather, terribly soft, delicate, vulnerable. His body was not like any of theirs: he was altogether without fur, a naked pink creature with long slender arms and frail little legs that could never have carried him anywhere. And he had no sensing-organ at all.

"Ryyig? Ryyig?" Koshmar whispered. "Open your eyes again! Tell me what you are meant to tell!"

He seemed to wriggle a bit in his cradle, as though annoyed that she was trespassing on his slumber. His bare forehead furrowed; through his thin lips came a faint little whistling sound. His eyes remained closed.

"Ryyig? Tell me: is the time of falling stars over? Will the sun shine again? Is it safe for us to go outside?"

Koshmar thought that his eyelids might be flickering. Boldly she rocked him by the shoulder, and then more boldly still, as if she meant to pull him awake by force. Her fingers dug deeply into his sparse flesh. She felt the frail bones just beneath. Would Thekmur have taken such risks? she wondered. Would Nialli? Perhaps not. No matter. Koshmar shook him again. Ryyig uttered a little mewing noise and turned his head away from her.

"You tried to say it before," Koshmar whispered fiercely. "Say it! *The winter is over.* Say it! Say it!"

Suddenly the thin pale lids pulled back. She found herself staring into strange haunting eyes of a deep violet hue, shrouded by dreams and mysteries of which she knew she could never comprehend a thing. The impact of those eyes, at this close range, was so overwhelming that Koshmar fell back a pace or two. But she recovered quickly.

"Come!" she called. "Everyone, come! He's waking up again! Come! Come quickly!"

The slender fragile figure in the cradle seemed to be struggling once more to a sitting position. Koshmar slipped her arm behind his back and drew him upward. His head wobbled, as if too heavy for his neck. Once more that gurgling sound came from him. Koshmar bent low, putting her ear to his mouth. The People were entering from both sides of the chamber now, gathering close around her. She saw Minbain, and little Cheysz, and the young warrior Salaman. Harruel came in grandly, pushing others aside, staring with blazing eyes at the Dream-Dreamer.

And Ryyig spoke.

"The—winter—"

His voice was feeble but the words were unmistakable.

"The—winter—"

"—is over," Koshmar prompted. "Yes! Yes! Say it! Say, *Why do you wait? The winter is over!*"

A third time: "The—winter—"

The thin lips worked convulsively. Muscles flickered in the fleshless jaws. Ryyig's body sagged against her arm; his shoulders rippled strangely; his eyes went dull and lost their focus.

"Is he dead?" Harruel asked. "I think he is. The Dream-Dreamer's dead!"

"He's only gone back to sleep," said Torlyri.

Koshmar shook her head. Harruel was right. There was no life to Ryyig at all. She put her face close to his. She touched his cheek, his arm, his hand. Dead, yes. Cold, limp, dead. That must surely mean the end of one age, the beginning of another. Koshmar lowered his flimsy form to the cradle and turned triumphantly to her people. Her breast throbbed in exultation. The moment had come. Yes, and it had come in the chieftainship of Koshmar, as she had long prayed it would.

"You heard him!" she declared. "'*Why do you wait?*' is what he said. '*The winter is over!*' he said. We will leave our cocoon. We will leave this mountain: let the stinking ice-eaters have it, if that is what they want. Come, we should begin collecting our possessions. We have to make ready for the journeying! This is the day we go outside!"

Torlyri said in her mild way, "All I heard him say was 'the winter,' Koshmar. Nothing more than that."

Koshmar stared at her, amazed. Now she was certain that this was truly a time of great changes, for twice this day the gentle Torlyri had put her will in opposition to that of her twining-partner. Holding back her temper, for she loved Torlyri dearly, Koshmar said, "You heard wrong. His voice was very faint, but I have no doubt of his words. What do you say, Thaggoran? Is this not the Time of Going Forth? And you? And you?"

She looked about the chamber sternly. No one dared to meet her gaze.

"Then you agree," she said. "The winter is over. No more stars will fall. Come, now. The dark time has ended and now by grace of Yissou and Dawinno we humans reclaim our world."

She lashed her thick, strong sensing-organ from side to side in great sweeping thumping movements of authority. Those fierce movements defied them all to speak against her. And no one spoke. Koshmar saw the boy Hresh gazing fixedly at her, eyes gleaming with intense excitement. It was agreed, then. This was the day. She would have to consult Thaggoran about the actual procedure, which she knew was going to be elaborate and time-consuming. But the preparations for departure, the complex round of rites and ceremonies and all the rest, would begin as soon as possible. And then the people of Koshmar's cocoon would go forth to take possession of the world.

From the niche where the shinestones were kept Thaggoran took the five oldest, the ones known as Vingir, Nilmir, Dralmir, Hrongnir, and Thungvir, and placed them in the pentagram pattern on the altar. They were the holiest ones, the most effective ones. He touched each stone in turn, building the link between them that produced the divination. Their mirror-bright black surfaces gleamed brilliantly beneath the clusters of glowberries that illuminated the dwelling-chamber, a fierce hard gleam though the glowberry light itself was soft; it was as though that mild illumination from without had kindled some cool but intense fire within the shinestones themselves.

Thaggoran had come to resign himself now to the awareness that no new shinestone would be added to the collection, despite the thrice-repeated dream that told him he was destined to find one. What he had found in the maze of caverns below was ice-eaters, not a new shinestone. And there was no time now for him to continue the search.

But dreams were not always exact in their prophecies. He had had auguries of a great discovery, at least; and a great discovery was what he had made.

He touched Vingir, and Dralmir, and Thungvir, and felt the force of the gleaming black stones. He touched Nilmir. He touched Hrongnir. He began the incantation. *Tell me tell me tell me tell me—*

"Tell me," said a voice behind him.

He leaped up, stung by the way the words in his mind had burst into his hearing from without. Hresh stood at the entrance to the chamber, balancing in his strange way on one leg alone, staring wide-eyed, looking skittish, ready to flee at a frown. "Please, Thaggoran, tell me—"

"Boy, this is no moment for questions!"

"What are you doing with the shinestones, Thaggoran?"

"You didn't understand what I said?"

"I understand," Hresh said. His lip quivered. His huge eerie eyes grew moist. He started to back away. "Are you angry with me? I didn't know you were doing anything important."

"We're getting ready to leave the cocoon, do you understand that?"

"Yes. Yes."

"And I need to seek the counsel of the gods. I need to know if our venture will succeed."

"The shinestones will tell you that?"

"If I ask the questions the correct way, they will," Thaggoran said.

"May I watch?"

Thaggoran laughed. "You're insane, boy!"

"Am I, do you think?"

"Come here," said the chronicler. He crooked his fingers beckoningly, and Hresh scampered into the holy chamber. Thaggoran slipped an arm around the boy's waist. "When I was your age," he said, "if you can imagine me as young once as you are now, Thrask was the chronicler. And if ever I had walked in here while Thrask was with the shinestones he would have had my hide pegged out on the wall an hour later. Lucky for you that I'm a softer man than Thrask."

"Were you like me when you were my age?" Hresh asked.

"Nobody has ever been like you," said Thaggoran.

"What do you mean?"

"We are quiet folk, boy. We live as we are told to live. We obey the laws of the People. You obey nothing, do you? You ask questions, and when you're told to be quiet you ask why you should be. There was much that I too wanted to know when I was a boy, and in time I came to learn it: but no one ever caught me prying and peeping and poking where I didn't belong. I waited until it was my proper time to be taught, which is not to say that I didn't feel curiosity. But not the way you do. Curiosity's a disease in you. You nearly died for that curiosity of yours the other day, do you realize that?"

"Would Koshmar have really made me go outside that time, Thaggoran?"

"I think she would."

"And I would have died, then?"

"Most certainly you would."

"But now we're all going outside. Are we all going to die?"

"A boy like you, you'd never have lasted half a day by yourself. But the whole tribe—yes, yes, we'll be all right. We have Koshmar to lead us, and Torlyri to comfort us, and Harruel to defend us."

"And you to show us the will of the gods."

"For a little while longer, yes," Thaggoran said.

"I don't understand."

"Do you think I can live forever, boy?"

He heard Hresh gasp. "But you're so old already!"

"Exactly. I'm near the end, don't you see that?"

"No!" Hresh was trembling. "How can that be? We need you, Thaggoran. We *need* you. You have to live! If you die—"

"Everyone dies, Hresh."

"Will Koshmar die? Will my mother? Will I?"

"Everyone dies."

"I don't want Koshmar to die, or you, or Minbain. Or anyone. Especially not me."

"You know about the limit-age, don't you?"

Hresh nodded solemnly. "When you come to be thirty-five, and you have to go outside. I saw the bones, when I was outside the hatch. There were bones scattered all over. They all died, everybody who had to go out there. But that was during the Long Winter. The Long Winter's over now."

"Perhaps. Perhaps."

"You aren't sure, Thaggoran?"

"I was hoping the shinestones would tell me."

"Then I interrupted you. I should go."

Smiling, Thaggoran said, "Stay. A little while. There's time yet for me to ask questions of the shinestones."

"Will there still be a limit-age after we go from the cocoon?"

The shrewdness of the boy's question startled the chronicler. After a moment he said, "I don't know. Perhaps not. It's a custom that won't be needed, will it? It isn't as if we'll be crowded into this little place any longer."

"Then we won't have to die! Not ever!"

"Everyone dies, Hresh."

"But why is that?"

"The body wears out. The strength goes. You see how white my fur has turned? When the color leaves, it means the life is leaving. Inside me, too, things are changing. It's a natural thing, Hresh. All creatures experience it. Dawinno devised death for us so that we could find peace at the end of our toil. It's nothing to fear."

Hresh was silent, digesting that.

"I still don't want to die," he said, after a while.

"At your age it's an unthinkable idea. Later you'll understand. Don't try to make sense of it now."

There was another silence. Thaggoran saw the boy staring at the casket of the chronicles, which more than once he had allowed Hresh to peer into, even to touch, though it was against all propriety. The boy was eager; the boy was persuasive; there did not seem to be harm in letting him see the ancient books. Thaggoran more than once had found himself wishing that Hresh had been born earlier, or that he himself had come later to his post; for here was a natural-born chronicler, no question of it, the kind that came along once in a generation at best. And yet he was just a child, years away from any possibility of the succession. I will be long gone, Thaggoran thought, before this boy is a man. And yet—and yet—

"You should do what you have to do with the shinestones," Hresh said finally.

"I should, yes."

"May I stay and watch?"

"Another time, perhaps," Thaggoran said, and smiled and touched the boy's slender arm, and gave him the lightest of gentle pushes, and sent him from the room. Once more he turned his attention to his shinestones. Once more he touched Vingir, and then Dralmir. But something felt wrong. The tuning was discordant; the shimmer that precedes divination was absent. He looked around, and there was Hresh, peering around the edge of the chamber door. Thaggoran choked back a laugh, and said, as sternly as he could, "Out, Hresh! *Out!*"

By the dim sputtering light of a sooty lamp fueled with animal fat Salaman saw the dark passageways twisting and forking in front of him. Awe rose in him like a rock-serpent slithering upward within his spine. He was ten years old, nearly eleven, just approaching the first threshold of manhood. He had never been down here before; he had never actually believed these caverns existed.

"Are you afraid?" Thhrouk asked, behind him.

"Me? No. Why should I be?"

"I am," said Thhrouk.

Salaman turned. He had not been expecting such frankness. Warriors were not supposed to admit fear. Thhrouk, like Salaman, was of the warrior class, and he was older by at least a year, perhaps more, old enough almost to be of twining-age. But his face was tense and rigid with anxiety. By the murky light of the lamp Salaman saw Thhrouk's eyes, glistening and smarting from the smoke. They were as bright as shinestones in his head, glassy, unblinking. Bunched muscles were working in his jaws, and those of his throat were clenched, protuberant, proclaiming his uneasiness.

"What's to worry about?" Salaman said boldly. "Anijang will get us out of here!"

"Anijang!" Thhrouk said. "A mindless old worker!"

"He's not so mindless," Salaman said. "I've seen him keeping his calendar. He keeps good count of the time, the years and everything, let me tell you. He's smarter than you think."

"And he's been down here before," said Sachkor, farther back in the line. "He knows his way."

"Let's hope so," Thhrouk said. "I'd hate to spend the rest of my life lost in these tunnels."

From up ahead came the sharp clink of a falling rock, and then a louder and more muffled sound, as though the roof of the passage had begun to fall in. Thhrouk leaned forward and caught Salaman by the shoulder, his fingers digging in tightly in his alarm. But then Anijang's voice could be heard in front of them, tunelessly bellowing the Hymn of Balilirion. So he was all right.

"You still there, boys?" the older man called. "Keep closer to me, will you?"

Salaman moved forward, crouching to avoid an overhanging boss of low rock. The other two kept pace. Small skittering creatures with beady red eyes ran past their legs. A trickle of cold water oozed across the path. They were down here on a mission of deconsecration; for in these musty old caverns were sacred objects that must not be left behind when the People left the cocoon. It was not a job that anyone could enjoy; but Sachkor and Salaman and Thhrouk were the three youngest warriors, and such tasks as this were part of their discipline. It was nasty work. Harruel himself would loathe doing it. But Harruel did not have to.

Anijang was waiting for them just around the bend. Some rocks had indeed fallen—they lay ankle-deep beside him—and Anijang was staring into the open place from which they had come. "New tunnel," he said. "Old one, rather. Very old. Old and forgotten. Yissou only knows how many passages there are altogether."

"Do we have to go into this one?" Thhrouk asked.

"Not on the list," said Anijang. "We'll keep going."

There were alcoves dedicated to each of the Five Heavenly Ones in this labyrinth, each with holy artifacts that had been placed there in the early days of the cocoon. Already they had found the Mueri alcove and the one of Friit; but those were the easy gods, the Consoler, the Healer. The shrine of Emakkis the Provider should be next, and then, on deeper levels, that of Dawinno and, finally, of Yissou.

The intricacy of this gloomy subterranean world astonished Salaman. For the first time, now that the People were about to leave the cocoon, he comprehended something of what it meant to have occupied this one place for seven hundred thousand years. Only across vast spans of time could all of this have been constructed. Each of these tunnels had been scraped out by hand, by folk just like himself, patiently chipping and scrabbling at the dark cold rock and earth for day after day, carrying away the debris, smoothing the walls, building archways to support them—it must have taken forever and a half to cut each one. And look how many passageways there were! Dozens, hundreds—used for a time, then abandoned. Salaman wondered why they had not simply kept the same group of chambers and corridors all the time, since the tribe had grown no larger during all the centuries of its stay in the cocoon. The answer, he thought, must lie in the human need for having some continued occupation to pursue, other than the mere acts of eating and sleeping. For a span of time beyond understanding the People had been prisoners in this mountain beside the great river, dormant, hiding from the bitter winter outside in a long comfortable repose; they had their crops to grow and their animals to tend and their drills and rituals to perform, but even that was not enough. They had to have other ways of expending their energies as well. And so they had built this maze. Yissou! What labor it must have been!

As they proceeded, Salaman saw strange shadows everywhere. Mysterious sparks of light drifted in the depths. Occasionally he saw enigmatic features in the glimmering distance—squat pillars, heavy arches. The forgotten works of forgotten men. There was a whole universe of caverns down here. Ancient rooms, abandoned altars, rows of niches, stone benches. For what? How old? How long ago abandoned?

Now and then he heard the far-off sound of roaring, as if some monstrous beast lay chained in the far recesses of the mountain's great heart. Salaman heard the sound of his own harsh breathing counterpointed against that distant roar. The world hung suspended all about him. He was at its center, entombed in rock.

"We turn left here," Anijang said.

They had arrived at a place where half a dozen irregular tunnels radiated out from a central gallery. The stone floor was rough and steep here, descending at a disturbing angle: it strained the knees to go downward so swiftly. And as they went down the passage narrowed. Salaman began to see why they had sent boys for this job, and a shriveled oldster like Anijang. Men like Harruel and Konya were too big for these corridors. Even he, wide-shouldered and husky for his age, was having trouble crawling through some of the tight places.

"Tell me, Salaman—what do you think it'll be like when we go outside?" Thhrouk asked suddenly, apropos of nothing at all.

Salaman, surprised by the question, glanced back over his shoulder.

"How would I know? Have I ever been out there?"

"Of course not. Except for your naming-day, and that wasn't for very long. But what do you think it'll be like?"

He hesitated. "Strange. Difficult. Painful."

"Painful?" Sachkor said. "Why so?"

"There's the sun out there. It burns you. And the wind. They say it cuts you like a knife."

"Who says?" Thhrouk asked. "Thaggoran?"

"Don't you remember how it was on your naming-day? Even if you were only outside for a moment or two then. And you've heard Thaggoran reading from the chronicles. How exposed everything is out there. Sand blowing in your eyes. Snow as cold as fire."

"As cold as fire?" Sachkor said. "Fire is *hot,* Salaman."

"You know what I mean."

"No. No, I don't, not at all. That's the sort of thing Hresh would say. Cold as fire: it makes no sense."

"I mean that snow burns you. It's a different kind of burning from the burning that fire does, or the sun," Salaman said. He saw them staring at him as though he had lost his mind. It was a bad idea, he thought, to be telling them these things, though he had speculated a great deal about them privately. He was a warrior; it was not his task to think. They would see a side of him that he did not care to have them see. With a shrug he said, "I don't really know anything about any of this. I'm just guessing."

"Here," Anijang called. "This is the way!"

He plunged into a black opening barely larger than he was.

Salaman looked back at Sachkor and Thhrouk, shook his head, and followed Anijang. There were marks on the walls here, blood-colored stripes and deeply engraved triangles, holy signs, intimations of the presence of Emakkis nearby. So Anijang still knew what he was doing: they were approaching the third of the five shrines.

Now that Thhrouk had awakened the thought in him, Salaman found himself once more pondering the changes that lay ahead. Part of him still could not believe that they truly were going to leave the cocoon. But all these weeks of preparation could not be argued away. They *were* going outside. To perish of the cold? No, not if Thaggoran and Koshmar were right: the New Springtime had come, they said, and who could say otherwise? Yet he found himself fearing the Going Forth. To leave the snug safe cocoon, to cast aside everything that was familiar and comforting in his life—Mueri! It was a frightening thing. And now he had frightened himself even more, with all his own talk of the burning sun, and the burning snow, and the sharp wind blowing sand in your eyes—

"What's that sound?" Thhrouk said, digging his fingers into Salaman's shoulders yet again. "You hear it? A rumbling in the walls? Ice-eaters!"

"Where?" Salaman asked.

"Here. Here."

Salaman put his ear to the wall. Indeed he heard something in there, an odd rippling, sliding sound. He imagined an enormous snorting snuffling ice-eater just on the far side of the wall, chomping away as it rose mindlessly toward the top of the cliff. Then he laughed. He could make out a distant splashing, a quiet wet murmur. "It's water," he said. "There's a stream running through the wall here."

"A stream? Are you sure?"

"Just listen to it," Salaman said.

"Salaman's right," said Sachkor, after a moment. "That's no ice-eater. Look, you can see the water running out of the wall a little way up there."

"Ah," Thhrouk said. "Yes. You're right. Yissou! I'd hate to meet an ice-eater while we're wandering around down here!"

"Are you coming?" Anijang called. "Follow me or you'll get lost, I promise you!"

Salaman laughed. "We wouldn't want that."

He hurried onward, so quickly that in his haste he nearly blew out his own lamp. Anijang was waiting by the entrance to a chamber that branched from the one they were in; he pointed inside, to the holy ikon of Emakkis on an altar within it. Of the four of them only Sachkor was slender enough to go in to get it.

While Sachkor carefully slipped into the shrine of the Provider, Salaman stood to one side, thinking still of the Going Forth and its perils and discomforts and strangenesses, thinking once more of the sun against his face, the snow, the sand. It was an awesome thing to undertake, yes. But somehow it began to seem less terrible, the longer he thought of it. Going outside had its risks, yes—it was *all* risk, it was nothing but risk—but what was the alternative? To live out your life in this tangled warren of dark, musty caverns? No! No! They were going to make the Going Forth, and it was glorious to contemplate. All the world stood before them. His heart began to race. His fears fell away from him.

Sachkor emerged from the tiny alcove, clutching the ikon of Emakkis. He was trembling and his face looked strange.

"What is it?" Salaman asked.

"Ice-eaters," said Sachkor. "No, not another stream this time. The real thing. I heard them chewing on the rock just beyond the inner wall."

"No," Thhrouk said. "That can't be."

"Go in and listen for yourself, then," Sachkor said.

"But I don't fit."

"Then don't go in. Whatever pleases you. I heard ice-eaters."

"Come along," said Anijang.

"Wait," said Salaman. "Let me go in. I want to hear what Sachkor heard."

But he was too husky to enter; and after a moment of trying to slide his shoulders past the narrow opening he gave up, and they moved along, wondering what it was, in truth, that Sachkor had heard in there. Just around the bend Salaman had the answer. The cavern wall here was throbbing with a deep, heavy vibration. He put his hand to it and it seemed as though something were shaking the entire world. Cautiously he lifted his sensing-organ and extended his second sight. What he felt was bulk, mass, power, movement.

"Ice-eaters, yes," Salaman said. "Just back of this wall. Eating the stone."

"Yissou!" Thhrouk whispered, making a cluster of holy signs. "Dawinno! Friit! They'll destroy us!"

"They won't get the chance," said Salaman. He smiled. "We're leaving the cocoon, remember? We'll be halfway across the world before they even get close to the dwelling-chamber level."

Minbain woke quickly, as she always did. About her she heard the morning sounds of the cocoon, the familiar clatterings and clamorings, the laughter, the buzz of talk, the slap of running feet against the stone floor of the dwelling-chamber. Rising from her sleeping-furs, she made her morning prayer to Mueri and said the words that were due the soul of her departed mate Samnibolon.

Then she fell about her tasks. There were so many things to do, a million things to do, before the People could actually leave the cocoon.

Hresh was already awake. She saw him grinning at her from the sleeping-alcove down the way where the young ones stayed. He was always up before anyone else, even before Torlyri arose to make the sunrise offering. Minbain wondered sometimes if he ever slept at all.

He came scampering over, skinny arms and legs flailing, sensing-organ jutting out behind him in a strange awkward way. They embraced. He is all bones, she thought. He eats, but nothing sticks: he burns himself up by thinking too much.

"What do you say, Mother? Will today be the day?"

Minbain laughed gently. "Today? No, Hresh, no, not yet. Not today, Hresh."

When he heard Koshmar declare, "This is the day we go outside," Hresh had assumed that they really were going to set out that very day. But of course that could not be. The death-rites for the old Dream-Dreamer had had to be performed first, an event of great pomp and mystery. No one knew what the proper rite for the burial of a Dream-Dreamer should be—it seemed wrong simply to take him outside and dump him among the bones on the slope—but finally Thaggoran had found something in the chronicles, or had pretended to find something, that involved much singing and chanting and a torchlight procession through the lower caverns to the Chamber of Yissou, where his body was laid to rest beneath a cairn of blue rock. All that had taken several days to prepare and execute. Then the rituals of deconsecration of the cocoon had had to be carried out, so that they would not leave their souls behind on the long march to come. And then the packing of all the sacred objects; and then the slaughtering of most of the tribe's meat-animals, and the curing of the meat; and after that would come the gathering-up of all useful possessions into bundles light enough to be carried, and then—and then—this rite and that, this task and that, everything according to instructions that were thousands of years old. Oh, it would be many days more, Minbain knew, before the Going Forth actually happened. And you could already hear the ice-eaters champing on the rock just below the dwelling-chamber, a dull ugly rasping sound that went on night and day, night and day. But the ice-eaters could have the place now, for whatever good it was to them. The tribe would never return to the cocoon. It was this time of waiting that was the difficult part, and for no one was it more difficult than Hresh. To Hresh a day was like a month, a month was like a year. Impatience chattered through him like a fire rushing through dry sticks.

"Will they be killing more animals today?" he asked.

"That's all done now," Minbain told him.

"Good. Good. I hated it when they were doing that."

"Yes, it was hard," Minbain said. "But necessary." Ordinarily one of the beasts was butchered every week or two for the use of the tribe, but this time Harruel and Konya had taken their blades and gone into the pen for hours, until blood ran down the sloping drainage channel and out into the dwelling-chamber itself. Only a few could be taken along as breeding stock; the rest must be slaughtered, and their meat cured and packed to sustain the tribe on the march. Hresh had gone to watch them at work at the butchering. Minbain had warned him not to go, but he had insisted, and he had stood there solemnly staring as Harruel seized the animals and lifted their heads to Konya's knife. And afterward he had trembled in terror for hours; but the next day he was back, watching the killings. Nothing Minbain could say would keep him from it. Hresh baffled her, always had, always would.

"Will you be packing the meat again today?" he asked.

"Probably. Unless Koshmar's got some other job for me today. What she tells me to do is what I do."

"And if she told you to walk upside down on the ceiling?"

"Don't be foolish, Hresh."

"Koshmar tells everyone what to do."

"She is the chieftain," Minbain said. "Are we supposed to rule ourselves? Someone must give the commands."

"Suppose you did instead. Or Torlyri, or Thaggoran."

"The body has only one head. The People have one chieftain."

Hresh pondered that a moment. "Harruel's stronger than anybody else. Why isn't he chieftain?"

"Hresh-full-of-questions!"

"Why isn't he, though?"

With a patient smile Minbain said, "Because he's a man, and the chieftain must be a woman. And because being big and strong isn't the most important thing a chieftain needs. Harruel's a fine warrior. He'll drive off our enemies when we're outside. But you know that his mind is slow. Koshmar thinks quickly."

"Harruel thinks more quickly than you'd imagine," said Hresh. "I've talked to him. He thinks like a warrior, but that doesn't mean he doesn't think. Anyway, I think more quickly than Koshmar. Maybe I ought to be chieftain."

"Hresh!"

"Hold me, Mother," he said suddenly.

The swift change in his mood startled her. He was shivering. One moment babbling in his Hreshlike way, the next huddling up against her, a small frightened bundle seeking comfort. She stroked his thin shoulders. "Minbain loves you," she murmured. "Mueri watches over you. It's all right, Hresh. Everything's all right."

A voice said over her shoulder, "Poor Hresh. He's afraid of the Going Forth, isn't he? I don't blame him."

Minbain looked around. Cheysz had come up beside her, small timid Cheysz. Yesterday Minbain and Cheysz and two of the other women had worked for hours, packing chunks of meat in bags made of skin.

Cheysz said, "I've been thinking, Minbain. As we do all this preparing for the Going Forth. What if they're wrong?"

"What? Who?"

"Koshmar. Thaggoran. Wrong that this really is the New Springtime."

Minbain pulled Hresh even closer against her breast, and clapped her hands over his ears. In fury she said to Cheysz, "Have you gone crazy? You've been *thinking*? Don't think, Cheysz. Koshmar thinks for us."

"Please don't look at me like that. I'm afraid."

"Of what?"

"Outside. It's dangerous out there. What if I don't want to go? We could die in the cold. There are wild animals. Yissou only knows what we'll find out there. I *like* it in the cocoon. Why must we all leave, simply because Koshmar wants us to? Minbain, I want to stay here."

Minbain was aghast. This was profoundly subversive talk. It horrified her that Hresh was taking it all in.

"We all want to stay here," said a deep new voice behind her. It was Kalide, Bruikkos' mother, another of the meat-packers of yesterday: like Minbain, a woman past middle years whose mate had died and who had shifted from breeding status to that of a worker. She was perhaps the oldest woman in the cocoon. "Of course we want to stay, Cheysz. It's warm and safe in here. But it's our destiny to go outside. We're the chosen ones—the People of the New Springtime."

Cheysz swung around, glaring, and laughed harshly. Minbain had never seen such fire in her. "Easy for you to say, Kalide! You're practically at the limit-age anyway. One way or another, you'd be outside the cocoon before long. But I—"

"Don't talk to me like that!" Kalide snapped. "You little coward, I ought to—"

"What's going on?" said Delim, stepping forward suddenly. She was the fourth of the packers, a sturdy woman with deep orange fur and heavy, sloping shoulders. She put herself between Cheysz and Kalide, pushing them apart. "You think you're warriors, now? Come on. Come on. Back off. We have work to do. What is this, Minbain? Are they going to have a fight?"

Softly Minbain said, "Cheysz is a little overwrought. She said an unkind thing to Kalide. It'll pass."

"We're on packing detail again today," Delim said. "We ought to go."

"You go," said Minbain. "I'll be there in a little while."

She glowered at Cheysz and made a quick brushing gesture with her hand, urging her away. After a moment Cheysz moved off toward the animal pen, Delim and Kalide close behind her. Minbain released Hresh from her grasp. He stepped back, looking up at her.

"I want you to forget everything you just heard," she said.

"How can I do that? You know I can't forget anything."

"Don't speak about it to anyone, is what I meant. The things Cheysz said."

"About being afraid to leave the cocoon? About wondering whether Koshmar's wrong about the New Springtime?"

"Don't even repeat them to me. Cheysz could be punished very severely for saying such things. She could be cast out of the People. And I know she didn't actually mean them. She's a very kind woman, Cheysz—very gentle, very frightened—" Minbain paused. "Are *you* frightened about leaving the cocoon, Hresh?"

"Me?" he said, and his voice rang with disbelief. "Of course not!"

"I didn't think so," Minbain said.

"Form the line there!" Koshmar called. "Shape it up! You all know your places. Take them!" She held the Wand of Coming Forth in her left hand, and an obsidian-tipped spear in her right. A brilliant yellow sash was wrapped over her right shoulder and across her breast.

Hresh felt himself beginning to shiver. At last the moment had arrived! His dream, his wish, his joy. The whole tribe stood assembled in the Place of Going Out. Torlyri, the sweet-voiced offering-woman, was turning the wheel that moved the wall, and the wall was moving.

Cool air came rushing in. The hatch was open.

Hresh stared at Koshmar. She looked strange. Her fur was puffed up so that she seemed to be twice her normal size, and her eyes had turned to little slits. Her nostrils were flaring; her hands moved urgently across her breasts, which appeared bigger than usual. Even her sexual parts were swollen as if they were hot. Koshmar was not a breeder; it was odd to see her heated up like that. Some powerful emotion must be sweeping her, Hresh thought, some excitement brought on by the arrival of the Time of Going Forth. How proud she must be that she was the one to lead the tribe out of its cocoon! How excited!

And he realized that he felt some of the same excitement himself. He looked down. His own undeveloped mating-rod was stiff and jutting. The little balls beneath it felt heavy and hard. His sensing-organ tingled.

"All right, forward, now!" Koshmar boomed. "Move along and keep your places, and sing. *Sing!*"

Terror showed plainly in the eyes of many about him. Their faces were frozen with fear. Hresh looked at Cheysz and saw her trembling; but Delim had her by one arm and Kalide by the other, and they moved her along. A few of the other women looked just as frightened—Valmud, Weiawala, Sinistine—and even some of the men, even warriors like Thhrouk and Moarn, were definitely uneasy. Hresh was hard put to understand it, that dread they must be feeling as they stared into the unknown frosty wilderness that awaited them. For him the Going Forth had come none too soon. But for most of the others the departure seemed to be striking with the force of a hatchet. To step out into this vast mystery beyond the cocoon—to leave behind the only world that they and their forefathers had known throughout a span of time that seemed to take in all eternity—no, no, they were scared out of their skins, all but a handful. Hresh could see that easily. He felt contempt for their timidity and compassion for their fear, inextricably mixed in one muddled emotion.

"*Sing!*" Koshmar cried again.

A faint, straggling sound came up from a few voices, Koshmar's, Torlyri's, Hresh's. The warrior Lakkamai, who was always so quiet, suddenly began to sing. Now came Harruel's harsh heavy tuneless voice too, and Salaman's; and then, surprisingly, that of mother Minbain, who hardly ever sang at all, and one by one the others picked it up too, uncertainly at first and then with more vigor, until at last from sixty throats at once came the Hymn of the New Springtime:

Now ends the darkness
Now shines the light.
Now comes the warm time.
Now is our hour.

Koshmar and Torlyri passed through the hatch side by side, with Thaggoran hobbling along right behind them, and then Konya, Harruel, Staip, Lakkamai, and the rest of the older males. Hresh, marching third from the end, threw his head back and bellowed the words louder than anyone:

Into the world now
Fearless and bold.
Now are we masters
Now shall we rule.

Taniane gave him a scornful look, as though his raucous singing offended her dainty ears. Haniman, that waddling plump boy, sticking close beside Taniane as he usually did, made a face at him also. Hresh stuck his tongue out at them. What did he care for Taniane's opinion, or glassy-eyed Haniman's? This was the great day at last. The exodus from the cocoon was finally under way; and nothing else mattered. Nothing.

> *The springtime is ours*
> *The new time of light.*
> *Yissou now gives us*
> *Dominion and sway.*

But then he passed through the hatch himself, and the outside world came rushing toward him and struck him like a great fist. He was overwhelmed despite himself, shaken, stunned.

That first time when he had crept outside it had all been too fast, too jumbled, a flash of images, a swirl of sensations, and then Torlyri had seized him and his little adventure was over, almost before it had begun. But this was the real Going Forth. He felt the cocoon and all that it represented dropping away behind him and plunging into an abyss; or else it was he that was falling into the abyss, drifting downward now into a vast well of mysteries.

He fought to regain his poise. He bit down hard on his lip, he clenched his fists, he drew slow, deep breaths. He looked around at the others.

The tribe was crowded together on the rocky ledge just outside the hatch. Some were crying softly, some were gaping in wonder, some were lost in deep silences. No one was unmoved. The morning air was cool and crisp and the sun was a great frightful eye high in the heavens on the far side of the river. The sky pressed down on them like a roof. It was a sharp hard color, with thick swirls of dust-haze making spiral patterns in it as the wind caught them.

The world stretched away before them, a vast empty desolation, open in all directions as far as Hresh could see: there were no walls, there was nothing at all to confine them. That was the most frightening thing, the *openness* of it. No walls, no walls at all! There had always been walls to press yourself against, and a roof over your head, and a floor beneath your feet. Hresh imagined that he could simply leap forward into the air beyond the ledge and go floating on and on forever, never striking anything. Even the roof that the sky made was so far above them that it scarcely provided any sense of boundary. It was truly terrifying to be staring into that immense open place.

But we will get used to it, Hresh thought. We will have to get used to it.

He knew how lucky he was. Lifetime after lifetime had gone by, thousands of generations of lifetimes, and all that while the People had huddled in their snug cocoon like mice in a hole, telling each other tales of the wondrous beautiful world from which the death-stars had driven their ancestors.

He turned to Orbin beside him. "I never thought I'd be seeing this, did you?"

Orbin shook his head—a tiny stiff movement, as though his neck had become a rigid stalk. "No. No, never."

"I can't believe we're outside," Taniane whispered. "Yissou, it's cold! Are we going to freeze?"

"We'll be all right," Hresh said.

He stared into the gray distance. How he had yearned for even a single glimpse of the outside world! But he had resigned himself to his fate, knowing that he was surely destined to live and die in the cocoon, like everyone else who had existed since the beginning of the Long Winter, without ever having had that glimpse of the world of wonders that lay beyond the hatch, other than the fleeting ones they promised him for his naming-day and his twining-day later on. He was stifling in the cocoon. He hated the cocoon. But there had seemed to be no escaping the cocoon. Yet here they were beyond the hatch.

Haniman said, "I don't like this. I wish we were still inside."

"You would," said Hresh scornfully.

"Only someone crazy like you would want to be out here."

"Yes," Hresh said. "That's right. And now I'm getting my wish."

From old Thaggoran he had learned the names of all the ancient lost cities: Valirian, Thisthissima, Vengiboneeza, Tham; Mikkimord, Bannigard, Steenizale, Glorm. Wonderful names! But what was a city, exactly? A great many cocoons side by side? And the things of nature out there: rivers, mountains, oceans, trees. He had heard the names, but what did they mean, really? To see the sky—just the sky—why, he had almost been ready to give his life for that, the day he had slipped past the sweet offering-woman and out the hatch. He nearly *had* given his life for that. Would Koshmar really have had him thrown out of the cocoon, if the Dream-Dreamer had not awakened just then? Probably she would. Koshmar was hard. Chieftains had to be. In another moment or two, but for the sudden outburst of the Dream-Dreamer, he would have been outside, yes, and the hatch forever shut behind him. That had been close, very close indeed. Only his luck had saved him.

Hresh had always thought of himself as gifted with unusual luck. He never spoke of it to anyone, but he believed he was under the special protection of the gods, all of them, not just Yissou, who protected everyone, or Mueri, who consoled the sorrowful, but also Emakkis, Friit, Dawinno, those more remote deities who governed the subtler aspects of the world. In particular Hresh thought Dawinno guided his days. It was Dawinno the Destroyer who had brought the death-stars upon the world, yes, but not in any malevolent way, he believed. He had brought them because they had needed to be brought. It was the time, and they had to come. Now the world would be resettled, and Hresh thought that he would have an important role in that; and so he would be doing the task that Dawinno had set aside for him. The Destroyer was the guardian of life, and not its enemy as simpler people believed. Thaggoran had taught Hresh these things. And Thaggoran was the wisest man who had ever lived.

Still, it surely had seemed to Hresh as if he had run out of luck that day of his attempt to go outside. If they had pushed him out the hatch into the world he so much yearned to see—and they would have, Torlyri or no, he was certain of that, the law was the law and Koshmar was a hard one—what would have become of him? Once outside, Hresh suspected, he wouldn't have survived half a day on his own. Maybe three quarters of a day if his luck held out. But nobody's luck was good enough to let him live long by himself in the outside world. Only Torlyri's quickness had spared him—that and the mercy of Koshmar.

His playmates had mocked him when they learned of what he had done. Orbin, Taniane, Haniman—they couldn't understand why he would have wanted to go outside, nor why Koshmar had not punished him for it. They had thought he was trying to kill himself. "Can't you wait for your death-day?" Haniman asked. "It's only another twenty-seven years." And he laughed, and Taniane laughed with him, and even Orbin, who had always been such a good friend, made a jeering face and punched him in the arm. Hresh-full-of-questions, Hresh-who-wants-to-freeze, they called him.

No matter. They forgot about his little exploit in a few days. And everything was altered now. The tribe was truly going forth. For the second time in just a few weeks Hresh was seeing the sky, and not just a glimpse this time. He would see the mountains and the oceans. He would see Vengiboneeza and Mikkimord. All the world would be his.

Now comes the warm time.
Now is our hour.

"Is that the sky?" Orbin asked.

"That's the sky, yes," said Hresh, proud of having been out here before, if only for a few minutes. Orbin, stocky and very strong, with bright eyes and a quick, shining smile, was Hresh's age exactly, and his closest friend in the cocoon. But Orbin would never have dared to try to slip outside with him. "And that's the river down there. That green stuff is grass. The red stuff is grass of another kind."

"The air tastes funny," Taniane said, wrinkling her nose. "It burns my throat."

"That's because it's cold," Hresh told her. "You won't mind it after a while."

"Why is it cold, if winter is over?" she asked.

"Don't ask stupid questions," Hresh said. But he found himself troubled about that too, all the same.

Up ahead, by the offering-stone, Torlyri was busy performing some sort of rite: the last one, Hresh hoped, before the march got really under way. It seemed to him that they had been doing almost nothing but rites and ceremonies these past weeks since that day when the Dream-Dreamer awakened and Koshmar announced that the tribe was going to leave the cocoon.

"Are we going to cross the river?" Taniane asked.

"I don't think so," Hresh said. "The sun's in that direction, and if we go toward it we can get burned. I think we're going to go the other way."

He was simply guessing, but he turned out to be right, at least about the direction of the march. Koshmar—wearing now the Mask of Lirridon that had hung so long on the dwelling-chamber wall, yellow and black with a great beak that made her look like some sort of huge insect—raised her spear and called out the Five Names. Then she stepped forward on a narrow track that led up from the ledge to the top of the hill, and from there over the far side and down the western slope toward a broad bare valley beyond. One by one the others fell into line behind her, moving slowly under the burdens of their heavy packs.

They were outside. They were on their way.

They marched down the long slope and into the valley in steady formation, following the same sequence in which they had emerged from the cocoon: Koshmar and Torlyri up front, then Thaggoran, then the warriors, then the workers, then the breeders, and Hresh bringing up the rear with the other children. The valley was much farther away than it seemed, and sometimes appeared to be retreating before them as they marched. Koshmar set a cautious pace. Even the strongest of the marchers, the ones who were up front, seemed to grow weary quickly; and for some of the others, the breeding-women especially, and poor fat Haniman, and the smaller children, it was a struggle almost from the beginning of the trek. Now and again Hresh heard the sound of weeping ahead of him, though whether it was out of fear or from fatigue, he could not tell. None of them, after all, had ever done this much walking, except back and forth within the cocoon, which somehow was different. Here you had to put your feet down on a rough trackless surface that could sometimes shift and slide beneath you. Or go up rises and down slopes, or move around or over obstacles. It was much more difficult than Hresh had imagined. He had thought you simply put one foot forward and then the other, and then the first one again. Which was basically what you did do; but he hadn't realized how tiring that could be.

The cold air was a hindrance, too. It was thin and it seemed to sting and burn with every breath. It went down your throat like a bundle of knives. It left you dry-mouthed and dizzy, and nipped your ears and nose. After a time, though, the cold seemed not to matter as much.

There was a great stillness, and that was more troublesome than Hresh could have expected. In the cocoon you heard the sounds of the tribe all around you all the time. There was a feeling of safety in that. Out here the tribesfolk were quieter, their voices stifled by awe, but even when they did speak the wind would blow their words away, or the vast dome of cold air overhead and the huge open spaces seemed to swallow them up. The silence had a hard, oppressive, metallic quality that no one liked.

From time to time someone halted as though unwilling to go on, and had to be comforted and consoled. Cheysz was the first, crumpling into a little sobbing heap; but Minbain knelt by her, stroking her until she rose. Then the young warrior Moarn dropped down and dug his fingers into the ground as though the world were spinning wildly about him; he clung desperately, cheek to the cold earth, and Harruel had to pry him loose with kicks and harsh words. A little later it was Barnak, one of the workers, a dull-witted man with huge hands and a thick neck: he turned and began to run back toward the cliff, but Staip went loping after him and caught him by one arm, and slapped him, and held him until he was calm. After that Barnak marched without looking up or speaking. But Orbin said, "It's a good thing Staip caught him. If he had gotten away, a dozen more would have gone running back there too."

Koshmar left her place at the head of the procession and came back, talking with everyone, offering encouragement, laughter, prayers. Torlyri moved through the line too to speak with those who were most frightened. She stopped by Hresh, to ask how he was doing, and he winked at her; and she laughed and winked also.

"This is where you always wanted to be, isn't it?"

He nodded. She touched his cheek and went back up front.

The day moved along. Time seemed to hurry. The sun did a strange thing. It moved in the sky, instead of hanging there in the east where Hresh had first seen it. To his surprise the sun seemed to be pursuing them, and somewhere about midday it actually overtook them, so that in the afternoon it lay before them in the western sky.

Hresh was puzzled to find the sun traveling like that. He knew that it was a big ball of fire that hovered overhead all day and went out at night—"day" was when the sun was there, "night" was when it wasn't—but it was hard for him to understand how it could move. Wasn't it fastened in its place? He would have to ask Thaggoran about that a little later. For now, his discovery that the sun could move was simply an inexplicable surprise. But he suspected that there would be other and bigger surprises ahead.

2

They Will Have Your Flesh

Thaggoran shuffled onward, keeping his place just behind Koshmar and Torlyri. There was a throbbing in his left knee and a stiffness in both his ankles, and the chill wind cut through his fur as though he had none at all. His eyes were swollen and pasty from the glaring sunlight. There was no hiding from that great angry blare of light. It filled the sky and reverberated from every rock, every patch of ground.

This was a hard business for a man of nearly fifty, to give up the comforts of the cocoon and march through so strange and bleak a countryside. But it was that very strangeness that would keep him going, hour after hour, day after day. For all his studies in the chronicles he had never imagined that such colors existed in the world, such smells, such shapes.

The land here was harsh and almost empty, a broad barren plain. Its deadness was a disheartening thing. He saw frightened faces all about him. Fear was general among the People. There was a terrible nakedness in having gone out from the cocoon, in being this far from that friendly sheltering place that had housed them all their lives. But Koshmar and Torlyri were working hard to keep panic from engulfing the marchers. Thaggoran saw them going again and again to the aid of those whose fears were overwhelming them. He felt little fear himself, only the threat of exhaustion; but he forced himself on, and smiled bravely whenever anyone looked his way.

The sky darkened steadily as the day went along: from a pale hard blue to a deeper, richer color, then to a dark gray, almost purple, as the shadows gathered. He had not expected that. He knew of such things as day and night from the chronicles, but he had imagined that night would fall like a curtain, cutting off the light at a single stroke. That it might come on gradually through the hours was not something he had considered, nor that the sun's light would change also, growing ruddier through the afternoon, until when the sky was just beginning to turn gray the sun would become a fat red ball hanging low above the horizon.

Late on the afternoon of the first day, as the long purple shadows were beginning to fall across the land, the front line of marchers came upon three large four-legged beasts with great scarlet pronglike horns sprouting in triple pairs from their snouts. They were grazing elegantly on a hillside, moving with careful high-stepping gestures as if in some formal dance. But at the first scent of the humans they looked up in terror and fled wildly, taking off at astonishing speed across the plain.

"Did you see those?" Koshmar asked. "What were they, Thaggoran?"

"Grazing beasts," he said.

"But their names, old man! What are such creatures called?"

He ransacked his memory. The Book of the Beasts said nothing about long-legged creatures with three pairs of red prongs on their noses.

"I think they must have been created during the Long Winter," Thaggoran ventured. "They are not animals that were known in the Great World."

"Are you certain of that?"

"They are unknown creatures," Thaggoran insisted, growing irritated.

"Then we must name them," Koshmar said resolutely. "We must name everything we see. Who knows, Thaggoran? We may be the only people there are. The naming of things will be one of our tasks."

"That is a good task," said Thaggoran, thinking about the fiery pain in his left knee.

"What shall we call them, then? Come, Thaggoran, give us a name for them!"

He looked up and saw the tall graceful things outlined sharply against the dark sky on the crest of a distant hill, peering cautiously down at the marchers.

"Dancerhorns," he said unhesitatingly. "Those are called dancerhorns, Koshmar."

"So be it! Dancerhorns they are!"

The darkness deepened. The sky was nearly black now. Thaggoran, looking up, saw some broad-winged birds flying east in the twilight, but they were too high overhead for him even to try to identify them. He stood staring, imagining himself soaring like that with nothing but air beneath him; for a moment it was an exhilarating idea, and then it became a terrifying one, and he felt a surge of nausea and vertigo that nearly knocked him to the ground. He waited for it to pass, breathing deeply. Then he crouched, digging his knuckles against the solidity of the dry sandy earth, leaning forward, putting his weight against the ground. It supported him as the floor of the cocoon once had done, and that was comforting. He rose after a time and went onward.

In the thickening blackness hard bright points of burning light began to emerge. Hresh, coming up beside him, asked him what they were.

"They are the stars," Thaggoran said.

"What makes them so bright? Are they on fire? It must be a very cool fire, then."

"No," said Thaggoran, "a fiery fire, a blazing fire like the fire of the sun. What they are is suns, Hresh. Like the great sun that Yissou has placed in the day-sky to warm the world."

"The sun is much larger than they are. And very much hotter."

"Only because it's closer. Believe me, boy: what you see are globes of fire hanging in the sky."

"Ah. Globes of fire. Are they very far away, then?"

"So far that it would take the sturdiest warrior all his life to walk to the nearest of them."

"Ah," said Hresh. "Ah." He stood staring at them a long while. Others had stopped too, and were studying the dazzling points of pulsating light that had begun to break out all over the sky. Thaggoran felt a chill, and not only from the evening air. He beheld a sky full of suns, and he knew there were worlds around all those suns, and he felt like dropping down to touch his head against the earth in recognition of his smallness and the greatness of the gods who had brought the People forth into this immense world, this world that was only a grain of sand in the immensity of the universe.

"Look," someone said. "What's that?"

"Gods!" cried Harruel. "A sword in the sky!"

Indeed something new was appearing now—a hook of dazzling white light, an icy crescent gliding into view above the distant mountains. All about him the tribe was kneeling, murmuring, offering up desperate prayers to that great silent floating thing that glowed with a frigid blue-white gleam above them.

"The moon," Thaggoran called. "That is the moon!"

"The moon is round, like a ball, so you always told us," Boldirinthe said.

"It changes," said Thaggoran. "Sometimes it is like this, and sometimes its face is fuller."

"Mueri! I feel the moonlight on my skin!" one of the men wailed. "Will it freeze me, Thaggoran? What will it do? Mueri! Friit! Yissou!"

"There's nothing to fear," Thaggoran said. But he was trembling now too. There is so much that is strange here, he thought. We are in another world. We are naked under these stars and this moon, and we know nothing, not even I, not even I, and everything is new, everything is frightening.

He found Koshmar. "We should make camp now," he said. "It's too dark to go on. And camping will give them something to do as the night comes over us."

"What will happen in the night?" Koshmar asked.

Thaggoran shrugged. "Sleep will happen in the night. And then will come morning."

"When?"

"When night is done," he said.

They camped that first night in a depression beside a thinly flowing stream. As Thaggoran had thought, the work of halting and unpacking and building a campfire distracted the tribe from its fears. But they had hardly settled down when some sort of pale many-jointed insects as long as a man's leg, with huge bulging yellow eyes and powerful-looking green legs tipped with nasty claws, came scuttering out of low mounds of earth nearby. The creatures were attracted by the light, it seemed, or perhaps the warmth of the fire. They looked fierce and ugly, and made a hideous clicking sound with their glossy red mandibles. The children and some of the women ran screaming away from them; but Koshmar came forward without fear and speared one with a quick contemptuous thrust. It pounded its two ends sadly against the ground a few moments before it became still. The others, seeing what had happened to their companion, crawled backward a dozen paces or so and stared sullenly. After a while longer they backed away into their holes again and were not seen again.

"These are greenclaws," Thaggoran said, quickly inventing the name before Koshmar could question him. It embarrassed him not to know the names of the first two creatures they had encountered in the Time of Going Forth. There was nothing in the Book of the Beasts about these, either. He was sure of that.

Koshmar roasted the dead greenclaws in the fire that night, and she and Harruel and some of the other braver ones tasted its flesh. They reported that it had no particular taste at all; yet a few went back for second helpings. Thaggoran declined his share with tactful thanks.

In the night came another annoyance, small round creatures no larger than the ball of a man's thumb, which moved in great lunatic leaps although they had no legs that could be seen. When they landed on someone they dug immediately in, deep down into the fur, and sank their little teeth into the flesh with a sensation that burned like a hot coal. From here and there about the camp outcries of annoyance and pain were heard, until everyone was awake, and the People gathered in a circle to groom one another, snapping the things between forefinger and thumb and pulling them free of the fur with no little difficulty. Thaggoran gave them the name of fireburs. They vanished with the dawn.

The pale light of morning brought Thaggoran out of uneasy sleep. It seemed to him almost that he had not slept at all, but he could remember dreams: visions of faces floating in midair, and a woman with seven dreadful red eyes, and a land where teeth grew from the ground. His body ached everywhere. The sun, looking small and hard and unfriendly, lay like an unripe fruit atop the jagged range of hills to the east. He saw Torlyri far away, making her morning offering.

Scarcely anyone spoke as they made ready to break camp. Wherever he looked, Thaggoran saw bleak faces. Everyone seemed to be struggling visibly against the cold, the fatigue of yesterday's march, the nuisance of the sleep-destroying fireburs, the strangeness of the landscape. The oppressive openness of the view was troublesome to many; Thaggoran saw them with their hands held before their faces, as if they were striving to create a private cocoon for themselves.

His own spirits were cast down by the barren terrain and the bitter stinging weather. Was this truly the New Springtime? Or had they given up their little nest in the mountain too soon, making a premature departure into inhospitable winter and certain death? Perhaps they were writing the Book of the Unhappy Dawn or the Book of the Cold Awakening all over again.

The shinestones had given him no clear answer. His attempt at divination had ended in ambiguities and uncertainties, as such attempts often did. "You must go forth," the stones had told him, but Thaggoran already knew that: were the ice-eaters not practically upon them? Yet the stones had not said they would go forth happily, or that this was the proper time.

He moved apart from the others and wrote for a time in the

chronicles. Hresh came to him as he squatted by the open casket with his hands on the book, but the boy stood silent, as if fearing to interrupt. When Thaggoran was done he glanced up and said, "Well? Would you like to write something now on these pages, boy?"

Hresh smiled. "If only I could."

"I know that you can write."

"But not in the chronicles, Thaggoran. I don't dare touch the chronicles."

Thaggoran said, laughing, "You sound so pious, boy."

"Do I?"

"I'm not fooled, though."

"No," Hresh said. "I wouldn't want to injure the chronicles by trying to write in them. I might put down nonsense, and then in all the years to come they would see what I had written, and they would say, 'Hresh the fool wrote that nonsense there.' What I want is to be able to read the chronicles, though."

"I read them to the People every week."

"Yes. Yes, I know. I want to read them for myself. Everything, even the oldest books. I want to know more about how the cocoon was built, and who built it."

"Lord Fanigole built our cocoon," said Thaggoran. "With Balilirion and Lady Theel. You know that already."

"Yes, but who were they? Those are only names."

"Ancient ones," Thaggoran said. "Great, great beings."

"Sapphire-eyes, were they?"

Thaggoran gave Hresh a strange look. "Why would you say a thing like that? You know that all the sapphire-eyes died when the Long Winter began. Lord Fanigole and Balilirion and Lady Theel were people of our own kind. That is, they were humans: all the texts agree on that. They were the greatest of heroes, those three:

when the panic came, when the deathly cold began, they were the ones who remained calm and led us into shelter." He tapped the casket of the chronicles. "It's all written in here, in these books."

"I would like to read those books someday," Hresh said again.

"I think you will have that opportunity," said Thaggoran.

Gray wisps of fog drifted toward them. Thaggoran began to pack away his holy things. His fingers were numb with cold, and his hands moved clumsily over the locks and seals of the casket. After a moment he beckoned impatiently to Hresh, asking him to help, showing the boy what to do. Together they closed the casket, and then Thaggoran put his raw hands to its lid as though he might be warmed by what it contained.

Hresh said, "Will we ever go back to the cocoon, Thaggoran?"

Again Thaggoran looked at him in a puzzled way. "We have left the cocoon forever, boy. We must go forward until we have found what we are instructed to find."

"And what is that?"

"The things we must have in order to rule the world," said Thaggoran. "As it has been written in the Book of the Way. Those things wait for us out there in the ruins of the Great World."

"But what if this isn't the true New Springtime? Look how cold it is! Don't you ever wonder if we've made some kind of mistake and come out too soon?"

"Never," Thaggoran said. "There can be no doubt. All the omens are favorable."

"It is very cold, though," said Hresh.

"Indeed. Very cold. But do you see how night gradually overtakes the day, and day is gradually born out of night? So too with the New Springtime, boy. A springtime does not arrive in a single great burst of warmth, but it happens moment by moment, bit by bit." Thaggoran shivered and wrapped his arms about himself as the fog touched his bones. "Come, Hresh. Help me with this casket, and let's rejoin the others."

It troubled him that Hresh seemed to have doubts about the wisdom of the trek, for there often was a seer's keenness in the things this strange little boy said, and Hresh's misgivings echoed Thaggoran's own. Koshmar, he thought, might well have been too quick to designate this as the Time of Going Forth. The Dream-Dreamer had not actually said that this was the moment, had he? He had only blurted a few words. Koshmar had finished the sentence for him, and she had put words in the Dream-Dreamer's mouth. Even Torlyri had accused her of that. But no one dared to cross Koshmar. Thaggoran was aware that she had been determined for a long time to be the chieftain who accomplished the Going Forth.

Besides, there were the ice-eaters: not only an omen of springtime, but an immediate threat to the cocoon. Still, might it not have been better to seek shelter somewhere else and wait for warmer weather, rather than to set out across this trackless wasteland?

Too late. Too late. The march had begun, and Thaggoran knew it would not end until Koshmar attained the glory that she had always sought, whatever it might be. Or else it would end with the deaths of them all. So be it, Thaggoran told himself. Whatever would come would come, as was usually the case.

The second day was harsh and difficult. In midday angry swarms of winged creatures with eerie white eyes and furious blood-seeking beaks swooped down. Delim suffered a slashed arm, and the young warrior Praheurt was cut in two places on his back. The People drove them off with shouts and rocks and firebrands, but it was an ugly task, for they kept coming back again and again, so there was no peace for hours. Thaggoran gave them the name of bloodbirds. Later there were others even more vile, with leathery black wings tipped with savage horny claws, and fat little bodies covered with stinking green fur. At night there were fireburs again, a maddening multitude of them. To keep spirits high Koshmar ordered everyone to sing, and sing they did, but it was a joyless singing that they did. There was sleet in the depths of the night, cold hard stuff that raked one's skin like a spray of fiery embers. Torlyri, when she had finished with her offering in the morning, made the rounds of the People, offering the comfort of her warmth and tenderness. "This is the worst of it," she said. "It will be better, soon."

They went on.

On the third day, as they were descending a series of bare gray rolling hills that opened into a shallow green meadow, keen-eyed Torlyri spied a strange solitary figure far in the distance. It seemed to be coming toward them. Turning to Thaggoran, she said, "Do you see that, old man? What do you think it is? No human, surely!"

Thaggoran narrowed his eyes and stared. His vision was not nearly so far-reaching as Torlyri's, but his second sight was the sharpest in the tribe, and it showed him plainly the bands of yellow and black on the creature's long shining body, the fierce beak, the great glittering blue-black eyes, the deep constrictions dividing head from thorax, thorax from abdomen. "No, not a human," he muttered, shaken to the depths of his spirit. "Don't you recognize a hjjk-man when you see one?"

"A hjjk-man!" said Torlyri in wonder.

Thaggoran turned away, trying to conceal the way he was

trembling. He felt as though this were some phenomenally vivid dream. He could scarcely believe that a hjjk-man, an actual living hjjk-man, was even now crossing that meadow. It was like a book of the chronicles jumping up from the casket and coming to life, with figures out of the lost Great World pouring forth and dancing about before him. The hjjk-folk had been only a name to him, a concept, something dry and ancient and abstract, a mere remote aspect of a vanished past. Koshmar was real; Torlyri was real; Harruel was real; this barren chilly countryside was real. What was in the chronicles was only words. But that was no mere word out there that was approaching them now.

And yet it came as no great surprise to Thaggoran that the hjjks too had survived the winter. That was just as the chronicles had predicted. The hjjk-folk had been expected to see the hard times through. They were innate survivors. In the days of the Great World they had been one of the Six Peoples: insect-beings, they were, bloodless and austere. Thaggoran had heard nothing likable about them. Even at this distance he could feel the hjjk-man's emanation, dry and cold like this land they were passing through—indifferent, remote.

Koshmar came over. She had seen the hjjk-man too.

"We'll need to speak with him. He must know useful things about what lies ahead. Do you think you'll be able to get him to talk?"

"Do you have any reason to think I won't?" said Thaggoran gruffly.

Koshmar grinned. "Getting tired, old man?"

"I won't be the first to drop," he replied in a surly tone.

They were crossing now a parched terrain: the soil was sandy and its surface crunched underfoot, as though no one had walked here in thousands of years. Sparse tufts of stiff blue-green grass sprouted here and there, tough angular stuff that had a glassy sheen. Yesterday Konya had tried to pull up a clump and it had cut his fingers; he had come away bloody and cursing.

All afternoon long as they descended the last hill in the group they could discern the hjjk-man stolidly advancing in their direction. He reached them just before twilight, when they had arrived at the meadow's eastern edge. Though they were sixty and he was only one, he halted and waited for them with his middle pair of arms crossed over his thorax, seemingly unafraid.

Thaggoran stared intently. His heart thundered, his throat was parched with excitement. Not even the Going Forth itself had had such an impact on him as the advent of this creature.

Long ago, in the glorious days of the Great World before the coming of the death-stars, these insect-beings had built vast hive-like cities in the lands that were too dry for humans and vegetals or too cold for sapphire-eyes or too moist for mechanicals. If no one else wanted a territory, the hjjk-folk would claim it, and once they did there was no relinquishing it. And yet the chroniclers of the Great World had not considered the hjjk-folk the masters of the earth, for all their sturdiness and adaptability: that was the place held by the sapphire-eyed ones, so it was written. The sapphire-eyes were the kings; after them came all the rest, including the humans, who had been the kings themselves in some even more ancient time. And would be again, now, with the Coming Forth. But the sapphire-eyes, Thaggoran knew, could not have survived the winter, and the humans had gone into hiding. Were the hjjk-folk the masters now by default?

In the failing light the hjjk-man's body had a dull glimmering sheen, as though he were made of polished stone. He was banded in alternating strips of black and yellow from the top to the bottom of his long body—he was slender and tall, taller even than Harruel—and his hard, angular, sharp-beaked face looked much like the Mask of Lirridon that Koshmar had worn on the day of leaving the cocoon. His eyes, enormous and many-faceted, gleamed like dark shinestones. Just below them dangled the segmented coils of bright orange breathing-tubes at either side of his head.

The hjjk-man regarded them in silence until they drew near. Then he said in a curiously incurious way, "Where are you going? It is foolish of you to be here. You will meet your death out here."

"No," Koshmar said. "The winter is over."

"Be that as it may, you will die." The hjjk-man's voice was a dry rasping buzz; but it was not, Thaggoran realized after a moment, a spoken sound. He was speaking within their minds: speaking with second sight, one might say. "Just beyond me in the valley your death is waiting. Go forward and see whether I am lying."

And without another word he began to move past them, as if he had given the tribe all the time he felt it deserved.

"Wait," Koshmar said, blocking his way. "Tell us what perils lie ahead, hjjk-man."

"You will see."

"Tell us now, or you will travel no farther in this life."

Coolly the hjjk-man replied, "The rat-wolves are gathering in this valley. They will have your flesh, for you are flesh-folk, and they are very hungry. Let me pass."

"Wait a little longer," said Koshmar. "Tell me this: have you seen other humans in your crossing of the valley? Tribes like ours, emerging from their cocoons now that the springtime has come?"

The hjjk-man made a droning sound that might have been one of impatience. It was the first trace of emotion he had shown. "Why would I see humans?" the insect-creature asked. "This valley is not a place where one finds humans."

"You saw none at all? Not even a few?"

"You speak words without sense or meaning," said the hjjk-man. "I have no time to spare for such discourse. I ask you now again to allow me to pass." Thaggoran picked up an odd scent, suddenly, sweet and sharp. He saw droplets of a brown secretion beginning to appear on the hjjk-man's striped abdomen.

"We should let him go," he said softly to Koshmar. "He'll tell us nothing more. And he could be dangerous."

Koshmar fingered her spear. Harruel, just to her side, took that as a cue and hefted his own, running his hands up and down its shaft. "I'll kill him, eh?" Harruel murmured. "I'll put my spear right through his middle. Shall I, Koshmar?"

"No," she said. "That would be a mistake." She walked slowly around the hjjk-man, who appeared unperturbed by this turn of the discussion. "One last time," Koshmar said. "Tell me: are there no other tribes of humans in this region? It would give us great joy to find them. We have come forth to begin the world anew, and we seek our brothers and sisters."

"You will begin nothing anew, for the rat-wolves will slay you within an hour," replied the hjjk-man evenly. "And you are fools. There are no humans, flesh-woman."

"What you say is absurd. You see humans before you at this very moment."

"I see fools," said the hjjk-man. "Now let me go on my way, or you will regret it."

Harruel brandished his spear. Koshmar shook her head.

"Let him pass," she said. "Save your energies for the rat-wolves."

Thaggoran watched in keen sorrow as the hjjk-man stalked away toward the hills out of which they had just emerged. He longed to sit down with the strange creature and speak with him of ancient times. Tell me what you know of the Great

World, Thaggoran would have said, and I will tell you all that is known to me! Let us talk of the cities of Thisthissima and Glorm, and of the Crystal Mountain and the Tower of Stars and the Tree of Life, and of all the glories past, of your race and mine and of the sleek sapphire-eyes folk who ruled the world, and of the other peoples also. And then let us speak of the swarms of falling stars whose great tails streamed in fire across the sky, and of the thunder of their impact as they struck the earth, and the clouds of flame and smoke that arose when they hit, and the winds and the black rain, and the chill that came over the land and the sea when the sun was blotted out by dust and soot. We can talk of the death of races, thought Thaggoran—of the death of the Great World itself, whose equal will never be seen again.

But the hjjk-man was nearly out of sight already, disappearing beyond the crest of the hills to the east.

Thaggoran shrugged. It was folly to think that the hjjk-man would have taken part in any such courteous exchange of knowledge. In the time of the Great World it was said of them, so Thaggoran understood, that they were beings who had not the slightest warmth, who knew nothing of friendship or kindness or love, who had, in fact, no souls. The Long Winter was not likely to have improved them in those regards.

A few days farther westward the tribe camped one afternoon in what appeared to be the bed of a dry lake, scooped low below the valley floor. For everyone, no matter how young, there were tasks to do. Some were sent off to gather twigs and scraps of dried grass for the main fire, some looked for greenery to build the second, smokier fire that they had learned kept the fireburs away, some set about herding the livestock into a close group, some joined Torlyri in chanting the guarding-rites to ward off the menaces of the night.

Hresh and Haniman were given tinder-gathering duties. That offended Hresh, that he should be assigned the same sort of job as fat, useless Haniman. He envied Orbin, who had gone off with the men to round up the livestock. Of course, Orbin was very strong for his age. Still, it was humiliating to be paired with Haniman this way. Hresh wondered if Koshmar really thought so little of him.

"Where shall we look?" Haniman asked.

"You go wherever you want to," Hresh replied bluntly. "Just so long as it isn't where I'm going."

"Aren't we going to work together?"

"You do your work and I'll do mine. But you keep out of my way, understand?"

"Hresh—"

"Go on. Move. I don't want to have to look at you."

For a moment something almost like a spark of anger showed in Haniman's little round eyes. Hresh wondered if he was actually going to have to fight him. Haniman was slow and awkward, but he was at least half again heavier than Hresh. All he needs to do is sit on me, Hresh thought. But let him try. Let him try.

Haniman's moment of anger, if that was what it was, passed. Haniman was no fighter. He gave Hresh a reproachful look and went off by himself, kicking at the ground.

Carrying a little wicker basket, Hresh headed out into the territory just west and a little north of the campsite and began foraging about for anything that looked as though it could be burned. There seemed to be very little. He moved farther outward. It was still a barren zone. He went farther still.

Night was coming on swiftly now, and great jagged streaks of violent color, rich purple and angry throbbing scarlet and a somber heavy yellow, made the western sky beautiful and frightful. Behind him everything had turned black already, a stunning all-engulfing darkness broken only by the dim flickering smoky flare of the campfire.

Hresh went a little farther, creeping carefully around a wide shoulder of rock. He knew that what he was doing was rash. He was getting very far from camp now. Too far, perhaps. He could barely make out the sound of the chanting from here, and when he looked back over his shoulder none of the other tribesfolk were in sight.

But still he roamed on and on through this mysterious chilly domain without walls or corridors, where the dark sky was an astounding open dome that went up beyond all comprehension to the distant stars that hung from heaven's roof.

He had to see everything. How else would he be able to understand what the world was like?

And seeing everything necessarily meant exposing himself to certain dangers. He was Hresh-full-of-questions, after all, and it was in the nature of Hresh-full-of-questions to seek answers, regardless of the risk. There is great merit, he thought, in having a soul as restless as mine. They didn't understand that about him, yet, because he was only a boy. But one day they would, he vowed.

It seemed to him that he heard voices in the distance, borne toward him on the wind. Excitement surged in him. What if he were to find the campsite of another tribe just up ahead?

The thought made him giddy. Old Thaggoran claimed that other tribes existed, that there were cocoons just like theirs all over the world; and Thaggoran knew everything, or almost.

But nobody, not even Thaggoran, had any real way of knowing whether that was true. Hresh wanted to believe that it was: dozens or even hundreds of little tribes, each in its own cocoon, waiting through generation after generation for the Time of Coming Forth. Yet no evidence for such a thing existed except in the chronicles. Certainly there had never been any contact with another tribe, at least not since the earliest days of the Long Winter. How could there be, when no one ever left his home cocoon?

But now Koshmar's people were making their way in the open world. There might well be other tribes out here too. To Hresh that was a fantastic notion. He had known only the same band of sixty people all the eight years of his life. Now and then someone new was allowed to be born, at those times when someone old had reached the limit-age and was thrust outside the hatch to die—but otherwise it was just the same people all the time, Koshmar and Torlyri and Harruel and Taniane and Minbain and Orbin and the rest. The idea of stumbling upon a band of completely other people was wondrous.

Hresh tried to imagine what they would look like. Maybe some would have yellow eyes, or green fur. There might be men taller than Harruel. Their chieftain would not be a woman but a young boy. Why not? It was a different tribe, wasn't it? They would do everything differently. Instead of an old man of the tribe they would have three old women, who kept the chronicles on bright sheets of grassglass and spoke in unison. Hresh laughed. They would have different names from ours, too. They will be called things like Migg-wungus and Kik-kik-kik and Pinnipoppim, he decided, names that no one in Koshmar's tribe had ever heard. Another tribe! Incredible!

Hresh moved less cautiously now. In his eagerness to find

the source of the voices ahead, he broke into a half-trot, jogging through the gathering darkness.

Another tribe, yes! The voices grew more distinct.

He pictured them sitting around a smoldering campfire just beyond the next clump of rocks. He saw himself stepping boldly into their midst. "I am Hresh of Koshmar's cocoon," he would say, "and my people are just over there. We mean to begin the world anew, for this is the great springtime!" And they would embrace him and give him velvetberry wine to drink, and they would say to him, "We too mean to begin the world anew. Take us to your chieftain!" And he would run back to camp, laughing and shouting, crying out that he had found other humans, a whole tribe of them, men and women and boys and girls, with names like Migg-wungus and Kik-kik-kik and—

Suddenly he halted, nostrils flaring, sensing-organ rigid and quivering. Something was wrong.

In the stillness of the night he heard the sounds of the other tribe very clearly, now. Very odd sounds they were, too, a high-pitched cluttering sort of squeak mixed with a thick snuffling sort of noise—a peculiar sound, an ugly sound—

Not the sound of some other tribe, no.

Not human sounds at all.

Hresh sent forth his second sight in the way that Thaggoran had taught him to do. For a moment everything was muddled and indistinct, but then he tuned his perceptions more carefully and things came into focus for him. There were a dozen creatures just on the far side of those rocks. Their bodies were about as long as a man's, but they moved on all fours, and their limbs looked quick and powerfully muscled. Their glaring red eyes were small and bright and fierce, their teeth were long and keen and protruded like daggers from their whiskery snouts, their hides were covered in dense gray fur, and their sensing-organs were held out straight and twitching behind them like long narrow whips, pink and almost hairless.

Not human. Not at all.

They were moving in a circle, around and around in a creepy shuffling way, pausing now and then to raise their snouts and sniff. Hresh could not understand the language they were speaking, but the meaning of their words rode clearly to him on his second sight:

"*Flesh—flesh—flesh—eat—eat—eat—eat flesh—*"

The rat-wolves are gathering in the valley, the hjjk-man had said. They will have your flesh, for you are flesh-folk, and they are very hungry. Koshmar had not seemed especially alarmed by that. Perhaps she had thought that the hjjk-man was lying; perhaps she thought there were no such creatures as rat-wolves at all. But what else could these snuffling shuffling bright-eyed long-toothed things be, if not the rat-wolves of whom the hjjk-man had tried to warn them?

Hresh turned and ran.

Around the jutting fangs of rock, past the low sandy hummocks, down into the dry lake bed—scrambling desperately in the dark, losing his basket of tinder in his haste, running as fast as he could back toward the campfire of the tribe. Strangenesses of the darkness assailed him. Something large with wings and bulbous greenish-gold eyes buzzed around his head. He slapped it away and kept running. A hundred paces farther on, another something that looked like three long black ropes side by side rose up before him, coiling and swaying in the cold faint starlight. Hresh darted to one side and did not look back.

Breathless, gasping, he rushed into the midst of camp.

"The rat-wolves!" he cried, pointing into the night. "The rat-wolves! I saw them!" And he went tumbling, exhausted, almost at the feet of Koshmar.

He feared that they would not believe him. He was only wild Hresh, troublesome Hresh, Hresh-full-of-questions, was he not? But for once they paid attention.

"Where were they?" Koshmar demanded. "How many? How big?"

Harruel began handing out spears to all but the smallest children. Thaggoran, squatting by the fire, aimed his sensing-organ out across the dry lake to read the rat-wolves' emanations.

"They're coming!" the old man called. "I feel them, heading this way!"

Koshmar, Torlyri, and Harruel, spears in hand, took up positions shoulder to shoulder at the western side of the camp. How magnificent they look, Hresh thought: the chieftain, the priestess, the great warrior. Nine more stood behind them, and then another row of nine, with the children and the childbearing women huddled in the middle.

He heard Koshmar invoking the Five Heavenly Ones, saw her making the Five Signs, and then the sign of Yissou the Protector over and over. He murmured a prayer to Yissou himself. Alone of his tribe he had seen the rat-wolves, their long snouts, their fiery little eyes, the sharp blades of their teeth.

There was a long timeless time when nothing happened. The warriors guarding the approach to the camp paced in tense circles. Hresh began to wonder if he had dreamed the rat-wolves out there in the dark. He wondered, too, how severely Koshmar would punish him if this proved to be a false alarm.

But then abruptly the enemy was upon them. Hresh heard terrible high-pitched chittering cries, and smelled a strange loathsome musky smell; and an instant later the camp was invaded.

"Yissou!" Koshmar bellowed. "Dawinno!"

The rat-wolves came bounding in from every side at once, screeching, leaping, snarling, flashing their teeth.

Women began to scream, and some of the men also. No one had ever seen animals like this, animals that lived on flesh and used their teeth as weapons. And no one had ever had to fight in this manner before, a true fight, not just a little social brawl among friends but a battle for life. It had been so easy in the cocoon, so sheltered. But they were not in the cocoon any longer.

The wolf-pack circled round and round as if seeking to find the weaker members of the tribe and cut them off. The sour smell of them was heavy on the air. By the flickering firelight Hresh saw their beady red eyes, their long naked sensing-organs, looking just as they had when he had seen them by second sight a little while before, but perhaps even more repellent. What ugly things, what monsters!

He shrank back toward the center of the group, holding the spear that Harruel had given him but not very sure what to do with it. Grasp it here, was that it? And thrust—upward? Let a rat-wolf come near him and he'd figure it out fast enough, he told himself.

The huge figure of Harruel was outlined against the darkness, thrusting, grunting, thrusting again. And there was Torlyri valiantly holding one rat-wolf at bay with robust kicks while skewering another on the tip of her spear. Lakkamai fought well, and Konya, and Staip. Salaman, who was not much older than Hresh himself, struck down two with two successive strokes of his weapon. Koshmar seemed to be everywhere at once, using not only the sharp end of her spear but its butt as well, ramming it with bloodthirsty joy into the toothy mouth of this wolf and that one. Hresh heard dreadful howling sounds. The rat-wolves were calling to one another in what could only be a sort of a language:

"*Kill—kill—kill—flesh—flesh—flesh—*" And someone human was moaning in pain; and someone else was uttering a low whimpering sound of fear.

Then, as swiftly as it had begun, the battle seemed to be over.

Between one moment and the next all grew still. Harruel stood leaning on his spear, breathing hard, wiping at a runnel of blood that streamed from his thigh. Torlyri crouched on her knees, shivering in horror and saying the name of Mueri over and over. Koshmar, clutching her spear at the ready, was prowling about looking for more attackers, but there were none. Dead rat-wolves lay strewn all around, already stiffening, looking even more hideous in death than they had when living.

"Is anyone hurt?" Koshmar asked. "Answer when I call out your name. Thaggoran?"

There was silence.

"*Thaggoran?*" she repeated uneasily.

Still no answer came from Thaggoran. "Look for him," Koshmar ordered Torlyri. "Harruel?"

"Yes."

"Konya?"

"Konya here."

"Staip?"

"Staip, yes."

When it was Hresh's turn, he could barely speak, so amazed was he by all that had occurred this evening. He managed to croak his name in a hoarse whisper.

Everyone was accounted for, in the end, except two—three, actually, for one of the dead was Valmud, a kindly if not overly intelligent young woman, one of the breeding couples; and she had been carrying an unborn. That was serious enough; but the other death was catastrophic.

It was Hresh who found him, lying sprawled in some straggly dead weeds just beyond the edge of the camp. Old Thaggoran had defended himself well. The wolf who had ripped out his throat lay beside him, eyes bulging, tongue black and swollen. The chronicler had strangled it even as he died.

Stunned and numbed, Hresh stared somberly at the dead man, unable even to cry. The loss was too great. He felt almost as if his own throat had been ripped out. After a time he managed a little dry choking sound, and then a sort of a sob. He could not move. He dared not even breathe. He wanted time to unhappen itself, this day to roll backward upon its foundations.

Finally he knelt and tremblingly touched the old man's forehead, as if hoping that the knowledge that was packed so deeply behind it might leap from Thaggoran's spirit to his at a touch, before Thaggoran had cooled. But Thaggoran's spirit was gone.

It was beyond belief. Hresh had never known such a loss. His own father, Samnibolon, had been only a name to him, dead long ago. But this—this—

"Dawinno—" he began uncertainly.

Then the dammed flood of his feelings broke through. A terrible cry came welling up out of the depths of his body and he let it come forth, a great curdled furious wailing sound that almost tore him apart as it erupted from him. Tears poured down his cheeks, plastering his fur into damp spikes. He shook, he moaned, he stamped his feet.

For a long moment after the worst spasm had passed, he crouched, trembling and sweating, thinking of all that was lost to the People, all that had slipped through his own hands, by the death of this wise old man.

This was more than the death of one man: everyone had to die someday, after all, and Thaggoran had lived a long while already. But this was the death of knowledge. An immense vacant place in Hresh's soul could never now be filled. There was so much he had hoped to learn from Thaggoran about this strange world into which the tribe had plunged, and he would never learn it now. Some things were in the chronicles, many things, yes, but some had been passed down only by spoken words, from one chronicler to the next across the hundreds of thousands of years, and now that line of transmission was broken, now those things were lost forever.

But I will learn all I can nevertheless, Hresh told himself.

I will make myself chronicler in Thaggoran's place, he said boldly to himself, in that moment of grief and shock and intolerable loss.

He reached down and coolly probed the bloodied fur just below Thaggoran's torn throat. There was an amulet that looked like a piece of green glass there, a small oval thing, very old, with tiny signs inscribed on it, something that Thaggoran once had told him was a piece of the Great World. Carefully Hresh slipped it free. It seemed to burn with a cold glow against his palm. He held it, heart pounding, tightly clenched in his hand for a time. Then he popped it into the little purse he carried on his hip.

He was not willing to put it around his own throat: not yet. But he would, someday soon.

And he resolved: I will go everywhere upon the face of this world and see everything that exists and learn everything that can be learned, for I am Hresh-full-of-questions! I will master all the secrets of the times gone by and the times to come, and I will fill my soul with wisdom until I nearly burst of it, and then I will set all my knowledge down in the chronicles, for those who are to follow after us in this the New Springtime.

And, thinking those things, Hresh felt the pain of Thaggoran's death beginning to ebb.

All night long the whole tribe chanted the death-chants over their two fallen tribesfolk, and at dawn's first light they carried the bodies eastward a little way into the hills and said the words of Dawinno for them and the words of Friit and Mueri for themselves. Then Koshmar gave the signal, and they broke camp and headed out into the broad plains to the west. She would not say where they were going: only that it was the place where they were destined to go. No one dared to ask more.

3

The Place Without Walls

A scouring wind cut across the dry plains, lifting the thin sandy oil and whirling it into dark clouds. Here scarcely anything grew: it was as if the surface of the world had been cut clean by a great blade passing close across it, stripping away all topsoil and every seed.

To the right of the marchers, not far away, lay a line of low rounded hills, blue-gray and barren. To the left an endless flatland stretched away toward the horizon. There was a sharp edge to the air, and its flavor was an acrid one. Yet the day was significantly warmer than any that had preceded it. This was the third week of the march.

In the stillness of the afternoon came a strange grunting sound, a distant dull noise like none that anyone of the People had ever heard.

Staip turned to Lakkamai, who marched beside him. "Those hills are talking to us."

Lakkamai shrugged and said nothing.

"They're saying, *Go back, go back, go back,*" said Staip.

"How can you tell that?" Lakkamai asked. "It's just a noise."

Harruel had noticed it too. He paused and turned, shading his eyes against the glare. After a moment he leaned forward into the wind and shook his head and laughed, and pointed to the hills.

"Mouths," he said.

His eyes were extraordinarily keen. The other warriors shaded their eyes as he had done, but they saw only hills. "What do you mean, mouths?" Staip said.

"In front of the hills. Big peculiar animals sitting there, making that barking sound. They don't have any bodies," Harruel said. "Just mouths. Can't you see?"

Koshmar by now had seen also. Coming to Harruel's side, she said, "Look at those things. Do you think they're dangerous?"

"They just sit there," said Harruel. "If they don't move from the spot they can't hurt us, can they? But I'll go over and check them out at closer range." He turned. "Staip! Salaman! Come with me!"

"May I go too?" Hresh asked.

"You?" Harruel chuckled. "Yes. We'll toss you in, and see what happens to you."

"No," said Hresh. "But may I come?"

"Keep back out of harm, if you do."

They went loping across the plain toward the hills, the three warriors and Hresh, who was hard pressed to keep up with them. At close range the grunting, barking sound was oppressively loud, sending a shivering vibration through the ground, and it was clear to everyone now that Harruel was right about its origin. At the foot of the line of hills sat a row of perhaps a dozen immense blue-black hump-shaped creatures spaced equidistantly at wide intervals. They seemed to have no limbs or bodies at all, but were mere immobile giant heads with dull staring eyes. In a steady, regular rhythm they opened the vast caverns of their mouths and emitted their booming, croaking cries.

All across the plain, small animals were moving toward them as though gripped with hypnotic fervor by those dull flat sounds. One by one they strode or crawled or hopped or slithered unhesitatingly toward the great heads, and up over the rims of their dark red lower jaws, and into the black maw beyond.

"Keep back," Harruel said sharply. "If we get too close we may be drawn in like that too."

"I don't feel any pull," said Staip.

"Nor I," said Salaman. "Just a little tickle, maybe. But—Hresh! Hresh, come back!"

The boy had edged forward until he had moved out in front of the warriors. Now he was walking out across the plain toward the heads in an odd jerky way, shoulders twitching, knees rising almost to his waist with each step. His sensing-organ was twisted around his body like a sash.

"*Hresh!*" Harruel yelled.

Hresh was no more than fifty paces from the nearest of the heads now, moving as if in a dream. The rhythm of the booming sounds picked up. The ground shook violently. With an angry toss of his head Harruel rushed forward and caught the boy around the middle, snatching him off the ground. Hresh stared at him with unseeing eyes.

"One of these days your curiosity will kill you," Harruel said in annoyance.

"What? What?"

"The boy's in a daze," Staip said. "That sound—it was sucking him right in—"

"I feel it too, now," said Salaman. "It's like a drum summoning us. *Boom—boom—boom—*"

Harruel looked back and stared in fascination and horror. Salaman was right: the sound had a kind of magnetic force, pulling in creatures from all over the plain to be devoured. Bending suddenly, Harruel snatched up a rock the size of his hand and hurled it furiously toward the gaping mouth. But it fell short by five or ten paces.

"Come," he said, his voice loud, rasping. "Let's get away from these things before it's too late."

Back toward the marchers they ran, Harruel carrying Hresh lest he be hypnotized a second time and go dashing off again to his doom. Behind them the sound of the great heads grew louder and more insistent for a time, then faded with distance.

When the men reached the tribe they found everything in chaos and confusion. A new attack of bloodbirds had commenced. The fierce white-eyed creatures had come suddenly out of the darkness to the east in a dense swarm and were whirling and shrieking above the tribe, darting down to thrust with their razor-keen beaks. Delim was struggling with one that had engulfed her entire head in its beating wings, and Thhrouk was fighting with two at once. Lakkamai, hurrying forward, pulled the bloodbird away from Delim and tore it in half. The woman crouched down, holding both hands to an eye streaming with blood. Harruel chopped the air with his spear, skewering one and then another. Koshmar cried encouragement, fighting among the others. The dull booming of the far-off mouth-creatures still could be heard, and the wild piercing cries of the bloodbirds above it.

The battle lasted ten minutes. Then the birds disappeared as quickly as they had come. Six of the tribe had been wounded, Delim the most seriously. Torlyri bandaged her eye, but she would not have the sight of it again. Harruel had sustained two deep gouges on his spear-arm. Konya too had been injured. Everyone was weary and dispirited.

And now night was coming on. The last light of the dying sun drenched the flatland in a flood of crimson.

"All right," Koshmar said. "It's too late to continue. We'll pitch our camp here."

Harruel shook his head. "Not here, Koshmar. We need to get farther away from those mouth-things. Can you hear them? The sound they make is dangerous. We'll have people going to them in the night, walking right into their jaws like sleepwalkers, if we stay here."

"Do you mean that?"

"We nearly lost Hresh," Harruel said. "He was heading straight for one."

"Yissou!" Koshmar contemplated the great heads on the horizon for a moment, frowning. Then she spat and said, "Very well. Let's move on."

They marched until it was too dark to go any farther. The booming of the great heads was only faintly audible here. Aching, sore of foot, blistered of soul, the People dropped down in relief in a place where a feeble stream seeped from the sand.

"It was a mistake," Staip said quietly.

"Leaving the cocoon, you mean?" Salaman asked. "You think we should have stayed? Taken our chances against the ice-eaters?"

Harruel glowered at them. "We were right to make the Coming Forth," he said firmly. "There is no question but that it was the right thing to do."

"I meant coming this way," said Staip. "Koshmar was wrong to bring us out into these miserable plains. We should have turned south, toward the sunlight."

"Who knows?" Harruel said. "One way is as good as another."

In the darkness there were strange sounds all night: hissings, cacklings, far-off shrillings. And always the distant throb of the giant heads, booming their song of hunger as they waited by the base of the barren hills for their helpless prey to come to them.

It was the fifth week of the journey. Torlyri, rising at daybreak as always so that she could make the sunrise-offering, rolled and stretched and clambered to her feet. The sun bathed her in a cheerful glow. Quietly she went out of the camp where everyone still lay sleeping, and searched until she found a suitable site for performing her offering, a little way to the west. It seemed a holy place: a sheltered declivity where thousands of small red-backed insects were industriously building an intricate turreted structure out of the sandy earth. She knelt beside it, said the words, named the Names, prepared the offering.

The dawn sunlight felt strong and warm and good. She had begun to notice, in the past few days, that the weather seemed to be growing more agreeable. At first she had awakened stiff and shivering in a cold mist every day, but now the morning air seemed softer and milder, though not yet soft, not yet mild.

It was a sign that stirred hope in her. Perhaps this really was the New Springtime, after all.

Torlyri had never been certain of that. Like all the rest of the tribe she had allowed herself to be swept along out of the cocoon by Koshmar's insistent optimism. Out of love for Koshmar she had not voiced any strong opposition, but Torlyri knew that there were some within the tribe who would have preferred to remain in the cocoon. Going forth was a tremendous step. It was such a change that Torlyri could scarcely believe they had done it. The tribe had lived in its cocoon forever; or almost forever, which was the same thing. Hundreds of thousands of years, so poor old Thaggoran had always said! It was impossible for Torlyri to imagine what sort of span of time hundreds of thousands of years might be, or even a thousand years. A thousand years was forever. A hundred thousand years was a hundred times forever.

But they had obediently come marching out, after living a hundred times forever in their cocoon. Like people walking in their dreams they had followed Koshmar outside, into a world of sudden dangers.

Those ferocious snarling chittering rat-wolves: a lucky thing the tribe had had some warning of them, or they would have taken more lives than just two, that was certain. Then the blood-birds—what a ghastly task that had been, beating them off! And the leathery-winged ones who followed them. And then after them, there had been—

There was no end, Torlyri knew, to the perils that lurked in these plains. And it was cold out here, even now, and dry and dis-hearteningly bleak, and there were no walls. *There were no walls.* The cocoon offered total security: here there was none at all.

What if they had come out of the cocoon too early?

True, it had been centuries since the last great cataclysm, according to Thaggoran. But this might just be one of the quiet intervals between one death-star and the next.

Minbain had expressed the same anxiety a day or two before, when she had come to Torlyri to have the communion of Mueri. It was the third time in a week that Minbain had asked for that communion. The march seemed harder on her than on most of the other women, perhaps because she was older, though there were others even older than Minbain who were bearing up well. But she was haggard and dejected, and full of uncertainties.

"Thaggoran used to tell us," Minbain said, "that as much as five thousand years would go by in peace, in the time when the death-stars were falling. But that didn't mean that it was all over. Always, after a time of no death-stars, a new death-star would come. How can we be sure that the world has seen the last of them?"

"Yissou the Protector has brought us forth," said Torlyri soothingly, hating herself for the smoothness with which she spoke the comforting lie.

"And if it wasn't the Protector who brought us forth?" Minbain asked. "If it was the Destroyer?"

"Peace," Torlyri whispered. "Come close to me, Minbain. Let me ease your soul."

But there was little repose for her own. Though she strived to hide it, she was as fearful as Minbain. There was no assurance that this was the true Time of Coming Forth. Torlyri believed that the gods did mean them well; but there was no comprehending the workings of the gods, who might in their great wisdom have led the tribe into fatal error. How could anyone know what was to come? Why, tomorrow or the next day or the day after that the terrible fire of a death-star's tail might be seen streaming across the heavens, and then the whole world would shake with the force of the collision, and the sky would grow black and the sun would be hidden and all warmth would flee and all warmth-loving creatures that were unable to find shelter in time would perish. That had happened so often before, in the seven hundred thousand years of the Long Winter: how could they be certain it would not happen again? The tribe owed it to humanity to preserve itself until the world's long nightmare was finally over.

It is possible that we are the only ones left anywhere, Torlyri thought.

The idea was frightening. Just one fragile little band of some sixty men and women and children standing between human-kind and extinction! Can we dare take any risk of destruction, she wondered, if we are the sole remnant of our kind? It was as though they bore the burden of all the millions of years of humanity's stay upon the earth: everything coming down to this one little band, these few frail stragglers wandering the bleak plains. And that was terrifying.

Still, the days *were* growing warmer.

It would have been folly for the People to huddle in their cocoon until the end of time, waiting for absolute knowledge that it was finally safe to emerge. The gods never gave you absolute knowledge of anything. You had to take your chances, and have faith. Koshmar believed it was safe to have come forth. The omens told her so. And Koshmar was the chieftain. Torlyri knew she could never see things with the clear, bold sight of Koshmar. That was why Koshmar was chieftain, and she a mere priestess.

She busied herself now with the sunrise-offering. Gradually she began to feel better. Yissou *did* protect and nourish. The gods had *not* betrayed them by allowing Koshmar to bring the People forth. All would be well. They had passed through great danger, and dangers aplenty still waited for them ahead: but all would be well. They dwelled in the protection of Yissou.

The Time of Going Forth had made the invention of a new sunrise rite necessary. No more the daily interchange of things from within the cocoon and things from without. Instead, now, Torlyri filled a bowl every evening with bits of grass and soil from whatever place they happened to have been spending the night at, and in the morning she waved it toward the four corners of the sky and invoked the protection of the gods, and then she carried that bowl's contents onward to empty it that evening at the next campsite. That way Torlyri constructed a continuity of sacredness as the People made their way across the face of this unfamiliar world.

Creating that continuity seemed vital to her. With Thaggoran dead, it was as though the whole past had been lopped away, and the tribe orphaned, left now without ancestors or heritage. They were stumbling forward in the dark, guessing at all they must do. With their yesterdays so cruelly severed from them by the death of their chronicler, they must build a new skein of history stretching into the years to come.

When Torlyri was done with that morning's rite she rose to return to camp. Unexpectedly something moved beneath her feet, in the earth. She looked down, scuffed at the sandy ground, felt it quiver in response to her probing. Putting down her bowl, she brushed away the surface soil and exposed what looked like a thick glossy pink cord buried a short distance underneath. It wriggled in a convulsive way as if annoyed. Gingerly she touched a fingertip to it, and it wriggled again, so vigorously that two arm's lengths of it burst free of the ground and arched into the air like a straining cable. The head and the tail of the thing remained hidden.

"What a nasty worm!" came a voice from above. "Kill it, Torlyri! Kill it!"

She looked up. Koshmar stood at the top of the slope.

"Why are you here?" Torlyri asked.

"Because I didn't want to be there," Koshmar said, smiling in an oddly self-conscious way.

Torlyri understood. There was no mistaking that smile. Koshmar must want to twine, something that they had not done since leaving the cocoon.

In the cocoon there had been twining-chambers for such intimacies; here no privacy was to be found under the great open bowl of the sky. And in the tensions and strangeness of the trek twining somehow had seemed inappropriate. Still, twining was essential to the welfare of one's soul. For Koshmar, apparently, it could be put off no longer. So she had followed Torlyri to the offering-place; and Torlyri was glad of it. Warmly she extended a hand to her twining-partner. Koshmar scrambled down the slope beside her.

The cable-creature in the ground was still writhing. Koshmar drew her knife. "If you won't kill it, I will."

"No," Torlyri said.

"*No?* Why not?"

"It hasn't harmed us. We don't know what it is. Why don't we just let it be, Koshmar, and go somewhere else?"

"Because I hate it. It's a hideous thing."

Torlyri stared strangely at her. "I've never heard you talk that way before. Killing for the mere sake of killing, Koshmar? That isn't like you. Let it be. All right? To kill without need is a sin against the Provider. Let the creature be." Something was troubling Koshmar deeply, that was clear. Torlyri sought to divert her. "Look over here, at the castle these insects have built."

Indifferently Koshmar said, "How amazing."

"It is! Look, they've made a little gate, and windows and passageways, and down here—"

"Yes, it's wonderful," said Koshmar without looking. She put her knife away; evidently she had lost interest in the cable-creature also. "Twine with me, Torlyri," she said.

"Of course. Right here, do you think?"

"Right here. Now. It's been a million years."

"Yes. Yes, of course."

Torlyri nodded. Tenderly she brushed her hand against her partner's cheek and they lay down together. Their sensing-organs touched, withdrew, touched again. Then gently they wound their sensing-organs one about the other in the delicate and intricate movements of the twining, and they entered into the first stages of their joining.

One by one they achieved the levels of linkage, easily, readily, with the skill born of long knowledge of each other. They had been twining-partners since they were girls; they had never wanted anyone else, as though they had been born as the two halves of a single whole. For some it was difficult to attain twining, but never for Koshmar and Torlyri.

Still, there were little hesitations and missed connections this time that Torlyri did not expect. Koshmar was unusually tense and taut; her whole soul seemed rigid, like a bar of some pliant metal that has been left in a cold place. Perhaps it is simply that we have not twined for a long time, Torlyri thought. But more likely the problem was something more complex than mere abstinence. She opened herself to Koshmar and as their souls merged she strove to take from Koshmar whatever dark troublesome thing had invaded her soul.

It was a communion far more intimate than mere coupling, which was an act that Koshmar had always scorned and which Torlyri had tried two or three times over the years without finding much reward in it. Most members of the tribe coupled rarely, for coupling often led to breeding, and breeding was necessarily a rare event, since the need for replacement of tribesfolk was so infrequent in the cocoon. But twining—ah, twining, that was something else! Twining was a way of love, yes, and a way of healing, and in some instances a way also of attaining knowledge that could not be had by any other means; and it was much more besides.

Their bodies held each other and their souls held each other and together they floated down and down and down, through all the levels that led to their goal of warm dark union, drifting like feathers on warm gusts, weightless, effortlessly carried onward, passing without difficulty around the rocky scarps and jagged boulders of the soul, negotiating with pure simplicity the treacherous canyons and gullies of the mind. Until at last they were fully joined and they were at oneness within each other, each encompassing and enclosing the other, each fully open to the flow and rush of the other's soul. Torlyri sought for the source of Koshmar's anguish, but she could not find it; and then in the joyous union of twining she no longer could devote herself to anything but the twining itself.

Afterward they lay close together, warm, fulfilled.

"Is it gone from you now?" Torlyri asked. "The shadow, the cloud that was on you?"

"I think it is."

"What was it? Will you tell me?"

Koshmar was silent for a while. She seemed to be struggling to articulate the anguish within her, which Torlyri had been able to perceive in their twining only as a dark, hard knot that could neither be penetrated nor understood nor made to uncoil.

After a time Koshmar dug her fingers lightly into Torlyri's dense black fur and said, as if from a great distance, "Do you remember what the hjjk-man said, his last words to us? *There are no humans, flesh-woman,* is what he said."

"I remember that, yes."

"It remains in my mind, and it burns me, Torlyri. What could he have meant by that?"

Torlyri turned so that her eyes were close to Koshmar's shining intense ones. "He was speaking mere idle mischief. He wished to trouble our souls, that's all. He was impatient, he was bothered because we weren't letting him pass. So he said something that he hoped would hurt us. It was only a lie."

"He spoke the truth about the rat-wolves," Koshmar pointed out.

"Even so. That doesn't mean that anything else he said was true."

"But what if it was? What if we're the only ones, Torlyri?" Koshmar seemed to force the words from the pit of her chest.

The chilling thought echoed Torlyri's own baleful speculations of a little while before. Somberly she declared, "The same thing has occurred to me, Koshmar. And also the thought of the responsibility that lies upon us to survive, if we sixty are the only humans left in the world. If all the others perished in the hardships of the Long Winter."

"The responsibility, yes."

"How heavily it must weigh on you, Koshmar!"

"But I am less troubled, now. I feel stronger, now that we have twined, Torlyri."

"Are you?"

Koshmar laughed. "Perhaps all I needed was to twine with you, eh? I was so full of gloom, such foreboding, such a sense that I had committed some crazy folly and that the punishment for folly is always terrible—and I knew that I was the only one responsible, that I was the one who had decided that we had to leave the cocoon, that Thaggoran had had his doubts and so had you—" She shook her head. "As always you've cheered me, Torlyri. You've shared your strength with me and enabled me to go on. The hjjk-man was lying, eh? We're not the only ones. And we'll find the others and together we'll rebuild the world. Isn't that so? Of course. Of course. Who could doubt it! Ah, Torlyri, Torlyri, how much I love you!"

And she embraced Torlyri joyously. But Torlyri responded

halfheartedly. In the last few moments she had felt some change come over her soul, darkening it with a grim heavy shadow. The uncertainties of the day before had returned. The fate of the People once again seemed to her to be precariously suspended above an infinite abyss. She was lost now in doubts and despairs, as if Koshmar's anguish had passed from her to her twining-partner in their communion.

"Is *your* spirit troubled now?" Koshmar asked after a time, pulling back.

"Perhaps it is."

"I won't allow it. Have you raised up my soul at the expense of your own?"

"If I've taken your fears from you, it pleases me greatly," said Torlyri. "But now, yes, I suppose that the fears that troubled you lie heavy on me." She scooped handfuls of sandy soil and tossed them about irritably. At length she said, "What if we *are* the only humans, Koshmar?"

"What if we are?" said Koshmar grandly. "Then we will inherit the earth, we sixty! We will make it our kingdom. We will repeople it with our kind. We must be very wary, that is all, for we are a rare precious thing, if we are the only humans there are."

Koshmar's sudden buoyance was irresistible. Almost at once Torlyri felt the dark moment beginning to lift.

"Still," Koshmar went on, "it's the same either way, whether we are the only humans or just a few out of millions. We must always go warily, past all the perils this world holds for us. For above all else we have to guard and preserve one another, and—"

"Oh, look—look, Koshmar!" Torlyri cried suddenly.

She pointed to the insect-castle. The cable-creature had yanked itself completely free of the ground at one end. It was enormously long, three or four times the length of a man. Looping high and swooping down, it was striking again and again at the elaborate walls and turrets of the structure. Its featureless, eyeless face ended in a gaping maw, and once it broke the castle open it began to devour the small red insects and their shattered ramparts of earth as well in a series of voracious gulps that would soon leave no trace of the builders or their work.

Koshmar shivered. "Yes: perils on all sides. I told you I wanted to kill it."

"But it hasn't harmed you."

"And the insects whose castle it has destroyed?"

Torlyri smiled. "You owe them no favors, Koshmar. Every creature must eat, even nasty cable-things. Come, let it finish its breakfast in peace."

"There are times I think you are less gentle than you seem, Torlyri."

"Every creature must eat," said Torlyri.

Leaving Torlyri to complete the sunrise rite that she had interrupted, Koshmar returned to the place where the tribe lay encamped. It was well past the sunrise hour now, and all the tribesfolk were up and moving about.

She stood atop a low hillock and peered toward the west. It was good to feel the warmth of the morning sun on her back and shoulders.

The land that lay before them was flattening out into a broad shallow bowl without mountains, without trees, almost without features of any kind. It was very dry here, sandy soil, no lakes, no rivers, only the most trifling of streams. Here and there the rounded stumps of little hills could be seen. They looked as though they had been ground down, polished smooth, by some gigantic force, as indeed most likely they had. Koshmar tried to imagine how it had been, deep layers of ice lying everywhere on the land, ice so heavy that it flowed like a river. Ice cutting into mountains, turning them to rubble, sweeping them away during the hundreds of thousands of years of the Long Winter. That was what Thaggoran said had happened in the world while the tribe nestled in its cocoon.

Koshmar wished she had Thaggoran with her now. No loss could have been more painful. She had not realized how much she relied upon him until he was gone. He had been the mind of the tribe, and the soul of it, and its eyes also. Without him they were like blind folk, lurching this way and that, knowing nothing of the mysteries that surrounded them on every side.

She brushed the thought away. Thaggoran had been important but he was not indispensable. No one was. She had refused to let his death subdue her spirit. Thaggoran or no Thaggoran, they would go on, and on and on and on, until they had strung their path clear around the round belly of the world if necessary, for it was their destiny to move forward until they had achieved whatever it was that they had been called into the world to achieve. They were a special folk, this tribe. That she knew. And she was a special leader. Of that too Koshmar was certain. Nothing could dissuade her of that.

Sometimes these days of the march, when she wavered even a little, when fatigue and sun-glare and dry cold winds carried doubt and fear and weakness into her soul, she summoned up Thaggoran out of death in her mind and used him to bolster her resolve. "What do you say, old man?" she would ask. "Shall we turn back? Shall we find a safe mountain somewhere and carve a new cocoon for ourselves?"

And he would grin. He would lean close to her, his rheumy

red-rimmed old eyes searching hers, and he would say, "You speak nonsense, woman."

"Do I? Do I?"

"You were born to bring us from the cocoon. The gods require it of you."

"The gods! Who can understand the gods?"

"Exactly," old Thaggoran would say. "It's not our place to try to understand the gods. We are here simply to do their bidding, Koshmar. Eh? What do you say to that, Koshmar?"

And she would say, "We will go on, old man. You could never talk me into turning back."

"I would never try," he would say, as he turned misty and transparent and faded from her sight.

Staring now into the west, Koshmar tried to read the omens in the hard, flat blue sky. To the north there was a line of soft white clouds, very high, very far apart. Good. The gray clouds, low and heavy, were the snow-clouds. She could see none of those now. These were harmless. To the south there was a line of swirling dust on the horizon. That could mean anything. High winds knifing into the dry soil, maybe. Or a band of huge heavy-hooved beasts thundering this way. Or an enemy army on the march, even. Anything. Anything.

"Koshmar?"

She swung around. Harruel had joined her on the hillock without her hearing him. He stood looming behind her, a huge, powerful broad-shouldered thick-wristed figure half again her size, casting an enormous shadow that stretched off to the side like a black cloak flung across the ground. His fur was a dark brick-orange, clustering in bunches at his cheeks and chin to form a savage heavy red beard that all but concealed his features, leaving only his cold blue-black eyes blazing through.

It angered Koshmar that he had come up to her that way, in silence, and that he was standing so close to her now. There was a certain lack of respect in his standing so close.

Coolly she said, "What is it, Harruel?"

"How soon will we be breaking camp, Koshmar?"

She shrugged. "I haven't decided. Why do you ask?"

"People are asking me. They dislike this place. It seems too dry to them, too dead. They want to pick up and move along."

"If people have questions, they should bring them to me, Harruel."

"You were nowhere to be found. You were off with Torlyri, we supposed. They asked me. And I had no answer for them."

She regarded him steadily. There was a tone in his voice that she disliked and that she had never heard before. With the sound of his voice alone he seemed to be implying criticism of her: it was a sharp, fault-finding tone. There was almost a challenge in it.

"Do you have some problem, Harruel?"

"Problem? What kind of problem? I told you: they were asking me when we were going to leave here."

"They should have asked me."

"I said, you were nowhere to be found."

"Better yet," Koshmar said, going on as if Harruel had not spoken, "they should have asked no one, but simply waited to be told."

"But they did ask me. And I had nothing to tell them."

"Exactly," said Koshmar. "There was nothing you could have told them. All you needed to say was 'We will leave here when Koshmar says we are going to leave here.' Such decisions are mine. Or would you prefer to make them for me, Harruel?"

He looked startled. "How could I do that? You're the chieftain, Koshmar!"

"Yes. You'd do well to keep that in mind."

"I don't understand what you're trying to—"

"Let me be," she said. "Will you? Go. Go, Harruel."

For an instant there was something like fury in his eyes, mixed with confusion and, perhaps, fear. Koshmar was uncertain about the fear. She had always thought she could read Harruel with ease, but not now. He stood for a moment glowering at her, parting his lips and clamping them again several times as though considering and rejecting various angry speeches; and then, making a grudging gesture of respect, he turned ponderously about and stalked away. She stood watching him, shaking her head, until he had descended into the camp.

Strange, she thought. Very strange.

Everyone seemed to be changing out here under the pressures of life in this place without walls. She could see the changes in their eyes, their faces, the way they held their bodies. Some seemed to be thriving on the hardships. She had noticed Konya, who had always been a quiet and private man, suddenly laughing and singing in the midst of the group on the march. Or the boy Haniman, always so soft and lazy: yesterday he had gone running past her and she had barely recognized him, so vigorous had he become. And then there were some who were growing faded and weary on the march, like Minbain, or the young man Hignord, who went slouching along with their shoulders down and their sensing-organs trailing in the dust.

And now Harruel, swaggering around demanding to be told her schedule for the march, and behaving almost as though he felt he should take her place as chieftain. Big as he was, strong as he was, he had never before let Koshmar see any ambitions of that sort in him. He had always been courteous in his gruff way, obedient, dependable. Here in this land without walls something black and dour seemed to have entered his soul and of late he appeared barely able to disguise his wish to command the tribe in her stead.

Of course that could never be. The chieftain was always a woman: it had never been otherwise since the tribe had been founded, and that would never change. A man like Harruel was bigger and stronger than any woman could be, yes, but the tribe would scarcely trust a man as its leader no matter how strong he was. Men had no cunning; men had no sense of the long view of things; men, at least the strong ones, were too blunt, too hasty, too rash. There was too much anger in them, Yissou only knew why, and it kept them from thinking properly. Koshmar remembered Thekmur telling her that the anger flowed from the balls they carried between their legs, and went constantly to their brains, making them unfit to rule. That was in the last weeks of Thekmur's life, not long after she had formally named Koshmar to be her successor. And Thekmur had probably learned her knowledge of men at close range, for she had often known men in the way of women, which Koshmar had never done herself.

Gods, she thought. Is that it? Does Harruel desire me?

It was a startling and horrifying idea. She would have to watch him closely. Something plainly was on Harruel's mind that had never been there before. If he could not be chieftain himself, perhaps he meant to make himself the chieftain's chieftain. Which she would never permit; but she needed Harruel, needed his great strength, needed his bravery, needed his anger, even. This would take some careful thinking.

4

The Chronicler

It required all the courage Hresh could summon to go to Koshmar and ask to be made chronicler in Thaggoran's place. Not that he feared being refused so much, since, after all, he would be asking an extraordinary thing. It was being mocked that he dreaded. Koshmar could be cruel; Koshmar could be harsh. And Hresh knew that she already had cause to dislike him.

But to his surprise the chieftain appeared to receive his outrageous request amiably. "Chronicler, you say? That's a task that customarily is given to the oldest man of the tribe, is it not? And you are—"

"I will be nine soon," Hresh said staunchly.

"Nine. Something short of oldest." Was Koshmar hiding a smile?

"The oldest man now is Anijang. He's too stupid to be chronicler, isn't he? Besides, what does my age matter, Koshmar?

Everything is different for us out here. There are dangers on all sides. All the men must be on constant patrol. We have had the rat-wolves, the bloodbirds, the fireburs, the leather-wings, almost every day some new creature to fend off. And they will all be back again and again. I'm too small to fight well yet. But I can keep the chronicles."

"Are you sure of that? Can you read?"

"Thaggoran taught me. I can write words and I can read them. And I can remember things, too. I have much of the chronicles by memory, already. Try me on anything. The coming of the death-stars, the building of the cocoons—"

"You've read the chronicles?" Koshmar asked, looking amazed.

Hresh felt his face grow hot. What a blunder! The chronicles were sealed; no one was permitted to open the chest that contained them except the chronicler himself. Indeed, even in the days of the cocoon Hresh had managed sometimes to study a few pages that Thaggoran had happened to leave open in his chamber, for the old man had been careless sometimes or indulgent, though Thaggoran had not seemed aware of what Hresh was doing. But Hresh had carried out most of his investigations of history since Thaggoran's death, surreptitiously, while the older tribesfolk had been out foraging for food. The baggage was often left unguarded; there was no longer any chronicler to keep a special eye on his treasure; no one appeared to notice the boy slipping open the sacred casket, or to care.

Lamely Hresh said, hoping Koshmar would not see through the blatant lie, "Thaggoran let me see them. He made me promise never to say anything to anyone about that, but once in a while as a special favor he would—"

Koshmar laughed. "He did, did he? Does no one keep oaths in this tribe?"

Desperately improvising, Hresh said, "He loved to tell the old stories. And I was more interested than anyone else, so he—he and I—"

"Yes. Yes, I can see that. Well, it matters very little now what oaths were kept or broken in the time before we came forth." Koshmar looked down at him from what seemed like an enormous height. She seemed lost in private musings for a long while. Then at last she said, "Chronicler, then? And not even nine? A strange idea!" And then, just as Hresh readied himself to slink away in shame, she said, "But go, get the books. Let me see how you write, and then we'll decide. Go, now!"

Hresh rushed off, heart pounding. Was she serious? Did she actually take *him* seriously? Would she give it to him? So it seemed. Of course she might simply be playing some cruel joke on him; but Koshmar, though she could be cruel, was not one who was known to make jokes. Then she must be sincere, he thought. Chronicler! He, Hresh! He could scarcely believe it. He would be the old man, and not even nine!

This day Threyne was in charge of the sacred things. She was a small wide-eyed woman, vastly swollen by the unborn that sprouted in her belly. Hresh pounced upon her, crying out that Koshmar had told him to fetch the holy books. Threyne was skeptical of that, and would not give them to him; and in the end they went together to the chieftain, carrying the heavy casket of the chronicles between them.

"Yes," said Koshmar. "I meant to let him bring the books." Threyne stared at her in astonishment. Plainly such a thing was blasphemy to her; but she would not defy Koshmar, even in this. Muttering, she yielded the casket to Hresh.

"Go," Koshmar said to Threyne, waving her away as if she were a mote of dust. When Threyne was out of sight the chieftain said to Hresh, "Open it, then, since you seem already to know the way it's done."

Eagerly Hresh put his hands to the casket, maneuvering its rounded bosses and interlocking seals this way and that. Though his fingers quivered nervously, he achieved the opening in just a moment. Within lay the Barak Dayir in its pouch, and the shinestones nearby it, and the books of the chronicles piled as Thaggoran liked to keep them, with the current volume on top and the Book of the Way lying just beneath it.

"Very well," Koshmar said. "Take out Thaggoran's book and open it to the last page, and write what I tell you."

He drew forth the book, caressing it with awe. As he opened it he made the sign of the Destroyer: for it was Dawinno, he who leveled and scattered, who was also the god of the keeping of knowledge. Carefully Hresh turned through it until he came to the final page, where Thaggoran had begun in his elegant way to write the story of the Coming Forth on the left-hand leaf. Thaggoran's account ended abruptly, incomplete, in midpage; the right-hand leaf was blank.

"Are you ready?" Koshmar asked.

"You want me to write in this book?" said Hresh, not believing her.

"Yes. Write." She frowned and pursed her lips. "Write this: '*It was decided then by Koshmar the chieftain that the tribe would seek Vengiboneeza the great city of the sapphire-eyes, for it might be possible there to find secret things that would be of value in the repeopling of the world.*'"

Hresh stared at her and did nothing.

"Go on, write that down. You *can* write, can't you? You haven't wasted my time in this? Have you? Have you? Write, Hresh, or by Dawinno I'll have you skinned and made into a pair of boots for these cold nights. Write!"

"Yes," he murmured. "Yes, I will."

He pressed the pads of his fingers to the page and concentrated the full force of his mind, and sent the words that Koshmar had dictated hurtling onto the sensitive sheet of pale vellum in one furious, desperate burst of thought. And to his wonderment characters began to appear almost at once, dark brown against the yellow background. Writing! He was actually writing in the Book of the Coming Forth! His writing was not as fine as Thaggoran's, no, but it was good enough, real writing, clear and comprehensible.

"Let me see," Koshmar said.

She leaned close, peering, nodding.

"Ah. Ah, yes. You do have it, do you not? Little mischief-maker, little question-asker, you truly can write! Ah. Ah." She pursed her lips and gripped the edges of the book tightly and narrowed her eyes and ran her finger along the page, frowning, and murmured, after a moment, "'*So Koshmar the chieftain decided that the tribe would search for the great city Vengiboneeza of the sapphire-eyes—*'"

It was close, but the words Koshmar was reading were not quite the words that she had spoken a moment before and that Hresh had written down. How could that be? He craned his neck and stared at the book in her hands. What he had written still began, "*It was decided then by Koshmar the chieftain—*" Was it possible that Koshmar was unable to read, that she was quoting from her own memory of what she had dictated? That was startling. But after a bit of thought Hresh saw that it was not really so surprising.

A chieftain did not need to know the art of reading. A chronicler did.

A moment later Hresh realized a second startling thing, which was that he had just been permitted to learn the identity of the goal toward which they had marched all these months. Until this moment the chieftain had been steadfast in her refusal to divulge the destination of their trek to anyone. So intent had Hresh been on the act of writing itself that he had paid no attention to the meaning of the words Koshmar had uttered. Now it sank in.

Vengiboneeza! He felt his heartbeat quicken.

They were soon to set out in search of the most splendid city of the Great World!

I should have guessed it, Hresh thought, chagrined; for Thaggoran had spoken of such matters, how in the Book of the Way it was written that at winter's end the People would go forth from their cocoons and find amidst the ruins of the Great World the things they would need to make themselves masters of the planet. What better place to search for such things than at the ancient capital of the sapphire-eyes folk? Perhaps Koshmar had realized that too; or, rather, Thaggoran very likely had suggested it to her. Vengiboneeza! Truly life has become a dream, Hresh thought.

He looked up at her. "Am I the new chronicler, then?" he asked.

She was studying him quizzically. "How old did you say you were? Nine?"

"Not quite."

"Not quite nine."

"But I read. I write. I have learned many things already, and for me it is only the beginning, Koshmar."

She nodded. "Yes," she said. "Perhaps this is the only way I can keep you under control, eh, Hresh? Hresh-full-of-questions? You will read these books, and they will answer some of your questions and fill you full of new ones, and you will be so busy with your books that you will no longer go stealing off, seeking new ways of making trouble."

"I was the one who found the rat-wolves, that time I went off by myself," he reminded her.

"Yes. Yes, you did."

"I can be useful as well as troublesome."

"Perhaps you can," said Koshmar.

"This isn't some game you're playing with me? I really am the new chronicler, Koshmar?"

Koshmar laughed. "You are, boy, yes. You are the new chronicler. We will proclaim you today. Even if you're not yet old enough to have had your naming-day. These are new times, and everything is different now, eh? Or almost everything. Eh, boy? Eh?"

So it was done. Hresh took up his new tasks with great zeal. As best he could, he brought Thaggoran's unfinished account of the Going Forth up to date, telling of the tribe's adventures at this point and that. He attempted to reconstruct the calendar of days, so that the rituals could properly be observed; but in the confusions following Thaggoran's death no one had bothered with that duty and Hresh suspected that he had not properly made up the tally, so that henceforth perhaps naming-days and twining-days and other ritual events would not be celebrated on precisely the correct date. He did his best to remedy that, though without much confidence that his work was accurate.

Each day now Hresh would come to the chieftain and she would speak with him, and those things that seemed to be of high importance he would set down in the vast book. And whenever he had the opportunity he burrowed with the burning eagerness of a cave-mole to the deeper levels of the casket, hungry to discover all that was. He reveled in the overflowing treasure of history. It might take him half his life to read through all those books, but he meant to try. In a kind of fever of knowledge-hunger Hresh turned the pages, stroking them, absorbing them, barely allowing himself time to scan more than a few lines on this page before he went on to that, and to the one beyond it. The truths that the books held became blurred and tangled as he wandered among them, turning into mysteries even deeper than they had been for him before he knew anything of them at all; but that was not important, for he would have plenty of time to master this knowledge later. Now he wanted only to gobble it.

He slipped the amulet of Thaggoran around his neck now, and wore it day and night. It was a strange presence at first, thumping against his breastbone, but soon he grew accustomed to it and then it came to seem virtually a part of him. Wearing it, he felt the nearness of Thaggoran. Touching it, he imagined that he could feel the wisdom of Thaggoran entering into him.

He went back to the oldest books, which he could barely understand, since they were written in a strange kind of writing that would not tune itself easily to his mind. But he ran his trembling fingertips over the stiff pages and a sort of sense came up out of them after a while, though always ambiguous, elliptical, elusive. Fragmentary accounts of the Great World is what they were: what seemed to be tales of how the Six Peoples had lived in harmony on the earth, humans and hjjk-folk and vegetals and mechanicals and sea-lords and sapphire-eyes. It was dim and faint, an echo of an echo, but even that echo resounded in his soul like a clarion fanfare out of the dark well of time. Surely it had been the most astounding of epochs, the peak of Earth's lost splendor, when all the world was a festival. He trembled just to think of it: the multitudes of people, the many races, the glittering cities, the ships sailing between the stars. He could scarcely begin to comprehend it. He felt the knowledge of it, partial though it was, swelling within him so that he feared he would choke on it. And then he skipped forward to the Great World's tragic end, when the death-stars began to fall, as had been foretold so long before. Why did they allow it to happen, they who had achieved such grandeur? Had they been unable to turn the plummeting stars aside? Surely that would have been within their power, since all other things were. Yet nothing was done. No mention was made of any of that, only of the coming of the doom itself. That was when the sapphire-eyes perished, for their blood was cold and they could not abide freezing weather, and the vegetals died also, having been fashioned out of plant cells and being unable to bear the frost. Hresh read the noble account of the voluntary death of the mechanicals, who had not wanted to survive into the new era, though that would have been possible for them. He read it all, swallowing it down in great intoxicating gulps.

He took out the shinestones, too, and arranged them in patterns, and stroked them and squeezed them and murmured to them, hoping to be able to draw some wisdom from them. But they remained silent. They seemed to him to be no more than dark gleaming stones. Try as he would, they told him nothing. Sadly he realized that the People no longer would have their guidance. That was lost forever to the tribe. Whatever secret governed the shinestones' use had died with Thaggoran.

The Barak Dayir, the Wonderstone, was the one thing in the casket that Hresh did not dare to examine at all. He left it undisturbed within its pouch of green velvet, not even daring to touch it. It would, he knew, open doors to realms of knowledge beyond even those that reading could make available to him; but he feared to do too much too soon. The Wonderstone was star-stuff, so Thaggoran had said. He had said that it had its dangers, too. Hresh chose to let it be until he had found some clue to the safe means of using it. In the privacy of his spirit he praised himself warmly for this one act of prudent renunciation, so alien to his character, and then laughed at his own absurd pride.

To the others of the tribe Hresh's ascent to the rank of chronicler was more a matter for amusement than anything else. They had heard Koshmar's proclamation, and they could see him every day puttering around in the baggage-train where the chronicles were kept; but they had trouble comprehending the fact that a small boy now was the chronicler. Minbain laughed and asked him, "Am I supposed to call you old man?"

"It's only a title, Mother. It makes no difference to me whether it's used or not."

"But you are chronicler? You are truly chronicler?"

"You know that I am," Hresh said.

Minbain put her hands over her breasts. Through gusts of laughter she said, in a way that seemed loving without being kind, "How could such a strange thing as you have come out of me? How? How?"

Torlyri was kinder to him, telling him that he was the proper choice and that to be chronicler was clearly what he had been born to be; but then Torlyri was kind to everyone. Orbin, who had been his playmate and friend, looked at him now as though he had grown an extra head. The others of his own age, or near to it, had never felt comfortable with Hresh to begin with. Now they kept their distance entirely, all except Taniane, who seemed utterly unimpressed with his new glory. She still would talk with him and march beside him on the trek as if nothing had changed, although lately she had begun spending a great deal of time with Haniman, of all people. What she found interesting in that oaf was hard for Hresh to see, although Haniman was at least growing less flabby as he marched, and showing signs of developing some coordination and grace, though not very much.

Anijang, who might have become chronicler in the old days simply because he was the senior tribesman now, only chuckled when Hresh went by. "What trouble you've saved me, lad! What a nuisance it would have been for me to have to learn to read!" He seemed honestly relieved. And the younger men, the warriors, generally ignored Hresh, all but Salaman, who sometimes paused and stared at him as though he could not bring himself to believe that a boy even younger than he was had become the chronicler and old man of the tribe. The other warriors paid no attention. For them the chronicler was a figure to revere, but they were not going to revere Hresh, and so he had no importance to them. Of them all only Harruel bothered to speak to Hresh at all, looking down from his vast height and gruffly wishing him success at his tasks. "You are very young," said Harruel, "but customs change with changing times, and if you are to be our chronicler then I have no quarrel with that." For which Hresh returned proper thanks, although Harruel was so huge and so strange these days—bitter over some sharp disappointment, it seemed, going about all the time with a black look in his eyes and a scowl on his lips—that Hresh preferred to stay away from him.

Naturally Hresh was supposed to keep everything that Koshmar dictated to him a secret until the chieftain was ready to divulge it to the entire tribe. But he was, after all, not quite nine years old. And so one day soon after he had become chronicler, when he was with Taniane, he said to her, "Do you know where we're heading?"

"No one knows that but Koshmar."

"I know it."

"You do?"

"And I'll tell you, if you keep it a secret." He put his head close to hers. "We're going to Vengiboneeza. Can you believe it? *Vengiboneeza*, Taniane!"

He thought the revelation would stun her. But it drew nothing from her but a blank look. "Where?" she asked.

They marched west, on and on through a changing land, warmer every day though still far from hospitable.

Never once did they encounter other human beings, only the savage and strange beasts of the wilderness. Koshmar was of more than one mind about that. She would have liked to meet some other tribe in order to have confirmation that it had not been foolish for her to lead her people out of the cocoon before the true end of winter; and also she wished to be free of the uncomfortable possibility that her sixty souls were all that was left of the human race. And in truth she was eager to join with some other bands of wanderers with whom the People could share the risks and hardships of the journey.

But at the same time the idea of finding others was less than entirely pleasing to her. She had long been the master, absolute and unchallenged. Harruel's surly glares and malcontent mutterings were no real threat to her: the People would never accept him in her place. But if they met another tribe and formed some kind of alliance with them there might well be rivalries, disagreements, even warfare. Koshmar had no desire to share her power with any other chieftain. To some degree, she realized, she *wanted* her people to be the only humans who had managed to survive the downfall of the Great World.

That way—if all went well—she would go down in the chronicles as one of the greatest leaders in history, the one who had singlehandedly engineered the revival of the human race. That was vanity, yes, she knew. Yet surely it was not an unpardonable sin to have such ambitions.

Still, the responsibilities were heavy. They were heading through a perilous land toward an unknown destination. Each day brought something new and troublesome to tax the tribe's resolve, and often Koshmar felt herself uncertain of her course. But those doubts had to be hidden from her people.

She called them together, and told them at last that Vengiboneeza was their destination. The older ones knew the name, from stories that Thaggoran had told them in the days of the cocoon; but the young ones merely stared.

"Tell them of Vengiboneeza," she commanded Hresh.

He came forward and spoke of the ancient city's great towers, its shining stone palaces, its wondrous machines, its warm radiant pools and shimmering gardens. These were all descriptions that he had found by touching his hands to the pages of the chronicles and letting the images rise to his mind.

"But what good is Vengiboneeza to us?" Harruel asked, when Hresh was done.

Koshmar said sharply, "It will be the beginning of our greatness. The chronicles tell us that machines of the Great World are still to be found there and the finders will be made powerful by them. So we will enter Vengiboneeza and search it for its treasures. We will take from it what we need, and make ourselves masters of the world, and build a grand and glorious city for ourselves."

"A city?" Staip asked. "We will have a city?"

"Of course we will have a city," said Koshmar. "Are we to live like wild creatures, Staip?"

"Vengiboneeza has been dust for seven hundred thousand years," Harruel said darkly. "There'll be nothing there that's useful for us."

"The chronicles say otherwise," Koshmar retorted.

There was grumbling on several sides. Staip continued to murmur, and Kalide, and a few of the other older ones. Koshmar saw Torlyri looking at her in sorrow and distress, and knew that her power over the tribe was in the deepest jeopardy. She had asked too much of them in making this doleful trek. She had taken them from the comfort of the cocoon into hard winds and bitter cold. She had exposed them to the cruel glare of the sun and the chilling light of the moon. She had given them over to a world of bloodbirds and fireburs and things whose mouths gaped like caverns. Patiently they had abided all these strangenesses and ordeals, but their patience was coming to an end. Now she must promise them rewards if she wished them to follow her farther.

"Listen to me!" she cried. "Do you have any reason to doubt me? I am Koshmar daughter of Lissiminimar, and you chose me your chieftain in Thekmur's time, and have I ever failed you? I will bring you to Vengiboneeza and all the wonders of the Great World will be ours! And then we will go forth again and make ourselves masters of everything! We will sleep in warm places and drink sweet drinks, and there will be food and fine robes and an easy life for everyone! That I pledge you: that is the pledge of the New Springtime!"

Still the sullen eyes, here and there. Staip shifted his weight restlessly. Koshmar saw Konya whisper something to him. Kalide too looked uncertain, and turned to say a word or two to Minbain. Harruel seemed far away, lost in brooding. But no one spoke out openly against the idea. She sensed a turning-point in their sentiments.

"On to Vengiboneeza!" Koshmar cried.

"On to Vengiboneeza!" Torlyri echoed. "Vengiboneeza!" Hresh called.

An uneasy moment, then. The others were still silent. The

eyes were still sullen. She saw weary people, troubled, rebellious. Only Torlyri and Hresh had spoken for her; but Torlyri was her twining-partner; Hresh was her creature, her servant. Would anyone else take up the cry?

"Vengiboneeza!" finally, a high strong voice: Orbin, that good robust boy. And then, surprisingly, from Haniman too, and then a few of the older ones, Konya, Minbain, Striinin, and then all of them, even Harruel, even the reluctant Staip. They were a tribe once more, speaking with one voice: "Vengiboneeza! Vengiboneeza!"

They went onward. But how long, Koshmar wondered, before she would have to win them to her side all over again?

There were more losses as they marched. On a day of strange hot gusty winds the young man Hignord was carried off by something green and writhing and many-legged that came hurtling out of a concealed pit in the ground. A few days later the girl Tramassilu, who had gone off to snare little tree-dwelling yellow toads, was speared by a huge lunatic hopping thing with a long red beak that came bouncing down upon her like an avalanche and danced babbling over her body until Harruel smashed it with a club.

That made four deaths now, out of sixty that had begun the trek. The bellies of the breeding pairs were swelling with replacements for the lost ones, but a birth took a long time and death was quick out here. Koshmar fretted over the dwindling of the tribe, fearing that their numbers might become dangerously low if more women perished. Two of their dead so far had been fertile females. One male was all it took to impregnate an entire tribe, Koshmar knew; but it was the females who bore the children, and they were a long time in carrying them.

The heavy clouds opened and it rained for ten days and ten

nights, until everyone was sodden and reeking from the wetness. There had been no rain before on the trek. But the sight of water falling from the sky quickly lost its fascination. Rain ceased to be a novelty and became a burden and a torment.

"Vengiboneeza," they began to say. "How long until Vengiboneeza?"

There were those who insisted that a new death-star had struck the earth far away, too far away for the impact to have been heard here, and that the rain was the beginning of yet another time of darkness and cold. "No," said Koshmar vehemently. "This is only something that happens in this particular place. It was dry where we were before, and here it is wet. Do you see how thick the grass is here, how heavy the foliage?" Indeed that was so. They went on, bowed and soggy, smelling of damp fur. And after a time the rain stopped.

Then the days began to grow shorter. Ever since they had left the cocoon, each day had been a little longer than the one before it; but now, beyond any dispute, the sun could be seen to drop below the western horizon earlier and earlier every afternoon.

"Vengiboneeza?" the tribesfolk began to mutter again.

Koshmar nodded, and pointed to the west.

"I think we are entering a land of eternal night," said Staip. He had always been a jovial man, to whom doubt and pessimism were unknown. Not now. "A dark land will be a cold land," he said.

"And a dead one," said Konya, who no longer laughed and sang. His natural reserve of spirit had returned in recent weeks and had deepened greatly, so that he seemed now not merely aloof and private, but bleak and lost in some terrible realm of his soul. "Nothing can survive in such a place," he said. "We should turn back."

"We must go onward," Koshmar insisted. "What is happening

now is normal and natural. We have entered a place where the darkness is stronger than the light. Beyond it things will change for the better."

"Will they?" Staip asked.

"Have faith," said Koshmar. "Yissou will protect us. Emakkis will provide. Dawinno will guide us."

And they went on.

But inwardly the chieftain was not so sure that her confidence was justified. In the cocoon the day and the night had been of identical lengths. Out here things were different, obviously. But what did it really mean, this dwindling of the hours of daylight? Perhaps Staip was right and they were marching into a realm where the sun never rose and they would meet their death of freezing.

She wished she could consult Thaggoran, who would have known the explanation or at least invented something reassuring. But she had no Thaggoran now, and her old man was a child. Koshmar sent for him anyway, and, taking care not to let him see how baffled she was, said to him, "I need to know an ancient name, chronicler."

"And what name is that?"

"The name that the ancients gave to the changing of the times of light and dark. It must be in the chronicles somewhere. The name is the god: we must call the god by his rightful name in our prayers, or the sunlight will never return."

Hresh went off to examine the archives. He looked through the Book of the Way, the Book of Hours and Days, the Book of the Cold Awakening, the Book of the Wrongful Glow, and many another volume, including very old ones that were without names. He found a part of the answer in this book and another part in that one, and after three days he came to Koshmar and said, "It is called the seasons. There is the season of daylight and it is followed by the season of darkness and then the daylight season comes 'round again."

"Of course," said Koshmar. "The seasons. How could I have forgotten the word?" And she summoned Torlyri and ordered her to pray to the god of seasons.

"Which god is that?" the gentle offering-woman asked.

"Why, the god who brings the time of light and the time of the dark," said Koshmar.

Torlyri hesitated. "Friit, do you think? Friit is the Healer. He would bring light after darkness."

"But Friit would not bring the darkness," said Koshmar. "No, it is another god."

"Tell me, then. For I have no idea which one to make my offerings to."

Koshmar had hoped that Torlyri would know; but she saw now that Torlyri, rather, was looking to her. "It is Dawinno," Koshmar said shortly.

"Yes, the Destroyer," Torlyri replied, smiling. "The darkness and then the light: that would be Dawinno's way. He holds everything in balance so that it will be right in the end."

Each day at midday, then, when the sun stood straight overhead, Torlyri made an offering to Dawinno the Destroyer, god of seasons. She would burn some scraps of old fur and a bit of dried wood in a fine ancient bowl of polished green stone shot through with golden veins. The smoke rising toward the sun was her message of gratitude to the god whose subtlety was beyond human comprehension.

Though the days continued to grow shorter, Koshmar would hear no further discussion of the phenomenon. "It is the seasons," she said, waving her hand imperiously. "Everyone knows that! What is there to fear? The seasons are natural. The seasons are normal. They are Dawinno's gift to us."

"Yes," muttered Harruel, not so quietly that Koshmar could not hear him. "And so were the death-stars."

The land was changing too. It was flat for a long while; then it became broken and wild, with ridges of blazing scarlet rock that were as sharp as knives along their summits. Just on the far side they found a strange sight: a dead thing of metal, twice as wide as a man but not half as tall, standing by itself on a bare stony slope. Its head was a broad one-eyed dome, its legs were elaborately jointed. Once it must have had a thick, gleaming metal skin, but now it was rusted and pitted by the rains of an uncountable number of years. "It is a mechanical," Hresh announced, after studying his books. "This must be where they came to die." And indeed in the lowlands a little way beyond that there were many more, hundreds, thousands, of the squat metal creatures, a forest of them, an ocean of them, covering the land in all directions, each standing upright in a little zone of solitude, a private empire. All were dead and rusting. They were so corroded that they dissolved at a touch, and toppled into a scattering of dust. "In the time of the Great World," said Hresh solemnly, "these creatures lived in the mighty cities of great kingdoms where everyone was a machine. But they did not care to go on living once the death-stars began to fall."

"What's a machine?" Haniman asked.

"A machine," Hresh said, "is a device that performs work. It is a metal thing with a mind, and strength, and purpose, and a kind of life that is not like our life." That was the best he could manage. They accepted it. But when someone else asked why something that had life, even if it was not like our life, would be willing without struggle to yield up that life when the death-stars came, Hresh could not say. That was beyond his understanding, willingly to yield up life.

Koshmar prowled among the horde of dead mechanicals, thinking that she might find one that still had life enough in it to be able to tell her how to reach the city of Vengiboneeza; but their blind rusted faces mocked her with silence. They were dead beyond hope of awakening, every one of them.

After that there was an awful sandy wasteland worse than any of the dry places they had passed through before. Here there was no water at all, not even a rivulet. The ground crackled and crunched when the weight of a foot pressed against it. Nothing would grow here, not the slightest tuft of grass, and the only animals were low coiling yellow things that left blade-sharp tracks as they slithered through the sand. They stung Staip and Haniman, raising painful purple swellings on their legs that did not go down for several days. They stung some of the livestock, too, and the animals died of it. There were very few beasts left to the marchers by this time. They had had to slaughter for food most of the ones they had brought with them out of the cocoon, and many of the others had strayed and vanished, or had been killed by creatures along the way. In this dry place throats were parched and eyes became sunken, and the tribesfolk said over and over again that they would be glad now to have some of the rain that they had found so bothersome not long ago.

Then they left the dry place behind and entered a green land broken by chains of lakes and a turbulent river which they crossed on rafts of light wood, bound by the bark of a slender azure creature that seemed half serpent, half tree. Beyond the river was a range of low mountains. One day during the journey across that range keen-sighted Torlyri had a glimpse of a huge band of hjjk-folk far away, a whole enormous army of them, marching toward the south. By the coppery glint of twilight they looked no larger than ants as they made their way along a rocky defile; but there must have been thousands of them, a terrifying multitude. If they noticed Koshmar's little band they gave no sign of it, however, and soon the insect-people were lost to view beyond the folds of the mountains.

The days grew longer again. The air became warmer, and then much warmer. Now and again new wintry blasts came out of the north, but they were fewer, and came ever more rarely. No one could doubt that the death-grip that winter had held on the world was easing, had eased, no longer was a significant thing. There was still winter in the world somewhere, but this was a springtime land, and the farther west they went, the gentler the weather became. Koshmar felt vindicated. The god of seasons smiled upon her.

Where, though, was great Vengiboneeza? According to the chronicles, the lost capital of the sapphire-eyes was in the place where the sun goes to rest; but where was that? In the west, surely. But the west was a huge place that went on and on without end. Each night the tribe was many weary leagues farther westward, and when the sun vanished beyond the end of the world at the day's close it was evident that all their marching had brought them no nearer to its resting-place.

"Search the books again," Koshmar said despairingly to Hresh. "There is some passage you have failed to find that will tell us how to reach Vengiboneeza."

He ran his hands again and again over the pages. He sought through the dustiest and most ancient of the books, those that spoke only of the Great World. But there was nothing. Perhaps he was looking in the wrong places. Or perhaps the writers of the chronicles had not seen any need to set down the location of that great city, so famous had it been. Or possibly the information had simply been lost. These oldest chronicles were not the original texts, he knew. Those had crumbled to dust hundreds of thousands of years ago; the ones he possessed were the copies of copies of copies, made from tattered earlier versions by generations of chroniclers during the long night within the cocoon, and who knew how much of the text had been changed by error, or discarded altogether, in that constant process of recopying? Much of what they contained was impossible for him to understand; and what was there, though often quite clear, sometimes had the deceptive eerie clarity of a dream, where everything seems orderly and straightforward but in fact nothing makes sense at all.

It might be time, Hresh thought, to risk using the Barak Dayir. But he was afraid. He had never been afraid of anything before, even when he had tried to sneak out of the cocoon. No, that was a lie. He had been afraid then that Koshmar would kill him; death did frighten him, he would not deny that. But death was the only question that contained its own answer, and when you asked the question and had the answer you were gone, you were nothing. So that was the one answer he feared. The question of how to use the Wonderstone might well be the same as the question of understanding death; and the answer, if he did not protect himself properly, might also be the same. He left the Barak Dayir in its velvet pouch.

"Tell me how to reach Vengiboneeza," Koshmar said again.

"I continue to search," said Hresh. "Give me another few days and I'll tell you what you wish to know."

Harruel came to Hresh while he searched the books. He loomed above him as Harruel always did, and said, "Old man! Chronicler!"

Hresh looked up, startled. Automatically he turned the book

he was reading away from Harruel, and shaded it with his hand. As though Harruel could possibly be able to read it!

"Sit down, if you want to talk to me," Hresh said. "You stand too far above me and it hurts my neck to see you."

Harruel laughed. "You are a bold one!"

"Is there something you want to know from me?"

Harruel laughed again. It was a harsh laugh that burst from him with a sound like that of rocks tumbling down a mountainside, but his eyes were twinkling. Indeed Hresh knew he was playing an absurd game, if not a dangerous one. A boy not yet nine years old was giving orders to the strongest man of the tribe: how could Harruel not laugh, or else hurl him angrily across the field? But I am the chronicler, Hresh thought defiantly. I am the old man. He is only a fool with muscles.

The warrior knelt down beside him and came close, too close for Hresh's comfort. There was a sharp biting smell about Harruel, and the sheer size of him was disturbing.

In a low voice Harruel said, "I need knowledge from you."

"Go on."

"Tell me about the thing called kingship."

"Kingship?" Hresh echoed. That was an ancient word, one that he had never heard spoken aloud in his life. It was strange hearing it now from Harruel. "You know of kingship?"

"Some," he said. "I remember Thaggoran spoke of it once, when he was reading from the chronicles. You were a babe, then. He talked of Lord Fanigole and Lady Theel and Balilirion, and the other founders of the People in the time of the coming of the death-stars. They were men, all but Lady Theel, and they ruled. I asked if men had often ruled, in those old days. That day Thaggoran said that in the time of the Great World there were many kings who were men like me, and not only among the humans—

the sapphire-eyes had kings too, said Thaggoran—and he told me that when the king spoke, his words were obeyed."

"As a chieftain's words would be today."

"As a chieftain's words would, yes," said Harruel.

"Then you already know about kingship," Hresh said. "What more can I tell you?"

"Tell me that such a thing existed."

"That there were men who were kings in the Great World?" Hresh shrugged. He had not studied these things. And even if he had, he doubted that he should be giving information about such matters to Harruel, or to anyone but Koshmar. The chronicles were here mainly for the guidance of the chieftain, not for the amusement of the tribesfolk. "I know little about kingship," he said. "What you have said is perhaps the extent of it."

"You can find more about it, can't you?"

"There may be more in the chronicles," said Hresh cautiously.

"Search it out, and tell me, then. It seems to me that kingship is something that should not have been forgotten. The Great World will be born again; and we must know how it was in the time of the Great World if we are to bring it to life a second time. Search your books, boy. Learn about the kings, and teach them to me."

"You must not call me boy," Hresh said.

Harruel laughed again, and this time his eyes were not twinkling.

"Search your books on these matters," he said. "And teach me what you learn—old man. Chronicler."

He stalked away. Hresh looked fearfully after him, thinking that this meant nothing but trouble, and probably danger. Worriedly he fondled Thaggoran's amulet. That day he began to search out the meaning of kingship in the casket of books, and what he found confirmed what he had guessed.

Perhaps I should tell Koshmar about this, he thought.

But he did not; nor did he report anything back to Harruel on his research. Harruel made no further inquiries just then into the matter of kingship. The conversation remained a private matter between them, secret, festering.

Koshmar felt the beginning of defeat. If only Thaggoran were here to guide her! But Thaggoran was gone and her chronicler was a boy. Hresh was quick and eager, but he lacked Thaggoran's depth of wisdom and familiarity with all the ages that had gone before.

She was coming to face the truth that she could not hope to sustain the trek much longer. The grumbling had begun again, and this time it was more heated. Already there were those, she knew, who said they were marching to no purpose. Harruel had emerged the leader of that faction. Let us settle down in some good fertile place and build us a village: so he was saying behind Koshmar's back. Torlyri had overheard him haranguing four or five of the other men. In the cocoon it was unthinkable that the tribe would even consider countermanding a chieftain's word, but they were no longer in the cocoon. Koshmar began to imagine herself cast down from power: not the savior of the reborn world but merely an overthrown chieftain.

If they deposed her, would they even let her live? These were all new thoughts. There were no traditions about the deposing of chieftains, or what to do with a deposed one afterward.

Koshmar had left behind, in the cocoon, that strip of glossy black stone that contained the spirits of the chieftains who had gone before her. All she had brought with her were their names, which she recited again and again; but perhaps the names had no strength without the stone, just as the stone had no strength without the names.

Thekmur, she thought. *Nialli. Sismoil. Lirridon. If you still are with me, guide me now!*

The departed chieftains did not make themselves known to her. Koshmar turned to Hresh for counsel. With him, though with no one else, she had ceased to pretend that she was following the clear mandate of the gods.

"What can we do?" she asked.

"We must ask for help," the boy replied.

"Of whom?"

"Why, of the creatures we meet as we go along."

Koshmar was skeptical. But anything was worth trying; and so from that day onward, whenever they encountered some being that seemed to have a mind, no matter how simple, she would have it seized and would soothe it until it grew calm, and then, by second-sight and sensing-organ contact, she would strive to get from it the knowledge she needed.

The first was an odd round fleshy creature, a head with no body and a dozen plump little legs. Vivid ripplings of excitement ran through it when Koshmar plumbed its mind for images of Vengiboneeza, but those ripplings were all that was forthcoming from it. From a trio of gawky stilt-legged blue furry things that seemed to share a single mind came, when they were asked about cities in the west, a pattern of thought that was like an intense buzzing and snorting. And a hideous hook-clawed forest creature twice the height of a man, all mouth and jutting nose and foul-smelling orange hair, gave a wild raucous laugh and flashed the image of lofty towers wrapped in strangling vines.

"This is of no use," the chieftain said to Hresh.

"But how interesting these animals are, Koshmar."

"Interesting! We'll die a hundred deaths in this wilderness and you'll find that interesting too, won't you?"

All the same, she had Hresh give each of these creatures names before they were released, and had him write the names down in his book. The giving of names was important, Koshmar believed. These must all be new beings, beasts that had come into existence since the time of the Great World, which was why there was nothing in the chronicles about them. Giving them names was the beginning of attaining power over them. She still clung to the hope that she, and her tribe through her, would be the masters of this New Springtime world. Thus the giving of names. But even as Hresh spoke the names, each time after deep cogitation, she felt a sense of the futility of the act. They were lost in this land. They were without purpose or direction.

The deepest pessimism invaded Koshmar's soul.

Then, as the tribe was going around the rim of a huge black lake in the midst of a zone of dank boggy land, the dark waters stirred and boiled wildly and out of the depths a bizarre colossus began slowly to rise, a thing of enormous height but so flimsily constructed that it seemed a gust of wind could shatter it—pale limbs that were no more than thin struts, a body that was only a filmy tube interminably extended. As this thing rose up and up until it half blotted out the sky in front of them Koshmar threw her arm across her face in astonishment, and Harruel roared and brandished his spear, and some of the more timid members of the tribe began to flee.

But Hresh, holding his ground, called out, "This must be one of the water-strider folk. It's harmless, I think."

Higher and yet higher it mounted, erupting from the lake to a height ten or fifteen times that of the tallest man. There it halted, hovering far above them, balancing with wide-splayed feet on the surface of the water, which it seemed barely to disturb. It peered down out of a row of glaring green-gold eyes, surveying them in a melancholy way.

"You! Water-strider!" Hresh shouted. "Tell us how to find the city of the sapphire-eyes!"

And, amazingly, the huge creature replied at once in the silent speech of the mind, saying, "Why, it lies just two lakes and a stream from here, in the sunset direction. Everyone knows that! But what good will it do you to go there?" The water-strider laughed in horrible clangorous tones, a shrill hysterical laugh, and began to fold itself, section upon section, down toward the lake. "What good? What good? What good?" It laughed again; and then it disappeared beneath the black water.

5

Vengiboneeza

On the afternoon of the day of the water-strider Threyne came to Torlyri, holding her hands to her sides, and announced that her time was upon her. Indeed Torlyri could see that it was true: the unborn was moving eagerly against the girl's distended belly, and there were other signs of imminent birth.

"We can't go onward so soon," Torlyri told Koshmar. "Threyne has come to her time."

For an instant unconcealed disappointment flickered in Koshmar's eyes. Koshmar was in a fever to race onward to Vengiboneeza, Torlyri knew, now that she had learned the great city was so close. But she would have to wait. The birth of a child took precedence over everything. Threyne must be made comfortable; the child must be brought safely into the world.

In the cocoon days the birth of each new child had carried with it not only joy but also a hidden darker aspect, for the only time someone new was allowed into the world was when someone else was nearing the time when it was necessary to leave it: there was no room for expansion within the cocoon, and birth was inextricably mixed with death. Thus the limit-age, so that the People would not be faced with a choice between an intolerable smothered existence and a virtual prohibition against new births. Out here, where so much was altogether different for the tribe, there was no need to fear overcrowding. Quite the opposite: they needed all the new life they could produce, and more beyond that. No one would have to die to make room for children any longer. Whoever had the childbearing power, Torlyri thought, owed it to the tribe to be hatching an unborn of her own. She was beginning to toy with the idea even for herself.

They went as far as they could get from the bog and its black lake. No one wanted the water-strider bursting forth again to fill the air with its horrifying laughter while Threyne was having her baby.

Some of the men cut down saplings to make a leafy bower for her. Minbain and Galihine and a couple of the other older women washed her and held her hands as the pains grew strong. Preyne, who was the child's father, crouched beside her for a while, touching his sensing-organ to hers and taking some of the discomfort from her, as was his obligation and privilege. Torlyri prepared birth-offerings to Mueri in her role as Comforter and to Yissou the Protector and also to Friit the Healer, for afterward. The labor was a long one, and Threyne groaned more than most women did. It was the hardship of the trek, Torlyri thought, that had put this pain in her.

Koshmar, who had been pacing tensely all afternoon, came to the bower toward sunset and stared down at Threyne's swollen middle. To Torlyri she said, "Well? Is everything going as it should?"

Torlyri beckoned Koshmar aside, out of Threyne's hearing, and said, "It's taking too long. And she's in great pain."

"Let Preyne take the pain from her."

"He's doing his best."

"Is she going to die?"

"No, I don't think so," Torlyri said. "But she's suffering. She'll be very weak for days afterward, if she lives."

"What are you saying, Torlyri?"

"We won't be able to break camp for a while."

"But Vengiboneeza—"

"—has waited seven hundred thousand years for us," Torlyri said. "It can wait another few weeks. We can't risk Threyne's life with your impatience. And Nettin's baby is almost due also: two days, three. We might as well stay here until they're strong enough to go onward. Or else divide the tribe, send Harruel and some of the other men ahead to look for the city, and we stay here to care for the mothers."

Koshmar looked bothered. "If anything happens to Threyne I'd never forgive myself. But can you see how I feel, with the city so close?"

Tenderly Torlyri put her hands to Koshmar's shoulders a moment, and held her. "I know," she said softly. "You've fought so hard to bring us here."

From Threyne just then came a new sound, higher, sharper.

"Her time has arrived," Torlyri said. "I'll have to go to her. We'll be on the march again soon, I promise you that."

Koshmar nodded and walked off. Torlyri, watching her go, shook her head. It amazed her that Koshmar, ordinarily so level-headed and clear-minded, had needed to be told that they would have to halt here for a while, and probably even now was having trouble accepting the idea. But Koshmar lacked all aptitude for these matters of women. She had never let a man put his hand to her thighs; she had never thought for a moment of bearing a child; she had aimed herself from childhood on for the chieftainship and nothing but the chieftainship, and to Koshmar that had excluded the idea of motherhood. Chieftains did not bear children: it was the tradition. But only because it had been necessary to regulate population within the cocoon so strictly, Torlyri thought. All sorts of traditions about who could bear children and who could not had sprung up over the centuries, but the underlying reason was always the fear that unlimited breeding would choke the cocoon and drive the tribe out into the harshness of winter before the true time.

Minbain called to her. The child was coming.

Torlyri hurried to the bower, just barely soon enough. Already a tiny head was jutting from between Threyne's thighs. Torlyri smiled. Koshmar could never bear to watch the moment of birth, but Torlyri thought it was beautiful. She knelt at the foot of the bower, holding Threyne lightly by her ankles as she uttered the prayers to Mueri the Mother.

"A boy," Minbain announced.

He was very small, noisy, wrinkled, pink all over, with scattered patches of thin grayish fur that would eventually expand to cover his entire body. His little sensing-organ moved stiffly from side to side, beating the air: a good sign, a sign of vigor and passion. Torlyri remembered when she had helped at Minbain's own childbed nine years before, when Minbain had been delivered of Hresh, how Hresh had whipped the air furiously with his sensing-organ. Certainly he had lived up to the omen, had Hresh.

"The old man," one of the women said. "We need the old man here now, to give the birth-name."

Minbain made a muffled sound, a smothered laugh. Some of the other women laughed also.

"The old man!" Galihine said. "Who ever heard of a child as old man!"

"Or a child presiding at a childbirth," said Preyne.

"Nevertheless," Torlyri said firmly. "We need him to do what must be done."

She turned to a girl named Kailii, who was almost of the age of motherhood herself and watching the delivery with fascination, and sent her off to fetch Hresh.

He arrived in a moment. Torlyri saw his sharp little eyes take in the scene in a series of quick sweeps: the women clustering close about the bower, the exhausted Threyne with streaks of blood staining the fur of her thighs, the little wrinkled babe, more like a radish than a man. Hresh looked uneasy, perhaps because his mother was here, or perhaps because he knew these matters were not ordinarily things for boys to witness.

"A child has been born, as you can see," Torlyri said. "A name must be provided, and it is your office to do so."

At once Hresh seemed to put his uneasiness beside him. He stood tall—though how absurdly small he still was, Torlyri thought!—and appeared to cloak himself in the majesty of his position.

Solemnly he made the sign of Yissou, and then that of Emakkis the Provider, and then that of Mueri the Mother, and then that of Friit the Healer. And then, finally, the sign of Dawinno the Destroyer, subtlest of gods.

Torlyri felt a surge of pride and delight. Hresh was doing the proper things, and in the right order! Old Thaggoran would have

145

done no better. And Hresh had never been present at the giving of a birth-name. He must have looked up the rite in his books. The shrewd boy: how remarkable he was!

"A male child has been given us," said Hresh resonantly. "By Preyne, from Threyne, to us all. I name him for the great one who has been taken from us so cruelly. Thaggoran shall he be."

"Thaggoran!" Preyne boomed. "Thaggoran son of Preyne, Thaggoran son of Threyne!"

"Thaggoran!" cried the women at the bower. "Thaggoran!" said Threyne faintly.

Hresh held out his hands to the mother, to the father, to Torlyri, as the rite required. Then he went around to each of the women in the group, one by one, even his mother Minbain, touching them on each cheek in a sort of blessing. Torlyri had never seen that done: it was something that Hresh must have invented, unless he had revived some ancient rite described in his books. He came last to Torlyri and touched her in the same way. His eyes were shining. What a splendid moment this must be for him, she thought: this boy-chronicler of ours, this strange little Hresh-full-of-questions, who seemed now both man and child, man in a child's body. She thought of him that day at the cocoon's hatch when she had seized him before he could flee, and remembered the terror in his eyes when she had told him that he must be taken before Koshmar for judgment. How utterly different everything had become for them all, since that day! And here was that same Hresh, in a land far from the cocoon, proclaiming a new Thaggoran to the world with all the seriousness of the old one.

Afterward Hresh took her aside and said, "Did I do it well? Did I do it properly?"

"You were magnificent," she told him; and, impulsively, she

swept him up against her bosom, holding him dangling off the ground, and kissed him twice.

He seemed ruffled by that. He gave her an odd look when she set him down, and preened his fur with a distinct attitude of offended dignity. But when she smiled and put her hands to his shoulders in a more seemly caress he looked less irked. No one could stay irritated at Torlyri for long.

"There's another ceremony we must do soon," Hresh said.

"Nettin's baby, you mean."

"That too. But I meant one for me."

"And what is that?" Torlyri asked.

"My naming-day," he said. "I will be nine, you know."

She struggled against laughter, could not suppress it, let it finally burst out.

Hresh stared at her, offended all over again.

"Did I make some joke?"

"No, there was no joke, Hresh, nothing funny at all—but—but—" She started to laugh again. "I'm sorry. It's wrong of me."

"I don't understand," Hresh said.

"Your naming-day. You are the old man of the tribe; you have just given a child a name yourself. Without even having had your own naming-day! Oh, Hresh, Hresh, these are truly strange times!"

"Nevertheless," he said. "It is the proper time for me."

She nodded. "Yes. You're absolutely right, Hresh. I'll speak to Koshmar about it this afternoon. Which day should it be, do you know?"

Sadly he said, "I've lost count, Torlyri. In these weeks and months of wandering. I think it may have gone past already. Some days back."

"Well, no matter. I'll speak to Koshmar," she told him.

*   *   *

What might be the correct procedure for a naming-day in this new life was a puzzle to Torlyri and Koshmar both. There had been no occasion to perform such a rite since the Going Forth.

In the cocoon times the naming-day, which marked a child's formal entry into adult life, had been one of the three sacramental days on which it was permissible for a member of the tribe to pass the threshold and briefly enter the outer world. Accompanied only by the offering-woman, the trembling nine-year-old would step through the hatch, proclaim the name that he or she had chosen to wear thenceforth, and—though dazed, astounded, by the view of the cliff and the river and the open vault of the sky, by the clutter of bleached old bones, and by the intoxicating impact of fresh cold air—perform the appropriate offering to the Five. A few years later would come a second rite, the twining-day, to mark the formal acknowledgment of maturity of soul; and the next time that most tribe members would go outside would be at the time of their death, when if they were strong enough to walk they would be escorted to the hatch by the offering-woman and the chieftain or sometimes the senior warrior, and otherwise would simply be carried out by the offering-woman and left to await the wind and the rain.

But how could Hresh go outside the cocoon for the rites of his naming-day, if he was outside it to begin with?

The old rite had become meaningless. But the naming-day was important. Once again, Torlyri realized, it had fallen to her to invent a rite. There was something strange and a little troublesome about that—simply making up a rite. Was that how all the old rites had come into being? she wondered. Invented by priestesses on the spot, or the old man, to meet some sudden need? Not decreed by a god at all?

The god, she told herself, speaks through the offering-woman.

So be it. She excused herself from Koshmar and went apart, back to the lake of the water-strider, and knelt there to Dawinno and asked for guidance. And Dawinno gave her a rite. It sprang clear and bright into her mind.

The water-strider appeared once again, while she still knelt there. She looked to it fearlessly, smiling as it unfolded its vast flimsy self. You could not harm me if you wished to, she thought. But even if you could, I would smile at you this day, and you would not do me injury. The strider, weaving slowly about at its great height, studied her somberly. And then it seemed to her that the strider smiled to her, and took pleasure in her presence there.

She nodded to it.

"The Five be with you, friend," she said. And the strider laughed; but the laugh seemed more gentle than it had been that other time.

As Torlyri returned to the camp she saw a flock overhead of the creatures that Thaggoran had named bloodbirds, which had swarmed upon them more than once far back in the plains, trying to pierce the marchers with their beaks. She remembered their frightful swoops, their screeching cries, the wounds they had inflicted. But this time she felt no cause for alarm. She looked upon them unafraid, as she had with the water-strider, and they stayed far above, circling without swooping.

This is the proper way to dwell in this place, she told herself. Meet these creatures without fear, meet them if you can with love, and they will do you no harm.

"Now, this is the rite," she said to Koshmar. "I will go off with him into the forest, deep, far from the tribe, to a place where we are all by ourselves with only the creatures of the forest around us. That will be like leaving the safety of the cocoon in the old days. And he will make the offerings to the Five, and then he must go before some creature of the wilderness, it makes no difference which one, a snake, a bird, a water-strider, anything, so long as it is a creature not like us: and he will go to it in peace and tell that creature his new name."

Koshmar looked troubled.

"What purpose does that have?"

"It says that we are people of the world and in the world, and that we live among its creatures again. That we come to them in love, without fear, to share their world with them now that the winter is over."

"Ah," said Koshmar. "I see." But Torlyri could tell from the way she said it that she was not convinced.

Even so, it was the time of Hresh's naming-day, and there was no cocoon for him to step out from, and this was the new rite that Torlyri had devised, and she was the only offering-woman the tribe had. So who was to say that the rite was incorrect? Torlyri gave Hresh instruction in what he was to do and they set forth together at dawn, just the two of them. He had an offering-bowl in his hand and as they walked he gathered blossoms and berries to give to the gods.

"Tell me when we are at the place," he said.

"No, you must tell me," said Torlyri.

His eyes were aglow with life and energy. It seemed to Torlyri that she had never known anyone so much alive as this boy, and her heart overflowed with love for him. Surely the force of the gods flowed in his veins!

"Here," Hresh said.

It was dark in the place he had chosen, for the trees were stitched together high above by networks of vines thicker than a man's arm. The ground was soft and damp. They could have been the only people in the world.

Hresh knelt and made his offerings.

"Now I will take my new name," he said.

Then he searched about for a creature to be his name-creature; and after some time a beast of fair size came padding into the grove, an animal about the size of a rat-wolf, but far more appealing, with bright eyes and a long tapered head and two shovel-like golden tusks alongside its snout and a row of pale yellow stripes down its tawny back. Its legs were slender and ended in three sharp-tipped toes: a digging animal, perhaps, that fed on insects in the ground. It looked at Hresh as if it had never seen anyone of his sort before.

He went close to it.

"*Your* name is goldentusks," Hresh said.

Torlyri smiled. How like him, to name the animal first, on his own naming-day!

The animal stared, unafraid, perhaps curious.

"And I," Hresh went on, "I am Hresh-full-of-questions, and this is my naming-day, and I have chosen you as my naming-beast. And I tell you, goldentusks, that the name I take is—Hresh! Hresh-of-the-answers!"

Torlyri gasped. The audacity of him!

Once in a while it happened that someone chose his birth-name to be his grown-name as well, but it was rare, it was almost unheard-of, for to do such a thing spoke of an inner confidence, a security, that bordered almost on the foolhardy. Hresh who chooses to be named Hresh! Had there ever been anyone like this child?

And yet—and yet—was it the same name? Hresh-full-of-questions before, which was the name that others had come to call him; and Hresh-of-the-answers now, which was the name he had called himself.

He was talking to the goldentusks, standing close beside it, stroking it, patting it. Then he tapped its haunch and sent it padding off into the underbrush. He turned to Torlyri.

"Well?" he said. "Am I properly named?"

"You are properly named, yes." She pulled him close to her and hugged him. "Hresh-of-the-answers, yes." He accepted his nearness to her a little stiffly, a little reluctantly, as if uneasy with her affection. Releasing him, she said, "Come now: we must return to the camp, and tell the others what you have chosen for yourself. And then it will be time to go in search of great Vengiboneeza."

But they could not set out for Vengiboneeza just yet, for now Nettin had been brought to childbed: a girl this time, and Hresh, presiding again, named her Tramassilu, after the girl who had been speared by the red-beaked hopping thing. It was his plan to name all the new children for those who had died on the trek, to indicate that the losses had been made up. They needed a new Hignord and a new Valmud, therefore; and then other names could be used as other children were born. Already Jalmud, whose mate had been killed by the rat-wolves, had asked leave to take the girl Sinistine to couple with, and Hresh supposed that other pairs would be forming soon, now that everyone realized they need not fear engendering new life, but must come to see it as a sacred duty.

For a few days more the tribe remained camped near the water-strider pond, until Threyne and Nettin were strong enough to move onward. It was a hard time for Koshmar, who yearned to see Vengiboneeza. It was hard for Hresh, too. More than any of the others he had some idea of what to expect at Vengiboneeza, and he boiled with eagerness.

Indeed he was the first of all of them to glimpse its towers, four days after they resumed the march. Heading westward, they came to a lake, of such a deep blue that it seemed black, and then another lake, just as the water-strider had said; and then they came to a stream, which plainly meant that Vengiboneeza must be near. It was only a small stream, but swift and cold with jutting fangs of rock everywhere. Crossing it with the baggage was an intricate task that took many hours, so that even Koshmar thought it was wisest to make camp and rest on the far side. But Hresh was unable to wait. Once they were across he slipped off by himself when no one was watching, and ran quickly through the trees until sudden amazement brought him to a halt.

The gleaming towers of a splendid city soared before him, rising like great slabs of shinestone above the jungle, and there were more of them than he could count, row upon row—this one an iridescent violet hue, this one a burning gold, this one scarlet rimmed with balconies of midnight blue, this one utter jet. Some were wrapped in strangling coils of vine, as the forest creature had said, but most stood clear.

Hresh resisted the urge to go plunging forward into the city itself. He stared at it a long while, drinking in its astonishing beauty.

Then, heart pounding, he hurried back toward the camp, crying out, "Vengiboneeza! I've found Vengiboneeza!"

He was less than halfway back to the camp when something thick and furry and incredibly strong snared him around the throat and hurled him to the ground.

Desperately Hresh struggled for air. He was choking. His eyes bulged in their sockets. Everything was a blur. He could barely make out his assailants. There were three of them, it appeared. Two were jumping up and down and the third held him prisoner with its long, ropy sensing-organ. If they were human, Hresh thought, they belonged to some very different tribe: their arms and legs were extraordinarily long, their bodies were thin and compact, their heads were small, their eyes were large and hard and gleaming, but without the light of intelligence in them. All three were covered from the crowns of their heads to their slender black toes by soft rank grayish-green fur of an unfamiliar texture.

"I—can't breathe—" Hresh murmured. "Please—"

He heard coarse mocking laughter and a fierce babble of sounds in an unknown language, shrill and turbulent. Desperately he tugged at the whiplike sensing-organ that was choking him. He dug his fingertips in hard. Strangely, that produced no response, except perhaps a tightening of the grip. Hresh had never known of a sensing-organ so insensitive. The other seemed hardly to feel a thing.

"Please—please—" he said feebly, with what he knew to be his last breath. Everything was going black for him.

There was a sudden wild screeching sound. The pressure at his throat relented and he rolled free, doubling over, gasping and gagging. His head spun. The world reeled wildly beneath him. For a moment he was unable to see clearly: his eyes showed him nothing but spots and whirls. After a little while he felt himself recovering, and looked up.

Harruel and Konya stood above him. They had speared two of the three strangers and cast their bloody bodies aside like so much trash; the third had fled into the trees, and dangled there from its sensing-organ, screaming at them.

"Are you all right?" Harruel asked.

"I think so. Just—out—of—breath." He sat up, kneeling, and

rubbed his aching throat and filled his lungs as deeply as he could. "Another moment and it all would have been over for me." He looked at the two crumpled-up dead things, and shuddered. "But you saved me. And see, there? The city! The city!" Hresh pointed with a trembling hand. "Vengiboneeza!"

Vengiboneeza, yes. The two warriors glanced toward the towers. The tips of them were barely visible from here. Konya grunted in surprise and dropped down and made the sign of the Protector. Harruel leaned in silence on his spear, shaking his head slowly in wonder.

Then Koshmar came running, and Torlyri, and most of the others after them. Hresh, though still wobbly and uncertain of foot, led them all through the tangles of vines and saw-edged grasses to the place where he had seen the shining towers piercing the sky. But the chattering gray-green folk were everywhere, scrambling by dozens in the trees, dangling by their sensing-organs, leaping from bough to bough, cackling, laughing, calling out defiance. They must have been watching me all the while, Hresh realized.

"What tribe is this?" Torlyri asked.

"A very stupid one, I think," said Hresh.

"They look something like us," Torlyri said.

"Very little like us," snapped Koshmar.

"But they move swiftly, this strange tribe," Hresh said.

"Not so swiftly that we can't slaughter them if they bother us," Koshmar said. "Gods! This is no tribe! These are no humans! All they are is animals. Vermin. And look: the city! Vengiboneeza will be ours. Spears, everyone! Torches! On to Vengiboneeza!"

Vermin they might be, and stupid vermin also, yet the strange animals proved very troublesome. They would not descend from the trees, but pelted Koshmar's people with fruit and branches and even their own green dung, crying out incomprehensible insults all the while. Galihine was knocked down by a heavy purple fruit that struck her between the shoulders, and Haniman was struck by a huge papery gray globe that turned out to be the nest of a swarm of angry stinging insects half a finger's length long.

But Koshmar and her warriors advanced steadily, using spears, throwing-sticks, darts, and the rest of their weapons; and gradually the other tribe retreated. Hresh, watching the battle from a safe place, was dismayed and horrified by these forest-folk. How ugly they were, how debased, how—inhuman! They had the shape of people, or something almost like it, but they acted and carried themselves like mere beasts. The torches terrified them, as if they had never seen fire before. They used their sensing-organs simply as a tail, like any trivial wild creature, as though that organ had no powers at all except that of allowing them to swing through the treetops.

All the same, Hresh thought, they look not so very different from us. That was the worst part. We are human, they are beasts; and they are not so very different from us! There but for the grace of the gods go we!

In half an hour the battle was over. The forest-chatterers were gone; the way to Vengiboneeza lay open.

"Let me go in first," Hresh begged. "I found it. I want to be first."

Koshmar, chuckling, nodded amiably. "You are still Hresh-full-of-questions, aren't you? Yes. Go."

Suddenly taken aback at having been granted with such ease the thing he had requested, Hresh nevertheless turned without hesitation, and slipped through the massive gate of three heavy green pillars that stood open at the threshold of Vengiboneeza.

To his astonishment, three figures that he recognized at once as members of the sapphire-eyes race waited just within. He had seen their like many times, when running his hands over the pages of the books of the chronicles: massive beings, standing upright on great thick-thighed legs, supported by heavy sensing-organs—or were they simply tails? They held their small forearms outstretched in a gesture that seemed plainly to be one of invitation. Their huge heavy-lidded eyes, of a blue so deep they seemed to be not eyes but seas, were radiant with wisdom and power.

Hresh reared back, startled. Twice these beings had ruled the world: once in the ancientmost times, before any humans had even existed, in a long-ago civilization that an earlier onslaught of death-stars had destroyed; and then again late in the human era, when the few survivors of that first lost sapphire-eyes empire had brought themselves back to greatness a second time. Reptiles by ancestry, of crocodilian stock, descended from creatures that had long been content to lie torpid in the mud of tropical rivers, they had managed to rise far above that level; but the return of the death-stars had shattered the sapphire-eyes' realm once again, and this time there had been no survivors in that new terrible cold. Or so the chronicles in their misty difficult way declared, and so Thaggoran had taught.

"No," Hresh whispered. "You can't exist. You all died with the Great World!"

The sapphire-eyes on the left raised one of its little forearms inquiringly.

"How could we have died, little monkey, when we were never alive?" It spoke in a stiff, antiquated way, strange but understandable.

"Never alive?"

"Only machines," said the one on the right.

"Placed here to welcome human beings at winter's end into the city of our masters, in whose image we were made," said the center sapphire-eyes.

"Machines," said Hresh, absorbing it, digesting it. "Made in the image of your masters. Who died in the Long Winter. I see. I see." He came up as close to them as he dared, craning his neck to peer into the deep mysteries of their gleaming eyes. "We can go into the city, then? You'll show us all that it holds?"

He was trembling with awe. He had never seen anything so majestic as these three. And yet he felt an obscure sense of disappointment. All they were were clever artificials of some sort. Not really alive. He had wanted them to be true sapphire-eyes folk, miraculously sustained through the time of cold. But it was impossible. He put that hope aside.

Then he said, after a moment, "Why did you call me 'little monkey'? Don't you recognize a human being when you see one?"

The three sapphire-eyes made strange hissing sounds, which Hresh felt to be laughter. He heard another sound from behind him: little gasps and sighs of wonder. He glanced quickly back and saw Koshmar and Torlyri and the rest, standing with mouths agape.

"But you *are* a little monkey," said the center sapphire-eyes. "And those are larger monkeys, standing behind you. And it was monkeys of a different and more foolish kind that attacked you in the forest."

"*They* were monkeys, perhaps. We are human beings," said Hresh firmly.

"Ah, no," said the left-hand sapphire-eyes, and made the little hissing sound again. "Not humans, no. The humans departed long ago, at the outset of the Long Winter."

"Departed?"

"They are gone, yes. You are only their distant cousins, do you see? Both you and the forest-folk who chatter in the treetops."

Hresh felt his face flaming with bewilderment and dismay.

"I believe none of this."

"It is so. You and the forest folk—"

"I forbid you to speak of us and them in the same breath!"

"But they are your kin, little monkey."

"No! No!"

"Oh, your kind is far superior in matters of the mind, that I will grant. But never confuse yourselves with humans, child. You are not made from human stock, but of something other, something similar, perhaps something of a different line of descent from the ancient ancestor of humans and monkeys both: a second attempt, perhaps, at achieving what the gods achieved with humans."

Hresh stared. Confusion and wrath choked his throat. These are malicious lies, he thought. Intended to confound and discomfort him, because he had been so rash as to intrude on the age-old solitude of these three malevolent artificials.

"You are somewhat like the humans," said the left-hand sapphire-eyes, "but not very much so. I assure you of that. They had no hair on their bodies, the humans, and they had no tails, and they—"

"This isn't a tail!" cried Hresh, indignant. "It's a sensing-organ!"

"A modified tail, yes," the sapphire-eyes went on implacably. "It is quite good, it is truly remarkable, in fact. But you are not human. There no longer are humans here. What you are is monkeys, or the children of monkeys. The humans are gone from the earth."

The incredible words were crushing. They had to be lying, they were toying with him, trying to torment and humiliate him with this hideous impossible slur. But he could not throw it off with the contempt it deserved. He felt his anger giving way to despair.

"Not—human?" Hresh said, close to tears, feeling very small and ugly. "Not—human? No. No. It isn't possible."

"What is this?" Koshmar burst in, at last. "Who are these creatures? Sapphire-eyes, are they? And still alive?"

"No," said Hresh, gathering himself. "Only artificials in the form of sapphire-eyes, guardians of the gate of Vengiboneeza. But did you hear what they said, Koshmar? Crazy stuff. That we aren't human. That we're only monkeys, or descended from monkeys, that our sensing-organs are nothing but monkey tails, that the real humans are gone from here—"

Koshmar looked startled. "What nonsense is this?"

"They say—"

"Yes, I heard what they say." She turned to Torlyri. "What do you make of this?"

The offering-woman, plainly uncertain, blinked, smiled a nervous smile, frowned. "These are ancient creatures. Perhaps they have knowledge which—"

"It's absurd," Koshmar said bluntly. She gestured at Hresh. "You! Chronicler! You've studied the past. Are we humans or aren't we?"

"I don't know. The early chronicles are very difficult. The humans are gone, these artificials say," Hresh murmured. He was shivering in the forest warmth. His eyes felt hot and swollen: the tears were a moment away.

Koshmar seemed to puff up with fury. "And what would humans be, then, if we are not humans?"

"The artificials say that they had no tails—no sensing-organs—they were without fur—"

"That is some other kind of human," said Koshmar with a

grand dismissing swoop of her arm. "A different tribe, long vanished, if they even existed at all. How do we know they ever lived? We have nothing but the word of these—these things here, these artificials. Let them say whatever they like. We know what we are."

Hresh was silent. He tried to summon his knowledge of the chronicles, but all that would rise to his mind was cloudy ambiguities.

"We are the children of Lord Fanigole and Lady Theel, who led us to the cocoon," said Koshmar vehemently. "They were humans and we are humans, and so be it."

From the sapphire-eyes' artificials, once again, came that hissing laughter.

Koshmar rounded on them fiercely. She made an angry sweeping gesture, as though brushing cobwebs out of the air before her face. "We are humans," she repeated, and there was something terrible and awesome in the way she said it. "Let no creature, living or artificial, deny it!"

Hresh hovered between fierce agreement and numb disbelief. He felt as though his soul were fluttering in the balance. Not human? Not human? What did that mean? How could it be? A monkey, nothing but a monkey, a superior kind of monkey? No. No. No. He looked toward Torlyri, and the offering-woman took his hand in hers. "Koshmar is right," Torlyri whispered. "The sapphire-eyes wish to mislead us. Koshmar speaks the truth."

"Yes," cried Koshmar, overhearing. "It is the truth. If ever there were humans once without fur, without sensing-organs, well, they were some misbegotten mistake, and they are gone now. But we are here. And we are human, by right of blood, by right of succession. It is the truth. By Yissou, it is the truth!" She came forward and faced the three hulking reptiles just within the gate. "What do you say, sapphire-eyes? You tell us we are not humans. But are we not the humans now? Humans of a different kind from the sort you claim to have known, perhaps, but humans of a better kind: for they are gone, if ever they lived at all, and we are here. We have endured, where they have not. We have survived to winter's end, and now we will take back the world from the hjjk-folk, or whoever else may have seized it in the time of coldness. What do you say, sapphire-eyes? Are we not humans? May we not enter great Vengiboneeza? What do you say?"

There was a long aching silence.

"I tell it to you again," declared Koshmar unwaveringly. "If we are not the humans you knew, we are the humans now. Admit it! Admit it! Humans by right of succession. It is our destiny to have this city. Where are they, the ones you call the real humans? Where? Where? We are here! I tell you, we are the humans now."

There was silence again, mighty and profound. Hresh thought that he had never seen Koshmar look more majestic.

The center sapphire-eyes, which had been staring toward the remote horizon, turned now to Koshmar. It regarded her with distant interest for a long while.

"So be it," it said finally, just as it seemed the air itself would crack and split apart under the strain. "You are the humans now." And the creature appeared to smile.

Then the three reptilian forms bowed and moved aside.

They have yielded, Hresh thought in joy and astonishment. They have yielded!

And Koshmar the chieftain, holding her sensing-organ aloft like a scepter, led her little band of humans through the gate and toward the shining towers of Vengiboneeza.

6

The Art of Waiting

In wonder and in jubilation Koshmar and her people took up lodg-
ings in the great city of the lost sapphire-eyes folk. Shattered and
crumbling though it was, Vengiboneeza still was a place of splendor
beyond anyone's imagining. Its location was superb, in a sheltered
bowl bordered on the north and partly on the east by a golden-
brown mountain wall, on the south and east by the dense jungle
that the tribe had just left, and on the west by a dark lake, or perhaps
a sea, so broad that it was impossible to look across it to the far side.
Warm winds blew steadily out of the west, carrying moisture from
the sea. Rain was frequent and the land was green and lush. This
was winter, the season of short days, which seemed to be the rainy
season, and it was a very wet season indeed. But the air was mild by
day and only a few of the nights saw frost, and then merely in the
hour just before dawn. When the days began getting longer there
was a distinct quickening of growth and the weather grew even

warmer. It was all very different from those early bleak months in the first days after leaving the cocoon, when they were crossing the sad and barren plains at the heart of the continent. Plainly the time of the Long Winter was over. No one doubted that now.

Vengiboneeza itself was everywhere, sprawling, vast, incomprehensible, a world unto itself, lying under an awesome silence. From the edge of the sea to the rim of the jungle to the forested foothills of the mountains the dead city spread in all directions, without apparent plan, without discernible order. In some districts the streets ran in grand open boulevards that afforded magnificent views of the mountains beyond, or the sea; in others, there were networks of tiny alleys that coiled one upon another in a sort of desperate cringing secrecy, or high walls that were set at odd angles to block ready access to the plazas beyond. There were great towers in many places, rising generally in serried rows of ten or twenty, but sometimes—and these were the biggest—the towers stood in grand isolation above a neighborhood of low squat buildings with green tiled domes.

Much of the city, especially in the seafront districts, was in ruins. Much was not.

The Long Winter had left fewer scars here than in the unsheltered plains to the east, but there were scars aplenty. The sea had risen more than once during the winter years and had swept devastatingly through the low-lying neighborhoods. There were ancient gray waterstains on high walls and swirling carpets of sandy rubble on third-story balconies. The scattered and crumbled bones of sea-creatures lay in drifts on the flat rooftops. It was clear also that sluggish rivers of ice must have come flowing down the sides of the mountain wall at some time to fold and crush the buildings on the higher slopes. And it looked as if the earth itself had heaved upward from its depths in many parts of the city, where the pavements were vertically displaced and buildings stood at precarious angles or lay fallen in shattered segments and shards of iridescent metal.

"The wonder of it is," Torlyri said, "that any of it survives at all, after seven hundred thousand years."

"It has been cared for," said Koshmar. "It must have been."

Indeed that seemed to be true. In many places signs were visible of repair and even of reconstruction on a large scale, as though the keepers of the city were expecting the sapphire-eyes folk to return at any moment and were striving to maintain the place in fit condition for them. But who were the keepers? No mechanicals were in evidence, no artificials of any kind: the place seemed deserted except for the three gigantic guardians who sat before the gate, and they never left their posts.

"Search the chronicles," Koshmar commanded Hresh. "Tell me how this city has been preserved."

Most diligently did he search. But though he discovered a great deal about the founding and glory of Vengiboneeza, there was no clue to any understanding of its survival. For all he could find out, the ghosts of the sapphire-eyes themselves might well have flitted invisibly through the streets, doing what had to be done.

At first the tribe did not venture to the more remote parts of the city. Koshmar led them inside just far enough so that they would feel safe from the creatures of the jungle, but not so far that they would become confused in the labyrinth of ruined streets. There was time to risk such things later; patience was essential now, in these early mysterious days. They had had the patience to live seven hundred thousand years in a single cocoon in a mountainside. Koshmar herself was not an extraordinarily patient woman; but she strived constantly to master the art that any wise chieftain must learn, which is the art of waiting.

She chose a district close by the southern gate that was not very badly ruined. Here a stupendous six-sided many-windowed tower of smooth purple stone dominated a sprawling neighborhood of the little green-domed buildings. These she assigned to the tribe in what she thought was a clever way. Each of the breeding couples was given a house of its own. The warriors were sent to live in a group, so they would jostle against each other and consume some of the restless energies that might otherwise lead to trouble. The older people were allowed to dwell in units of three or four, to look after one another, and all the children were placed together in a house adjoining that of the unmated worker-women. Koshmar and Torlyri took the building closest to the great tower for themselves. The tower would become the tribe's temple, and later it could serve as a beacon to lead them back to their home district when they traveled through the city, since there was no region of Vengiboneeza, apparently, from which it could not be seen.

This was the happiest time that Koshmar had ever known. There was some problem to solve every day, some decree to issue, some decision to make.

In the cocoon she had often felt uneasy and uncertain. Her powerful urge toward leadership had mainly gone unfulfilled. Since girlhood she had been shaped toward the chieftainship, and she exercised her powers with strength and incisiveness. But she had been a leader with no leading to do. Things were too easy in the cocoon. She played her proper role in all the rites, she passed judgment when disputes or quarrels broke out, she acted as counselor to the weak and pacifier to the strong and the headstrong. That was what the life of the cocoon was like, and that was what the role of the leader was.

But she had seen her days going by without real purpose,

and the end of them had been coming into view with her rest-lessness still aching within her. Though at thirty she was still as vigorous as a girl, she knew she had no way of avoiding the onrushing limit-age. The law was absolute. Only the chronicler might live beyond the thirty-fifth year. There was no exemp-tion for chieftains. Koshmar had often considered how it would be for her a few years hence, when she must be thrust through the exit hatch, vigorous or not, to meet her death in the world outside.

That was all changed now. Now it was essential for them all to live as long as they could, and for those who were capable of bear-ing young to bring them forth with zeal.

Some of the tribesfolk did not understand that, at first. Ani-jang, who was the oldest, came to Koshmar not long after their arrival in Vengiboneeza and said, "It is my death-day this day. What shall I do, go out into the jungle alone?"

"Anijang, there are no more death-days!" Koshmar said, laugh-ing.

"No death-days? But I am thirty-five. I have kept the count very carefully." He displayed a tattered old strip of leather, marked with notches. "This is the day."

"Are you not still strong and healthy?"

"Well—" He shrugged. Anijang's shoulders were bent and his muzzle was beginning to turn gray; but he looked sound enough to Koshmar.

"There's no reason for you to die until your natural time comes," she said. "This isn't the cocoon any more. There's room for everyone now, for as long as he can live. Besides, you are needed. There's work to do for all of us here, and in the times to come there'll be even more. How can we spare you, Anijang?"

The baffled and forlorn look in the man's eyes astonished

her. Then Koshmar realized that he had long ago made his peace with death and was unable to welcome or even to comprehend this reprieve. For him, for this ordinary man, this plain slow-witted hardworking man, the thirty-five years was enough. He saw no reason to go on. Death to him was only an unending sleep, restful, pleasing.

"I am not to go?" Anijang said.

"You must not go. Dawinno forbids it."

"Dawinno? But he is the Destroyer."

"He is the Balancer," said Koshmar. "He takes and he gives. He has given you your life, Anijang, and you will hold it for many years to come." She pulled him close, gripping his arms tightly. "Rejoice, man! Rejoice! You will live a long time! Go, find your twining-partner, celebrate this day!"

Anijang went shuffling away from her. He seemed not to understand; but he would accept.

Some of the others, Koshmar knew, would be confused in the same way. This matter had to be dealt with by a decree. She spoke a long while with Torlyri, devising what must be said. It was so difficult for them to work it out that they resorted to twining, which gave them the necessary depth of understanding. Then Koshmar called the tribe together to explain the new order of things.

It would be wrong, she told them, to believe that the gods had ever required early death of them. She reminded them of the teachings by which they had been reared. The gods had asked only that the People live within the cocoon in an orderly way until the Time of Going Forth arrived. Since the gods loved life, it had been important that new life occasionally enter the cocoon; but since the tribe could not easily expand the cocoon and their supplies of foodstuffs were limited, the gods had ordered them to maintain a balance of population. Thirty-five years was all that they could live, and then they must leave the cocoon to face their destiny, so that new life might enter. For every child, a death. No one, said Koshmar, had ever questioned the necessity and the wisdom of that.

But the gods in their mercy had brought them forth now into the world and the old strictures no longer applied. The world was huge; the tribe was small; food was easy to find. Now it was the desire of the gods that they be fruitful and multiply. Death would come when the gods willed it, but only then. This now was the season of life, of joy, of the growth of the tribe, said Koshmar.

"And how long will we live, then?" Minbain asked. "Will we live forever?"

"No," said Koshmar, "not forever. Only for the natural time, however long that is."

"Yes," called Galihine, "and how long is that?"

"As long as the chroniclers have lived," Koshmar said. "For they alone have lived their natural time."

Still the faces were blank.

"How long is *that*?" Galihine repeated.

Koshmar looked toward Hresh. "Tell me, boy: what was the name of the chronicler who kept the casket before Thaggoran?"

"Thrask," Hresh said.

"Thrask, yes. I had forgotten, because I was so young when he died. Hardly any of you were born in Thrask's time, but I tell you this, that he lived to be old and bent, and his fur was entirely white. And that is the natural time."

"To be old and bent," Konya said, shivering a little. "I'm not sure I like that."

"For warriors," young Haniman said with sudden impudence, "the natural time will be much shorter, Konya."

The meeting dissolved in laughter. Koshmar could see that

there was more uneasiness than she had anticipated: death for some was freedom, she realized, and not the brutal interruption of life that it seemed to her. They would learn. They would come to understand the new ways. And even if they struggled with these ideas, their children would not, and their children's children would have trouble so much as believing that anything like a limit-age and a death-day had ever been imposed on the tribe.

But Koshmar saw that she could not only abolish death; she must encourage life. And so another of her new laws revoked the restrictions on childbearing. No longer, she decreed, would breeding be limited to just a few couples of the tribe, and then only a single child apiece, to be conceived whenever the tribe needed a replacement for one who had reached the limit-age. From now on anyone above the age of twining might have children in any number. Not only might: *should.* The tribe was too small. That must change.

At once new couples began coming to her to ask for the coupling-rites. The first were Konya and Galihine, and then Staip and Boldirinthe. Then, most surprisingly, Harruel came with Minbain, who had brought forth Hresh by her mate Samnibolon. Samnibolon had died of a fever long ago. Did Minbain truly mean to breed again? Koshmar wondered if there had ever been a woman of the tribe who had borne two children, let alone two by different fathers. But this was a new age, she reminded herself for the thousandth time. Had she not said that it was everyone's obligation to breed who could? Then why not Minbain, since she was still of childbearing age? Why not any of us?

Why not you, Koshmar? a voice within her unexpectedly asked.

It was so odd an idea that she burst out laughing. I am a chieftain, she answered herself, trying to imagine herself lying in a bower with her belly grown huge and women clustered around to comfort her while a baby tried to force its way out of her body. For that matter, she could not even think of herself in a man's embrace, his hands on her breasts, his hands pushing her legs apart. Or—how did they like to do it? The woman thrust down against the ground on her face, the man's weight descending on her from behind—no, no, it was not for her, the chieftainship was enough of a burden for her—

And why not Torlyri? the same mischievous voice asked.

Koshmar caught her breath and clutched her side as though she had been kicked in the stomach. Warm good Torlyri, *her* Torlyri? Why, she was the mother of the whole tribe, was Torlyri. She had no need to bring forth babes of her own. How could the offering-woman take time for childrearing, anyway? She had so much else to do.

Still, the image would not go from her: Torlyri in the arms of some warrior whose face she could not see, Torlyri gasping and sighing, Torlyri's sensing-organ thrashing about the way they did during coupling, Torlyri's thighs opening—

No. No. No. No.

Why not Torlyri? the voice said again.

Koshmar clenched her fists.

These are new times, yes, she told herself. But Torlyri is mine.

Taniane said, "What did those sapphire-eyes things mean, when they said we were monkeys and not humans?"

"Nothing," Hresh told her. "It was just a stupid lie. They were only trying to belittle us."

"Why would they want to do that?"

"Because we are alive," said Hresh. "And they are things that never were, built by a race that is dead."

Harruel said, "They called us monkeys. I know what monkeys are. I killed the two that attacked you in the jungle. I killed more when we were entering the city. I wish I had killed them all, the filthy dung-throwing beasts. What are these things, these monkeys, that are supposed to be our kin?"

"Animals," Hresh said. "Just animals."

"And we are just animals too?"

"We are human beings," said Hresh.

He said such things as though there could be no question of their truth. But in fact he felt no certainty, only a dark morass of confusion.

To be human, he thought, was a grand and glorious thing. It was to be a link in an infinite chain of achievement descending from the world's most ancient times. To be a monkey, or even the cousin of a monkey, was to be scarcely better than one of those foul-smelling chattering stupid things that swung by their sensing-organs—no, Hresh corrected himself, by their *tails*—from the trees of the jungle beyond the city's edge.

Are we humans, then, Hresh asked himself, or are we monkeys?

In the chronicles, in the Book of the Way, it was written that at winter's end the humans would come forth from their hiding places and journey to ruined Vengiboneeza, and obtain there the things they needed to gain power over all the world. So Hresh understood the text to say; and he understood the chronicles to mean the People, where the Book of the Way spoke of "humans."

But was that so? The chronicles were not written in the simple words of everyday speech; they were composed of encapsulated thought-packets to which a reader had access by the powers of mind. There was much scope for misinterpretation in that. What leaped from the vellum page to his fingers and from his fingers to his mind, when he studied the Book of the Way, was a concept that seemed to mean the People, that is, those-for-whom-this-book-has-been-written. But it could just as readily mean humans-who-are-distinct-from-the-People. When Hresh examined the text more closely, he saw that the only unarguable reading was one which said that those-who-deem-themselves-to-be-humans would come to Vengiboneeza at winter's end to claim the treasures of the city.

One could *deem* oneself to be human, though, without truly *being* human.

The sapphire-eyes' artificials, Hresh told himself, say that we are monkeys, or the descendants of monkeys. Koshmar angrily replies that we are human. Who is right? Does the Book of the Way mean that *we* will come to Vengiboneeza, or some mysterious *they*?

Everything else in the Book of the Way appeared to be intended for the People. It was their book, written by them, for them. When the Book of the Way says "humans," Hresh thought, it must surely be referring to us. But does the Book of the Way really say "humans" Hresh wondered? Or was that merely the reading that the People had given the word, because they had come over the centuries to regard themselves as human, when in fact they were not?

He was lost in confusion.

He asked himself: Does it matter, really, whether we are human or something else? We are what we are, and what we are is far from contemptible.

No. No.

Better than anyone else he knew what the monkey-beings of

the jungle were like. He had looked them straight in the eyes, and had seen the beastliness there. He had been seized around the throat by a powerful furry tail and nearly done to death. He had heard their cackling gibberish. With all his soul he detested them; and with all his soul he prayed that the artificials had been lying, that there was not even the most distant of kinships between his people and the monkeys of the jungle.

He told himself fiercely that he and his people were human beings, just as Koshmar insisted. But, he wished he could be as sure of that as she seemed to be. He wished he had some proof. Until then he must live in doubt and torment.

The People shared Vengiboneeza with other, smaller creatures, some of them very troublesome.

The monkeys of the jungle occasionally entered, dancing along the high ledges and cornices of the nearby buildings and tossing things at those below—pebbles, pellets of dung, little prickle-edged scarlet berries that burned like hot coals. Serpents with ruffled green mantles behind their heads were everywhere, coiling sleepily between rocks, but now and again uncoiling to hiss and strike. The girl Bonlai was bitten, and also the young warrior Bruikkos, and both were ill for many days, feverish and pain-racked, despite the medications and spells that Torlyri used on them.

Salaman, prowling between two slope-roofed three-sided alabaster buildings a hundred paces behind the main tower, came upon a slab in the ground with a metal ring set into it, and made the mistake of tugging on it. The slab lifted easily, and immediately a horde of gleaming iridescent blue-and-gold creatures no larger than a thumb came swarming up from the depths of the earth. Their eyes were huge and glittered like fiery red jewels, and their clacking little jaws were sharp as blades. Salaman endured a dozen bites, from each of which blood began to stream. He yelled in pain and Sachkor and Moarn came running, and the three of them were able to free him of his attackers, but by then the small beasts were everywhere. Their bodies were soft, though, and easily smashed by a blow from a broom of straw. An hour's work by half a dozen of the tribe and all of them were dead. During the night unseen scavengers gathered the hundreds of pulpy little corpses from the plaza and by dawn none were to be seen.

Each day brought some new annoyance. There were stinging insects of many kinds, small and difficult and persistent. There were venomous little lizards that sang soft hissing sounds. There were birds with filmy tapering wings and pale, delicate blue bills that perched in high trees and bombarded anyone who passed beneath them with a shining sticky spittle that raised painful welts wherever it struck.

All in all, though, the city was not an unpleasant place to be. There were some who said that life here was almost as good as dwelling in the cocoon. And others declared that life in Vengiboneeza, for all its little annoyances and the strangeness of an existence beneath the terrifying open sky, was in truth to be preferred to the old days in the snug burrow in the heart of the mountain.

One day in the fifth week of their stay in Vengiboneeza, Koshmar called Hresh to her and said, "Tomorrow you and Konya will begin to explore the city."

"Konya? Why Konya?"

"Did you expect to go out alone? We can't risk losing you, Hresh."

That was maddening. He had assumed that when Koshmar finally sent him out into Vengiboneeza he would be able to move at his own pace, thinking his own thoughts and poking his nose wherever he felt like poking it, without having to put up with some great hulking impatient warrior who had been given the job of protecting him. He argued, but it was useless. The sapphire-eyes folk, Koshmar said, might have filled the city full of deathtraps; or perhaps the outlying districts were occupied by the screeching monkeys, or some new kind of noxious insect or reptile with a poisonous bite. He was too valuable to the tribe. She would take no chances. One of the warriors would accompany him. Either that, she told him, or he could stay in the settlement and let the older and stronger men do the exploring without him.

Hresh was wise enough now to know when he could try to oppose Koshmar's decisions and when it was best simply to abide by her wishes. He let the issue drop.

When morning came the day was warm and bright, with low-hanging mists quickly burning off. "Which way do you plan to go?" Konya asked, as they stood in the plaza before the great tower.

Hresh had no plan. But he peered in his most serious way to the right and to the left, as though deep in contemplation, and then pointed his forefinger straight ahead, toward a broad and awesome boulevard that seemed to lead to one of the grandest sectors of the city.

"That way," he said.

In the beginning Konya walked ahead of him, stamping his foot against the pavement to see if it would hold their weight, peering into doorways and down alleys in search of hidden enemies, prodding with the butt of his spear against the sides of buildings to make certain that they would not topple as he and Hresh went past. But after a while, when it was obvious that no lurking beasts were waiting to spring, that the streets would not give way beneath them or buildings come tumbling down, Hresh began to sprint ahead, going wherever his curiosity took him, and Konya made no objection.

To Hresh it was like entering an enchanted world. He was dizzy with excitement and his eyes flickered so wildly from one thing to another that his head began to throb. He wanted to take in everything at once, in a single greedy gulp.

He saw buildings everywhere whose grandeur and massive forms took his breath away. The Great World seemed almost still to be alive. Any moment, he imagined, sapphire-eyes or vegetals or sea-lords might come sauntering out of that building of swooping parapets over there, or this one that rose in delicate filigreed arches that looked like frozen music, or that one of the yellow towers and wide-jutting wings.

"In here," he called to Konya. "No, this one! No, this looks better yet! What do you think, Konya?"

"Whichever you want," the warrior said stolidly. "They all look good to me."

Hresh grinned. "We're going to find all sorts of marvelous things. The chronicles say so. Everything's been preserved, the miraculous machines that the Great World used. We're going to find it all sitting right where the sapphire-eyes left it when the death-stars came."

But very quickly Hresh found out that it was not like that at all.

Many of the buildings that appeared so amazingly well preserved on the outside were mere ruins within. Some were empty shells, containing nothing more than a trickle of ancient dust.

Others had collapsed inside so that one floor lay piled upon another in chaos, and it would have taken an army of strong diggers to penetrate the mounds of debris. In others, seemingly intact facades and cabinets came apart at the lightest touch, dissolving into clouds of dark vapor when Hresh approached them.

"We should be going back now," said Konya finally, as the purple shadows of afternoon began to gather.

"But we haven't found anything!"

"There'll be other days," Konya told him.

It was intensely embarrassing to return from the expedition empty-handed. Hresh could scarcely bear to look at Koshmar's face as he made his report.

"Nothing?" Koshmar said.

"Nothing," said Hresh, mumbling sheepishly. "Not yet."

"Well, there'll be other days," said Koshmar.

He went out nearly every day, except when it rained. Usually it was Konya who went with him, sometimes Staip; never Harruel, for he was too huge, too overbearing, and Hresh told Koshmar bluntly that he would never be able to accomplish anything with Harruel breathing down his neck. Hresh would have preferred not to have Konya or Staip with him either, but Koshmar absolutely forbade that, and grudgingly he had to admit that she was right not to let him go off into the city alone. Hardly anyone else in the tribe knew how to read at all, let alone how to interpret the chronicles. If anything happened to him the People would be left helpless, cut adrift from all knowledge of the past and any hope of comprehending what the future might hold.

After a time, when some of Koshmar's fears of the city's dangers had subsided, he went out sometimes with Orbin as his companion. Orbin, though no older than Hresh, had always been bigger and sturdier, and now he was growing so fast that it looked as if he would be as big and strong as Harruel himself before many more years had gone by. Later still, Hresh took Haniman as his companion and bodyguard. To everyone's surprise, Haniman too was growing tall and strong, and even in a way agile. He had become very unlike the Haniman Hresh had known in the cocoon, slow and pudgy and clumsy and, so it seemed, irritatingly stupid. The trek across the continent appeared to have transformed him, or, Hresh thought, perhaps there had been more to Haniman all along than he had been willing to see.

It made no difference who he went with, Konya or Staip, Orbin or Haniman, or where in the city he went, north or south, east or west. To his shame and consternation he could discover nothing of any imaginable value, only an occasional useless scrap of twisted metal or bit of dull glass.

"You look sad," Taniane said. "It's very disappointing, isn't it?"

"There's plenty out there. I'll start finding things soon."

"I know you will." Taniane seemed very interested in his explorations. He wondered why. Perhaps he had underestimated her, too. She was taller than he was, now, growing up fast, and her mind seemed to be broadening, deepening, extending itself. There was an unusual expression about her eyes, a strange searching gleam that seemed to hint at hidden complexities. It was as if her coltish girlishness were only a mask for something more somber and strange. One day she asked him to teach her how to read, which surprised him greatly. He began to give her lessons. There was unexpected pleasure in going off with her to some quiet place and explaining the mysteries of the holy craft. But then a little while afterward Haniman expressed interest in learning how to read also, which spoiled everything. Hresh could hardly refuse him, but that was the end of his going off alone with Taniane, for there was no time to give each of them private instruction; and after a time he began to think that Haniman had asked Hresh to teach him to read for precisely that reason.

The great round of the seasons moved on. The mild rainy winter gave way to a drier, hotter time, and then a time of cooler east winds foretokening the return of winter. Resolutely Hresh went on searching the ruined city. Through one dark empty dusty shell of a building after another he prowled, finding nothing. He seethed with impatience. He wondered if he would ever find anything worthwhile at all.

It was beginning to seem as though Vengiboneeza was entirely useless.

What about the prophecy of the Book of the Way? Was it only a lie and a deception? Suppose he never discovered a thing in these ruins, as was beginning to seem likely? Did that mean, then, that the treasures of the city truly were reserved only for the real humans, whoever and wherever they might be? And that the People were in fact nothing more than glorified monkeys who had intruded where they did not belong?

Hresh fought bitterly against that dismal conclusion. But again and again it came swimming up from the depths of his mind to plague him.

He searched on and on, ranging farther and farther from the home settlement. Often now he went too far to return in a single day, and he begged and won permission to pitch camp overnight at some distant site of exploration. For those journeys he had to take two bodyguards, usually Orbin and Haniman, so that one might remain awake, sitting sentry through the dark hours. But they never encountered danger, though occasionally some wandering animal of the jungle browsed by, and once or twice a flock of monkeys went noisily through the upper stories of the buildings around them, swinging hand to hand in and out of empty windows and leaping wildly from one tower to another.

The size and complexity of the city still bewildered him, but after nearly a year Hresh knew it far better than any of the others. He was the only one for whom Vengiboneeza was something other than a wholly incomprehensible maze. He divided the city into zones, naming each sector for one of the Five Heavenly Ones, and subdividing each of the five into ten lesser zones that he named for members of the tribe. Then he drew a simple map which he carried with him at all times: a roughly sketched outline on an old strip of parchment.

Taniane saw it once, when he took it by accident from his sash. "What's that?" she asked. "Are you learning how to draw pictures now?"

"It isn't anything important."

"Can I look?"

"I'd rather you didn't."

"I won't make fun of it, I promise."

"It's—a sacred thing," he said lamely. "Something only the chronicler can look at."

He wondered why he had told her that. There was nothing sacred about the map. Indeed, not only was there no reason to conceal it from her, but he knew that he probably should make copies of it, so that the others could at least begin to gain some understanding of the city. But somehow he found himself reluctant. The map gave him power over the city, and power too over the rest of the tribe. The pleasure he took in his private knowledge of it was not, Hresh knew, particularly admirable. But it was real pleasure all the same and he prized it.

On a day in early winter when he felt oppressed to the depths of his soul by the disappointment and frustration of his fruitless search, Hresh returned to the main southern gate, where he had encountered the three gigantic artificials that the sapphire-eyes had left behind. They stood just where they had been, near the great pillars of green stone, silent, motionless, majestic.

He walked around them until he stood before them. He stared up at them without fear or awe this time.

"If you were anything more than machines," he said, "you'd know that you've been wasting your time standing guard here all these thousands of years."

The one on the left looked at him with something like amusement in its huge shining blue eyes.

"Is that the truth, little monkey?"

"You mustn't call me that! I'm a human! A human!" Hresh pointed angrily at the center sapphire-eyes, the one who had finally granted Koshmar and her people permission to enter the city. "You admitted it yourself! 'You are the humans now,' you told us."

"Yes. That is correct," said the center sapphire-eyes. "You are the humans now."

"Do you hear that?" Hresh said to the left-hand one.

"I do. And I agree: you are the humans now. For whatever that may be worth to you. But why do you say we have wasted our time, little monkey?"

Hresh fought back his annoyance.

"Because," he said frostily, "you guard an empty city. Our books say that useful things are supposed to be stored here. But there's nothing but ruined buildings, calamity, chaos, dust, trash."

"Your books are correct," said the center one.

"I've searched everywhere. There's nothing. The buildings are empty. One good sneeze would bring half the place toppling down."

"You should search more deeply," said the left-hand sapphire-eyes.

"And search with that which can help you find what you seek," said the right-hand one, speaking for the first time.

"I don't understand. Tell me what you mean."

The hissing sound of their laughter showered down about him.

"Little monkey!" said the left-hand one, almost affectionately. "Ah, impatient little monkey!"

"Tell me!"

But all he could get from them was the hissing of their laughter, and their indulgent, patronizing crocodile smiles.

Hresh was with Haniman, a month or two afterward, in the sector of the city that he called Emakkis Boldirinthe, when finally he made his first discovery of a working artifact out of the Great World.

Emakkis Boldirinthe was a northern district of extraordinary grace and beauty, midway between the sea and the foothills, where three dozen slender tapering towers of dark blue marble were arrayed in a circle around a broad plaza paved with shining black flagstones. The windows of the towers were intact in their triangular frames, yielding a dazzling pink glint as they reflected the light of late afternoon. Intricately carved metal doors twice the height of a man rested still on their massive hinges, seemingly ready to swing open at a touch. The buildings looked as if they had been abandoned only the day before yesterday. Staring at them in wonder, Hresh felt the weight of the inconceivable ages pressing down on him, a sense that all time was compressed into this single moment. A prickling sensation ran along the back of his neck, as though myriad invisible eyes were watching him.

"What do you think?" Haniman asked. "Do we try to go inside?"

They had been searching all day. A wet wind was blowing. Hresh felt weary and dispirited.

"I've already been in them," he said, though it was untrue. Several times now he had seen these towers at a distance, and once had come this close to them; but in a perverse way their very intactness had discouraged him from trying to enter. Somehow there had seemed no point in it. They would be as empty as all the rest; and his disappointment would be all the more keen because they seemed so well preserved.

"You have? All of them? Every single one?"

"Do you doubt me?" Hresh said sourly.

"It's just that there are so many—and there's always the chance that one of them somewhere around the circle will have something, anything—"

"All right," Hresh said. He lacked heart for sustaining the lie any longer. It was only his weariness, he thought, that made him not want to peer inside these buildings, he who had explored so many less promising places. Hresh who called himself Hresh-full-of-questions and Hresh-of-the-answers should not need to be urged by the likes of Haniman to undertake this exploration now. "We'll give them a look. And then we'll call it a day."

Haniman shrugged.

"I'll go first," he said.

Without waiting for permission from Hresh he loped toward the nearest tower and stood for a moment in front of its great door. Then he flung his arms out as far as they would go, as though he were trying to embrace the building, and pressed himself against it, pushing hard. The door rose so swiftly that Haniman, with a shout of surprise, tumbled forward into the vestibule and vanished in the darkness within.

Hresh rushed after him. By a long shaft of light he saw Haniman sprawling face down just inside the door.

"Are you all right?" Hresh called.

He watched Haniman slowly pick himself up, dust himself off, stare upward. Hresh followed Haniman's gaze and gasped. The building was hollow within, a great dark open space containing nothing but a spiraling arrangement of thin metal struts and tubes that began a few feet from the ground and ran in leaping zigzags from wall to wall, higher and higher, in a design so complex that it dizzied him to trace its pattern. At first he could track it only for a few stories, but as his eyes grew accustomed to the dimness he saw that the crisscrossing structures went up and up and up, possibly to the very top of the tower. It was like a great web. Hresh wondered whether some enormous quivering spider waited for them in the remote upper reaches. But this was a web of metal, unquestionably metal, shining airy silvery stuff, cool and smooth to his hand.

"Should we climb it?" Haniman said.

Hresh shook his head. "Let's try to see what sort of place this is meant to be, first."

He reached up and tapped the strut nearest him. It rang with a rich musical tone, deep and astonishingly beautiful, that rose slowly and solemnly to the next layer of the web and the next, and the next, touching off reverberations at each level. Wondrous shimmering sounds echoed all about them, growing steadily in intensity as they penetrated the higher reaches of the tower, until they became a deafening roar that filled the entire interior of the building.

Hresh stared in wonder and in delight, and in fear, too, thinking that in another moment the tone would succeed in reaching the top and under the force of that tremendous climactic clamor the entire structure might come crashing down.

But all that happened was that the tone, after it had attained a breathtaking mind-filling peak of volume, rapidly began to grow fainter and more delicate again. In moments it faded away entirely, leaving them in startling silence.

"Light your torch," Hresh said. "I want to see what's on the far side."

Cautiously they circled the interior of the building, staying close to the line of the outer wall. But the shimmering metal structure overhead seemed to be the only thing the building contained. At ground level there was nothing remarkable anywhere. The floor was bare brown dirt, dry and hard. When they came around to the entrance again Hresh, beckoning to Haniman, stepped outside, and they crossed the plaza to the next building in the circle. It was identical inside to the first, intricate metalwork within a dark hollow shell. So was the third, and the fourth, and the fifth. Not until they reached the tenth building in the series did they come upon anything that was different.

This one had a rectangular slab of glossy black stone, the same kind of stone that had been used to pave the plaza outside, set flush with the ground in the center of its bare floor. It could have been some sort of altar; or perhaps it was the hatch covering a subterranean chamber.

You should search more deeply, the sapphire-eyes' artificial had said.

Hresh scowled and shook his head. Surely the creature hadn't meant anything so stupidly literal as to look underground.

He knelt and rubbed his hand over the rectangle of black stone. It was cool and very smooth, like some sort of dark glass, and it bore no inscriptions that Hresh could see, or even the traces of them. Stepping out into the middle of it, he looked up into the dizzying strutwork overhead. Here in the center of the tower the lowest struts were just beyond his reach.

"Come here and crouch down," Hresh said. "I want to try something."

Haniman obligingly went to his knees. Hresh scrambled to Haniman's shoulders and told him to rise; and when Haniman stood erect Hresh gave the nearest metal strut a sharp two-fingered tap that set the whole building to ringing with brilliant echoing tones.

At once the black rectangular slab responded with a deep groaning sound and a kind of mechanical sigh; and then it began to move, gliding slowly downward.

"Hresh?"

"Steady," Hresh said. "Here. Let me down." He jumped from Haniman's back and stood stiffly beside him, uneasily struggling to maintain his balance as the stone block went on unhurriedly descending, seeming to float, down and down and down through the darkness.

Finally it came to rest. Sudden amber light glowed about them. Hresh looked around. They were at the lowest level of a high-vaulted cavern that seemed to stretch away through the depths of the earth forever. Its roof was lost in the shadows far overhead. The air was stale and dry, with a sharp stabbing quality to it that reminded Hresh of the cold air in the first days after they had left the cocoon, although it was not cold in this place.

To the right and to the left along the cavern walls and rising as far as he could see was a great clutter of graven images, huge carvings half shrouded in darkness, climbing in tier upon tier. It was difficult at first to make out the shapes that were portrayed, but gradually Hresh began to discern that they were sapphire-eyes folk, mainly, carved from some green stone in high relief, their heavy jutting jaws and rounded bellies savagely exaggerated. The figures were grotesque, bizarre, with an aspect that was both comic and terrifying. Some were enormously fat, or had absurdly elongated limbs, or eyes as big across as a dozen saucers. Many of them had five or six smaller versions of themselves sprouting like boils from their bellies or shoulders. Their sinister daggerlike teeth were bared. Silent laughter seemed to boom from their gaping mouths.

But the statues that rose in uncountable numbers on both sides of them were not only those of sapphire-eyes. There was a whole world here—a cosmos, even—dense, congested, statue upon statue in crazy profusion, all manner of beings packed tightly together in crowded groups.

Here and there Hresh saw the carved figures of hjjk-men interspersed with the sapphire-eyes, and some dome-headed mechanicals not very different from the ones the tribe had found rusting in the lowlands just beyond the mountains of scarlet rock, and other creatures that looked like walking shrubs, with petals for faces and leafy branches for arms and legs.

"What are those?" Haniman asked.

"Vegetals, I think. A tribe of the Great World that perished in the Long Winter."

"And those?" said Haniman. He pointed to a group of pale

elongated beings that reminded Hresh very much of Ryyig Dream-Dreamer, that strange hairless creature who had dwelled in slumber in the cocoon for, so it was said, hundreds of thousands of years. These walked upright on two long thin legs and looked something like the people of the tribe, but they had no fur and no sensing-organs, and their attenuated bodies, even in stone, seemed flimsy and soft.

Hresh stared a long while at them.

"I don't know what they're supposed to be," he said finally.

"They're like the Dream-Dreamer, aren't they?"

"I thought so too."

"A whole race of Dream-Dreamers."

Hresh pondered that. "Why not? Before the Long Winter, all sorts of beings may have lived on Earth."

"So Dream-Dreamers were one of the Six Peoples of the Great World that the chronicles talk about?" Haniman began to count on his fingers. "Sapphire-eyes, sea-lords, hjjks, vegetals, humans— that's five—"

"You left out mechanicals," said Hresh.

"Right. That's all six, then. So who were the Dream-Dreamers?"

"From some other star, maybe. There were all sorts of people here from other stars in those days."

"What was somebody from another star doing living in our cocoon?"

"I don't know that either."

"There's a lot you seem not to know, isn't there?"

"You ask too many questions," said Hresh irritably.

"Ah, but you are Hresh-of-the-answers."

"Ask me this one another time, will you?" Hresh said.

He turned away, stepping down cautiously from the slab of stone that had borne them to this place and tentatively advancing a few paces up the floor of the cavern. As he moved forward the amber glow preceded him, illuminating his path. It seemed to radiate from invisible outlets that might have been set fifteen or twenty paces apart, activated by his proximity.

Though overwhelmingly intricate masses of statuary rose along the walls on both sides far into the distance, the cavern floor itself seemed bare. But as Hresh continued he began to make out a blocklike object, high and broad, sitting in his path far up in the dimness. When he was closer he saw it to be a complex and significant structure, perhaps a machine, set all about with knobs and levers fashioned from a shining tawny substance that looked almost like bone.

"What do you think?" Haniman asked.

Hresh chuckled. "Haniman-full-of-questions, they'll call you!"

"Is it dangerous?"

"It could be. I don't know. There's nothing about any of this in anything I've read." He raised his hands and let them hover above the nearest row of knobs, not daring to touch anything. He had a sudden clear sense of this thing as a master control unit to which all the metal webwork of the three dozen towers of the plaza was connected. Those spirals of struts and braces might serve to collect and funnel energy to it.

And if I touch the knobs? he wondered. Will all that energy go roaring through my body and destroy me?

To Haniman he said, "Stand back."

"What are you going to do?"

"Conduct a test. It could be dangerous."

"Shouldn't you wait, and study it a little first?"

"This is how I will study it."

"Hresh—"

"Stand back. Farther. Farther still."

"This is craziness, Hresh. You're talking nonsense and your eyes look wild. Get away from that thing!"

"I have to try it," Hresh said.

He put his hands to the nearest knobs and squeezed them as tightly as he could.

He expected anything: lightning cutting through the cavern like a bright sword, the crash of terrible thunder, the roar of the winds, the screaming of dead souls. Himself burned to a cinder in an instant. But all he felt was a faint warmth and a vague tingle. For an instant a startling, dizzying image flashed through his mind. It seemed to him that all the myriad statues on the walls had come to life, moving about, gesturing, talking, laughing. It was like being plunged into a turbulent stream, being swept down a wild whirlpool of life.

The sensation lasted only for a moment. But in that moment it seemed to Hresh that he himself was a citizen of the Great World. He was in the midst of all its wondrous surge and vigor. He saw himself striding down the throbbing streets of Vengiboneeza, moving through the turmoil and frenzy of a marketplace where members of the Six Peoples jostled one another by the thousands, sea-lords, vegetals, hjjks, sapphire-eyes, shoulder to shoulder. There was the sultry feel of warm moist air against his cheeks. Slender trees bent low under the weight of their thick, heavy, glossy blue-green leaves. Strange music tingled in his ears. The scent of a hundred unfamiliar spices astonished his nostrils. The sky was a tapestry of brilliant colors, azure, turquoise, ebony, crimson. It was all there. It was all real.

He was stunned by it, and humbled, and shamed.

All at once he understood what a true civilization was like: the immense bustling complexity of it, the myriad interactions, the exchange of ideas, the haggling in the marketplace, the schemes and plans, the conflicts, the ambitions, the sense of a great many people simultaneously moving in a host of individual directions. It was so very different from the only life he had known, the life of the cocoon, the life of the People, that he was stricken with profound awe.

We are really nothing, he thought. We are mere simple creatures who lived in hiding for century upon century, going through endless repetitious rounds of trivial activity, building nothing, changing nothing, creating nothing.

His eyes grew hot with tears. He felt small and lowly, a cipher from a tribe of ciphers deluded by their own pretentions. But then his chagrin gave way suddenly to defiance and pride and he thought: We were very few. We lived as we had to live. Our cocoon thrived and we kept our traditions alive. We did our best. We did our best. And when it was the Time of Coming Forth we emerged to take possession of the world that had been left to us; and when we have had a little time we will make it great again.

Then the vision slipped away and the astounding moment was over, and Hresh stood trembling, blinking, bewildered, still alive.

"What happened?" Haniman asked. "What did it do?"

Hresh made an angry gesture. "Let me be!"

"Are you all right?"

"Yes. Yes. Let me be."

He felt dazed. The world of this dark musty cavern seemed only a hateful phantom, and that other world, so bright, so vivid, was the true world of his life. Or so it had seemed, until the cavern had sprung up about him once more and that other world had been swept away beyond his grasp. Just then he would have given everything to have it back.

He suspected that he had tasted only the merest slice of what this machine could give him. The Great World lived anew within it! Some ancient magic was kindled here, some force drawn downward through the three dozen towers and the enormous jumble of statuary, a force that had roared through his mind and carried him back across the bygone centuries to a lost world of miracles and marvels. And he could make that leap through the eons again. All it took was a touch.

He held his hands above the knobs a second time.

"No, don't!" Haniman cried. "You'll be killed!"

Hresh waved him away and seized the knobs.

But nothing happened this time. He might have been holding his own elbows, for all the effect he felt.

He reached around, touching this knob, that one, this one, that one. Nothing. Nothing.

Perhaps the machine had burned itself out in order to allow him that one miraculous glimpse.

Or perhaps, he thought, he was the one who had burned out. It might be that his mind was so numb from the inrush of that force that it could absorb no more.

He stepped back and studied the thing thoughtfully. Maybe it took time to build up its power again after having discharged it. He would wait, he decided, and try it once more a little later.

The sapphire-eyes artificials at the gate had not deceived him, then, when they had told him to search more deeply. They had meant it in the most literal way. Perhaps all the wonders that Vengiboneeza still contained were to be found in hidden caverns like this, beneath the great buildings.

Then Hresh remembered the other thing the sapphire-eyes had told him.

Search with that which can help you find what you seek.

That advice had made little sense at the time. Now, suddenly, it did. He caught his breath sharply as fear and excitement swept through him in equal measure.

The Barak Dayir, did they mean? The Wonderstone?

That magical talisman which the generations of chroniclers kept hidden in the casket that held the books? The instrument that Thaggoran himself had handled with such fear and reverence?

It was worth trying, Hresh thought.

Even if he died in the attempt, the attempt would be worthwhile; for there were great questions to be answered here, and if he had to risk everything in the hope of gaining everything, so be it.

"Come on," he said. "Let's get out of here—if we can."

"You aren't going to fool around with it any more?"

"Not now," said Hresh. "I need to do some research first. I think I know how to make this thing work, but I have to consult the chronicles before I try it."

"What did you see just now?"

"The Great World," said Hresh.

"You did?"

"For an instant. Only an instant."

Haniman stared at him, jaws slackening with amazement.

"What was it like?"

Hresh shrugged. "Grander than you could ever imagine," he said in a low, weary tone.

"Tell me. Tell me."

"Another time."

Haniman was silent. After a moment he said, "Well, what will you do now? What is it you need to know to make the machine work?"

"Never mind that," Hresh said. "What we need to know just

now is how to make that stone block rise and get us out of this place."

In the heat of his eagerness to explore the cavern he had given that problem no consideration at all. Getting down here had been easy enough; but what were they supposed to do to get out again? He beckoned to Haniman and they jumped on the slab of black stone. But the slab remained where it was on the cavern floor.

Hresh slapped his hand against the stone. No response. He groped along its edges for some lever that might operate it, akin to the wheel that had opened the hatch of the tribal cocoon in the old days. Nothing.

"Maybe there's some other way up," Haniman suggested. "A staircase somewhere."

"And maybe if we flap our arms hard enough, we'll fly right out of here," Hresh said sharply. He squinted into the dimness. A lever sticking out of the wall, perhaps—run to it, pull it, run back quickly to the slab—

No lever. What now? Pray to Yissou? Yissou himself might not know the way out of this place. Or care that two inquisitive boys had stranded themselves in it.

"We can't just sit here all day," said Haniman. "Let's get off and see if we can find something that controls it. Or a different way out. How do you know there *isn't* a staircase around here some-where?"

Hresh shrugged. It cost nothing to look. They began to make their way along the cavern floor in the direction opposite from the one they had taken before, peering here and there at the base of the statuary groups in search of a control unit, a hidden door-way, a staircase, anything.

Suddenly there was a groaning sound, as of a heavy vibra-tion in the ground beneath them. They halted and stared at each other in surprise and fright. A dry, dusty odor spread like a stain through the thick stale air.

"Ice-eaters?" Haniman said. "Coming up underneath us, the way they did under the cocoon?"

"Ice-eaters here?" said Hresh. "No, that can't be. I thought they lived only in mountains. But the ground is shaking, all right. And—"

Then came a sighing sound of a sort that he had heard before, and another deep groan; and Hresh realized what was happening. There were no ice-eaters here. The sounds they heard were those of the unseen machinery that had carried them into these depths.

"The stone!" he yelled. "It's taking off all by itself!"

Indeed it had begun slowly to rise. Desperately he rushed for it. It was already as high as his knees when he caught it by the edge and pulled himself up. Looking around for Haniman, he saw him lumbering and thundering along in a strange sluggish way, as though running through water. It was the Haniman of old returned, the fat clumsy boy out of whom this Haniman had grown; that fat Haniman might be gone, but evidently even this new improved version was still a slow runner. Hresh leaned over the edge of the slab, furiously gesticulating at him.

"Hurry! It's going up!"

"I'm—trying—" Haniman grunted, head down, arms flailing.

But the slab was nearly as high as Haniman's shoulders when he reached it, an eternity later. Hresh reached down to catch him by the wrists. He felt a terrible hot wrenching pain, as though his arms were being yanked out at the sockets; and he thought for a moment that Haniman's weight would pull him forward and off the slab. Somehow he anchored himself on the smooth glossy stone and heaved. In one terrible burst of exertion Hresh hauled Haniman up until he was able to hook his chin over the edge of the slab, and after that it was easier. The slab rose into the dome of blackness above them. They lay sprawled side by side, both of them gasping, shaking, exhausted. Hresh had never felt such pain as he was feeling all along his arms now, pulsating fiery tremors that went on and on and on; and he suspected that was going to get worse before it healed.

The slab glided up and up. When he dared, Hresh looked over the edge and saw only empty darkness below; the amber light must have gone off once they were in midair. Above was darkness also. But before long they were back in the tower of the metal webwork, and the slab was fixed once more on the tower's bare dirt floor.

They rose from it in silence. In silence they made their way back to the tribe. Night had come, heavy, starless, mysterious. Hresh could not recall ever feeling so weary in his life, not even during the worst days of the long march. But in his mind there blazed the brilliant images he had seen, in just that single moment, of the Great World alive. He knew he would return to the cavern under the tower soon. Not at once, no, however much he wanted to do that, for there were certain preparations he knew he must make first. But soon.

And this time he would bring the Barak Dayir.

Taniane, studying Hresh and Haniman in the days that followed, sensed that something extraordinary must have happened on their last trip to the heart of the city. They had come back with eyes glowing and faces strange with amazement. Hresh had gone straight to Koshmar, simply brushing aside anyone who tried to speak with him before he found her, as if brimming with urgent things to report. But when Taniane asked him that evening what he had seen, he glared as if she were one of the hjjk-folk and said, almost angrily, "Nothing. Nothing at all."

It seemed to her that she had been trying to get Hresh to tell her things all her life, but he had always kept her at arm's distance. That was, she knew, not strictly true. In the days of the cocoon they had played together often and he had told her many things, fanciful things, his visions of the world outside the cocoon, his dreams of life in the ancient times, his versions of the tales that the old chronicler Thaggoran related to him. And all too often she had not been able to understand what Hresh was talking about, or had simply not been interested. Why should she have? She was only a child then. That was what all of them had been then, she, Orbin, Haniman, Hresh. But Hresh had always been the strange one, far beyond them all, Hresh-full-of-questions.

He must think I am a fool, Taniane thought bleakly. That I am empty, that I am simple.

But she was no longer a child. She was rapidly rising toward womanhood now. When she ran her hands over her body she could feel the buds of her breasts sprouting. Her fur was deepening in tone, a rich glossy dark brown with undertones of red, and it was growing thick and silken. She was becoming tall, almost as tall as such full-grown women as Sinistine and Boldirinthe. Certainly she was taller than Hresh, whose growth was coming on him more slowly.

It was the time when Taniane was beginning to think of finding her mate.

She wanted Hresh. She always had. Even when they were children in the cocoon, bouncing from wall to wall in the wild games they played, the kick-wrestling and the arm-standing and the cavern-soaring, she had dreamed of being grown up, dreamed of becoming a breeding-woman, dreamed of lying in the dark breeding-chambers of the cocoon with Hresh. Even though he was so small, even though he was so strange, there was a force about him, an energy, an excitement, that had caused Taniane to desire him although she had not yet known what desire meant.

Now she was older, and she still desired him. But he seemed still to treat her casually, with little show of interest. He was wholly absorbed with being the chronicler. He lived in a realm apart.

And chroniclers never took mates, anyway. Even if Hresh loved her the way she loved him, what chance was there that they would ever form a couple? No, she would probably have to mate with someone else, when her time came.

Orbin? He was big and strong, and gentle within his strength. But he was slow-minded and stolid. She would be bored with him quickly. Besides, he was unmistakably interested in little Bonlai, though Bonlai was two or three years younger than they were. Bonlai was the sort of easygoing, sturdy girl that someone like Orbin would prefer. And calm patient Orbin would be quite willing, Taniane guessed, to wait for Bonlai to grow up.

That left Haniman, then: the only other young man of their group. It struck her as odd, the idea of mating with Haniman. He had been such a woeful thing when they were younger, so slow, so fat, always tagging along behind the others. In the cocoon days she could not imagine that anyone would want to mate with Haniman, or twine with him, or do anything much else with him. But there was something likable about him, or at least unthreatening, that had drawn her to him for companionship. Now he was greatly changed. He was still a little slow and awkward, always fumbling things and dropping them, but he was strong now, and all that soft childish flesh was gone from him. There was nothing fascinating about him, as there was about Hresh. But he was acceptable, she supposed. And he might well be the only choice she had.

I will mate with Haniman, she told herself, trying the thought out to see how she liked it. Taniane and Haniman, Haniman and Taniane: why, the names had similar sounds! They went well together. Taniane and Haniman. Haniman and Taniane.

And yet—yet—

She couldn't quite bring herself to it. To mate with Haniman, merely because he was the only one—Haniman the slow, Haniman the outsider, always the last one to be chosen in any game—no matter that he was different now, he would always be the same Haniman to her, a boy she liked to have as a friend, but not as her mate, no, no—

Maybe someday soon they'd meet some other tribe of people, as Hresh was always speculating. And she would find a mate in that new tribe, since she couldn't have Hresh himself.

Or maybe she wouldn't mate at all. There was always that possibility. Torlyri had never mated. Koshmar had never mated. A person didn't *have* to mate. Koshmar was a magnificent leader, Taniane thought, though she seemed sometimes a driven person, narrow-souled, hard. There was no room in Koshmar's life for a mate: the closest she could come to it was what she did with Torlyri, which was twining, not mating. But she was the chieftain. The chieftain did not mate, by custom. Or perhaps by law. And in Koshmar's case by preference as well.

It was sad to think of never having a mate at all. Though if that was the price of being chieftain, perhaps it wasn't too much to pay.

"Does the chieftain really never take a mate?" Taniane asked Torlyri.

"Maybe long ago," Torlyri said. "You could ask Hresh about it. But certainly no chieftain I've ever heard of has had one."

"Is it the law, or just the custom?"

Torlyri smiled. "There's very little difference. But why do you ask? Do you think Koshmar ought to take a mate?"

"Koshmar?" Taniane burst into laughter. The thought of Koshmar with a mate was absurd. "No, of course not!"

"Well, you asked."

"I was just speaking generally. Now that so many of our customs have changed, I wondered if that would too. Almost everyone is mating now, not just the breeders. Maybe a time will come when the chieftain mates also."

"Very likely it will," said Torlyri. "But not, I think, Koshmar."

"Would that trouble you, if Koshmar mated?"

"We are twining-partners. That wouldn't change, if she were to mate. Or if I were. The twining bond remains strong always, regardless. But Koshmar is not at all the sort to give herself to a man."

"No. Not at all." Taniane paused a moment. "Are you, Torlyri?"

Torlyri smiled. "I confess that I've been asking myself the same thing lately."

"The offering-woman is another one who by custom never has mated, am I right? Like the chieftain, like the chronicler. But everything's changing so fast. The offering-woman might take a mate too now. And even the chronicler."

Torlyri's eyes sparkled with gentle amusement. "Even the chronicler, yes. You'd like that, wouldn't you?"

Taniane looked away. "I was speaking in general terms."

"Forgive me. I thought you might have some special reason."

"No. *No!* Do you think I'd have Hresh even if he asked me? That weird boy, who pokes his nose in dusty places all day long, and never says a word to anyone any more—"

"Hresh is unusual, yes. But so are you, Taniane."

"Am I?" she said, startled. "How?"

"You are, that's all. There's more to you than I think most people suspect."

"Do you think so? Do you?" She considered the idea. Unusual? Me? Taniane preened herself. She knew it was childish and foolish to react with such obvious pleasure; but no one had ever praised her before, and to hear such things from Torlyri—from *Torlyri*—

Impulsively she embraced the older woman. They held each other tightly a moment. Then Taniane let go and backed away.

"Oh, Torlyri, I do hope you find the mate you want, if that's what you've decided to do."

"Wait, now!" cried Torlyri, laughing. "When did I say I had decided to do anything? Only that I was beginning to ask myself if such a thing was proper for me. That's all."

"You should mate," said Taniane. "Everyone should. The chieftain should—the next chieftain, the one after Koshmar. The chronicler should. In this New Springtime no one should be alone. Don't you think so, Torlyri? Everything is changing! Everything must change!"

"Yes," Torlyri said. "Everything is changing."

Afterward Taniane wondered if she had been too open, too naive. Things said to Torlyri might well go straight back to Koshmar; and Taniane found that thought troubling.

She shrugged and put her hands to her body. She slipped them over her smooth strong flanks and up over the firm little new breasts nestling in her lustrous auburn fur. Her growing body ached. A horde of unanswered questions bubbled in her mind. Time would answer them all, she thought. She needed now to study the art of waiting.

7

The Sounds of the Storm

The plaza of the three dozen blue towers in Emakkis Boldirinthe never left Hresh's mind, waking or dreaming. Often he awakened, shivering and sweaty, with that scene of Vengiboneeza alive once more glowing and throbbing in his soul, the crowded marketplace, those beings of the Six Peoples jostling against one another.

But it was many weeks before he would allow himself to return to it. He knew he was not ready. With all his strength he held himself back.

Eagerness and curiosity ate at him like a ravening worm. But he did not go to the towers. It was hard keeping away, but he did not go. He went everywhere else, anywhere, taking new turns and byways through the city. He found a terrace of radiant pools, glimmering and warm. He found an array of tall slender stone obelisks set in a diamond pattern around an onyx-rimmed pit of utter darkness, and when he dropped a rock into the pit it fell and fell and fell, without ever striking bottom. In the district of Dawinno Weiawala he found a somber brooding greenish-black edifice of enormous size that he called the Citadel, unlike any other building in the city, standing alone on a lofty greenswarded hillside and rising above Vengiboneeza like a guardian. Its length was far greater than its height, its walls were without ornament except for ten huge columns running along each of its two long sides to support its steep-vaulted roof, and it had neither doors nor windows, which made it seem blind and unapproachable, an inward-looking structure. Its function was not only unknown but, apparently, unknowable, though plainly it had been a structure of some high significance. Hresh could find no way of entering it, though he tried several times. Such discoveries as these led him nowhere useful.

"Why haven't you gone back to that vault yet?" asked Taniane, who had heard of it from Haniman.

"I'm not yet ready," Hresh said. "First I must master the Barak Dayir." And gave her a look that closed the discussion.

That was the problem: the Barak Dayir. Without it there was no point in returning, for he was convinced that only through the mastery of the Wonderstone could he solve the riddle of that machine of visions in the vault beneath the tower. But the Wonderstone made him uneasy—he, Hresh-full-of-questions!— as did few other things. He had never actually seen it. Like the rest of the People he knew of it by repute, that there was some fabulous instrument that the chronicler kept, made of star-stuff, which had extraordinary properties but which would snuff the life of any-one who used it wrongly. Thaggoran had called it the key to the deepest realms of understanding; but Thaggoran had taken care not to let Hresh see him using it, careless though he sometimes was in guarding the other secrets of his office, and Thaggoran too had spoken of its perils, saying that he did not dare to resort to it often. Since becoming chronicler himself Hresh had not yet been able to bring himself even to look upon it. Unable to find in his books of chronicles any sort of guide to its function or proper use, he left it alone. When it came to the Barak Dayir his natural curiosity gave way to his fear of dying too soon, of dying before he had learned all that he hoped to learn.

Now at last Hresh took the velvet pouch from the casket of the chronicles for the first time, and held it cupped in both his hands. It was small, small enough to fit in the palm of one hand, and it felt faintly warm.

Star-stuff, they said. What did that mean?

He had not known what a star was until the Time of Coming Forth, when he had seen them for the first time in the sky, those magical bright points of light burning in the darkness. Globes of fire is what they are, Thaggoran had said. If they were closer to us they would blaze with the heat of the sun. Was the Wonderstone a piece of a star?

But the stars that gave light, Hresh knew, were not the only stars in the sky. There were the death-stars, too, those dark terrible things that had come crashing down upon the world to bring the Long Winter. They weren't made of fire at all; they were spheres of ice and rock, so the chronicles said. Hresh hefted the pouch of the Barak Dayir. A piece of a death-star in here? He tried to imagine the furious trajectory of the plummeting star, the thunderous impact with Earth, the clouds of dust and smoke rising to blot out the light of the sun and bring the deadly cold. This? This little thing in his hand, a fragment of that monstrous calamity?

The chronicles also said that the distant stars of heaven had worlds in attendance on them, just as this world where the People dwelled was in attendance on its sun. Those other worlds had peoples of many kinds. Maybe, Hresh thought, the stone had been made on a world of one of those other stars. He touched it through the pouch and let some other world float into his mind, yellow sky, turbulent purple rivers, a red sun smoldering by day, six crystalline moons singing in the heavens by night.

Guesses. All guesses. He was stumbling about in the dark. There was information of all kinds in the chronicles but nothing that could help him with this.

He made the Five Signs. He called on Yissou, and then on Dawinno, who had always shown special favor to him. Then, slowly, fearfully, he took a deep breath and drew the Barak Dayir from its pouch, thinking that he might be taking his death into his hands. He was surprised at how calm he was.

If it killed him, well, then, it would kill him. A voice tolling like a gong in his head told him that he must do this all the same, that he owed it to his tribe and to himself finally to attempt the mysteries of this thing, whatever the risk.

The Barak Dayir was pleasing to look at, but not extraordinary. It was a piece of polished stone longer than it was broad, brown with purple mottlings, tapering to a point. Though it seemed so soft that it could be marred at a finger's touch, it was in fact hard, terribly hard. Except that it was so ornamental, it could have been a small spearhead. There was a dizzying network of intricately carved lines along its edges, forming a pattern so fine that it was all but impossible for him to make it out, keen as his vision was.

He held it in his left hand for a while, then in his right. It was warm, but not unpleasantly so. There was something almost benign about it. At least it did not appear to be planning to kill him. His fear of it diminished moment by moment, yet he continued to regard it with respect.

What did you do with it? How did you make it obey you?

He put it to his ear, thinking perhaps to hear a voice within it, but there was no sound. He pressed it between both his hands, to no avail, and held it firmly against his breast. He spoke to it, telling it his name and declaring that he was the successor to Thaggoran as chronicler. None of this produced any response. Then at last Hresh did the most obvious thing, the one thing he had held back from doing, and curled his sensing-organ about it and applied his second sight.

This time he heard distant music, strange, unearthly, not from the stone itself but from all about him. The music entered his soul and filled it to its depths, engulfing him, intoxicating him. He felt a hot prickling at the root of his tongue and his fur grew light, floating outward, spreading about him like mist. The sensations were so intense that they were frightening. Hastily Hresh released the Wonderstone and the music stopped. Putting his sensing-organ to it again brought the music back. But once more a moment was all he could stand. Again he broke the contact. All those tales of the power of the Barak Dayir had not been lies. The thing had great strength and magic to it.

Hresh took a deep breath. He felt drained and close to collapse. But he had taken the first step on an immense journey he knew not where. Gratefully he put the Wonderstone back in its pouch. He would continue these researches at another time. But at least he had made a beginning. A beginning, at last.

In a troubled dream Harruel saw himself grasping the towers of Vengiboneeza in his hands and tearing them out by their roots, and smashing them one against another like dry sticks, and hurling their fragments contemptuously aside.

In his dream Koshmar appeared and stood before him, defying him to overthrow her. He ripped a vast stone tower loose and wielded it as a club, swinging it high over Koshmar's head and smashing it down. She jumped deftly aside. He roared and swung the tower again. And again. And pursued her through the streets of the city, until he had her trapped between two broad black-walled buildings. Calmly she awaited him there, unafraid, a mocking smile on her face.

Bellowing in fury, Harruel grasped the tower under his arm now as though it were a spear. And began to thrust it at the chieftain; but as he started toward her he was seized about the throat and held in check. The tower fell from his hands, crashing to the ground. Who dared to interfere with him this way? Torlyri? Yes. The offering-woman held him with astonishing force, so that he felt his soul being squeezed upward and outward from his chest. Desperately Harruel struggled, and slowly he began to break her grip, but as they fought she shifted shape and became his mate, Minbain, and then that strange boy Hresh who was such a mystery to him, and then a roaring, snarling sapphire-eyes, huge and green and loathsome with blazing blue eyes and a great snapping mouth glistening with many rows of evil teeth.

"Become anything you want!" Harruel shouted. "I'll kill you anyway!"

He seized the long jaws of the sapphire-eyes and strived to wrench them apart with one hand and hold them apart, while reaching for a tower with the other, so that he might wedge it between and prop the terrible mouth of the creature open. It struck back with fierce raking blows of its clawed hands, but he paid no heed, he forced the jaws to part, he pushed the great head backward—

"Harruel!" it cried. "Please, stop, Harruel—Harruel—"

Its voice was strangely soft, almost a whimper. It was a voice he knew. A woman's voice, a voice much like that of Minbain, his mate—

"Harruel—no—"

He came swimming up toward consciousness, which lay like a stone pavement above him. When he broke through he found himself close by the side of the room where he and Minbain slept. Minbain was crushed up against the wall, struggling to push him away. His arms were wrapped about her in a frenzied grip and his head was jammed down into the hollow between her shoulder and her throat.

"Yissou!" he muttered, and released her, and rolled away. The dank biting stink of his own curdled sweat filled the room, sickening him. The upper muscles of his arms were jerking and popping as though they were trying to break free of his body and there was a ridge of flame running along his shoulders and neck. He wiped shining flecks of saliva from the coarse fur of his jaws. Great racking shivers ran through his body.

She said into the silence in an uncertain voice, "Harruel?"

"A dream," he said thickly. "My soul was gone from me, and I was in strange realms. Did I hurt you?"

"You frightened me," Minbain said. Her eyes, dark and solemn, stared into his. "You were like something wild—you made awful sounds, choking, gagging, and you thrashed around—and then you caught hold of me, and I thought—I thought you would—"

"I would not injure you."

"I was frightened. You were so strange."

"It frightens me also." He shook his head. "Have I ever done such a thing before, Minbain? This wildness, this fury?"

209

"Not like this. Dark dreams, yes. Stirrings, groanings, moanings, words in your sleep, curses, even sometimes slapping your hands against the floor as if you were trying to kill creatures moving around beside you. But this time—I was so frightened, Harruel! It was as if a demon had entered you."

"Indeed a demon has entered me," he said bleakly. He rose and went to the window. The night seemed less than half spent. A heavy darkness lay like a smothering veil over everything. The hideous scarred face of the moon blazed icily high overhead, and behind it, hanging in thick swirling bands at the zenith of the sky, were the stars, those dazzling malign white fires that gave no warmth. "I'm going outside, Minbain."

"No, stay here, Harruel. I'm afraid to be alone now."

"What harm can come to you? The only danger around here is me. And I will go out."

"Stay."

"I need to go off by myself for a time," he said. He looked back at her. In the darkness, by cool shimmering moonlight and starlight, there appeared to be a beauty to Minbain that Harruel knew she did not in fact possess. Her face, rounded and delicate, seemed to have shed the years: she was new and tender, a girl again. His heart flooded with love for her. It was difficult for him to express that love in words; but he went to her and crouched down beside her, and let his hands rove tenderly over her throat where he had hurt her, and her breasts, and her soft warm belly. It seemed to him that he could feel new life starting inside her there. It was too early to tell, but he thought that his fingers detected a quickening, a gathering of life-force, which would become the son of Harruel. As softly as he could he said, "I did not mean to hurt you, Minbain. A demon was with me in my sleep. It was not me. I would never injure you."

"I know that, Harruel. You are kind, behind your gruffness."

"Do you think so?"

"I know it," Minbain said.

He held his hand outspread across her belly for a time. He was calmer now, though his dark dream still oppressed him. Waves of deep love for her were coursing through his soul.

She was three years older than he was, and when he was growing up, not thinking at all about mates—for he was of the warrior class and in those days warriors had not mated—she had seemed to be more of his mother's generation than his own; but when the new matings had been allowed, Minbain was the one he had chosen. A younger woman would have had more beauty, but beauty goes quickly, and Minbain had virtues that would remain all her life. She was warm and kind, somewhat like Torlyri in that regard. Torlyri was not a woman for men; but Minbain was, and Harruel had reached for her quickly. It made no difference to him that she was older, or that she had had a child. If anything it was a favorable thing that she had had a child, since that child was Hresh, who at so supernaturally early an age had come to have such power in the tribe. Harruel saw many uses for Hresh; and perhaps one way to reach Hresh was through his mother. Not that that was his main reason for having chosen Minbain. But it had been a factor. It had definitely been a factor.

"Let me go now," Harruel said.

"Come back soon."

"Soon," he promised. "Yes."

Minbain watched him go, a huge hulking shadow moving with exaggerated care across the room and out the door. She touched her throat. He had hurt her more than she had wanted him to know. In his madness he had struck her with a flailing elbow, he had seized her by both shoulders and slammed her against the wall, and when he had burrowed down against her throat like that he had nearly choked her with the pressure of his heavy head. But that had been the madness, the demon. It had not been Harruel. Minbain understood that in his rough way he cared for her.

She was carrying his child. That she knew for a certainty, and, from the way he had touched her body just now, he must know it too. They would have to go to Torlyri soon to have the first words said over her.

Hresh would have a brother. She would have a second son. She was sure of it, that it was a son; Harruel's seed could bear nothing but sons, that much seemed obvious to her. She would be the first woman in thousands of years to bear two sons. Would the new one be anything like Hresh, she wondered?

No. There could never be anyone else like Hresh. Hresh was unique.

Nor had she ever known anyone else like Harruel. She loved him and she feared him, and some days it was the love that was stronger, and some days the fear, and there were times like this when both were mixed in equal measure. He was so strange. The gods had given her a strange child for her son and now a strange man for her mate: why was that? Harruel was so huge, so powerful, so far beyond all the others in strength—he was unusual in his strength, yes. He had the force of a falling mountain. But there was something else. He had a darkness in his soul. He had an anger. Minbain had never really seen that when they all lived in the cocoon, but once they had begun the trek it had become obvious. Some turbulent force roiled his soul day and night. He yearned for something—but what? What?

*   *   *

Harruel walked down one street and up another, not knowing where he was going and scarcely caring. He felt the cold sharp moonlight upon him like a scourge, driving him onward. He had promised Minbain he would return, and so he would. But not before dawn. There was no sleep in him.

The city was a prison for him. He had borne cocoon life easily enough, never imagining there was an alternative to it. But now that they were free of the cocoon and he had come to know what it was like to walk boldly under the open sky, it galled him to live penned up in this sleek dead place, which in his mind reeked with the stench of the extinct sapphire-eyes folk. And it galled him also, it stung him like a firebur against his skin, that he would live under the commands of the woman Koshmar to the end of his days.

This was the time to end the rule of women. This was the time to restore the power of kings.

But it seemed to Harruel that Koshmar would be his chieftain until he was old and bent and white of fur. For there were no more death-days. Koshmar was older than he was, but she was healthy and strong. She would live a long time. Nothing would ever rid him of her, unless he did it himself; and there Harruel drew the line. To kill a chieftain was beyond him. It was almost beyond his comprehension. But he could not bear living under her rule much longer.

Of late he had taken to roaming the city frequently, going off alone on long wanderings, seeking to come to know it. The city was his enemy, and he believed that it is important to know your enemy. But this was the first time he had gone forth by night.

Everything looked altered. The towers seemed taller, the lesser

213

buildings seemed more squat. Streets hooked away at strange angles. There was menace in every shadow. Harruel walked on and on. He had his spear. He was unafraid.

Some of the streets were paved with immaculate flagstones, as if the city had been abandoned by the sapphire-eyes only the day before yesterday. Others were cracked and rutted, with coarse grass rising through the paving-blocks, and still others had lost their pavements entirely and were mere muddy tracks bordered by crumbling buildings. This city made no sense to him. He detested it. It sickened him to think that his son would be born in it, in this hateful alien place, this place that had nothing human about it.

There were ghosts here. As he walked he kept watch for them.

Harruel was certain that ghosts hovered everywhere about. They were the ones who were making the repairs. It happened by night, though not when anyone could see it. Randomly, so it seemed, buildings that had fallen were shored up, given new facades, cleansed of debris. He saw the changes afterward. Some of the others had noticed it too—Konya, Staip, Hresh. Who was responsible?

He was wary, too, of creeping, crawling, stinging creatures of the night. Most of the pests that afflicted Vengiboneeza vanished with the coming of the darkness, except the ones that lived inside the buildings. But that did not mean that he could regard himself as altogether safe from them.

Early one evening not long before, wandering restlessly as he was tonight, Harruel had found himself at the edge of the warm sea that lapped the city on its western flank, and he had watched an invading army of ugly gray lizard-things come crawling up out of the water. They were evil little creatures with slim tubular bodies the length of his forearm and thick fleshy legs and wrinkled green wings folded back behind their necks, and they had a sinister glint in their bright yellow eyes. From them came a low growling hum of a sound, menacing and nasty, as if they were threatening him by name: "Harruel! Harruel! Harruel! We'll make a meal of you tonight!"

Jaws snapping, they advanced like a horde of insects in tight formation until they were no more than thirty paces from him, and he began to look around for something to defend himself with. Backing away, he scooped up handfuls of pebbles and pelted them with those, without halting them. But when they reached a row of square-hewn blocks of green stone, set into the seawall just below where he was standing, that had tiny mysterious faces carved into them, they pulled up short as if they had hit an invisible barrier. Then they turned, baffled, glum, and headed back toward the water. Perhaps they had picked up the scent of a swarm of some even nastier beast on the far side of those shattered columns, he thought. Or maybe they just didn't like my smell. Whichever it was, he knew he had been lucky to get off so easily.

Another time he saw clouds of flying creatures crossing over-head, so thick a flock that they darkened the sky at midday. It seemed to him that they were the fierce white-eyed things that were called bloodbirds, which had plagued the tribe far back when they had crossed the plains. He stood poised, ready to run to the settlement and give the alarm. But though they circled and circled far above the city, the birds never descended below the tops of the highest towers.

He was near the green stone pillars now where the three sapphire-eyes guardians sat. A short distance before him was the avenue that fronted the jungle.

Without any clear purpose in mind he began to walk toward the southern gate. But after a minute or two he halted abruptly. He heard a faint sound behind him: someone breathing, someone moving about. He grasped his spear. Had Minbain followed him? Or was this one of the ghosts that patrolled the city in the secrecy of the night? He whirled and peered into the shadows.

"Who's there?"

Silence.

"I heard you. Come out where I can see you."

"Harruel?" A man's voice, low and steady, familiar.

"Who else do you think it would be? Is that you, Konya?"

Laughter came from the darkness. "You have a good ear, Harruel."

Konya emerged and walked slowly forward. He was a tall man, though only shoulder-height to Harruel; but because he was so deep through his chest and back he did not seem as tall as he actually was. By the tribe he was regarded as the second-ranking warrior, generally deemed to be Harruel's rival, a man smoldering with envy for Harruel's preeminence. Only the two of them knew how untrue that was. Konya was strong enough to realize that it was all right not to be strongest. His nature was a calm, remote, quiet one. What he felt for Harruel was a respect growing out of the natural order of things, not envy; and what Harruel felt for him was an equal respect, though he knew Konya was not an equal.

"So you're out wandering tonight too," Harruel said.

"Sleep wouldn't come. The moon was too bright in my eyes as I lay in bed."

"In the cocoon that wasn't a problem."

"No," Konya said, with a little laugh. "The moon's brightness couldn't trouble us, when we dwelled in the cocoon."

They walked together in silence for a while. This was a street of shattered buildings whose golden-hued facades, perversely, were in perfect condition. Empty windowframes still bore their elegantly worked shutters of thin-cut white stone. Elaborate doors stood ajar, revealing rubble and emptiness behind them. Then they came to one building that was of the opposite condition: its facade was gone, so that each of its many floors was revealed along one side, but the interior was intact. Wordlessly Harruel entered it and began to ascend, not knowing what he was looking for. Konya went with him unquestioningly.

With difficulty they ascended a staircase that had been built for sapphire-eyes, with wide flat risers so low that it was more of a ramp than a stair. After a time Harruel developed the knack of taking the steps two and even three at a time in loping bounds, and the ascent became easier. Along the walls, all the way up, were carvings that troubled the eye. Seen from the side they seemed to show the figures of living creatures, sapphire-eyes and hjjks and other things that must have lived in the time of the Great World, but when you looked at them straight on they dissolved into jumbles of meaningless lines. The rooms of the building were empty. There was not even dust in them.

Eventually the staircase narrowed to a spiral passage that coiled upward for half a dozen bends and delivered them to the building's flat roof of dark tile. Here they were high above the surrounding district. The city lay behind them, to the north. Looking southward over the edge of the roof they saw the closely arrayed trees of the jungle glowing eerily in the harsh bright moonlight.

There were stirrings in the treetops, little snicking sounds.

"Monkeys, there," Konya said.

Harruel nodded. They were swinging through the treetops no more than a good stone's throw away, those shrieking stinking chattering things of the jungle. How he loathed them! He felt a rushing in his ears. If he could, he would march through the jungle from tree to tree, spearing them all and piling their repellent little bodies in heaps for the snuffling scavenger-beasts to devour.

"Filthy creatures," said Harruel. "I'd like to kill them all. A good thing that they keep out of the city, mostly."

"I see them sometimes. Not many."

"Just a few, yes, once in a while. It's not hard for them to get in. They just have to swing right over that open space there and they're inside. Good thing for us that it's usually only one or two at a time. Yissou, I detest them! Foul filthy things!"

"They're just wild animals, Harruel."

"Animals? They're vermin. You saw them yourself, right up close. They have no souls. They have no minds."

"The sapphire-eyes who guard the gate said that they are our cousins."

Harruel spat. "Dawinno! Do you believe that foolishness?"

"They look a little like us."

"Anything with two arms and two legs and a tail would look a little like us, if it walked on its hind legs. We are humans, Konya, and they are beasts."

Konya was silent a while. "You think that's so, Harruel? What about the thing the sapphire-eyes said, that we aren't human at all, that the humans were a different race altogether, that we're nothing but monkeys with a high opinion of themselves?"

"We are human, Konya. What else could we be? Do you *feel* like a relative of those things swinging from their tails out there?"

"The sapphire-eyes said—"

"Dawinno take the sapphire-eyes! They're dead lying things. They only want to make trouble for us!" Harruel turned toward Konya, glaring coldly. "Look: we think, we talk, we have books, we know the gods. Therefore we are human. I know it. I have no doubt of it. Regardless of what the sapphire-eyes may say. Besides, they let us enter the city, didn't they? The city is reserved for the humans who will come here at winter's end: that's what the prophecy said. And the winter is over, and we are here, by permission of the three guardians. Therefore we are the ones who were supposed to come here. The humans, that is."

"Koshmar made them let us in."

"*Made* them? When they have magic in their hands? No, Konya, it wasn't Koshmar's doing. She could have talked at them all day, and if they truly felt we weren't human beings they never would have accepted us. They let us in because it was our destiny to come in here, our *right* to come in here, and they knew it. They were only testing us with their idiotic lies, to see if we had the strength of spirit to claim our rights. If Koshmar hadn't spoken out, I would have done so, and they would have yielded. And if they hadn't yielded I would have slain the three sapphire-eyes to win admission here."

After another silence Konya said, "You would have slain them? When they have magic in their hands?"

"There's magic in this spear, Konya."

"But how can you slay what isn't alive? The boy Hresh says they're just artificials in the guise of sapphire-eyes, and not sapphire-eyes themselves."

Harruel nodded distantly. He had lost interest in this debate. Narrowing his eyes against the moonlight, he stared at the frolicking monkeys, thinking thoughts of slaughter.

After a time he said, "This city is full of mysteries. I find it a troublesome place."

"I find it hateful," said Konya, with sudden surprising vehemence. "I hate it the way you hate the monkeys of the jungle."

Harruel turned to him, eyes widening. "Do you?"

"It is a dead place. It has no soul."

"No, it lives," Harruel said. "It's dead, I agree, but somehow it lives. I hate it as much as you, but not because it is dead. It has a strange kind of life that is not our kind of life. It has a soul that is not a soul like ours. And it's for that that I hate it."

"Dead or alive, I'd be glad to leave it tomorrow, Harruel. I would have been glad never to have seen it at all. We shouldn't have come here in the first place." Something in Konya's tone made it seem as though he were seeking Harruel's approval.

But Harruel shook his head. "No," he said. "Not so, Konya. It was right to come. This city holds things that are important for us. You know what the chronicles say. In Vengiboneeza we will find ancient things of the sapphire-eyes that will help us to rule the world."

"We've been here many months, and we've found nothing."

With a shrug Harruel said, "Koshmar's too timid. She lets only Hresh search, and no one else. A vast city, one small boy—no, we should all be out there every day, everyone seeking in the hidden places. The things are here. Sooner or later we'll find them. And then we must take them and get out of this place. That's the important thing, to leave once we have achieved what we came here to achieve."

Konya said, "It seems to me that Koshmar is thinking of staying here forever."

"Let her stay, then."

"No. I mean she would have us all stay here. The city is becoming a new cocoon for her. She has no thought of leaving."

"We must leave," Harruel said. "The whole world is awaiting us. We are the new masters."

"Even so, I think Koshmar—"

"Koshmar doesn't matter any longer."

Sudden amazement gleamed in Konya's eyes. "What are you saying, Harruel?"

"What I'm saying is that we've come to this city for a purpose, which is to learn how to rule the world in the New Springtime, and we must strive with all our might to achieve that purpose. And then we must go forth so that we may continue to fulfill our destiny elsewhere. You hate this place. So do I. If Koshmar doesn't, she can make it her home forever. When the time comes—and it must come soon—I will lead the way out of here."

"And I will follow you," Konya said.

"I know that you will."

"Will you take all the others?"

"Only those who want to go," said Harruel. "Only the strong and the bold. The others can stay here to the end of their days, for all I care."

"So you will make yourself chieftain, then?"

Harruel shook his head. "Chieftain is a title out of the cocoon life. That life is ended. And chieftains are women. Koshmar can remain chieftain, if she likes, though she'll have precious little tribe to be chieftain over. I will call myself by another name, Konya."

"And what name will that be?"

"I will be called king," said Harruel.

The mild weather that the tribe had enjoyed since first coming to Vengiboneeza ended abruptly, and there were three days of heavy winds out of the north and cold, sweeping rains. The sky turned black and stayed that way. Creatures of the sky were seen beating raggedly against the wind, vainly trying to journey to the westward and constantly being driven far to the south.

"A new death-star has struck the earth," said Kalide to Delim. "The Long Winter is returning."

Delim, carrying this to Cheysz, said that the rain, so she had heard, would soon turn to snow.

"We will all freeze," said Cheysz to Minbain. "We need to seal things up the way the cocoon was sealed, or we will die when the Long Winter comes again."

And Minbain, summoning Hresh, asked him what he knew of these things. "Has this been nothing but a false spring?" she demanded. "Shouldn't we be storing food in the caverns beneath Vengiboneeza to tide us through the time of freezing?" Life in Vengiboneeza had been too easy, she said, a trap laid by the gods: now the sun would be blotted out for months or even years and they would all perish if they failed to take immediate steps. There was no way to return to the old cocoon; Vengiboneeza would have to be their refuge now. Even Vengiboneeza, grand though it was, might not be a fitting hiding place if the Long Winter were to fall upon the world once more. The sapphire-eyes folk had been unable to survive here; would the tribe fare any better?

Hresh smiled. "You worry too much, Mother. There's no danger of freezing. The weather has changed for the worse just now, and after a little while it will change for the better again."

But the rumor had traveled even to Koshmar, growing more ominous along the way. She too sent for Hresh. "Is this truly the coming of the Long Winter again?" she asked him, looking somber, grim, head drawn in close against her shoulders, eyes hooded and hard. "Is it true that the sun will not shine again for a thousand years?"

"It is only a bad storm, I think."

"If it's like this in sheltered Vengiboneeza, it must be much worse elsewhere."

"Perhaps. But in a few days it'll be warm here again, Koshmar. So I do believe."

"You believe! You believe! Can you be sure, though? There must be some way of finding out."

He gave her an uneasy look. Koshmar had built a fine nest for herself and Torlyri in this solid little building in the shadow of the great tower. There were fragrant hangings of woven rushes on the walls, and thick carpets of skins, and dried flowers everywhere. And yet the bitter wind now came whipping against the windows and down the air vents and brought a chill into the room. From the first, Koshmar had insisted that the Long Winter was over. She had invested all her soul in the abandonment of the cocoon and the making of the great trek to Vengiboneeza. It occurred to Hresh that something might crack within Koshmar if it turned out that she was wrong.

She wanted reassurance from him, her chronicler, her staff of wisdom. What could he tell her? He knew no more of winds and storms than anyone else. He had grown up in the cocoon, where no winds blew. Thaggoran, perhaps, might have read the portents and given Koshmar the truth of the situation. Thaggoran, steeped in the lore of the chronicles, had been equal to almost any situation. But Thaggoran had been old and wise. Hresh was young and clever, which was not at all the same.

There must be some way of finding out, Koshmar had said.

There was. The Barak Dayir might tell him; but in the weeks since he first had found the courage to pull the shining stone from its pouch and touch his sensing-organ to it, he had proceeded with unusual caution, extending his mastery over it in minute stages. He had learned how to bring it to life, and how to liberate the potent sweep of its music, and how to let its force approach the borders of his mind. But that was as far as he had dared to go. It was easy to see how the Wonderstone might engulf him, how it might submerge his mind entirely within the torrent of its incomprehensible power. Once he let himself be lost in that torrent there might be no returning. And so he had forced himself to resist the irresistible. He kept his mind alert, agile, defensive: he leaped back quickly whenever the song of the Barak Dayir became too guileful and tempting. Though he went a little deeper into it each time he drew forth the stone, he took care not to let it possess his spirit as he thought it was capable of doing; and therefore he knew that he was still far from attaining command of the mysterious instrument.

This storm is the punishment of the gods upon us for my sloth and my cowardice, he thought. And if the storm causes Koshmar to become angry in her panic, the gods will guide her to direct her anger against me. Therefore I must act.

He said, "I'll consult the Wonderstone, Koshmar. And it will tell me the meaning of this storm."

"Yes. That's what I hoped you would do."

He hurried into the six-sided tower that was now the holy temple, and into the chamber where he kept the casket of the chronicles, and where he now slept much of the time, for he felt out of place in the dormitory where the other unmated young people lived. Unhesitatingly he drew the Wonderstone from its pouch. Thunder cracked terrifyingly overhead.

He put his sensing-organ to the stone and quickly brought his second sight to bear on it. Delay could bring only failure now. From it, at once, came the strange intense music that he had experienced on a dozen or more other occasions. But this time, because he knew he dared not falter, he opened himself to it in a way that was new to him. He let the music possess him; he let himself become the music.

He was a column of pure sound, rising without resistance to the roof of the world.

He climbed above the storm. He towered over Vengiboneeza like a god. The city seemed a toy model of itself. The lofty mountain ranges that sheltered the city looked to him now like mere low ridges. The great sea west of the city was no more than a leaden wind-tossed puddle, half hidden by swirls of black cloud that clustered at his ankles. He saw land on the far side of it, and an even mightier sea beyond, a gleaming sea that stretched so grandly around the curve of the world that even he, colossal though he now was, could not make out its farther shore.

He saw the sun. He saw the sky, blue and radiant above the storm. He looked to the east, where the great river was and their old cocoon, and saw that the air was clear there and the warmth of the New Springtime still prevailed.

There was nothing to fear. The Barak Dayir had told him what he needed to know. He could descend now and bear the good tidings to Koshmar.

But he remained longer than was needful. The splendor of this ascent was not something he could relinquish easily. The music that was his new self crashed in majesty across the world, falling upon sea and upon land, upon mountains and upon valleys, with terrible grandeur. He looked toward the moon and reached a tendril of sound toward it as easily as in his old life he might have reached toward a ripe fruit hanging on a low branch. It would be simple, he knew, to encircle the moon with music and move it in its course, or bring it closer to the earth, or shatter it altogether. Or he could bypass it entirely, and send himself surging out into the depths of the void, and swim among the stars. He had never imagined such power. The stone could make you a god.

Then he understood why old Thaggoran had feared the Wonderstone, and why he had said it was dangerous. It was not that the stone would do any sort of harm to its user; but so great was its force that it could destroy all judgment, and the user, in the blindness of his borrowed godliness, might well do harm to himself. Overreaching was the danger.

With an effort that was greater than any he had made before in his life, Hresh hauled himself in. He descended to his body; he relinquished his godhead. He shrank down into himself until he lay limp and sweat-soaked on the stone floor of the chamber, quivering, stunned.

After a time he picked himself up and restored the stone to its pouch and hid it away where it belonged, and locked the casket with more than ordinary care. Rain was still falling heavily outside, perhaps even more heavily than before, although it seemed to him that it was less turbulent now, an obstinate hammering downpour but one with little wildness about it. The sky still was dark but he thought he saw a thinning of the darkness in places.

Heedless of the rain, he trotted back across to Koshmar's house. Torlyri was there now, and the two of them were huddling together like frightened beasts. Hresh had never seen either of them like that, eyes wide, teeth chattering, fur standing on end. When he came in they made an attempt at regaining some self-possession, but their terror still was manifest.

In a hushed voice Koshmar said, "Is this the end of the world?"

Hresh stared. "What do you mean?"

"I thought the sky would split open. I thought the lightning would set the mountain on fire."

"And the thunder," said Torlyri. "It was like a great drum. I thought it would deafen me."

"I heard nothing," Hresh said. "I saw nothing. I was busy in the temple, seeking the answers you required of me."

"You didn't hear anything?" Torlyri asked. "Not a thing?" They were still shivering. It must have been truly cataclysmic. They couldn't understand how he had failed to notice what was taking place.

"Perhaps the stone shielded me from the sounds of the storm," he said.

But he knew that that was only a part of the truth, and a small part at that. Whatever tremendous uproar had just happened had been of his own making. It was he who had brought the great thunder and the terrible lightning, while he was using—and perhaps somewhat misusing—the Wonderstone. Of course he had not heard the sounds of the storm at its height. He had *been* the sounds of the storm at its height.

It would not be good for them to know that, though.

He said simply, "I have the assurance you seek, Koshmar. The Wonderstone has shown me the boundaries of the storm. All is clear to the east and to the west, and the neighboring lands still are fair and mild. This is not the return of the Long Winter, nor has any new death-star fallen. It's only a storm, Koshmar, a very bad storm but not one that will endure much longer. There's nothing to fear."

And, indeed, within hours the winds were dying down, the rain was slackening, patches of blue were showing through the blackness overhead.

8

One Enormous Thing at a Time

After the storm the weather in Vengiboneeza became warmer even than it had been before. Flowers of a dozen kinds burst into explosions of color on the hills above the city, trees grew so quickly you could almost see their boughs waving like arms, and the air was heavy and rich with scent. It was as if those three days of black skies and howling winds had been the final convulsive throes of the Long Winter, and now it was truly the New Springtime and would be forever more.

But Koshmar was troubled, and her distress was deepening from day to day.

There was a private place that she had found for herself in a ruined part of the city, a place that she called her chapel and kept so secret that not even Torlyri knew about it. It was the place where she went when she was uncertain and needed the special counsel of the gods or of her predecessors as chieftain—the equivalent for her of the black stone in the wall of the cocoon's central chamber.

At first the chapel had been a diversion for her, a kind of amusement, that she visited at widely spaced intervals and forgot for weeks at a time. But now Koshmar found herself drawn to it almost every day, slipping away furtively in the early hours of the morning, or late at night, or even at midday sometimes instead of holding the regular judgment-sessions that were her custom as chieftain.

To reach her chapel Koshmar went eastward a little way toward the mountains, then north past a forbidding black tower that had broken to a jagged stump in some ancient earthquake, and down five flights of stupendous stairs which led to a saucer-shaped plaza of pink marble flagstones. At the far side of the plaza were five intact arches and six crumbled ones, each of which must have been the entryway to one of eleven rooms of some high ceremonial importance in the days of the Great World. Now they were empty, but all but two or three still were rich with gilded wall-carvings, strange and beautiful, of figures with bodies that seemed almost human and the faces of suns, of wraithlike animals with elongated limbs, of interwoven wreaths of unearthly long-stemmed plants. Pivoted stone doors gave admission to these chambers.

Koshmar had found out accidentally how to operate the doors, and she had chosen the midmost of the eleven rooms for her chapel. In it she had constructed a little altar and arranged objects of ritual importance or of sentimental value around it; and here she knelt in secret solitude, here she spoke with the gods—or, more usually, with Thekmur, who had been chieftain before her.

Kneeling now, she made an arrangement of dried flowers and set it afire. The fragrant smoke went up to Thekmur. Koshmar was wearing the ivory-hued mask of the former chieftain Sismoil, flat and glossy, with the merest of slits for her eyes.

"How much longer will it be," she asked the dead chieftain, "before we discover why we are here? You dwell with the gods now, O Thekmur. Tell me what it is that the gods intend for us. And what they intend for me, O Thekmur."

She could almost see the soul of Thekmur hovering in the air before her. Each time she came to the chapel Thekmur was a little more visible. A time would come, Koshmar hoped, when Thekmur's apparition was as real and as solid for her as her own arm.

Thekmur had been a small, compact woman, very strong of body and of mind, with grayish fur and gray eyes that looked outward in a calm, unwavering way. She had loved many men and many women also, and had ruled the tribe with quiet competence until the coming of her death-day; and then she had gone through the cocoon's hatch without a quiver. Koshmar sometimes thought that she herself was only a pale shadow of Thekmur, a poor substitute for the departed chieftain, though such dark moments came only rarely to her.

"The gods will not speak to me," she told Thekmur. "I send the boy Hresh out and he finds nothing, and now he has found something and nothing so far has come of it. And there was a terrible storm, and during the storm the sky split and the lightning was frightful. What does all this mean? What is it that we are waiting for here? Answer me, O Thekmur. Answer me just this once."

The smoke curled upward and the faint image of Thekmur swirled in the darkness. But Thekmur did not speak; or if she did, Koshmar was unable to hear her words.

Only gradually over the past months had Koshmar come to realize that she was sliding into gray despair, or something as close to despair as she was capable of feeling. Life had lost its forward thrust here in Vengiboneeza. Everything seemed to be standing still. And the happiness that she had felt in the first busy time of organizing the new life in the city had all melted away now.

In the cocoon you expected everything to stand still forever, unchanging, static. No one questioned that. You grew up, you did the things you were told to do, you kept the commandments of the gods, and you knew that in your proper time you would die and others would take your place; but you understood all the while that your life would be contained from first to last by the stone walls of the cocoon and that it would not be different in any fundamental way from the life of your grandparents or of your grandparents' grandparents, back for thousands upon thousands of years. Your purpose was only to continue the life of the People, to be a link in the great chain of the eons that stretched from the epoch of the Great World to the hoped-for coming of the New Springtime. You did not expect to see the New Springtime yourself; you did not think that you would ever have a life outside the cocoon.

But now—whatever the occasional doubts that arose—the New Springtime had arrived. The world was unfolding like a flower. The tribe had gone forth into it. But the predestined first stage in the Going Forth was the sojourn in Vengiboneeza; and so far nothing had come of that sojourn except restlessness, uneasiness, dismay. Even their humanity itself had been brought into question, thanks to those lying, despicable sapphire-eyes artificials at the gate. And though Koshmar was certain that what the three strange guardians had tried to assert about their not being human was complete nonsense, she suspected that for some of the others the question still stood unresolved, a great anguished discord of the soul.

"How can I make things happen?" Koshmar asked the woman who had ruled before her. "My life is going by; I wish to embrace the world, now that it is ours; I feel impatient, Thekmur, I feel as trapped as though I were still in the cocoon!" Some part of her longed to leave this place and move on, though she knew not where; and yet she felt the powerful spell of Vengiboneeza and feared going from it, even while she yearned for new ventures far away.

Many of the tribesfolk, Koshmar knew, were quite content here. But they were people who would be content anywhere. Instead of the cramped and intense environment of the cocoon, they had an entire huge city to serve as their stage. They lived well—there was abundant food to be had from the gardens that they had planted here, and from the meat that the warriors brought back from the slopes of what Hresh had named Mount Springtime, where animals of all kinds abounded and the hunting was easy. For them it was a happy time. They twined, they sang, they played. They were mating and beginning to bring forth young. Already the numbers of the tribe were past seventy and more children would be arriving before long. They could look forward to rich and comfortable lives untroubled by the grim promise of the limit-age.

But others were not fashioned of that placid stuff. Harruel, Koshmar saw, was seething with impatience and the hunger for change. Konya and a few of the younger men like Orbin seemed to be drifting toward Harruel and coming under his influence. Hresh, as he grew toward manhood, was more of an enigma to her than ever. And the girl Taniane was suddenly turning into a schemer, a whisperer, a hatcher of dreams. You could see the glint of ambition in her eyes. But ambition for what?

Even Torlyri seemed distant and strange. Torlyri and Koshmar twined rarely now, and when they did it was a strained, unrewarding thing. Koshmar knew that Torlyri wanted to mate; but she was keeping herself back from doing so, perhaps because she felt it would injure her relationship with Koshmar, perhaps because as offering-woman of the tribe she did not know how she could become mate and mother as well. Or perhaps she believed that there were no men in the tribe with whom she could mate as an equal, after having been their priestess so long. Whatever it was, it was causing trouble within Torlyri; and trouble within Torlyri was trouble for Koshmar.

"What can I do to make you speak?" she asked Thekmur. "Shall I make a special offering to one of the gods? Shall I go on a pilgrimage? Shall I bring Torlyri here, and twine with her, and approach you when we are twined?"

A small creature appeared through some opening in the wall, a slender blue animal with shining scaly skin, long fragile limbs, bright golden eyes. Seeing Koshmar, it paused, sniffing the air, balancing high up on its thin legs. It studied her intently. There was something calm and gentle about it, and its liquid gaze was steady and untroubled.

"Have you been sent?" Koshmar asked.

The animal continued to study her and to sniff.

"What creature are you? Hresh would know; or he would pretend to, and give you a name. But I can name you myself. You are the thekmur, eh? Do you like that name? Thekmur was a great chieftain. She was frightened of nothing, just like you."

The thekmur seemed to smile in agreement.

"And she was one who withstood anything, just as you must," Koshmar went on. "For you lived through the Long Winter, eh? You look frail but your kind must be tough. The sapphire-eyes died and the sea-lords died and all those other

233

great peoples died too, but here you still are. Nothing frightens you. Nothing is too much for you. I will follow your example, little thekmur."

The ground began to rock suddenly, a sidewise swinging motion that made the entire chapel sway. Another time, Koshmar might have made a dash for the safety of the open ground; but the thekmur held its place on the far side of the altar, and she held her place too, waiting without alarm for the earthquake to end. It was over in a moment or two. With great dignity the little creature strode from the room. Koshmar followed it outside. There had been little damage, only a few overhanging cornices of a ruined building thrown to the ground.

It is an omen, Koshmar said to herself. It speaks of the watchfulness of the gods, who have put their hands to the earth to remind me that they are there and that they are almighty, and that their plan is good and that in the fullness of time they will let their wishes be known.

The earthquake, following so soon upon the storm, left Hresh with no doubt that the time had come to return at last to the plaza of the thirty-six towers. These omens were too powerful, too urgent, to ignore. The gods were pressing upon him. It behooved him now to make use of the Wonderstone to gain the knowledge stored in that underground vault.

"Make yourself ready," he said to Haniman. "This is the day. I mean to go down into the hidden vault again."

Off they marched toward the district of Emakkis Boldirinthe. The morning was sunny and cloudless, with immense flocks of great-winged, long-necked purple birds, evidently bound on some vast migration, screeching far overhead. Haniman capered and whooped all the way, so eager was he to experience once again the mysteries of the vault.

They entered the tower of the black stone slab. At once Haniman ran toward the center and crouched down on the slab as he had done before, so that Hresh could mount him and strike the metal strut overhead that would cause the slab to descend. But Hresh waved him aside. He had brought a staff with him this time, so that there would be no need for him to clamber up on Haniman's back to reach the strut.

"Wait here for me," Hresh said. "I'll go down alone."

"But I want to see what's down there too, Hresh!"

"I suppose you do. But I want to be certain of getting out of there. The last time, the slab came up again of its own accord. It may not do that again. Stay here until I call to you; then strike the metal with this staff, and bring me up."

"But—"

"Do as I say," said Hresh, and gave the strut a quick rap with his staff. The slab grumbled and groaned as it began to move. Quickly he tossed the staff to Haniman, who stood by looking sour and disgruntled while Hresh disappeared into the depths of the vault.

Amber light glowed. Hordes of somber glowering figures came into view along the walls, that frantic population of monstrous carvings. Hresh caught his breath in an involuntary reaction of amazement, and sharp, stale, strange air filled his lungs.

Ahead of him lay the device of the knobs and levers. He ran to it.

Quickly he drew the Barak Dayir from its pouch, and quickly he seized it with his sensing-organ. Immediately the strange music of the stone flooded his soul, distant chimes and a languorous roar punctuated by sharp stabs of brazen clangor.

235

He understood better now how to control the device. This time there were no storms. This time he did not soar toward the heavens, but instead extended the zone of his perceptions laterally in all directions, so that he spread out to encompass the entire city of Vengiboneeza. His tingling mind felt the structure of the city as a series of interlocking circles, hundreds of them both great and small, which he perceived as clearly as though they were no more than half a dozen straight lines scratched on the floor. Brilliant points of hot red light blazed at many places along the circles.

Hresh would investigate those points of light at another time. His task now was the machine of knobs and levers. Grasping the same knobs he had seized before—he could see the mark of his own hands' heat on them from the last visit, a vivid throbbing yellow pulsation—he squeezed them with all his strength.

An irresistible force instantly took him and swept him up and carried him like a mote of dust into another realm.

The Great World erupted into glorious life all about him.

He was still in Vengiboneeza, but it was no longer Vengiboneeza of the ruins. Once more it was Vengiboneeza as it had been, the living city; but this time the vision was no fleeting one. It was vivid and tangible, with the unarguable density of the utterly real.

The city glistened with the hot sheen of its vitality, and he was everywhere in it, floating down all the streets at once, an unseen observer in the central marketplace, on the marble quays by lakeside, in the villas on the green slopes of the hill district.

I am there, he thought. I am truly there. I have been drawn down through the abyss and whirlpool of time like a dust mote through a straw, and thrust into the heart of the Great World.

He wondered if it would ever be possible for him to return to his own world.

He realized that he didn't care.

Wherever he looked he saw throngs of the sapphire-eyes folk. They moved calmly, confidently, strolling arm in arm. And why shouldn't they be confident and calm? They were masters of the world. Hresh looked upon them with awe. What great terrifying beasts they were, with their enormous jaws and their myriad gleaming teeth and their rough green scales and their bulging sapphire-blue eyes! How they swaggered about the streets on their powerful fleshy hind legs, propped up by those huge thick tails! And yet they could not truly be thought of as beasts, however fearsome they looked. The light of keen intelligence burned in the strange eyes. The long heads rose in startling domes, and Hresh felt the power of the large brains ticking within them.

A cold sluggish fluid that was like blood, but not blood at all, bathed those great brains. But the minds of the sapphire-eyes folk were neither sluggish nor cold. Hresh felt the thunder of those minds pounding against him from all sides. Merchants, poets, philosophers, sages, masters of the sciences and the wisdoms: they all were hard at work, recording, analyzing, comprehending, at every moment of the day and the night. He saw even more clearly than he had before what work it was to create and sustain a great civilization like this: how much thought was necessary, how much information must be gathered and stored and disseminated, how intricate the webwork of planning and execution. The People, with their little cocoon, their pitiful books of chronicles, their trifling oral traditions and sanctified customs, seemed more insignificant than ever to him as he contemplated the sapphire-eyes. Even when they sat basking in the stone-walled pools of pink radiance that they loved so much, they busied themselves in study, thought, passionate dispute. Had there ever been another race like this? How had it come to pass that such miraculous folk had sprung from the same stock as the lowly mindless lizards and serpents?

And why, he wondered, had they allowed themselves to die of the Long Winter, when surely they had had the power to fend off the disaster that was coming upon their world?

And he saw that the other five of the Six Peoples were represented in this lost ancient Vengiboneeza also.

Here were hjjk-folk, chilly and aloof, keeping close together in files of fifty or a hundred, like ants. Hresh sensed the dry rustle of their bleak thoughts, the click-clatter of their hard, brittle souls. It was easy to detest them. There was no singleness to them, no individuality. Each was part of the larger entity that was the group of hjjk-folk, and each group was part of the race of hjjk-folk as a totality.

From them radiated the stern conviction of their own enduring superiority. *We will be here after you are gone,* the hjjk-folk announced with every movement of their arrogant antennae. And it was clear that they would regard the instant disappearance of all members of the other races as a considerable boon. Yet no one begrudged the presence here of these inimical insect-people. Hresh saw them actively mingling, acquiring, trading.

Here too were the vegetals, the delicate flower-folk, gathering in little groups on sunny porches. The petals of their faces were yellow or red or blue, and in the center of each was a single golden eye. Their central stems were sturdy, their limbs much less so, pliant and soft. They spoke in mild whispering tones, with much rustling of leaves and elegant gesturing of branches. There was a soft poetry in their movements and sounds.

By what miracle had it happened, Hresh wondered, that plants had learned to speak and walk about? He was able to look within the souls of these vegetals and see the knotty fibers and sinews of true brains, little hard clumps nestling in the protected place where their head-petals joined their central stems. In his trek across the plains he had not encountered plants that had minds; but of course these vegetals that he saw were ancient creatures. Their kind had been swept away by the bitter storms of the Long Winter, and perhaps nothing like them had been capable of surviving into the era of the People.

The mechanicals were much in evidence. Hresh saw them hard at work in every district of the city, those massive dome-headed, jointed-legged metal beings. They were constructing, repairing, cleansing, demolishing. So they were the servants of the sapphire-eyes; and yet they had clear, strong minds and a sharp awareness of their own existence. Machines they might be, but to Hresh they were more comprehensible than the hjjk-folk. Each was an individual, with a distinct identity and no little pride in that identity.

A scarcer group were the sea-lords, but this, Hresh realized, must be owing to the difficulties they experienced in getting about on land. They were sleek brown tight-furred beings, tapered in a graceful way, with robust frames and flipperlike limbs. Plainly they were creatures of the water, though they breathed the air of Vengiboneeza with no sign of discomfort. Each was installed in a cunning chariot on silver treads, which was operated by deft manipulations of the sea-lord's flipper tips. Sea-lords were to be found mainly in the districts near the waterfront, sensibly enough, in taverns and shops and restaurants. Their look was a bold and haughty one, as if each regarded himself as a prince among princes. Perhaps it was so.

On and on he drifted, and the Great World glittered about him in the fullness of its brightness. What had existed only as the blurred memory of a memory in the oldest pages of the chronicles was alive for him. For him there was no time outside the time of his vision. This was the world as it had been before the disaster; this was the world at the summit of its highest civilization, when miracles were everyday things.

He had become a citizen of that world. Moving through the streets of ancient Vengiboneeza, he paused now to bow to some sapphire-eyes lord, paused to exchange pleasantries with a group of blushing twittering vegetals, paused to let a sea-lord in a magnificent gleaming chariot go past him. He knew himself to be at the hub of the universe. All epochs of every star converged here. There had never been anything like it in the universe before. It was his great and unique privilege to be seeing it. He wanted to roam every street, to inspect every building, to see and comprehend everything: to live in two worlds from now on, to retain, if he could, his citizenship in this doomed land of the long-gone past.

If this is a dream, he thought, it is the finest dream that anyone ever had.

Very little of what he saw bore much resemblance to the ruined Vengiboneeza he had come to know. Perhaps half a dozen of these great buildings, he thought, had survived into his own time. The rest were entirely different, as was the pattern of the streets. He knew that this place was Vengiboneeza, for the arrangement of the city between the mountains and the water was the same; but the city must have been built and rebuilt many times over during its long span of existence. He had a powerful sense of it as a living, changing thing, as a gigantic creature that breathed and moved.

More than ever, now, Hresh perceived the complexity of the Great World, and felt dismayed and disheartened by the task that he knew the People would face in attempting to achieve so lofty an ambition as to equal the achievements of that lost civilization. But once again he told himself that even the Great World had not been built in an afternoon. The labor of millions, across thousands of years, had created it. Given enough time, the People could do just as well.

He ventured onward, hovering like a wraith, peering here, peering there, trying to take it all in before this vision, like the last, was snatched from him.

And after a time he realized that there was one thing he had not seen here.

My own kind, Hresh thought. Where are we?

He counted carefully. Of the Six Peoples of whom the chronicles spoke, those who had shared this vanished world in peace, Hresh had seen five thus far: sapphire-eyes, hjjks, vegetals, mechanicals, sea-lords. Humans were the sixth people. He had seen none at all. Dazzled by the richness and strangeness of it all, he had not become aware of the absence of that one race until now.

He searched the city to its boundaries; and there were no humans to be found. Through one broad plaza after another, up this grand boulevard and that, into the wineshops of the harbor and the white marble villas of the foothills he sought them, hoping for a glimpse of dark thick fur, of bright alert eyes, of sensing-organs proudly erect. Nothing. Not one. It was as if humanity was wholly unknown in this antique Vengiboneeza of the high great era.

But during this quest Hresh came from time to time upon creatures of another kind familiar to him: curious frail beings sparsely distributed in the great city, scattered by twos and threes through Vengiboneeza like precious gems on a sandy shore. They were tall and slender, and walked upright as the People did. Their skulls were high-vaulted; their lips were thin; their skins were pale and bare of fur; their eyes glowed with a mysterious violet hue. And from them came an emanation of great antiquity and power, rooted in a sense of self so firm that it was overwhelming, it was crushing in its complacent force.

Hresh had seen these people before, carved on the walls of the subterranean vault where he had commenced this journey across time. He had seen one in the cocoon itself: that enigmatic sleeping creature who had dwelled so long among the People without ever entering into the life of the tribe. They were the Dream-Dreamer folk. Haniman, all innocence, had asked if they were one of the Six Peoples when he saw them amid the statuary of the vault, and Hresh had said no, no, they must be folk from some other star. But now he was not so sure. Now a dread suspicion of the truth began to hatch and grow within his soul.

He saw them moving through the city in silence, aloof mysterious creatures, like kings, like gods. They seemed almost to float a little way above the pavement. Then he came to a building that he recognized, the dark flat heavy-walled structure that he had called the Citadel, windowless, stark, looming in somber majesty on a great hill and looking just as it did in his own time. There he found dozens of the creatures going to and fro, as if this was their special hostelry, or perhaps their palace. They paid him no notice. He watched them approach the building one by one and touch their long fingers to its sides, and pass through as though the walls were mere insubstantial mist; and when they emerged it was the same way.

He let his mind drift down toward them, and he entered into the blaze of their dazzling aura, and he sank into the shadowy cloak that covered their souls.

And he felt their inwardness, and knew their nature. And the knowledge of it struck him with such force that it thrust him down to the ground, huddling on his knees as though a mighty hand had pressed against his back.

Once more Hresh heard the mocking voice of the sapphire-eyes artificial, saying in a voice of thunder, *You are not human. There no longer are humans here. What you are is monkeys, or the children of monkeys. The humans are gone from the earth.*

Was it so? Yes. Yes, it was.

These were the humans. These pale long-legged furless things, these Dream-Dreamers, these ghosts and phantoms floating through Vengiboneeza of old.

He touched their souls, and he knew the truth, and there was no way to hide from it.

He felt the ancientness of them. Their unending lifeline, falling backward, backward in time, across so many years that he had no name for a number that huge, millions of years, eternities. They had lived upon this world since the beginning of it, or so it seemed. He was crushed beneath the weight of that immense past of theirs, that staggering burden of their history. He looked into their souls and he beheld a vast procession of empires and realms that had risen and fallen and risen again, an endless immortal cycle of grandeur, kings and queens, warriors, poets, chroniclers, a host of accomplishments so great that they baffled his understanding. Surely they were gods. For, like gods, they were able to create and then to turn away from their creations; they could allow towering achievements beyond his comprehension to slip into oblivion, and then would create anew and turn away again, and again and again.

Surely these people, Hresh thought, must be the true masters of Vengiboneeza, rather than the sapphire-eyes whom we had thought were the rulers here.

But no. Not the masters, these humans. They did not need to

be. To the sapphire-eyes fell the responsibilities of planning and government; to the mechanicals fell the burden of labor; to the hjjk-men and the sea-lords and the vegetals fell the various functions of commerce that sustained the life of the Great World. The humans, Hresh saw, simply *were*. An ancient race, declining now in numbers, they warmed themselves with glories out of an unimaginable antiquity. This world had once been theirs, theirs alone, and they showed by nothing more than the look of their eyes that they had not forgotten that ancient supremacy of theirs, nor did they begrudge having surrendered it, for it had been a willing surrender. Perhaps they had created the other five races long before. Certainly the others, even the sapphire-eyes, deferred to them without hesitation. Surely they were gods. Surely. Whenever he touched the mind of one of them it felt as he imagined it would feel to touch the mind of Dawinno or Friit.

After a while Hresh could no longer bear to be near them. He backed away from them as he would from a blazing fire, and moved onward, still searching, still finding.

There were still other races in the city, in even smaller numbers than the humans. They were strange creatures, of many startling sorts. Of some he could find no more than four or five representatives, of some a single one only. They looked like nothing that his studies of the chronicles had prepared him to encounter. Hresh saw beings with two heads and six legs and beings with no heads at all and a forest of arms. He saw beings with teeth like a thousand needles set round circular mouths that gaped in their stomachs. He saw beings that lived in sealed tanks and beings that floated like bubbles above the ground. He saw ponderous things moving with an earthshaking tread, and light, fluttering ones whose motions dazzled his eye. From them all came the unmistakable glint of intelligence, though it was not an earthly intelligence, and the emanations of their souls were puzzling and disturbing to him.

In time Hresh realized what these beings were. Star-creatures. Visitors from the worlds that circled the bright cold fires of the night. In the era of the Great World there must have been constant comings and goings of star-travelers among the worlds of heaven. From one of these strangers, maybe, had come the very Wonderstone that had granted him this vision.

And us? he thought. The People? Are we nowhere to be found in this mighty Vengiboneeza?

Nowhere. Not a trace. We are not here.

It was shattering. His people were altogether absent from the splendor and grandeur of the Great World.

He struggled to absorb and comprehend it. He told himself that this scene he saw was unfolding itself in the unimaginable past, long before the coming of the death-stars. Perhaps whole peoples are born just as individuals are, he thought: perhaps, on this age-old day that I have journeyed to, our kind is yet unborn. Our time is not yet come.

But that was small consolation. The deeper truth resonated and reverberated with terrible force in his soul.

You are not human. What you are is monkeys, or the children of monkeys.

The proof lay before him, and still he could not accept it. Not human? Not human? His mind whirled. He knew what it meant to be human, or believed that he did; and to be excluded from that great skein of existence that stretched backward into the depths of time was an agony beyond endurance. He felt cut adrift, severed from every root that bound him to the world. For a long while he hovered motionless in some sphere of air above ancient Vengiboneeza, numb, bewildered, lost.

*   *   *

Hresh had no idea how long he stood by the device in the underground vault, gripping the knobs and levers, while the Great World poured in torrents through his dazzled mind. But after a time he felt the vision beginning to fade. The shining towers turned misty, the streets blurred and melted and ran in streams before his eyes.

He gripped the levers more tightly. It was no use. His spirit was drifting upward now toward the stony reality of the cavern beneath the tower.

Then ancient Vengiboneeza was gone. But he was still under the spell of the Barak Dayir, and as he rose he saw once more the pattern of the ruined city in his mind as he had seen it upon his descent, those interlocking circles, the blazing points of red light. Suddenly he understood what those red lights must be: the places where the life of the Great World still burned in the ruins. Wherever he saw those dots of hot light, there would he find caches of the treasure he sought.

Hresh had neither time nor strength to deal with that now. He felt dazed and weak. And yet a powerful exaltation lingered within his soul, mixed with great confusion, with self-doubt, with despair.

He looked around in disbelief at the huge hollow of the cavern: the dry earthen floor strewn with drifts of dust and cobwebs and bits of rubble, the dim lights, the half-seen statuary rising in insane profligacy along the walls. The Great World still seemed vivid and real to him, and this place only a shabby dream. But from moment to moment the balance was steadily shifting; the Great World slipped beyond his reach, the cavern became the only reality he had.

"Haniman!" he cried.

His voice came out cracked and ragged and thin, and half an octave too high.

Hresh tried again. "Haniman! Bring me up!"

There was no response from overhead. He stared up into the musty blackness, squinting, peering. He heard the sounds of chittering things moving about in the walls. But nothing from Haniman.

"Haniman!"

He bellowed it with all his strength. There was a sound as if of fine rain. Rain, down here? No, Hresh realized. Tiny pebbles, bits of sand and dirt, falling from the roof of the cavern. His voice alone had brought them down. Another such shout and he might bring the roof itself down upon him.

His nerves trembled like lute-strings. He wondered if Haniman had abandoned him in this tomb—simply walked off to leave him to rot and die. Or perhaps he had wandered away on some excursion of his own. Maybe it was just that Hresh was so far below the surface that Haniman was unable to hear his calls. Yissou! Hresh considered calling again. This place had endured the earthquakes of seven hundred thousand years; could it be tumbled by a single shout? "*Haniman!*" he called once more. "*Haniman!*" But once more his cries produced nothing but a further shower of fine particles from above.

What should he do? Starve? No. Climb? How?

He thought of using his second sight to catch Haniman's attention. That was a forbidden thing, to turn one's second sight upon a fellow member of the tribe, and thus to violate the sanctuary of his mind. But was he supposed to rot here in the darkness rather than go against custom?

Gathering his strength, Hresh sent forth his second sight.

Upward through the darkness went the tendrils of his perception. Someone was up there, yes. He felt life, he felt warmth. Haniman. Asleep! Dawinno take him, he had fallen asleep!

Hresh gave him a jab with his mind. There was a stirring overhead. Haniman murmured and grumbled. Hresh had a sense of Haniman turning in his sleep, perhaps brushing at his face as if trying to brush away a bothersome dream. He jabbed again, harder. *Haniman! You imbecile, wake up!* And harder yet. Haniman was awake now. Yes, sitting up, eyes open. Hresh saw the upper floor through Haniman's eyes. That was a weird sensation, being in someone else's mind. Hresh knew that he should withdraw. But he remained, lingering another moment, out of sheer curiosity. Feeling Haniman's mind all around his like a second pelt. Touching Haniman's little yearnings and hungers and angers. Discovering something of what it had been like to grow up fat and slow in a tribe of thin agile folk. Hresh felt an unexpected flood of compassion. This was almost like a twining; and in some ways it was more intense, more intimate. His annoyance with Haniman remained; but now it was like being annoyed at one's own self, an irritation tinged with amusement and forgiveness.

Then Haniman's mind shook itself angrily, tossing Hresh aside, and hastily Hresh withdrew, shivering at the impact of the breaking of the contact.

"Hresh? Was that you?"

Haniman's voice floated downward, faint, vague, shrouded in echo.

"Yes! Bring me up, will you?"

"Why didn't you say so?"

"I've been calling for ten minutes. Were you asleep?"

"Asleep?" came the voice from far above. But Hresh could not be sure whether it was Haniman repeating his word, or his own voice returning to him from the vault of the cavern.

In a moment the slab emitted its familiar groaning, sighing sound. Hastily Hresh scrambled aboard it, and it began to rise. He lay still, feeling the ache of fatigue in all his limbs.

He emerged into the upper level. Haniman stood beside the slab, arms folded, regarding him sourly.

"I don't care if you are the chronicler," he said. "You touch me like that again and I'll push you into the sea."

"I had to get your attention somehow. I was calling and you weren't answering."

"You weren't calling loudly enough, maybe."

"Enough to knock rocks loose from the cavern roof."

Haniman shrugged. "I didn't hear a thing."

"You were asleep."

"Was I? How could I have been? You weren't down there more than two minutes."

Hresh stared in amazement. "Are you serious?"

"Two minutes! No more than that! You went down below, I laid myself down to rest, and maybe I closed my eyes for a moment, and next thing I knew there you were, grubbing around inside my mind in that filthy way, and—" Haniman halted abruptly. He walked toward Hresh and peered at him closely. "Yissou! What happened to you down there?"

"What do you mean?"

"You look a hundred years old. Your eyes are strange. Your whole face—it's all different. As if you've been hollowed out inside."

"I had a vision," Hresh said. He touched his face, wondering if it had been transformed as Haniman said, wondering if he looked as old as old Thaggoran now. But his face felt the same as ever. Whatever transformation he had undergone must have been within.

"What did you see?"

Hresh hesitated. "Things," he said. "Strange things. Disturbing things."

"What kind of things?"

"Never mind," said Hresh. "Let's get out of this place."

A great weariness gripped him on the journey back to the settlement. He had to pause often to rest, and once he became sick and knelt behind a broken column, gagging and retching for an almost interminable spell. He felt old and feeble all the rest of the way, lagging behind as Haniman went bounding ahead, and then feeling abashed as Haniman found it necessary to come back and look for him. Only as they reached the settlement itself did his youthful vitality assert itself and his strength begin to return. He moved more quickly, he paused less frequently, though Haniman still turned again and again to beckon impatiently.

Hresh knew he would be a long time pondering what he had learned in the vault of the plaza of thirty-six towers. The jeering hissing laughter of that sapphire-eyes artificial by the south gate swelled in his soul until it seemed to fill the world.

Little monkey, little monkey, little monkey.

It was impossible now for him to clear his spirit of that bitter mockery. And yet he had found the key to lost Vengiboneeza as well. A great triumph, a shattering defeat, each wrapped in the other: it bewildered him. He resolved to keep his own counsel until he came to some deeper comprehension of these matters. But the treasures of Vengiboneeza lay open to him now. He had to tell Koshmar at least that much.

Just outside the chieftain's house he came upon Torlyri.

"Where's Koshmar?"

The offering-woman pointed toward the house. "Inside."

"I've got things to tell her! Marvelous things!"

"She's busy now," Torlyri said. "You'll have to wait a little while."

"Wait? Wait?" It was like a bucket of cold water in the face. "What do you mean, wait? I saw the Great World, Torlyri! I saw it alive, as it had been! And I know now where everything we came to Vengiboneeza to find is hidden!" In his sudden enthusiasm his fatigue and confusion fell away. "Listen, go to her, will you? Tell her to drop whatever she's doing and let me in. All right? Will you? What's she so busy doing, anyway?"

"She has a stranger with her," said Torlyri.

Hresh stared, not comprehending at first.

"A stranger?"

"A scout from a strange tribe, so it seems."

Hresh's hand went, as it so often did, to Thaggoran's amulet at his throat. A stranger!

He gaped. "What? Who?"

"A spy, in fact. Harruel and Konya caught him snooping around on Mount Springtime a little while ago." Torlyri smiled and put her hands over his. "Oh, Hresh, I know you're bubbling over with things to tell her. But can you wait? Can you wait just a little while? This is important too. It's an actual man from another tribe, Hresh. That's an enormous thing. She can't deal with more than one enormous thing at a time. Nobody can. Do you understand that, Hresh?"

Koshmar stood straight and tall in front of the dark rat-wolf skin that hung as a trophy on the wall of her room. Her wide shoulders were drawn tightly back, her face was set in determination. Harruel was at her left, Konya at her right, both of them armed and ready to protect her; but she knew that spears were useless in this situation. What was unfolding now was a challenge that intelligence alone could deal with. It was something that she had anticipated since the Time of Coming Forth; but now that it had finally arrived she was far from sure of the best way to proceed.

Now, if ever, she needed old Thaggoran. Another tribe! It was only to be expected; and yet it was almost beyond belief. Throughout all their history her people had thought of themselves as the only people in the world, and in essence that had been so. And now—now—

She stared across the room at the spy.

He was a formidable sight. There was an overwhelming strangeness about him. His face was a lean one, sharp cheekbones cutting away to a long narrow chin. His eyes, set very far apart, were a color that Koshmar had never seen, a startling bright red, like the sun at sunset. His fur was golden, and long and rank, not at all like the fur of anyone of the tribe. Though slender and graceful, he had a remarkable look of strength and resilience, like some fine cable that could never be broken. His legs were almost as long as Harruel's, although he was far less massive. And there was a curious helmet on his head that made him actually seem taller even than Harruel.

The helmet was a nightmarish thing. It was a high cone of a thick black leathery material, with a visor that went down almost to the stranger's forehead in front and a ridged plate running the length of his neck to the rear. Mounted in back at the helmet's summit was a circle of golden metal and five long metal rays jutting upward like five spears. In front, over the stranger's forehead, the sinister image of a huge golden insect was affixed, its four wings outspread, its gigantic eyes of red stone burning with a ferocious gleam.

At first glance the man looked like some sort of upright monster with a hideously frightful head; only when you looked again did you see that the helmet was a thing of artifice, mere headgear, strapped below his neck with a thick brown cord.

Konya and Harruel had stumbled upon him while hunting together in the foothills of the mountains. He was camped in a cave not far above the last line of ruined villas, and from the looks of things he had been there some time, perhaps as long as a week, for the bones of animals that had been recently butchered and roasted were scattered all around the place. When they found him—sitting quietly, wearing his helmet, staring out over the city—he sprang up immediately and ran past them into the high forest. They followed, but it was no easy chase. "He runs like one of those animals with red horns on their noses," Harruel said.

"Like a dancerhorn, yes," Konya put in.

Several times they lost him amid the tangles of the wilderness, but always the glint of the golden rays of his helmet revealed him in the distance. In the end they had trapped him in a pocket canyon that had no exit; and, though he was armed with a beautifully made spear and seemed capable of using it, he offered no resistance, but abruptly surrendered without a struggle and without saying a word.

Nor had he spoken yet. He met Koshmar's gaze evenly, fearlessly, and kept his silence as she attempted to question him.

"My name is Koshmar," she began. "I am the chieftain here. Tell me your name and who your chieftain is."

When that produced nothing but a calm stare, she ordered him by the names of the gods to speak. She invoked Dawinno, Friit, Emakkis, and Mueri without success. It seemed to her that the name of Yissou drew some response from him, a quick quirking of the lips; but still he said nothing.

"Speak, curse you!" Harruel growled, angrily stepping forward. "Who are you? What do you want here?" He shook his spear in the stranger's face. "Speak or we'll flay you alive!"

"No," Koshmar said sharply. "That is not how I mean to deal with him." She pulled Harruel back beside her and told the stranger in a soft voice, "You will not be harmed here, I promise you that much. I ask you again to tell us your name and the name of your people, and then we will give you food and drink, and welcome you among us."

But the stranger seemed as indifferent to Koshmar's diplomacy as he was to Harruel's bluster. He continued to stare at Koshmar as though she were uttering mere nonsense.

She tapped her breast three times. "Koshmar," she said, in a loud, clear tone. Pointing at the two warriors, she said, "Harruel. Konya. Koshmar, Harruel, Konya." She pointed now at the helmeted stranger and gave him a questioning look. "Thus we entrust you with our names. Now you will tell us yours."

The Helmet Man remained silent.

"We can go on like this all day," said Harruel in disgust. "Give him to me, Koshmar, and I promise you I'll have him talking in five minutes!"

"No."

"We need to find out why he's here, Koshmar. Suppose he's the lead man for an army of his kind that's waiting out there, planning to kill us and take Vengiboneeza for themselves!"

"Thank you," said Koshmar acidly. "It was a thought that had not occurred to me."

"Well, what if he is? It's almost certain that he means trouble for us. We've got to know. And if he won't tell us anything, we'll have to kill him."

"Do you think so, Harruel?"

"Now that he's been down here and seen everything, and he knows how few we are, we can't just let him go back to his people and give them his report."

Koshmar nodded. That had been clear to her all along, though only a brute like Harruel, she thought, would say such a thing to the stranger's face. Well, perhaps they would have to kill him. The idea held little appeal for her, but she would do it without hesitation if the safety of the tribe was at stake.

A thousand conflicting thoughts collided in her mind. Strangers! Another tribe! A rival chieftain!

That meant enemies, conflict, war, death, might it not? Or would they be friendly? Conflict was not inevitable, whatever Harruel believed. Suppose they settled here—Vengiboneeza was big enough for a second tribe, certainly—and entered into some kind of amiable relationship with her people. But what would that be like, she wondered—friends who are not of our kind? The two terms were close to being contradictory: *friends* and *not of our kind.* Different beliefs, strange gods, unfamiliar customs? How could there be other gods? Yissou, Dawinno, Emakkis, Friit, Mueri: those were the gods. If these people had different gods, what sense was there in the world?

And would there be matings between people of the two tribes? Where would the children live—with the mother's tribe, or with the father's? Would one tribe grow large at the expense of the other?

Koshmar closed her eyes a moment, and drew breath deep down into her lungs. She found herself wishing that this were only a dream.

Where this man came from, there must be many more just like him, an army of strangers camped on the far side of the mountain wall. Everywhere in the world right now, very likely, other tribes were making the Coming Forth as the new warmth flooded the air. She had lived all her life in a world of sixty folk. It was almost impossible for her to grasp the truth that there could be six thousand in the world, or sixty thousand, even—all those names, all those souls, all those unfamiliar selves, each clamoring for some place in the sun. But that might well be the case.

There was a knocking at the door.

She heard the voice of Torlyri, saying, "Hresh has returned, Koshmar."

"Bring him in," she said.

Hresh looked odd: worn and dusty, tired, suddenly much older than his years. His eyes were in shadows. He seemed almost ill. But at the sight of the stranger in the helmet the old Hresh glow returned to his face. Koshmar could almost hear the questions beginning to pop and click in his mind.

Quickly she told him of the capture and of the interrogation thus far. "We can get nothing out of him. He pretends not to understand what we say."

"Pretends? What if he actually doesn't understand you?"

"You mean, that he's stupid, like a beast?"

"I mean that he may speak some other language."

Koshmar stared at him, baffled. "Another language? I don't know what that means, 'another language.'"

"It means—well—another *language*," Hresh said lamely. His hands groped in the air as though they were searching. "We have our language, our set of sounds that convey ideas. Imagine that his people use a different set of sounds, all right? Where we say 'meat,' his people may say 'flookh,' or maybe 'splig.'"

"But 'flookh' and 'splig' are sounds without meaning," Koshmar objected. "What sense is there in—"

"They have no meaning to us," said Hresh. "But they might to other people. Not those sounds particularly. I just made them up as examples, you understand. But they could have some word of their own for 'meat,' and one for 'sky,' and one for 'spear,' and so on. Different words from ours for everything."

"This is madness," Koshmar said irritably. "What do you mean, a word *for* meat? Meat is meat. Not flookh, not splig, but meat. Sky is sky. I thought you might be of help, Hresh, but all you do now is mystify me."

"These ideas are very strange to me too," the boy said. He seemed to be extraordinarily weary, and struggling to express his thoughts. His hands groped the air, as if searching. "I have never known any language but ours, or even thought that there might be another. The notion leaped into my mind, out of nowhere, just as I looked upon this stranger. But think, Koshmar: what if the hjjk-men have a language of their own, and each kind of beast has its own also, and every tribe that lived through the long winter too! We were alone so long, cut off from others for hundreds of thousands of years. Maybe at first everyone spoke one language, but over so long a time, hundreds of thousands of years—"

"Perhaps so," said Koshmar uneasily. "But in that case, how will we communicate with this man? For we have to communicate with him somehow. We have to find out if he's friend or enemy."

"We could try doing it by second sight," Hresh said after a moment.

Koshmar stared at him, shocked. "Second sight is not used among people."

"In extreme cases it can be," said Hresh, looking uncomfortable. "We've got the tribe's safety to think about here. Shouldn't we use whatever abilities we have to find out what we need to know?"

"But it's such a violation of—"

Koshmar halted, shaking her head. She looked toward Torlyri, standing by the door.

"What do you say? Is it proper to attempt such a thing?"

"It seems strange. But I see no harm in it," the offering-woman said, a little doubtfully, after a moment's consideration. "He is not of our tribe. Our customs need not apply. No sin will attach to us on this account."

"The gods gave us second sight to help us where language and vision fail," said Hresh to Koshmar. "How could they object if we used it in a situation like this?"

Koshmar stood silent, examining the matter. The stranger, impassive as ever, gave no sign that he had comprehended anything of this. Maybe he really does speak an entirely different language, Koshmar thought. The idea made her head hurt. It seemed as strange to her as the idea that someone could be a man today and a woman tomorrow, or that rain would fall upward from the ground, or that the blessing of Yissou might be withdrawn from her in the twinkling of an eye and someone else named chieftain in her place. None of those things was possible. But this is a time of many strange things, Koshmar thought. Perhaps it was true, what Hresh said: that here was one who spoke with other words, if indeed he spoke at all.

After a time she turned to Hresh and said brusquely, "Very well. You're the expert on language here. Use your second sight on him, and find out who he is and what he seeks here."

Hresh stepped forward and confronted the stranger in the helmet.

He had never felt so tired in his life. What a day this was! And not finished yet. They were all watching him. He was far from sure he *could* muster second sight again, so tired was he.

The Helmet Man looked down at him from his great height in a cool, distant way, as though Hresh were nothing more than some bothersome little beast of the jungle. His eerie red eyes were disturbingly intense. Hresh imagined that he could see anger in them, and contempt, and an abiding sense of self-worth. But no fear. Not a trace of fear anywhere. There was something heroic about this helmeted stranger.

Hresh gathered his strength and sent forth his second sight.

He expected to meet some sort of opposition: an attempt to block his thrust, or to turn it aside, if that was possible. But with the same cool indifference as ever the stranger awaited Hresh's approach; and Hresh's consciousness sank easily and deeply into that of the Helmet Man.

The contact lasted no more than a fraction of a second.

In that instant Hresh had a sense of the great power of this man's soul, of his strength of character and depth of purpose. He saw also, for the briefest flicker of a moment, a vision of a horde of others much like this one, a band of warriors gathered on some heavily wooded hill, all of them clad in bizarre and fanciful helmets like his, but each of an individual design. Then the contact broke and everything went dark. Hresh felt his limbs turning to water. He staggered, tumbled backward, pivoted somehow at the last moment, and landed on his belly in a sprawling heap at Harruel's feet. That was the last he knew for some time.

When he awakened he was in Torlyri's arms on the far side of the room. She held him close, crooning to him, reassuring him. Gradually he brought his eyes into focus and saw Koshmar holding the stranger's helmet in both her hands, regarding it quizzically. The stranger was limp on the floor and Harruel and Konya, gripping him by the ankles, were dragging him out of the room as unceremoniously as if he were a sack of grain.

"Don't try to stand up yet," Torlyri murmured. "Get your balance first, catch your breath."

"What happened? Where are they taking him?"

"He's dead," Torlyri said.

"Fell right down the moment you touched his mind," said Koshmar from across the room. "So did you. We thought you were both gone. But you were just knocked out. He was dead before he hit the floor. It was to avoid being questioned, do you see? He had some way of killing himself with his mind alone." She slammed the helmet down angrily on the ledge of her trophy shelf. "We will never know anything about him now," she said. "We will never know a thing!"

Hresh nodded somberly.

The thought came to him that this was somehow his fault, that he should have anticipated some defensive maneuver of this sort from the stranger, that he should never have allowed himself to talk Koshmar into using second sight in this interrogation.

Perhaps it would have been a better idea to use the Wonderstone instead, he told himself.

But how was he to have known? Thaggoran might have known; but he, as he continued to discover, was not Thaggoran. I am still so young, Hresh thought ruefully. Well, time would cure that. A great sadness spread through him. He might have learned new and remarkable things from this man of another tribe. Instead he had merely helped to send him from the world.

Best not to think of it.

He went to Koshmar's side, where she stood glowering above the helmet, running her hand repeatedly along its golden rays in a stunned, angry way. After a moment she glanced at him. Her eyes were dull and sullen.

"I need to tell you something," Hresh said. "I've just come back from the heart of the city. Haniman and I. We went down into a vault beneath a building, where there is a machine of the sapphire-eyes, Koshmar. A machine that still works."

Koshmar looked at him more closely. The light of her spirit returned to her eyes.

"It's a machine that was meant to show pictures of the Great World," Hresh told her. "More than pictures. It was meant to show the Great World itself. I put my hands on it, Koshmar, and I used the Barak Dayir on it."

"And could you see anything?" she asked.

"Yes! Wonderful things!"

9

In the Cauldron

That was the beginning of Hresh's true penetration into the mysteries of Vengiboneeza. The machine in the vault of the plaza of the thirty-six towers had opened the way; that and the Barak Dayir.

Everyone knew that he had made some great discovery. Haniman had spread the story far and wide. It stirred even the most sluggish imagination. Hresh was the center of all attention. People stared at him as if he were newly returned from a dinner at the table of the gods. "Did you really see the Great World?" he was asked, twenty times a day. "What was it like? Tell me! Tell me!"

But it was Taniane who saw the real truth. "You came upon something terrible when you were down in that hole. It upset you so much that you don't want to say anything about it. But it's changed you, hasn't it, Hresh? Whatever it was. I can see it. There's a darkness about your spirit now that wasn't there before."

He looked at her, amazed. "Nothing about me has changed," he said tightly.

"It has. I can see it."

"You're imagining things."

"You can tell me," she said, cajoling. "We've always been friends, Hresh. It'll soothe your soul to tell someone."

"There's nothing to tell. Nothing!"

And he turned quickly away from her, as he always did when he was fearful that someone would see the lie on his face.

Not only was he unable to bring himself to share with any of the others the agonizing truth he had discovered in the vault of the thirty-six towers, he could scarcely bear even to think about it. Now and again he felt it like a dull pain close to his heart; and now and again he heard a harsh mocking voice whispering, *Little monkey, little monkey, little monkey.* But the revelation of the vault was too painful for Hresh to face just yet. He put it aside; he thrust it down beyond the reach of his conscious mind.

He eased his spirit by plunging deep into the exploration of the ruins of Vengiboneeza. The pattern created in his mind by the machine and the Barak Dayir was his guide. When he wielded the Wonderstone, the points of red light that glowed on the interlocking circles that he saw gave him the clues he needed; and he began now systematically to uncover the city's ancient caches of undamaged mechanisms, which he now knew lay all about at close hand, some in deeply hidden galleries, some virtually out in the open.

It amazed him that so many treasures of the Great World had survived the Long Winter. Even metal, he thought, should crumble to dust in so great a span of time. Yet wherever he looked—now that he knew the right places—he came up with wonders great and small. Most of the devices were far too big to remove; but many could be carried away and brought back to the settlement, where a special storeroom in the temple was set aside for them. Rapidly it filled with strange, glittering devices of mysterious function. Hresh examined them cautiously. Discovering these objects was one thing, determining how to make use of them was another. It was slow, difficult, frustrating work.

A group who became known among the People as the Seekers collected about Hresh to aid him in the task of exploration and discovery.

At first the Seekers were simply the handful of bodyguards— Konya, Haniman, Orbin—who usually went out to protect him as he roamed the city. Hresh had regarded them in the beginning as necessary nuisances and nothing more, mere spear-wielders. But before long they knew the city almost as well as he did. Though he tried to keep his map to himself, it was impossible to prevent others from learning their way around. Sometimes now they would go on expeditions of their own. It became a kind of competition for celebrity, now that they saw the fame that accrued to Hresh for having been out so often into the city. And occasionally they would actually return with some glittering little marvel out of antiquity, which they had pried out from under a fallen column, or excavated in some debris-choked undercellar.

Hresh protested to Koshmar about that. "They are ignorant," he said. "They might damage the things they find, if I'm not there to oversee the work."

"They'll cease being ignorant," Koshmar replied, "if they get into the habit of using their minds. And they can learn to be careful with what they find. This city is so big that we need all the searchers we can muster." And after a moment she added, "They need to feel that they are doing important things, Hresh. Otherwise they'll grow bored and restless, and that will endanger us all. I say let them wander where they want to."

Hresh had to obey. He knew when to be wary of disputing the chieftain's decisions.

The number of Seekers grew as time went along. There were many who were curious about the wonders of the city.

One day when he was searching with Orbin in the rich troves of the Yissou Tramassilu district, Hresh found a puzzling little container bound in intricately woven chains. He tried to open it, but the chains were too complex and delicate for his thick male fingers, or Orbin's, to unravel. A woman's hands, smaller and more adept at such work, were needed.

He brought the container back and let Taniane deal with it. Her fingers flew like whirling blades and within minutes she managed to get the container out of its wrappings. There was nothing inside but the dry bones of some small animal, hard as stone, and a bit of grayish powder, perhaps ash.

Taniane went to Koshmar and asked to be allowed to accompany the Seekers. "Probably they find many things like that little box," she said. "And they break them, or they toss them aside. My eyes are sharper than theirs, my fingers are cleverer. They are only men, after all."

"There is sense to what you say," Koshmar replied.

She told Hresh to include Taniane in the search party the next time he went forth. He had mixed feelings about that. Taniane, who had grown tall and silken and keen-witted, had begun to fascinate him in a strange, disturbing way that he scarcely understood. It gave him a mysterious feeling of warmth and excitement when she was close to him, but at the same time she stirred powerful discomfort in him, and sometimes he felt so ill at ease that he would go out of his way to avoid her. He accepted her into the Seekers, for Koshmar had ordered him to, but he took care always to have Orbin or Haniman with him also whenever Taniane was part of the exploration group. They distracted her and kept her from asking him uncomfortable questions.

After Taniane, it was Bonlai who wanted to be a Seeker: if Taniane could go, other girls could, she insisted. And it would give her a chance to be with Orbin. Hresh saw no merit in that, and this time he prevailed with Koshmar. Bonlai, Koshmar agreed, was too young to go exploring. But Hresh could raise no such objection in the case of Sinistine, Jalmud's mate, and she became the second woman of the tribe to join the group.

A little while later the shy and stolid young warrior Praheurt asked to be one of them, and then Shatalgit, a woman just entering childbearing age, who all too obviously was hoping to mate herself with Praheurt. So there were seven Seekers all told, almost a tenth of the entire tribe.

"Seven is certainly enough," Hresh said to Koshmar. "Pretty soon there'll be nobody left working in the vegetable fields or tending the meat-animals, and we'll all be out prowling in the ruins."

Koshmar frowned. "Are we here to raise crops or to find the secrets of the Great World that will show us how to conquer the world?"

"We've found any number of Great World secrets already."

"And they remain secret," said Koshmar sharply. "You don't know how to use a single one of those machines."

Hresh replied, trying to choke back his annoyance, "I'm working on that. But the secrets of the Great World will be of no value to us if we starve to death while trying to learn how to make use of them. I think seven Seekers is enough."

"Very well," said Koshmar.

Nothing more was heard from the Helmet People in all this time.

Harruel made it his special responsibility to keep watch for them. He was sure that more of the strangers were lurking in the mountainous country above the city's northeastern flank, and sure also that they were planning an eventual murderous descent on the tribe. That there would be a war he had no doubt. In truth the People should be turning themselves into an army right now: drilling and marching, preparing themselves for the conflict to come. But nobody, not even Koshmar, was interested in that. At the moment Harruel was an army of one. By default he held all the ranks from private officer up to general. And as general he sent himself out each day on reconnaissance missions along the highland side of Vengiboneeza.

At first he went alone, telling no one where he was going. All day long he would sweep through the ruined zones of the upper city and into the wilderness beyond, looking for the glint of helmets in the distance. It was lonely work, but it provided him with a sense of purpose. He had felt a grievous lack of that since the People had settled in Vengiboneeza.

After a time Harruel realized that it was foolish to go on these missions alone. If the Helmet People did come back, they would probably come in force. Strong as he was, he could hardly hold off more than two or three at a time. He needed a companion on his marches, so that if he was attacked the other might still be able to slip away and sound an alarm.

The first he tried to recruit was Konya. Konya had been with him, after all, when he had caught the first Helmet Man. He understood the nature of the enemy they were up against.

But to Harruel's disgust Konya now was preoccupied with this Seekers thing of Hresh's. He spent all his time wandering in the ruins of the city, prowling for useless incomprehensible objects, instead of training and strengthening himself as a proper warrior should. And he let Harruel know that he intended to go on doing that.

"We'll take care of the Helmet People well enough, if they come back. What's to fear? We'll just send Hresh out to hit them with his second sight. But meanwhile we're recovering amazing things in the ruins."

"You are recovering trash," Harruel said.

Konya shrugged. "Hresh thinks they have value. He says that these are the treasures of the prophecy, which will help us to rule the world."

"If we are all slain by the Helmet People, Konya, we'll rule nothing but our graves. Come and help me keep watch over the city's frontier, and forget this foraging in that dismal rubble."

But Konya would not yield. Harruel thought for a moment of ordering him, as his king, to march on patrol with him. But then he realized that he was not yet king of anything or anyone, except in his own mind. It might be unwise to test the depth of Konya's loyalty more severely just now. Let Konya go grubbing with Hresh for those shiny baubles; he would come to his senses soon enough.

The young warrior Sachkor was more willing to be swayed by Harruel. He was earnest and devoted, and had no interest in becoming a Seeker. Now that he had reached mating age— he seemed to have his eye on the girl called Kreun, who had also just come into her maturity—Sachkor was looking about for some way to distinguish himself in the tribe, to gain Kreun's attention. Attaching himself to Harruel could perhaps be the way. Harruel had his doubts about Sachkor's value as a warrior, for he was slender and did not seem very strong; but at least he was fast afoot and could be useful as a messenger.

"There are enemies hiding in the hills," Harruel told him. "They have red eyes and wear evil-looking helmets on their heads, and one of these days they'll try to kill us all. We must be on constant guard against them."

Sachkor now accompanied Harruel each morning into the hill country. He seemed overjoyed to have some sort of meaningful duty to perform, and sometimes his spirit grew so buoyant that he went running wildly up the forested slopes in an exuberant outburst of speed. Harruel, bigger and heavier and older and not nearly as fleet, found this irritating, and ordered Sachkor to stay closer to him. "It's unwise," he said, "for us to become separated out here. If we're attacked we must stand together."

But they were never attacked. They saw some strange beasts, few of which appeared unfriendly; of Helmet People there were none in evidence. Still they went forth searching every day. Harruel grew weary of Sachkor's callow babble, which centered mainly about the praise of Kreun's thick dark fur and long elegant legs. But he told himself that a warrior must be willing to endure all manner of discomforts.

Harruel made a few more recruits among the idle young warriors: Salaman and Thhrouk. Nittin, not a warrior at all but rather one of the breeder males, also joined. He was sick of spending his days among infants, he said. And there was no reason to maintain the old caste structure of the cocoon out here, was there? That startled Harruel at first, but after a moment he came to see merit in Nittin's offer. Ultimately, when he challenged Koshmar for control, he would need the support of as many different factions of the tribe as he could get. Nittin, with his connections among the women and other breeder males, opened new possibilities.

An attempt to recruit Staip, though, came to nothing. Staip, half a year older than Harruel, was strong and competent, but a colorless man who seemed to Harruel to have no spirit at all. He did as he was told and the rest of the time he did nothing. Therefore Harruel thought he would be easy to gather in; but when he spoke to Staip about the Helmet Man and the threat he represented, Staip merely looked at him in a blank way and said, "He is dead, Harruel."

"That was only the first one. There are others in the hills, making ready to pounce on us."

"Do you think so, Harruel?" Staip said, without interest.

He could not or would not grasp the importance of maintaining patrols; and after a time Harruel threw up his hands in fury and strode away.

With Lakkamai, the fourth of the senior warriors, Harruel had a similar failure. The silent, moody Lakkamai seemed barely to pay attention when Harruel approached him. Impatiently he cut in before Harruel had even finished. "This is no concern of mine. I will not go clambering around the mountain with you, Harruel."

"And if enemies hide there, preparing to do us harm?"

"The only enemies are in your troubled mind," said Lakkamai. "Let me be. I have things of my own to do, and they are things that must be done in the city."

Lakkamai walked away. Harruel spat after him. Things of his own to do? What could be more important than the defense of the tribe? But Lakkamai plainly would not be swayed, nor would any of the other older men. It seemed that only the young ones, full of surging juices and unfocused ambitions, were willing to pledge themselves to the task. Well, so be it, Harruel thought. So be it. They are the ones I will need when I set out to build my new kingdom, anyway: not Staip, not Lakkamai, not even Konya.

Koshmar had by now discovered that several of the men were going on mysterious excursions into the hills every day under Harruel's supervision. She sent for him and asked for an explanation.

Harruel told her exactly what he had been doing and why, and braced himself for a hot dispute.

But to his surprise there was none. Koshmar nodded calmly and said, "You've served us well, Harruel. The Helmet People may be the greatest danger we face."

"The patrols will continue, Koshmar."

"Yes. So they should. Perhaps some of the other men will want to join. All I ask," she said, "is that when you organize a project of this sort, you let me know what you're up to. There are some who thought you might be training an army of your own in the hills, with some plan to attack the rest of us and—who knows?—impose your will on us."

Harruel glared in fury. "Attack the tribe? But that's madness, Koshmar!"

"Indeed. I thought so too."

"Tell me who's been spreading such lies about me! I'll have him skinned and stuffed! I'll turn him into a footstool! An army of my own? Attack the tribe? Gods! Who is the slanderer?"

Koshmar said, "It was only a foolish whisper, and put forth simply as a guess. When it was told to me, I could only laugh, and then the teller laughed too, and admitted that there wasn't much likelihood of a thing like that. No one has slandered you, Harruel.

271

No one doubts your loyalty. Go, now: get your men together, take up your patrol. You do us all a great service."

Harruel walked away, wondering who had put such thoughts in Koshmar's mind.

Konya was the only one who had heard him speak of his ambition to push Koshmar from power and take control of the tribe under the name of king. And Konya had refused to join him on his patrols. Even so, Harruel found it impossible to believe that Konya could have betrayed him.

Who, then?

Hresh?

There had been that time long ago, Harruel remembered, when Hresh had first been made chronicler and he had gone to the boy with his questions about the meaning and history of kingship. Afterward Harruel had decided it could be dangerous to direct Hresh's attention to such matters, and he had never broached the topic with the boy again. But Hresh had a peculiar, simmering sort of mind. Things stewed in it a long while, and he drew profound connections between them.

If Hresh had been whispering suspicious thoughts in Koshmar's ear about him, though, Harruel did not immediately see what he could do about it. It was reasonable now to think that Hresh was his enemy, and to conduct himself accordingly. But this was not the time to move against him. Things had to be thought through first. You had to be wary of little Hresh: he was too sharp, he perceived things too clearly, he had great power.

It also occurred to Harruel that the reason Koshmar was so pleased that he was going out on his reconnaissance patrols every day was that it kept him out of her way. So long as he was off in the hills half the day, he was no threat to her authority in the settlement. She might think that was very obliging of him.

Harruel continued to go out daily, usually with Nittin or Salaman, less often with Sachkor. He had lost patience with hearing
how wonderful and beautiful Sachkor's beloved Kreun was.

The Helmet People remained invisible. For the first time
Harruel began to think, despite himself, that they might not be
there at all. Perhaps that first scout had simply been on his own,
a solitary wanderer far from the rest of his people. Or perhaps
the helmet-wearers, passing through the vicinity of Vengiboneeza
and discovering that it was occupied by Koshmar's people, had
sent him in here to see what sort of reception he would get; and
when he failed to return, they had simply moved along.

It was a hard thing to face. Secretly Harruel hoped the Helmet
People would turn up, and that they would be looking for trouble.
Or if not the Helmet People, then some other enemy—any enemy,
any enemy at all. This placid city life had made him restless to
the core. His bones ached with it. He was eager for a good lively
battle, for a fierce prolonged war.

During this tense period of unbroken peace, Harruel's mate
Minbain was brought to bed and delivered of a sturdy boy. That
pleased him, to have fathered a son. Hresh was summoned, and
did the naming-rite. Hresh gave his new half brother the birth-
name of Samnibolon, which did not please Harruel at all, for
Samnibolon had been the name of Minbain's earlier mate, Hresh's
own father. Harruel felt in some way cuckolded to have the name
return to the tribe in the person of his own son.

And it is Hresh who has done this to me, he thought angrily.

But the old man of the tribe had spoken the name, in the presence of the parents and the offering-woman, and the name was
irrevocable. Samnibolon son of Harruel it would have to be. The
gods be thanked, it was only the birth-name. When his naming-day arrived nine years from now the boy would be able to

273

choose his permanent name, and Harruel would see to it that it was something else. Still, nine years was a long time to be calling your firstborn son by a name that was a bitter reproach in your mouth. Harruel vowed he would pay Hresh back for that, someday, somehow.

It was a difficult time for Harruel: month after month of peace, and a son given a maddening name. Angers boiled and bubbled within him. It could not be long now before the cauldron boiled over.

There were few triumphs and many calamities as Hresh struggled to understand the things he had found in the ruins of Vengiboneeza.

The Great World folk—or the mechanicals who had been their artisans—had apparently intended to build their devices for all eternity. Most of them were simply constructed, strips of metal of different colors arranged in cunning patterns. They showed few signs of rust or other decay. Often they were inlaid with precious jewels that appeared to be part of the mechanism, rather than mere decorations.

In some cases operating them posed no difficulties. A few had intricate arrangements of pressure-points and levers, but most had the simplest of control panels, if they had any at all. Yet how could you tell what function a device was meant to have? Or what catastrophe you might cause by using it the wrong way?

Hresh's early experiments led to catastrophe more often than not. There was one instrument, no longer than his arm, that began weaving a web the moment he touched a coppery node on its snout. With fantastic speed it hurled thin sticky strands of a nearly unbreakable cord from its muzzle, tossing them in wild loops for thirty paces all around. Hresh released the command node as soon as he saw what was happening, but by then he had snarled Sinistine, Praheurt, and Haniman in a tight net of the stuff. It took hours to cut them free of it and it was days before their fur was completely clean.

Another device, which fortunately he tried at some distance outside the temple courtyard, seemed to turn earth into air. With one quick blast Hresh dug a pit a hundred paces across and fifteen paces deep, leaving no trace behind of what had been there, only a faint burned smell. Perhaps it was meant for clearing away rubble, or perhaps it was a weapon. In horror Hresh hid it where no one was likely to find it again.

A long narrow box with angular projections running down its side turned out to be a bridge-building machine. In the five minutes before Hresh, with some desperation, managed to switch it off, it constructed a bizarre swaybacked bridge from nowhere to nowhere, ending in midair, that filled an entire avenue of the city. For a building material it employed a stonelike substance that it created out of—so it seemed—nothing at all. A similar-looking machine proved to be a wall-builder: with the same lunatic zeal as the bridge-building device, it began at the touch of a stud to throw up high walls at random all along the street. Hresh retrieved the pit-digging machine to clear away the bridge and the walls; but despite all caution he cleared away three buildings of the avenue with them. He hoped they had been unimportant ones.

Then there were the devices that could not be made to work at all—that was most of them—and the ones that somehow looked so treacherous and unpredictable that it seemed rash even to try them. Hresh put those away for such time as he might have a clearer notion of what he was doing.

Then, too, there were the ones that would function once, and almost immediately destroy themselves. Those were the most maddening of all.

One of those set up a star-map: a sphere of soft darkness that was three times as wide as a man's body was long. On its surface all the stars of heaven were depicted in dazzling splendor. They moved as you looked at them; and if you pointed to one star with a shaft of light that came from the machine, a voice would utter a single solemn sound, which Hresh took to be the name of that star in the language of the Great World. He stared in awe and astonishment. But within five minutes curling wisps of pale smoke began coming from it and the brilliant panoply of the stars vanished in an instant, leaving Hresh gasping with the pain of irretrievable loss. He was never able to make that device work again.

Another played music: a tumultuous sky-filling music, full of heavy, clashing melodies, that brought everyone in the tribe running, as if the gods had come to Vengiboneeza and were playing in concert. It too died in smoke almost as soon as it had begun to function.

And there was one that wrote an incomprehensible message in the sky in letters of golden fire. Within moments the machine expired with a sad little sound and the wind blew the strangely fierce-looking sharp-angled characters away.

"We are ruining much and learning little," Hresh said bleakly to Taniane, one day when there had been three such disasters. But Vengiboneeza was proving to be an incredibly rich storehouse of Great World artifacts. New treasures came back with the Seekers virtually every day. It was a pity to waste any of them, Hresh knew. But perhaps a certain amount of destruction was an inevitable part of the process of learning. He had to go on with the experiments, whatever the losses, whatever the risks. It was his task. The destiny of the tribe was at stake. And perhaps his own destiny as well: for he was here not to find mere curious toys, but to discover the secrets by which the People would rule the world.

The warm wet season came round again. That was winter, and when the cool east winds ended and the heavy rains began Torlyri went forth to do the winter-offering. The sun was low in the sky every day, which was why Hresh had named this season winter; but that seemed strange to Torlyri, because the weather was so mild. Winter was supposed to be a cold time. They had called it winter, had they not, that bitter time which was just ended, the Long Winter of the world, when everything froze and all living things had had to take refuge.

But there was a difference, Torlyri was coming to see, between the Long Winter and an ordinary winter. There were great cycles and small ones. The Long Winter had been the world's dark calamity, brought by the falling death-stars, when dust and smoke in the sky had cut off the sun's rays and a terrible cold descended; but that had been an event of the great cycles, which span immense periods, carrying doom at vast and distant intervals. It had been sent from the remote heavens and all the world had fallen to its knees before it. Millions of years would pass before such a thing occurred again. Whole epochs of life would rise and fall, remembering nothing of the last Long Winter that the great cycle had brought, knowing nothing of the next catastrophe that lay far in the future.

Ordinary winter, though, was simply one of the seasons of the small cycle. It was a thing which might differ greatly in intensity from one part of the earth to another. Hresh had explained how the seasons were caused, though the idea was still hazy for her. It had something to do with the movement of the sun around the earth, or the earth around the sun, she was unsure which. There was a time of year when the sun barely reached above the horizon, and that was winter. Winter was generally cold—certainly it had been when they had crossed the plains, that first year—but in certain fortunate places winter was gentle and mild. This was one such place. That was why the sapphire-eyes, who could not stand cold, had chosen to build their great city here long ago, before the death-stars came.

And so the seasons went round. It is winter again, Torlyri thought, our warm wet Vengiboneeza winter. Time passes, and we all grow older.

The tribe was increasing rapidly. All those who had come to Vengiboneeza on the great trek from the cocoon were still alive, and the settlement was full of new children now. Those who had been children before were rising toward adulthood. Taniane, Hresh, Orbin, Haniman—they were almost old enough to be initiated into the mysteries of twining. And soon after that they would be mating. And having children of their own.

Torlyri wondered what it would be like, having a child. Feeling the life growing within her day by day. Pulsing. Pushing outward. And then to be reaching her time, lying down among the women, opening her legs to let the new one out.

She had never given much thought to mating or motherhood when she was a girl. But she had been toying with it for at least a year now. It was not an uncommon thing to think about, here in the New Springtime. There had been any number of matings among the People since the change of customs, and nearly all those who had not actually mated yet had at least flirted with the idea. Even Koshmar had joked about Torlyri's sudden playfulness with this man or with that one. But Koshmar did not seem to be seriously concerned. It was not the custom for the offering-woman to take a mate; and as for coupling, Koshmar knew that Torlyri had never had any great interest in that.

Torlyri had been chosen early to be the next offering-woman, when she was barely more than a girl. Thekmur had been chieftain then, and Gonnari the offering-woman. Those two were virtually the same age, so they would reach the limit the same month and go out the hatch within weeks of each other. Thekmur picked Koshmar to succeed her, and Gonnari chose Torlyri. For the next five years Koshmar and Torlyri, who had already become twining-partners, had undergone preparation for the great responsibilities that would be theirs; and then the death-days arrived for Thekmur and for Gonnari, and the lives of Koshmar and Torlyri changed forever.

That had been twelve years ago. Torlyri was thirty-two now, almost thirty-three. If they still were living in the cocoon, her own death-day would be only a couple of years away, and she would be busy training her own successor now. But no one spoke of limitages or death-days any longer. Torlyri would be offering-woman until death came to take her. And instead of thinking of dying, she was thinking of mating.

Strange. Very strange.

She had experimented with coupling now and then—almost everyone did, even those who had not been designated as breeders—but not very often, and not in a long time. There was said to be high pleasure in it, but Torlyri had never managed to find it. Nor displeasure, either: it had seemed merely an indifferent thing to her, a series of movements to perform with one's body, about as rewarding as kick-wrestling or arm-standing, perhaps not even that.

Her first experience of it had come when she was fourteen,

soon after her twining-day, the usual age for such initiations. Her partner was Samnibolon, later to be Minbain's mate. He came upon her in a far corner of the cocoon and beckoned to her, and held her, and stroked her dark fur, and at last she understood what it was he wanted to do. There seemed to be no harm in it. As she had seen older women do, she opened herself to him and let him put his stiff mating-rod inside her. He moved it swiftly and they rolled over and over in a tangle, and some impulse told her to draw her legs up and press her knees against his sides, which seemed to please him. After a time he grunted and released her. They lay still in each other's arms for a while. Samnibolon told her how beautiful she was and what a passionate woman she would be. That was all. He never approached her again. Not long afterward he and Minbain were mated.

A year or two later old Binigav the warrior drew her aside and asked her to couple with him; and because he was kindly and getting near to the limit-age, she did. He was tender and gentle with her, and once he had entered her he remained there a very long time, but all she felt was a vague warmth, pleasant but unexciting.

The third time was with Moarn, father of the Moarn who was a warrior of the tribe now. Moarn was already mated, so it surprised Torlyri when he reached for her after a feast. He had had too much velvetberry wine, and so had she. They grappled and embraced. Torlyri was never certain later whether they had truly coupled or not: she remembered that there had been some difficulties. Either way, it made little difference. Certainly it had not been memorable. And those were her three coupling-partners, Samnibolon, Binigav, Moarn. They were all long since dead; and she, once she had been chosen in her eighteenth year to be the next offering-woman, had never again ventured to explore such matters.

But now—now—

For weeks now, Lakkamai had been staring at her oddly. That quiet, intense, remote man: what was on his mind? No one had ever stared at her like that. His gray eyes were marked with flecks of lustrous green, which made him appear mysterious, unfathomable. He seemed to be trying to see deep inside her soul.

Whenever she glanced around suddenly, there was Lakkamai, peering toward her out of the distance. Hastily looking away, pretending he was busy with something, with anything. Sometimes she smiled at him. Sometimes she simply turned away; and when she turned toward him again, five or ten minutes later, there he was peering at her again.

She began to understand.

She found herself often looking at Lakkamai to see if he was looking at her. And then she found herself looking at Lakkamai for the sake of looking at Lakkamai, even when his back was turned to her. He was sleek and graceful and he looked strong: not strong in the thick-bodied manner of Harruel, but with a wiry, resilient power to him that reminded her of that poor Helmet Man who had died while he was being questioned by Koshmar and Hresh. Lakkamai was one of the older men of the tribe, a senior warrior, but his fur, a deep purple-brown, had not yet begun to show any gray. His face was long and sharp of chin and muzzle, his eyes were deep-set. Throughout all his days he had said very little. Small as the tribe was, intimate as life in the cocoon had been, Torlyri nevertheless had the feeling that she hardly knew him.

One night she dreamed that she was coupling with him.

It took her by surprise. In actuality she was lying with Koshmar. As it happened, they had twined that evening, for the first time in many weeks. Her mind should have been full of Koshmar while she slept. Instead Lakkamai came to her and stood silently over her, studying her intently. She beckoned to him and drew him down—he seemed to float to her side—and Koshmar disappeared and there were only the two of them on the sleeping-mat, and Lakkamai was inside her, and she felt sudden heat within her womb and knew that he had fathered a child upon her.

She gasped and woke, sitting up, trembling.

"What is it?" Koshmar asked at once. "A dream, was it?"

Torlyri shook her head. "A passing chill," she said. "The winter air brushing across my face."

She had never lied to Koshmar before.

But she had never desired a man before, either.

The next day, when Torlyri saw Lakkamai outside the temple, she could not bear to meet his eyes, so powerful was her feeling that she actually had coupled with him the night before. If the dream had been so vivid for her, he must also have felt it. It seemed to her that he must already know everything about her, the feel of her breasts in his hands, the taste of her mouth, the scent of her breath; and, old as she was, Torlyri felt suddenly like a girl, and a foolish girl at that.

That night she dreamed of Lakkamai again. She gasped and moaned and throbbed in his arms, and when she awoke Koshmar was staring at her, eyes bright in the darkness, as though she thought Torlyri was losing her mind.

On the third night the dream came again, even more real. She did things with Lakkamai that she had never seen others do while coupling, that she had never even imagined anyone would think of doing; and they gave her delight of the deepest and most intense kind.

She could not bear this any longer.

In the morning the rains that had been pelting the city for many weeks finally halted, and the bright blue winter sky burst through the clouds with the force of a trumpet-blast. Torlyri performed the sunrise-offering as she always did; and then, in utter calmness, she went to the house where the unmated warriors lived. There was a cage hanging on the porch at the corner of the building, with three small harsh-eyed black creatures in it that the warriors had caught, running around and around and crying out in angry, piercing, high-pitched tones. Torlyri gave them a sad compassionate smile.

Lakkamai was waiting outside as though expecting her. Silent as ever, seemingly at ease, he leaned back against the wall and watched her draw near. His eyes, cool and solemn, held no trace now of that fierce probing stare that he had so often turned on her of late. But the corner of his mouth was moving repeatedly in a quick short tic that betrayed inner tension. He appeared unaware of that.

"Come," Torlyri said softly. "Walk with me. The rains have relented."

Lakkamai nodded. They started off side by side, keeping so far apart that burly Harruel would have had room easily to walk between them. Past the houses of the tribe, past the entrance to the six-sided tower of purple stone that was the temple, past the garden of shrubs and flowering plants that Boldirinthe and Galihine and some of the others now maintained with such care, past the sparkling pool of pink radiance that once had given pleasure to the sapphire-eyes. Neither of them spoke. They looked straight ahead. It seemed to Torlyri that she caught sidewise glimpses of Hresh, of Konya, of Taniane, even perhaps of Koshmar, as she walked. But no one called to her and she did not turn her head to see anyone more clearly.

Beyond the garden of the women and the light-pool of the sapphire-eyes there was a second garden, a wild one, where tangled vines and crook-armed trees and strange swollen-bellied black-leaved shrubs grew in crazy profusion above a thick carpet of dense bluish moss. Here Torlyri entered, Lakkamai walking beside her, but closer now. Still neither spoke. They went inward perhaps two dozen paces, to a place where there was an opening, almost a bower, in the undergrowth. Torlyri turned now to Lakkamai and smiled; and he put his hands to her shoulders, as if to pull her downward with him to the moss, but no pulling was necessary. They descended together.

She could not say whether it was he who entered her, or she who enfolded him; but suddenly they were pressed close upon each other with their bodies joined. From the moss beneath them came a faint sighing sound. It was heavy with the stored moisture of the many days of rain, and as they moved Torlyri imagined that they were squeezing it out into the shallow declivity in which they lay, so that it was forming a pool around them. She welcomed that. Gladly would she submerge herself in that gentle warmth.

Lakkamai moved within her. She clung to him, clasping the ridged muscles beneath the thick fur of his back.

It was not quite as it had been in her dream. But it was not at all as she remembered its having been with Samnibolon and Binigav and Moarn, either. The communion was nowhere nearly as deep or as full as was twining—how could it have been?—but it was far more profound than she had ever known coupling could be. Holding tight to Lakkamai, Torlyri thought in wonder and surprise that this went beyond coupling: this must be in fact what mating is like. And in that moment of astonished realization there arose a discordant voice within her that asked, *What have I done? What will Koshmar say?*

Torlyri let the question go unanswered, and it was not repeated. She lost herself in the wondrous silence that was the soul of Lakkamai. After a time she moved free of him, and they lay a short distance apart, only their fingertips touching.

She thought of touching him with the tip of her sensing-organ, but no, no, that would be too much like twining. That would *be* twining. Koshmar, not Lakkamai, was her twining-partner. But Lakkamai was her mate.

Torlyri turned that thought over and over in her mind.

Lakkamai is my mate. Lakkamai is my mate.

She was thirty-two years old and had been the offering-woman of the tribe for a dozen years, and now, suddenly, after so long a time, she had a mate. How strange. How very strange.

On a cool bright winter day when the last storm had blown itself out to the east and the next had not yet come sweeping in from the western sea, Hresh went once more to explore the grim building he called the Citadel. It was Taniane's idea, and she went with him. Lately she had begun to accompany him on many of his journeys. Koshmar seemed to have no objection these days to his going into the ruins without a warrior to protect him. And Hresh had quickly come to accept Taniane's participation in the group of Seekers. There was still something about being close to her that made him uneasy and uncomfortable; but at the same time he felt a curious giddy pleasure at being alone with her in the distant reaches of the city.

Hresh had not wanted to return to the Citadel. He thought he knew now what it was, and he feared to know that he was right. But the strange building fascinated Taniane, and she insisted again and again, until at last he agreed. He dared not tell her why he had been keeping away. And having agreed to go, he resolved to force the mystery of the Citadel to its depths, no matter what the consequences. Tell her nothing, but let her see. Let her draw her own conclusions. Perhaps the time had come, he thought, to share some of the terrible truth that he had kept pent within himself. And perhaps Taniane was the one to try to share it with.

The path to the Citadel was a difficult one, paved with blocks of gray flagstone that had been heaved this way and that by time and earthquakes and made slippery during the winter rains by a thick furry coating of green algae. Twice Taniane lost her footing and Hresh caught her, once by the upper arm, once by her haunch and the small of her back; and his fingers tingled strangely from the contact each time. There was a stirring in his loins and in his sensing-organ. He found himself wishing she would slip a third time, but she did not.

They reached the top and stepped out onto the headland where the Citadel stood in solitary majesty overlooking Vengiboneeza. Hresh crossed the carpet of short dense thick-bladed grass that surrounded the building, going to the edge and looking out. The vast sprawl of the city lay before him, shining in the pale, milky winter light. He looked down at the broken white stubs of buildings, at delicate airy bridges that had collapsed into mounds of rubble, at roadbeds of gleaming stone shot through with livid greens and blues extending to the horizon. Taniane stood close by him, breathing harshly from the climb.

"I saw all this as it was when it was alive," Hresh said after a moment.

"Yes. Haniman told me."

"It was absolutely amazing. So many things happening at once, so many people, such energy. Amazing. And very depressing."

"Depressing?"

"I never understood what a real civilization was, before I saw the Great World. Or realized how far we are from having one. I thought it would be just like a cocoon, only a lot bigger, with more people doing more things. But that isn't it, Taniane. There's a difference in quality as well as quantity. There's a certain point at which a civilization takes off, where it begins to generate its own energy, it grows of its own accord and not simply from the actions of the people who make it up. Do you understand me at all? The tribe is too small to be like that. We have our little things to do, and we do them, and the next day we do them all over again, but there isn't the same sense of possibility, of transformation, of exploding growth. You need more people for that. Not just hundreds. You need thousands—millions—"

"We'll have that someday, Hresh."

He shrugged. "It's a long way off. There's so much work that has to be done first."

"The Great World also started small."

"Yes," he said. "I keep telling myself that."

"So that's what's been troubling your soul so much, since you came back from seeing the things you saw?"

"No," said Hresh. "That wasn't it. It was something else."

"Can you tell me?"

"No," he said. "I can't tell anyone."

She looked at him a long while without speaking. Then she smiled and touched him lightly on the shoulder. He shivered at the touch, and hoped she had not noticed.

He turned and studied the Citadel for a time. Those bare massive greenish-black walls, those gigantic stone columns, that low, heavy, sloping roof: it was a building that spoke of power and strength, of arrogance, even, of colossal self-assurance. Hresh closed his eyes and saw the tall pale furless humans of his vision drifting ghostlike through these doorless walls at the touch of a finger, as though the walls were walls of mist. How had they done that? How could he?

"Turn your back," he said.

"Why?"

"I have to do something that I don't want you to see."

"You're becoming so mysterious, Hresh."

"Please," he said.

"Are you going to do something with the Wonderstone?"

"Yes," he said, irritated.

"You don't need to hide it from me."

"Please, Taniane."

She made a wry face and turned her back to him. He reached into his sash and drew forth the Barak Dayir, and after a moment's uneasy hesitation he touched the tip of his sensing-organ to it, and heard its potent music rising through the chasms and abysses of the air to fill his soul. He began to tremble. He caught the force of the stone and tuned it and focused it, and thick whirls of red and yellow and white began to shine on the walls of the Citadel. Gateways, he thought.

"Give me your hand," he said.

"What are we going to do?"

"We're going to go inside. Give me your hand, Taniane."

She stared at him strangely and put her hand into his. The Wonderstone so amplified his sensations that her palm was like fire against his skin, and he could scarcely endure the intensity of the contact; but he found a way of tolerating it, and with a gentle tug he led her toward the nearest of the whirls of light. It yielded to his approach and he stepped through the wall without difficulty, drawing Taniane along behind him.

Inside was an immense empty space, illuminated by a dim ghostly light that sprang up everywhere without apparent source. They might have been in a cavern half the width of the world, and half a mountain high.

"Yissou's eyes," Taniane whispered. "Where are we?"

"A temple, I think."

"Whose?"

Hresh pointed. "Theirs."

Humans were moving to and fro in the air high above them, light as dust-motes. They seemed to emerge from the walls, and they traveled across the upper reaches of the huge room by twos and threes, evidently deep in conversation, to disappear on the far side. They gave no sign that they were aware of the presence of Taniane and Hresh.

"Dream-Dreamers!" she murmured. "Are they real?"

"Visions, probably. From another time. From when the city was still alive. Or else we're dreaming them." He was still clutching the Barak Dayir in his hand. He dropped it back into its pouch and slipped the pouch into his sash. At once the ghostly figures overhead vanished, and there was nothing to be seen but the four rough bare stone walls, glowing dully in the faint spectral light that they themselves emanated.

"What happened?" Taniane asked. "Where did they go?"

"It was the Wonderstone that let us see them. They weren't really here, only their images. Shining across thousands of years."

"I don't understand."

"Neither do I," said Hresh.

He took a few cautious steps, going to the wall at the place where they had entered and running his hand over the stone. It felt utterly unyielding, and faintly warm, like the Barak Dayir itself. A shiver ran along his spine. There was nothing in the great room, nothing at all, no shattered images, no toppled thrones, no sign of any occupants.

"I feel peculiar here," Taniane said. "Let's go."

"All right."

He turned away from her and drew forth the Wonderstone again, not bothering to hide it from her this time. She stared and made the sign of Yissou. The moment he touched it the walls began to blaze with light once more, and the eerie procession of the airborne humans was restored. He saw Taniane gaping at them in wonder. "Dream-Dreamers," she said again. "They look just like him. Ryyig. Who were they?"

Hresh said nothing.

"I think I know," she said.

"Do you?"

"It's a crazy idea, Hresh."

"Then don't tell me."

"Tell me what *you* think, then."

"I'm not sure," Hresh said. "I'm not sure of anything."

"You're thinking what I'm thinking."

"Perhaps," he said. "Perhaps not."

"We're thinking the same thing. I'm frightened, Hresh."

He saw her fur rising, and her breasts beginning to stir. He wished he dared to draw her close against him and hold her.

"Come," he said. "We've been in here long enough."

He took her hand again and led her through the gateway in the wall. When they were outside they looked back, and then at each other, without saying a word. He had never seen Taniane so shaken. And in his own mind that strange procession of Dream-Dreamer folk still drifted through the air above him, mysterious, tantalizing, magical, telling him once again the thing that he did not want to hear.

In silence they made their way down the slippery, tormented flagstone path. They said nothing to each other all the way back to the settlement.

As they approached it they heard angry shouts, loud cries, the high mocking cries of jungle monkeys. The place was full of them, dozens of them, swinging and capering through the rooftops.

"What's going on?" Hresh asked, as Boldirinthe ran by waving a spear.

"Can't you see?"

Weiawala, coming along behind her, paused to explain. The monkeys had come carrying the papery nests of insects of some sort. The nests broke when they hit the ground, releasing swarms of shining long-legged red nuisances with jagged nippers that dug deep. When they bit it burned like hot coals, and they couldn't be pulled free, only pried out with knives. The bugs were all over the settlement, and so were the monkeys, screeching and laughing high above, and occasionally tossing down yet another nest. The whole tribe was busy trying to drive them away and to round up the stinging things.

It was hours before the settlement was calm again. By then, no one seemed to care where he had been or what he had done. Later that evening he saw Taniane sitting by herself, staring into the remote distance; and when Haniman went over to her to say something she shook him off angrily and left the room.

There was a sawtooth ridge halfway up the slope of Mount Springtime that Harruel often used as a lookout point when he was standing sentry duty over Vengiboneeza. It hung above the flank of the mountain like a terrace, so that when he looked upslope he had a view down into the saddle that any invading force would have to cross as it descended from the summit. From there also, looking the other way, he could see all of Vengiboneeza spread out below him like its own map.

There he sometimes sat, hour after hour, even in the rain, perched in the fork of an enormous shiny-barked tree with triangular red leaves. He had begun going alone to the mountain again these days. His recruits, his soldiers, had become mere annoyances to him, for he could see the impatience in them, their disbelief that invaders ever would come.

Dark thoughts came to him often, now. He felt caught in some kind of dream in which no one was able to move. The months, even the years, were passing, and he was trapped in this old ruined city the way he once had been trapped in the cocoon. Somehow in the cocoon it had not mattered to him that each day was exactly like the day before. But here, with all the world gleaming just beyond his reach, Harruel felt seething impatience. He had come to understand that he had been born for great things. When would he begin to achieve them, though? When? When?

During the long rainy spell these feelings built in him until they became all but unendurable. He spent entire days in his forked tree, drenched, soggy, furious. He glared at the tribal settlement below him at the city's edge and roared his contempt for its dull pallid people. He glared at the mountain above him and screamed defiance at the invaders who obstinately refused to come. He grew stiff and sore. His body ached and his mind throbbed. Now and then he descended and plucked fruits from the nearby bushes. More than once he caught some small animal with his bare hands, and killed it and ate it raw.

He stayed crouched in his tree all one night long, though the rain came without a break in great heavy drops. What was the use of going home? Minbain was busy with her little one; she had no interest in coupling these days. And the rain, at least, cooled his anger somewhat.

In the morning sunlight struck him suddenly, like a slap across the mouth. Harruel blinked groggily and stared and sat up, wondering where he was. Then he remembered that he had slept in the tree.

For one startled moment he thought he saw golden-spiked helmets all along the jagged rim of the ridge to his left. The invasion at last? No. No. Only the morning light, low along the horizon, cutting through the droplets of water that glistened on every leaf.

He swung himself to the ground and went limping off toward the city to see about something to eat.

A figure came into view when he was about halfway down the mountain. He thought at first it might be Salaman or Sachkor, coming to look for him now that the rain had ended. But no: this was a woman. A girl. She was tall and slim, with fur of an unusual deep black hue. Harruel recognized her after a moment as young Kreun, Sachkor's beloved, the daughter of old Thalippa. She was waving to him, calling.

"I'm looking for Sachkor! Is he with you?"

Harruel stared, making no reply. He had coupled once with Thalippa, many years ago. A hot one, Thalippa had been, back then. After all this time the memory of it came gliding up out of the depths of his mind. She had scratched him with her claws, Thalippa had. He remembered the strong sweet musky odor of her. Amazing, after fifteen years, remembering that. Half his life ago.

"Nobody knows where he is," Kreun said. "He was here yesterday morning, and then he vanished. I went to the place where all the young men stay, but he wasn't there. Salaman thought he might be up here on the mountain with you."

Harruel shrugged. At another time all that might have mattered. But now a strange spell gripped his spirit.

"It's been such a long time, Thalippa."

"What?"

"Come here. Come closer. Let me look at you. Thalippa."

"I'm Kreun. Thalippa's my mother."

"Kreun?" he said, as if he had never heard the name before. "Oh. Yes. Kreun."

He felt red heat between his legs, and a terrible numbing ache. Days and days in that tree, and now a whole night too, sitting up there in the rain. Guarding these foolish people, these silly heedless people. Protecting them against an enemy they refused even to believe in. While the days of his life went idly ticking by, and all the world was waiting for his embrace.

"Is something wrong with you, Harruel? You look so peculiar."

"Thalippa—"

"No, I'm Kreun!" And now she was backing away from him, looking frightened.

Sachkor was right to babble so much about her. Kreun was very beautiful. Those long slender legs, that deep rich fur, the bright green eyes now sparkling with fear. Odd that he had never noticed that, how good-looking Kreun was; but of course she was young, and one paid no attention to girls until they had reached twining-age. She was a marvel. Minbain was warm and good and loving but she had left her beauty years behind her. Kreun was just growing into hers.

"Wait," Harruel called.

Kreun halted, frowning, uncertain. He stumbled down the path toward her. As he drew near she gasped and tried to run, but he reached out with his sensing-organ and caught her about the throat. There was a tingling coming from her: he felt it and it redoubled his frenzy. Easily he pulled her toward him, grabbed her by the shoulder, threw her facedown on the wet ground.

"No—please—" she cried.

She tried to crawl away, but she stood no chance against him. He fell on top of her and gripped her arms from behind. The heat in his loins was unbearable now. Somewhere deep within his mind a quiet voice insisted that what he was doing was wrong, that a woman must not be taken against her will, that the gods would exact a price from him for this. But it was impossible for Harruel to fight the fury, the rage, the need that had overwhelmed him. He pressed his thighs against her smooth furry rump, and thrust. She uttered a thick cry of pain and horror. "It is my right," Harruel said to her, over and over, as he moved against her. "I am the king. It is my right."

10

The River and the Precipice

Koshmar said, "so it is to be Lakkamai for you, is it?"

It was the third day since the end of the time of rains. Koshmar and Torlyri were together in the house they shared, at nightfall, after dinner, when all the tribe had gathered to observe the midwinter ceremony of the Provider: all but the mysteriously absent Sachkor, for whom daily searches were now being undertaken.

Torlyri, who had been lounging, sat swiftly upright. Koshmar had never seen such an expression on Torlyri's face before: fear, and a kind of sheepish guilt, and something close to defiance, all mixed together.

"You know?" she said.

Koshmar laughed harshly. "Who doesn't? Do you think I'm a child, Torlyri? The two of you making eyes at each other all over the settlement for weeks—and you, mentioning Lakkamai's name in every third thing you say, you who could go a year and a half without ever once having occasion to speak of him—"

Torlyri looked down, abashed. "Are you angry with me, Koshmar?"

"Do I sound angry? That you should be happy?" But in fact Koshmar was troubled more than she had imagined she would be. She had known for a long while that something like this was coming, and had told herself that she would be strong when it did. But now that it was here, it was like a huge weight on her heart. She said, after a moment, "You've been coupling with him already, have you?"

"Yes." Torlyri could barely be heard.

"You used to do that, a long time ago, when we were girls. It was Samnibolon you did it with, I recall. Minbain's Samnibolon, am I right?"

Torlyri nodded. "And one or two others, yes. But I was very young then. It has been an extremely long time."

"And you find pleasure in it?"

"I do now," said Torlyri softly. "There was nothing for me in it, those times long ago. But there is now."

"Great pleasure?"

"Sometimes," said Torlyri, huskily, guiltily.

"I am very glad for you," Koshmar said, her voice high and tight. "I never could see the sense of coupling, you know. But they tell me it has its rewards."

"Perhaps it must be done with just the right person."

Koshmar snorted. "For me there is no right person, and you know it! If you were a man, Torlyri, I'd couple gladly with you, I think. But we have our twining, you and I. We have our twining, and that's sufficient for me. A chieftain doesn't need coupling."

Nor does an offering-woman, Koshmar added silently.

She glanced away so that Torlyri would not see the thought in her eyes. She had sworn not to interfere with what Torlyri was doing, however painful it might become for her.

Torlyri said, "Speaking of twining—"

"Yes, speak of twining, Torlyri! Speak of it anytime." Sudden eagerness made Koshmar's breath come quickly. The deeper Torlyri's involvement with Lakkamai became, the more eager Koshmar was for any token of affection from her. "Now? Right now? Certainly. Come."

Torlyri looked surprised and perhaps not pleased. "If you wish, of course, Koshmar. But that was not what I was starting to say."

"Oh?"

"It's time for Hresh's twining-day, is what I was beginning to tell you. If I can manage to get him away from his machines and his Wonderstone long enough, I have to take him aside for his initiation."

"Already," Koshmar said, shaking her head. "Hresh's twining-day."

That was one of the offering-woman's tasks, to initiate the young people into the way of twining, and Torlyri had always performed it with great care and love. Koshmar had never minded all those shared twinings, though twining was so much more intimate than coupling. Initiating the young was Torlyri's god-given task. If any of this made sense, Koshmar thought, I should be more troubled by her twining with Hresh than by her coupling with Lakkamai. Yet it is the other way around. Torlyri's twining with the young was no threat to her. But her coupling with Lakkamai—her coupling with Lakkamai—

Coupling is nothing, Koshmar thought angrily.

She told herself that she was being illogical. And then she told herself that all these matters were far beyond logic. The heart has a logic of its own, she told herself.

"Taniane has had her first twining, and Orbin, and now it is Hresh's time," Torlyri said. "And then Haniman."

"How fast time moves. Sometimes I still think of him as that mischievous boy who tried to slip past you through the hatch, that day when the ice-eaters came and the Dream-Dreamer awoke. That strange day seems terribly long ago. And so does Hresh's boyhood."

"This has all been so odd," said Torlyri. "For the old man of the tribe to have been someone not even old enough to twine."

"Do you think it will change him, once he begins?"

"Change him? How so?"

"We depend on him so much," Koshmar said. "There's such wisdom in that strange little head of his. But children change, sometimes, when they first begin to twine. Have you forgotten that, Torlyri? And Hresh is only a child still. That is something we must never let ourselves forget. Once he finds a twining-partner he may give himself up to nothing but twining for many months, and what will happen to the exploration of Vengiboneeza? He might even begin showing interest in coupling."

Torlyri said, with a shrug, "And if he did? Would that be so bad?"

"He has responsibilities, Torlyri."

"He's a boy just becoming a man. Do you mean to take his youth away from him? Let him twine all he likes. Let him couple, if that's what he wants. Let him mate, even."

"Mate? The chronicler, taking a mate?"

"This is the New Springtime, Koshmar. There's no need to hold him to old customs."

"The old man should not mate," Koshmar said stiffly. "No more than the chieftain or the offering-woman. Twine, yes. Couple, if coupling is desired. But take a *mate*? How can that be? We are selected by the gods as people apart from others." Koshmar shook her head. "We've strayed from our subject. How soon are you planning to do Hresh's initiation?"

"Two days. Three. If he has no duties which will get in the way."

"Good," said Koshmar. "Do it as soon as you can. Tell me when you do. And then we must watch him, to see that he does not change."

Torlyri said, smiling, "I'm sure he'll be no different afterward. Remember that he has the Barak Dayir, Koshmar. What can twining do for him that the Wonderstone has not already done fiftyfold?"

"Perhaps. Perhaps."

There was a long moment of awkward silence.

"Koshmar?" said Torlyri, at last.

"Yes?"

Torlyri hesitated. "Do you still want to twine?"

"Of course," said Koshmar, softening, becoming eager.

"Before we do, one more question."

"Go on."

"The offering-woman, you said, should not mate."

Koshmar stared. This was something entirely new. She had not realized the situation was so bad.

"It has never been done," she said coolly. "Not the chieftain, nor the old man, nor the offering-woman. Coupling, yes, if they wished. And twining, certainly. But never mating. Never. We are people apart."

"Yes. Yes, I know."

There was a silence again, an ugly one.

Koshmar said at length, "Are you asking for permission to take Lakkamai as your mate, Torlyri?"

"We would like to take each other as our mates, yes," said Torlyri cautiously.

"You are asking permission of me."

Torlyri regarded her with a steady gaze. "It is the New Spring-time, Koshmar."

"Do you mean to say that you think not even my permission is needed? Say what's on your mind, Torlyri! Say what is in your soul!"

"I have never felt things like this before."

"No doubt that's true," said Koshmar sharply.

"What shall I do, Koshmar?"

"Perform your services to the gods and to the people," Koshmar said. "Take Hresh for his initiation. Make the daily offerings. Bring your goodness to those about you, as you always have."

"And Lakkamai?"

"Do as you wish with Lakkamai."

A third time Torlyri fell into silence. Koshmar allowed it to go on and on. Finally Torlyri said, "Do you want to twine with me now, Koshmar?"

"Another time," Koshmar said. "In truth I'm very weary this evening, and I think it would not be a good twining." She turned away. Bleakly she said, "I wish you joy, Torlyri. You understand that, don't you? I wish you nothing but joy."

Now Hresh began going into the ruins by himself, as if daring Koshmar to object; but she seemed not to care, or perhaps not even to notice. More often than not the Great World was his destination. The squat many-levered machine in the vault beneath the tower in the plaza of the thirty-six towers held an irresistible appeal.

By now he knew that the floating slab of stone that took him down to the lower-level vault would return automatically to the level above after a certain span of time; and so he no longer needed to bring Haniman or anyone else with him to operate the mechanism when he made his descents. Whatever risks there might be, he was willing to accept them for the sake of keeping others from sharing his journeys to the distant past. The Great World was his private treasure-trove, to mine as he pleased.

The procedure was the same every time. Activate the black stone slab; descend to the machine; grasp the Barak Dayir with his sensing-organ; seize the levers. And the Great World would spring to life, vivid and astonishing.

He never entered it at the same point twice. The physical structure of the city was different every time. It was as though all the long history of fabulous Vengiboneeza lay stored up in the machine, all its hundreds of thousands of years of growth and transformation, and it would randomly offer him any slice of the past that it wished, sometimes an early Vengiboneeza barely beginning its glittering expansion, sometimes a version of the city that surely must date from one of the final years, so close to the layout of the ruins was it.

There was no better evidence of how energetic and dynamic a place Vengiboneeza had been than the constant change Hresh observed in it. Only occasionally did he see any familiar landmarks—the waterfront boulevards, the thirty-six towers of the plaza, the tower that had become the temple of the People, the districts of villas on the mountainsides. Sometimes they were there, sometimes not. The squat potent Citadel was the only changeless and invulnerable place, whenever Hresh's soul soared back across the gulf of the ages.

On one occasion he might vanish into a time when tall white palisades rose like spears along the streets of the lower part of town, and the city was full of sea-lords, parading up from the quay by the scores in their gleaming silver chariots. Another time, banners of some intangible force, a crackling tumult of colored lights, would be whirling overhead, and a vast procession of hjjk-folk would be winding down into the mountain, unimaginable millions of them filing one by one into the city, which absorbed them as though its capacity were infinite. Or there would be some convocation of humans in progress—he grudgingly conceded now that that was what they were, for he saw little alternative, though still he hoped desperately that he had misinterpreted the evidence he had found—seventy or eighty of the hairless thin-limbed ones sitting in a wide circle in a central plaza of the city just below the Citadel. They were exchanging silent thoughts from which he was utterly excluded, however hard he tried to penetrate their mysteries.

But mainly Vengiboneeza was a city of the sapphire-eyes. They dominated it. For every ten members of the other races that Hresh saw, there might be a hundred of the reptilians, or a thousand. He saw them wherever he looked, heavy-thighed, long-jawed, monstrous of form, brilliant of eye, radiating strength and wisdom and contentment.

It was easy enough for Hresh to enter into conversations with those he met in Vengiboneeza, even sea-lords, even humans. Everyone understood him and everyone was unfailingly courteous. But gradually he came to understand that these were not real conversations. They were polite illusions engendered by the machine that was his gateway to the past. He was not actually there in the Great World that had died seven hundred thousand years before under the onslaught of the death-stars, but was, rather, enmeshed in some projection, some facsimile, which had all the semblance of life and which drew him into itself as though he were an actual wayfarer in that huge city.

This became apparent because he went among its inhabitants full of questions, as usual. But somehow the answers that he received had no substance. They appeared to hold meaning, but it would slip away into nothingness even as it entered his mind, like the food one enjoys in the banquets of dreams. He could not learn anything by questioning those whom he encountered on the streets of lost Vengiboneeza. It was truly lost, and cut off from him by the terrible barrier of time.

Still, what he saw dazzled and enriched him, and filled him with awe for the splendor of what had been.

The sapphire-eyes seemed to appear and disappear in old Vengiboneeza as they pleased, winking in and out of being with astonishing ease. *Pop* and they were here, *pop* and they were gone again.

For travel outside the city they had another wondrous thing, sky-chariots like shimmering pink-and-gold bubbles that came floating down without a sound and released their passengers from hatches opening magically in their sides. Hresh saw hundreds of these bubbles overhead, moving silently and swiftly. They never collided, though they often seemed to come close. Within them sat sapphire-eyes, in positions of ease.

A third means of travel—if indeed travel was what it was—was available at enigmatic devices mounted on small platforms of sleek green stone. These were narrow vertical tubes of dark metal, about as tall as a full-grown man, widening at their upper ends into hooded open-faced spheres no larger than a man's head. A strange fierce light, blue and red and green, played about the openings of these spheres as though emanating from some powerful apparatus within.

From time to time a sapphire-eyes, moving even more sedately and calmly than usual, would approach one of the platforms on which these tubes were stationed. Generally others of its kind would accompany it, walking close alongside, sometimes letting their little forearms rest against its heavy body. But always these companions would move away, allowing the departing sapphire-eyes to ascend the platform alone. It would draw near the sphere atop the tube until its great-jawed face was shining with the light that came from it; and then it would suddenly be drawn inside. Hresh could not see how that was accomplished, nor how there might be room for the immense bulk of a sapphire-eyes within that small glowing sphere. Never could he detect the moment when the transition was made, when the sapphire-eyes that stood peering into the sphere was swept from sight.

Whatever voyage the sapphire-eyes had undertaken was evidently a one-way journey: many went into the spheres atop the tubes, but Hresh never saw anyone emerge.

It appeared that none of these devices had survived into the modern-day Vengiboneeza. Hresh saw them only in his visions. In the real ruined Vengiboneeza he was unable even to find traces of the green stone platforms on which the tubes had been mounted.

After observing the rite of the hooded sphere many times, Hresh finally resolved to approach one of them himself. His dreaming spirit entered a deserted plaza on a moonless night. A tree stood nearby, its branches bowed down under the weight of enormous wedge-shaped brown nuts, each one bigger across than the span of his two hands. He made a heap of these, piling them high enough so that he could see into the sphere's opening. It was a difficult business. The nuts, packed edge to edge, kept slipping and sliding beneath him, and he had to grip the hood of the sphere to keep from falling. Holding tight, he put his head close to the opening.

He knew there was danger in this. He might be drawn in and swept away—where? To another world? To the home of the gods? Or he might be destroyed altogether, for he had begun to suspect that the sapphire-eyes used these devices to end their lives, when their death-day finally had come. But the temptation to look within one was irresistible. And he told himself that this was only a vision. How could he be harmed by a device that had no real existence, that had ceased to exist at least seven hundred thousand years before he was born?

But if you are not really here, a voice within him said, then how is it you were able to pull those nuts from the tree and pile them up like this?

Hresh brushed the question aside and looked within.

There was a strange thing at the heart of the hooded sphere: a zone of utter darkness, so black that it gave off a kind of light beyond light. He stared at it, dazzled, and knew that he was looking not merely into another world but into some other universe, something outside the domain of the gods entirely. Though the black zone was very small—he supposed that he could enclose it in the palm of one hand—there was a great power to it. They have captured little pieces of that other universe, he imagined, and installed them in these round metal containers; and when they wish to leave the realm of the gods they approach one of the containers and the blackness scoops them up and carries them off.

He waited calmly for it to carry him off. The spell of the thing held him completely. Let it take him where it would.

But it took him nowhere. He stared at it until his eyes hurt; and then two figures appeared out of the shadows, a sapphire-eyes and a vegetal, and beckoned to him.

"Come away from there," the vegetal said, in its whispering, rustling way. "There's danger there, little one."

306

"Danger? Where? I can put my head right in it, and nothing happens."

"Come away, all the same."

"I will, if you'll explain to me what this is."

The vegetal folded its petals; the sapphire-eyes laughed its hissing laugh. Then they explained the device to him, both of them speaking at once, and he understood perfectly what they said, at least so long as they were speaking. What they told him left him rapt with wonder; but it was like everything else he heard while visiting the Great World, no more nourishing than dream-food, and such meaning as it might have had in the first moment of its telling slipped away from him at once, hard as he struggled to hold to it.

He stepped down from the platform, and they led him away toward a place of lights and singing. The only thing he could remember afterward was something he had concluded for himself, and not anything they had told him. Which was that these were the devices that the people of the Great World employed to end their lives, when they knew that the time had come for them to die.

Why would they want to die? he asked himself. And had no answer.

Then he thought: they knew the death-stars were coming. And yet they stayed here, and let them come.

Why would they have done that?

And had no answer for that, either.

There was a place in the city of Hresh's visions where the whole world stood portrayed against the sky. A flat metal disk of a bright silvery metal was mounted at an angle in the outer wall of a low ten-sided building; and when he touched a knob beside it a shaft of piercing brightness came down out of somewhere and struck it, and a huge globe of the world sprang into brilliant life before him. He knew at once that this was the world, because he had seen pictures of it in the chronicles. Those pictures were flat, and this was round, but he knew it was the world because that was how the chronicles said the world really was. Hresh had never imagined there would be so much of it. He could walk completely around the globe that represented it, and there were places on every side. He saw four great landmasses, separated by vast seas. Vast sprawling cities were shown, laced with highways like rivers of light, and lakes and rivers, and mountains and plains. Even though this was only an image in the air, Hresh could feel the surging power of the mighty seas and the immense weight of the mountains, and when he looked at the representations of the cities he had the illusion that he saw tiny figures moving about on tiny streets.

One of the landmasses was gigantic, filling nearly an entire face of the world. When he went around to the globe's other side he saw two more, one above the other, and the fourth was at the bottom of the world, an icy place from which came a perceptible chill.

"Where is Vengiboneeza?" Hresh asked, and a dazzling green light appeared near the left-hand side of the uppermost landmass on the side of the globe that had two.

"And Thisthissima?" he asked. "Mikkimord? Tham?"

As fast as he could name other cities of the Great World, they sprang into light, and the globe turned to display them. Then his little store of names was exhausted, and he ordered the globe to show him every city all at once. It obeyed instantly; and so many blazing points of light sprang out on the globe, and it turned so rapidly, that he shrank back, blinded for the moment, covering his eyes in terror. When he dared to look again the globe was gone.

He never tried to summon it a second time. But the image of that round world with its immense seas and its colossal landmasses speckled everywhere with the blinding light of a myriad cities would remain with him forever. And he understood how great the Great World in fact had been.

Something else that showed him the immensity of what had been lost was a structure that he guessed to be the Tree of Life, of which Thaggoran had sometimes spoken.

It was not really a tree at all, but more of a tunnel, or set of tunnels, for it lay horizontally upon the ground for many hundreds of paces in an open parklike space. Its floor was below ground level, and it was roofed over with arches of some absolutely clear material, so that it did not appear to have a roof at all. A great central gallery was at its core, from which smaller passageways branched, and even smaller ones from those.

At the tip of each branch was a round chamber; and in each of those chambers a little family of animals lived, each in what must have been its natural surroundings, for some chambers were dry and desertlike, others were lush with moist foliage. It was possible to walk through the Tree of Life past branch after branch without disturbing the creatures in it in any way.

Hresh had seen no animals like these when the tribe was crossing the plains. But they resembled some that he had seen depicted in the Book of the Beasts in the chronicles. So these must be the creatures that had dwelled in the world before the coming of the death-stars: the lost animals, the vanished denizens of the former world.

There were huge slow ambling black-and-red ones with horns like trumpets that opened into wide bells at the tips, and there were delicate long-legged ones with pale yellow fur and round, startled eyes as big across as Hresh's hand, and there were fierce little low squat ones that seemed to be all snout and teeth and claws. There was something tawny with black stripes that waded in a marsh, standing high above it on four scrawny legs, and swooped down with its long neck and long toothy beak to snatch hapless green creatures from the mud.

There were round drumlike animals that made jovial booming sounds with their distended blue bellies. There were snakelike things with triple heads. There were shy huge-eared little beasts that were covered with green moss and thickets of small flat leaves, so that Hresh could not tell whether they were animals or plants.

He wandered wonderstruck through all these chambers, astounded by the abundance and complexity. A deep sadness came over him at the thought that all these beasts probably were gone from the world now, unless somehow they had been set aside in some cocoon to wait out the cold centuries. He doubted that. They all were gone, gone with the sapphire-eyes.

In a chamber near the uttermost tip of the Tree of Life he came to something that took him totally by surprise: a group of what seemed to be people of his kind, going about their lives in what appeared to be a miniature version of his old tribal cocoon.

They were not exactly like him. At first glance they seemed the same; but when Hresh looked more carefully he saw that their sensing-organs were thinner and hung at a different angle, that their ears were large and set back on their heads in a way that looked very odd to him, that their fur was exceptionally dense and very coarse. The adults were shorter than the adults of his tribe and their bodies were not as stocky. Their hands joined their wrists at a strange angle and had fingers that were long and black and palms that were bright red, not pink as Hresh's were.

He felt his chest constrict. This was a devastating revelation.

It was as though they were an earlier version of the People, a first attempt. They were as much unlike him as they were like. But he could not deny the similarities. The kinship. These were people of his own kind. They had to be. But they were ancient. This was the way the People had looked in the time of the Great World.

It said in the Book of the Beasts that Dawinno the Destroyer constantly altered the forms of all the creatures of the world. The changes were so small that from one generation to the next they could scarcely be observed, but over the great span of time they mounted up into significant differences. Now Hresh saw the proof of that. The race that had emerged from the cocoons at the end of the Long Winter was much different from the one that had entered them seven hundred thousand years before.

A deeper and more staggering truth lay behind that one. He would have hidden from it if he could. But it was inescapable.

Beyond much doubt the Tree of Life was nothing more than a collection of animals, assembled here, perhaps, for the amusement of the citizens of Vengiboneeza. There were no sea-lords here, no hjjks, no vegetals, none of any of the civilized peoples of the Great World: only simple beasts. And his own ancestors were here among those beasts.

Hresh's muscles writhed in angry protest. But there was no way he could reject the evidence. Step by step, this city had forced him to admit the thing that he had been struggling to deny since the People first had come to Vengiboneeza: that in the time of the Great World his own race had not been considered human at all, but mere beasts, not to be ranked with the Six

Peoples. Superior beasts, perhaps. But beasts nevertheless, that could be kept on display like this, one exhibit among many in this place where all the animals of the ancient world had been displayed.

He felt stunned and shaken and crushed. For a long time he stood in numb silence, staring. The people in the chamber—the *creatures* in the chamber—those beasts who were his kin— ignored him. Perhaps none of the animals on exhibit in the Tree of Life were able to see those who came to see them.

He waved to them. He drummed on the clear wall of their chamber. In a hoarse, ragged, defiant voice he called to them, "I am Hresh your brother! I have come to tell you good tidings, that your children's children's children will inherit the world!" But the words came out in a jumble, and the creatures in the chamber never once looked up.

After a time he crept away and wandered outside to the boulevard. He saw the green Citadel of the Dream-Dreamer folk crouching above him on the hill. Somber as it was, it blazed at him now with the fury of a thousand suns. He turned away from it, flinching. That was a place for humans. He knew that beyond question now. Their temple, their hostelry, their special headquarters, whatever. *Their* place, he thought. Not ours. A place for humans. And whatever we may think we are, we are not that.

Once more he imagined that he heard the awful hissing laughter of the guardians of the city gate.

Little monkey. Little monkey. Never confuse yourselves with humans, child.

He let the vision fade, and came up out of old Vengiboneeza like a drowning man flailing his way to the surface of the water.

When he returned to the settlement he said nothing to anyone,

312

not even Taniane, about what he had seen. But he felt strangely
transparent to her. She stared at him from a distance in a remote,
veiled way, as though telling him, *There's a terrible secret that you
don't dare share with me, but I know it anyway.* In his confusion
and grief he kept his distance from her for several days, and when
they spoke again it was of trivial things only, a vague and carefully
circumscribed conversation. He was unable to bear anything else
just now, and she appeared to know that.

A few days later the wild monkeys of the jungle swept through
the settlement again, howling and shrieking, smashing windows,
hurling gobbets of mud and dung and more of the nests of the
stinging insects. Hresh glared at the intruders with loathing and
fury. Everything within his soul cried out against the idea that the
People and these dirty screaming animals could possibly be close
kin, as the sapphire-eyes artificials had claimed. But when Staip
and Konya went to a rooftop and speared half a dozen of them
Hresh turned away, shivering in shock, fighting back tears. He
could not bear to see them killed like that. It seemed like murder.
He did not know what to think. It seemed to him that he was
unable to understand anything any more.

Minbain was at work in the fields, setting out the new season's young flameseed plants, when Torlyri came up to her and
said, "I'm trying to find Hresh. Do you have any idea where he
might be?"

Minbain laughed. "On the moon, maybe. Or swimming from
one star to the next. Who knows where Hresh takes himself? Not
me, Torlyri."

"I suppose he's wandering around in the ruins again."

"I suppose. I haven't laid eyes on him in two or three days." Minbain had long since ceased to think of Hresh as any child of hers. He was a being beyond her comprehension, as swift and strange and unpredictable as the lightning. She returned her attention to the flameseed bed. After a moment she looked up again and said, "You haven't seen Harruel, by any chance, have you? It's been a while since I've laid eyes on *him*, too."

"Doesn't he spend a lot of time patrolling in the hills?"

"Too much," Minbain said. "If he's with me one night out of five, that's a lot. There's something bad brewing in that man."

"Shall I speak with him? If I can help him in any way—"

"Be wary if you try it. He frightens me these days. Anger comes boiling out of him when you're least expecting it. And stranger things. He moans in his sleep, he thrashes about, he calls out to the gods. I tell you, Torlyri, he frightens me. And yet I wish he'd spend more of his nights at home." With a grin she said, "There are some things about him I miss very much."

"I think I know what you mean," said Torlyri, smiling.

"Why do you want Hresh? Has he done something wrong again?"

"It's his twining-day," Torlyri said.

"His twining-day!" Minbain looked up, astonished. "Imagine that! So Hresh is old enough to twine already! How time moves along! And I paid no attention." Then she shook her head. "Ah, Torlyri, Torlyri—if Hresh is old enough to twine, how old I must be getting, then!"

"Don't give it any thought. You carry your years well, Minbain."

"Yissou be praised for that."

Once more Minbain returned to her task.

Torlyri said, "If I run into Harruel, I'll tell him you'd like to see him now and then."

"And I'll do the same, if I run into Hresh."

314

*   *   *

The wound that had been inflicted on him at the Tree of Life was a long time healing. Hresh told himself that he would never go to the vault of the thirty-six towers again, that he would make no more journeys to the living Vengiboneeza. But as the days passed his innate curiosity began gradually to reassert itself, and he knew he would not keep his vow for long; but he swore that if he happened to stumble upon the Tree of Life a second time when he did go back, he would not set foot in it. He had no desire ever again to see that place where his ancestors had been penned like the beasts that they were, for the delight and instruction of civilized people.

When he did go back, he saw no sign of the place where the Tree of Life had been. Once again the city was much transformed, and of buildings that he recognized from his earlier visits there were only the Citadel and a handful of others. He felt great relief at that; for he suspected that if he had found the Tree of Life again, he would have entered it, despite his oath, despite everything.

Torlyri said, "There you are! I've been hunting for you all morning!"

Hresh, muddy and disheveled, came ambling toward her down the wide curving boulevard that led from the Emakkis Boldirinthe sector in the northern part of the city. He wore a remote, abstracted expression, the look of someone who was half in this world and half in some other.

He turned toward Torlyri as if he had no idea who she was. His eyes did not quite meet hers. "Am I late for something?"

"Do you know what day this is?"

315

10000000001000

"Friit?" he said hazily. "No, it's Mueri. I'm sure it's Mueri."

"It's your twining-day," Torlyri said, laughing.

"Today?"

"Today, yes." She held her arms out to him. "It's that unimportant to you, is it?"

Hresh hung back, looking down at his feet. He began to inscribe patterns in the soft earth with his left big toe. "I thought tomorrow was the day," he said in a low, anguished voice. "Honestly. Honestly, Torlyri!"

She recalled him that time on the ledge outside the hatch of the cocoon, trembling in the cold air, begging her not to tell Koshmar that he had tried to slip outside. He was years older now, very different, sobered by his responsibilities within the tribe; and yet he really had not changed at all, had he? Not in any essential way. He was almost a man, no longer a wild frightened boy, Hresh-of-the-answers now, keeper of the chronicles, leader of the Seekers, surely the wisest member of the tribe, and yet he remained Hresh-full-of-questions too, willful, unpredictable, ungovernable. Forgetting his own twining-day! Only Hresh would be capable of something like that.

She had told him, three days before, to make himself ready for his final initiation into adulthood. That meant fasting, purging, chanting, contemplation. Had he done any of that? Probably not. Hresh's priorities were determined only by Hresh.

If he has not made himself ready, she thought, how can he hope to attempt his first twining? Even he, even Hresh, must prepare himself properly. Even he.

She said, "You look strange. You've been using the Great World's machines again, haven't you?"

He nodded.

"And seen some disturbing things?"

316

"Yes," he said.

"Do you want to tell me about them?"

Quickly Hresh shook his head. "Not really."

He still had that not-entirely-here expression in his eyes. His gaze was aimed at a point somewhere beyond her left shoulder, as though he were politely tolerating this conversation without being in any significant way part of it. He was lost in some pain Torlyri could not begin to comprehend. She became more and more certain that it would be a mistake to take him for his first twining today.

But she could try to ease his pain, at least.

She reached toward him, touched him, sent energy and warmth to him. Hresh continued to look off into the distance. Something was twitching and throbbing in one of his cheeks.

After a moment he said, as though speaking from very far away, "I can see the past all around me as we stand here. The old Vengiboneeza that was. Vengiboneeza of Great World times." His voice was oddly husky. His lower lip trembled. For the first time now he looked straight at her, and she saw strangeness in his eyes, and fear such as she had never seen in them before. "Sometimes, Torlyri, I don't know where I am. Or *when*. The ancient city lies over this one like a mask. It rises like a vision, like a dream. And I become frightened. I've never been really frightened by anything before, do you know, Torlyri? I just want to learn things. There can't be anything frightening about that. But sometimes I see things when I go into Vengiboneeza that—that—" He faltered. "The ancient city comes to life for me. When it does that it lies over the ruined one like a shining golden mask, a mask so beautiful that it terrifies me. Then I return to this city, the ruined one, and it lies over the ancient one like a skull above a face."

"Hresh—" she said softly, taking him against her breast.

"I want to learn things, Torlyri. To learn everything about everything that ever was. But sometimes—sometimes the things that I find—"

He slipped free of her embrace and moved a few steps away, and stood with his back to her, staring toward the mountain.

"Maybe we should let your first twining wait for another time," she said after a while.

"No. Today is the proper day."

"Your soul is deeply troubled today."

"Still, we should do it on the proper day."

"If you're so distracted by other things that you're unable to enter the twining state—"

"I feel myself growing calmer already," Hresh said. "Simply from being near you. Talking with you." He swung around to face her. His back straightened. Abruptly he spoke in a deeper voice, quivering with determination. "Come. Come, Torlyri. It's growing late, and we have important things to do."

"You truly think we should?"

"Absolutely!"

"Ah, but have you done the preparations? Everything you were supposed to do?"

"Enough of it," said Hresh. He offered her a quick flashing smile. He looked suddenly eager, alert, animated. "So, now, Torlyri, we should go to your chamber. This is my twining-day! Will you forgive me for letting it slip my mind? You know I have many things to think about. But who could overlook his own twining-day? Come, now, teach me the art, Torlyri! I've waited all my life for this day to arrive!"

It was as though he had awakened between one moment and the next from a sleep, or risen from an illness. In an instant all his gloom and confusion seemed gone from him. Was it so, she wondered, or was this only a pretense? In truth he appeared swiftly restored to his usual self, the ebullient, impatient Hresh, Hresh-full-of-questions, hungry as ever for new experiences. Perhaps this morning among the mysteries of old Vengiboneeza he had had one experience too many; but whatever cloud had settled upon him there seemingly had lifted from him just now.

Still, she was uneasy about him.

"There's no harm in waiting another day," she said.

"Today, Torlyri. Today is the day."

She smiled and embraced him again. Hresh was irrepressible. How could she refuse him?

"Well, then, come. So be it: today is the day."

In the cocoon, twining had always been performed in special small chambers, set a little way apart from the main dwelling-chamber. It was a private thing, the most intimate act there was. Even coupling might be done in view of others without occasioning surprise, but never twining, no.

Since the tribe had lived in Vengiboneeza the old custom of maintaining distinct twining-chambers had fallen into disuse. One could always twine privately in one's own chambers, or in some abandoned building of the city. The chances were slight that anyone would intrude. But a first twining was a delicate thing, and Torlyri kept a chamber of her own for that, in a gallery below the temple, where there was no possibility of an accidental interruption. She led Hresh toward it now.

As they entered the main level of the temple, the tall slender figure of Kreun stepped from the shadows of the Mueri chapel. When she was close she halted and turned to Torlyri as though about to speak; but all that came from her lips was a sort of sob, and then she moved hurriedly onward. In a moment she was out of sight.

Torlyri shook her head. The girl had become very strange in the past few weeks. Of course she was deeply disturbed by the disappearance of Sachkor, who was to have been her mate: gone off into thin air, was Sachkor, and no one could find him anywhere in the city. Hresh, using his Wonderstone, had determined that Sachkor must still be alive. But even Hresh had no idea where Sachkor might be. That was odd; but the degree to which Kreun had retreated into herself seemed even more peculiar. Grief alone did not seem enough to account for it. She was a different person now, edgy, silent, brooding. She kept to herself, and wept a great deal. This had gone on much too long. Torlyri resolved to draw her aside and try, if she could, to ease whatever burden lay upon her.

But not today. This day belonged to Hresh.

A broad, winding stone ramp of the sort so often favored by the sapphire-eyes architects led down to Torlyri's twining-chamber. Bunches of glowberries set in sconces lit the way with pale orange light.

As they began to descend the ramp Hresh said abruptly, "I've been thinking about the gods, Torlyri."

She was taken by surprise by that. He should have twining on his mind now, and not such things as this. But her surprise did not surprise her. Many of the things Hresh said took her by surprise. Hresh rarely did as anyone expected.

"Have you?" she asked mildly.

"I saw a thing in my exploring," he said, "a machine of the ancients, that showed me animals which lived in the time of the Great World. Some of them were very much like animals of today, and yet they were different. In little ways or great, the animals that have survived down through the ages since Great World times have undergone many changes."

"Perhaps so," said Torlyri, wondering where any of this might be leading.

"I asked myself which god it is who brings about such changes," Hresh went on. "It's Dawinno who has changed them. He's the one, isn't he, Torlyri, who transforms all kinds of beings as the years pass? Dawinno makes new forms out of old."

Torlyri paused on the ramp, studying Hresh in puzzlement. To be only a boy, just becoming a man today, and to have such thoughts swarming in his head—surely there was no one else like Hresh, and surely there had never been another like him!

"Dawinno takes away the old, yes," Torlyri said cautiously. "He makes room for the new."

"He *brings forth* the new out of the old."

"Is that your understanding of it, Hresh?"

"Yes. Yes. Dawinno is the transformer of forms!"

"Very well," Torlyri said, feeling more and more lost.

"But transformation is only transformation," said Hresh. "It isn't creation."

"I suppose that that's so."

His eyes were bright, almost feverish-looking, now.

"Where does it all start, then? Consider, Torlyri, the gods we worship. We worship the Provider, and the Consoler, and the Healer. And the Protector and the Destroyer. But there's no god that we call the Creator. Who do we owe our lives to, Torlyri? Who is the maker of the world? Is it Yissou?"

Torlyri had been troubled since the beginning of this discussion; but now her uneasiness began swiftly to deepen.

"Yissou is the Protector," she said.

"Exactly. But not the Creator. We don't know who the Creator

321

is. We never even think about that. Have you ever thought on these things, Torlyri? Have you?"

"I perform the rites. I serve the Five."

"And the Five must serve a Sixth! But who is he? Why do we have no name for him? Why are there no rites to honor him? He made the world and everything in it. Dawinno merely reshapes that world. Seeing the evidence of his reshaping, I began to wonder about the first shaping, do you see? There's a higher god than Dawinno, and we know nothing of him. Do you see, Torlyri? Do you see? He keeps himself hidden from us. But his is the greatest power. He has the power of creation. He can make something out of nothing. And he can transform anything into anything else. Why, it might be that he's capable of taking beasts as stupid and nasty as these monkeys that have been plaguing us and turning them into something that's almost human. He can do anything, Torlyri. He is the Creator! Why, he might even have made the Five themselves!"

She stared at Hresh in shock.

She was not an unintelligent woman, but there were certain areas that she did not choose to explore. No one did. One did not speculate on the nature of the gods; one simply did their bidding. All her life that was what she had done, faithfully and well. The Five ruled the world; the Five were sufficient.

Now here was Hresh proposing things that were profoundly disturbing to her. A Creator, he said. Well, obviously there must have been a beginning to all things, now that she stopped to think about it, but it must have happened a long time ago, and what bearing could it have on those who lived today? It was folly to think about such matters. The notion that there might have been a time when the Five themselves did not exist, that they could have been summoned into existence by someone else, made Torlyri dizzy. If the Five had had a Creator, then the Creator might have had one too, and that Creator might have been created by some god even higher up the scale, and—and—

There was no end to it. Her head was spinning.

And then this business of turning monkeys into humans. What sense did that make?

Oh, Hresh, Hresh, Hresh!

Quietly but firmly she said, "Let's put our minds to twining, Hresh."

"If you wish."

"Not just because I wish it. But because it's why we are here."

"All right," he said. "Today we twine, Torlyri."

He smiled tenderly and took both of her hands in his. Now it seemed to her suddenly that she was the novice and he the one who would give instruction. She found it eternally bewildering to deal with this boy. Torlyri reminded herself that a boy was all that he was, that he was only thirteen and stood barely breast-high next to her, that what they had come here for was his first twining, not hers.

Together they proceeded on downward until they came to the low stone-walled gallery with the pointed arch that led to her little twining-chamber. As they made their way through the narrow passageway, she stooping a little to clear its roof, Torlyri became aware of a change in his scent, and knew that another subtle shifting of the situation was taking place. From the moment they had entered this place he had taken command. But at last, she realized, it might be starting to sink in that he was actually about to twine for the first time. The event was becoming real for him. That was the scent of apprehension about him. Hresh the chronicler he might be, Hresh the wise, but he was also only a mere boy, and he was beginning to remember that now.

The twining-chamber had twelve sides, each set off by a rib of blue stone; the ribs met overhead in a complex groined vault that was half hidden by shadows. It was a small room, perhaps once a storeroom for the sapphire-eyes; surely it must have been too tiny for such bulky folk as they had been. But there was space enough in it for her purposes. She had fashioned a couch of piled furs, and there were niches in the walls in which she had placed certain holy objects. Glowberry sconces cast a flickering greenish-yellow light, faint but sufficient.

"Lie down and make your calmness," Torlyri told him. "I have observances to perform."

She went from niche to niche, invoking each of the Five in turn. The holy amulets and talismans in the niches were old and familiar ones, things she had brought from the cocoon, greasy and smooth with much handling. It was essential to obtain the favor of the gods for a first twining: the novice would be wide open to forces from without, and if the gods did not enter him, then other powers might. Torlyri had no idea what those powers might be, but she took care to leave no opportunity for them.

So she moved about the room, making the signs, murmuring the words. She asked Yissou to protect Hresh from harm when his soul lay open. She called upon Mueri to take from the boy the anguish that seemed to trouble his spirit, and Friit to heal whatever scars his turmoil might have left upon him, and Emakkis to give him strength and resilience. She paused a long while at the altar of Dawinno, for she knew that the Destroyer was a god to whom Hresh had specially consecrated himself; and if indeed Dawinno was the Transformer, as Hresh had argued, then it would be good to summon his particular grace for the transformation about to take place.

The niches had been carved in every other facet of the twelve-

sided chamber, and so there were six in all. Torlyri, having never
found a use for the sixth one, had left it empty. But as she completed the circuit of the room she halted before it now, and to her
astonishment she found herself invoking a god she did not know,
the mysterious Sixth of whom Hresh had spoken a little while
before.

"Whoever you may be," she whispered, "if indeed you exist at
all, hear the words of Torlyri. I ask you to watch over this strange
boy who loves you, and to make him strong, and to preserve him
for all that he must do upon the face of this your world. That is
what Torlyri wishes of you, in the name of the Five who are yours.
Amen."

And she stared, amazed at what she had done, into the shadowy recess of the sixth niche.

She turned, then, and knelt beside Hresh on the furs. He was
watching her, wide-eyed, intent.

"Have you made your calmness?" she asked.

"I think so."

"You aren't sure?"

"I have made my calmness, yes."

Torlyri doubted that very much. The dreaminess that should
have been in his eyes was not there. Probably he had not even
studied the technique, though she had instructed him in it and
told him to practice. But perhaps the mind of Hresh was equal
to entering into twining even when not fully calm. There was
never any telling about anything, when you were dealing with
Hresh.

She had taken a sacred object from the niche of Dawinno, a
smooth white stone tied round its middle with a wisp of tough
green fiber. Now she pressed it into Hresh's left hand for a talisman, and folded his fingers about it. It would serve to focus his

concentration. He was already holding the amulet that once had been Thaggoran's in his other hand.

Formally she said, "This is the deepest joy of our people. This is the union of souls that is our special gift. We approach our twining with reverence and awe. We approach it with eagerness and delight."

Torlyri felt tension rising within her.

How many times she had done this, with so many of the tribe! She had instructed nearly half in their first twining; but never had she faced the prospect of joining her soul with someone like Hresh. To enter his mind, to have his mind enter hers—it filled her with unexpected disquietude. Here at the last moment she found it necessary to make a calmness herself, going through the simple exercises that ordinarily only novices would need to practice. Hresh seemed aware that she was unusually ill at ease: she saw his gleaming eyes peering at her worriedly, as if once again the balance had shifted and he was the master, she the young initiate.

The moment passed. She was calm.

She put her arms about him and they lay close together.

"Rejoice with me," she said softly. "Rest with me."

Their sensing-organs touched. He hesitated—she could feel it, that sudden quick rigidity of the muscles—but then he relaxed, and they began the twining.

He was awkward at first, as they always were, but in a little while he caught on to the movements, and after that it became easy. Torlyri felt the first tinglings of a communion and knew there would be no difficulty. Hresh was entering her. She was entering Hresh. The joining was unmistakable. She felt the unique texture of his soul, the color of it, the music of it.

He was even stranger than she had thought. She had expected

to find great loneliness in him, and that was there, yes. But his soul had a depth and a richness and a fullness that she had never encountered before. The power of his second sight was overwhelming, even here in the first levels of the twining. And already she could sense the might he held in reserve. The force of his mind was like that of a river in full spate plunging over a titanic precipice. Could it harm her, she wondered, to join with such a mind?

No. No. No harm could ever come from Hresh.

"Twine with me," Torlyri said, and opened fully to him.

11

The Dream That Would Not End

Afterward Hresh Rose and stood for a time looking down on the sleeping Torlyri. She was smiling as she slept. He had feared that he might have injured her when his mind went rushing with full power into hers. But no: she would sleep a little while, and then she would awaken.

He made his way by himself up the winding ramp and out of the temple. Better that he let her awaken alone. She might be abashed when she awoke to find him still lying beside her, as if they were twining-partners. She would need some time to return to herself, to regain her equilibrium. He knew that the unexpected intensity of their communion had had great impact on her.

For his part Hresh had found his first twining a pleasure and a revelation.

A pleasure, certainly: to lie in Torlyri's warm embrace, to feel her gentle soul mingling with his, to enter into that odd and delicious state of communion. Now at last he understood why twining was so highly regarded, why it was considered a delight more powerful even than coupling.

A revelation, too: he had known Torlyri all his life, but he saw now that until today he had known her in only the most general way. A good woman, a kindly woman, a gentle and loving presence in the tribe—she who performed the rites and spoke with the gods and gave comfort to all in need, a kind of mother to everyone. Yes: that was Torlyri. But now Hresh knew that there were other aspects to her. There was great strength in her, an astonishing toughness of spirit. He should have expected that, remembering how strong she was physically, nearly as strong as a warrior and in some ways stronger. That kind of strength usually reflected inner strength, but he had been so deceived by her warmth, her softness, her motherliness, that he had not noticed it.

Then too there were ordinary human things about Torlyri. She was not just a doer of rites and a giver of comfort, but also a person, with a private existence, with a private person's fears, doubts, needs, pains. He had not taken the trouble to consider that. Twining with her just now, he had detected the urgency of her desire for some warrior of the tribe—Lakkamai, he supposed; Torlyri and Lakkamai were always together these days—and the complexity of her relationship with Koshmar, and something else, an emptiness, a lonely place within her, that had to do with the fact that she had not borne a child. She was mother to all the tribe and yet not mother to anyone, and that seemed to trouble her, perhaps on such a deep level that she was not aware of it herself. Hresh saw it now, and seeing it had changed him. He was coming to realize what a difficult and intricate thing it was to be adult. There were so many aspects of life that refused to fit neatly into

329

any compartment, but kept squirming about and causing sub-terranean disturbances, when you were adult. That was, perhaps, the main thing that his first twining had taught him.

A pleasure and a revelation. And had it been something of a disappointment, too? Yes, that too. It had not been as awesome an experience as he had hoped. It had fallen short of his vision of what it might be, but only because he possessed the Wonderstone. When you twined you could reach the soul of only one other person; with the Barak Dayir you could reach the soul of the world. Already in his early uncertain experiments with the Wonderstone he had risen above the clouds, he had looked across seas, he had peered into the time before the coming of the death-stars. What was twining compared with that?

He realized that he was being unfair. The Barak Dayir offered him an almost incomprehensible reach. Twining was intimate, personal, small. Yet one did not negate the other. If he had found some disappointment in twining, it was only because the Wonder-stone had shown him already how to step beyond the boundaries of his own mind. Had he not had that experience, twining would probably have seemed overwhelming. The Wonderstone, it seemed, had spoiled him for that. But there was little reason, all the same, to take twining lightly. It was an extraordinary thing. It was an astonishing thing.

He wanted to twine again as soon as he could.

He wanted to twine with Taniane.

That thought, the thought of twining with Taniane, leaped into his mind with such force and such suddenness that he was stunned by it, as if he had been struck a terrible blow between the shoulders. His throat went dry, his breath came short. His heart began to pound, making a loud thumping sound like that of a drum, loud enough, he thought, for others to hear.

Twining with Taniane! What an amazing idea!

She was a mystery to him. He had long felt some sort of connection with her, some kind of attraction. But he had feared it as a distraction from his real work; and he feared also that it would lead him to something bad.

She was a woman now, a beautiful one, and one of unusual intelligence. And ambition. She dreamed of taking Koshmar's place as chieftain one day: no question of that. Anyone with any sense could see that, just from the envious way she looked at Koshmar. Sometimes also Hresh caught her looking at him from a distance, staring in that curious way that women use when they are interested in a man. And sometimes, too, he looked closely at her from far away, when he thought she was unaware of him. Often she was giddy and flirtatious with him. She followed him about, she demanded to go with him on his explorations in the ruins, she plied him with questions whose answers seemed to be of the highest importance to her. He was not sure how to interpret that. Sometimes he suspected that she was only toying with him, that it was Haniman who really interested her.

That would be agonizing, to be rejected in favor of *Haniman*. That was one risk he did not care to take.

But today everything seemed changed. He had twined, now. The whole world of adult complexities lay open to him. He might be the old man of the tribe but he was a young man, too. And he wanted Taniane.

He went in search of her.

It was midafternoon, and the day had become sunny and clear. The roof of the sky appeared to be twanging back and forth as though on strings. The edges of everything Hresh saw were peculiarly sharp, with knife-keen boundaries between one object and another. Colors were vibrant and throbbing. It was as if the twining had opened his soul to a host of powerful new sensory impressions.

Orbin emerged from a nearby passageway, whistling, sauntering. Hresh halted him. "Have you seen Taniane?"

"Over there," said Orbin, pointing to a building where some recent finds of the Seekers were being stored. He began to saunter on. Then he paused for a second look at Hresh. "Is anything wrong?"

"Wrong? Wrong?" Hresh felt flustered. "What do you mean, anything wrong?"

"You've got a strange look in your eye."

"You're imagining things, Orbin."

Orbin shrugged. "Maybe I am, yes."

He began whistling again. He strolled away, smiling in a way that seemed disagreeably knowing and supercilious.

Am I that transparent? Hresh wondered. One glance at me, and Orbin can read everything that's in my mind?

He hurried to the Seeker storehouse, where he found Konya and Praheurt and Taniane, but not Haniman, to his great relief. They all were bending over some unfamiliar piece of machinery with jutting odd-angled metal arms and legs, prodding it in a gingerly way.

"Hresh!" Praheurt called. "Come and see what Konya and Haniman brought back from—"

"Another time," Hresh said. "Taniane, may I speak with you?"

She glanced up. "Of course. What is it, Hresh?"

"Outside?"

"Can't we talk in here?"

"Please. Outside."

"If you insist," she said, looking puzzled, and signaled to Praheurt and Konya as if to say she would be right back. Hresh led her into the open.

The warm breeze was dizzying. He was astounded by the beauty of her thick fur and the shining splendor of her strange, haunting eyes. They stood for a moment in silence as he searched for a way to begin. Cautiously he peered about to make certain that Haniman was nowhere in the vicinity.

"You should have taken a moment to look at what we found today," she said. "We aren't sure about it, but—"

"Never mind that now," he said tightly. "Taniane, I did my first twining today."

She appeared surprised and perhaps even troubled by the sudden announcement. Her eyes looked hooded, guarded. Then her expression changed. A smile that did not seem entirely sincere appeared on her face and she said, perhaps too enthusiastically, "Oh, Hresh, how happy I am for you! It was a good twining, wasn't it?"

He nodded. Somehow this was not going the right way. He fell silent again.

"What do you want to say, Hresh?"

He took a deep breath. "Twine with me, Taniane," he blurted.

"Twine with you?"

"Yes. Right now."

For one horrified moment Hresh thought she was going to burst into laughter. But no, no, her eyes were wide, her lips were drawn back, her throat bobbed strangely.

She looks afraid, he thought.

"Now?" she said. "Twine?"

There was no turning back for him now. "Come on. We can go deep into the city. I'll show you a good place."

He reached for her. She backed away.

"No—please, Hresh, no—you're frightening me."

"I don't mean to. Twine with me, Taniane!"

She seemed shocked, or perhaps offended, or merely annoyed, he could not tell which.

"I've never seen you like this. Have you lost your mind? Yes. That must be it. You've gone out of your mind."

"All I said was—"

She flashed anger at him. "If you aren't crazy, then you must think I am. You can't just walk up and ask someone to twine like this, Hresh! Don't you know that? And that wild look on your face. You should see yourself." Taniane shivered and moved her hands in a gesture of dismissal, and something more than that. "Go away. Please. Please. Just let me alone, Hresh." There was a sob in her voice now. She moved farther from him.

Hresh stood motionless, miserable, appalled. A leaden sense of having bungled things began to take possession of him. He saw how hasty he had been, how clumsy, how foolish. And now all was lost for him, on this day which should have been a day of great joy.

What a fool I am! he thought.

There she was, ten paces away, standing as frozen as he was, staring at him as if he had been transformed into some beast of the wilderness, something ghastly with gnashing jaws and blazing eyes. He wished she would simply turn and run, and leave him alone with his shame, but no, she continued to stand there, staring at him in that strange way.

Then, while he stood there too, yearning to sink into the ground, there came a raucous outcry from far off, from the direction of the city's entrance, that spared him from further torment just then.

"Helmet People! Here come the Helmet People! The Helmet People are coming!"

*   *   *

Koshmar was drowsing in her bedchamber when the cry arose. The day had been a low one for her, the lowest in a succession of low days. Not even the end of the rains and the coming of this clear dry weather had buoyed her dank clogged spirit. Her mind was full of Torlyri and Lakkamai, Lakkamai and Torlyri.

It should not change anything. She had told herself that a thousand times. Torlyri would still be her twining-partner. Twining was the true communion. If Torlyri now felt the need for coupling too, or even for mating—though who had ever heard of an offering-woman taking a mate?—why, even that should make no difference. Torlyri would still need a twining-partner. And Koshmar would be that partner.

Or would she?

Among breeding couples, it was customary for the mate also to be the twining-partner. For the rest of the tribe, one coupled or did not couple with whomever one wished, and then one also had one's twining-partner. But that had been in the cocoon days. This was the time of the New Springtime.

Koshmar had yearned with all the force within her to be the one to lead the tribe out of the cocoon into the New Springtime. Well, now she had; and what had it brought her but confusion, doubt, misery? Here she was hunched down gloomily on her own bed in midafternoon, lost in despair, while bright shafts of sunlight danced on the towers of Vengiboneeza. Hour after hour, nothing but brooding. Brooding. The future seemed all mystery and despair to her now. She had never known such hopelessness before.

"The Helmet People! The Helmet People! Here come the Helmet People!" a hoarse voice cried outside her window.

335

Almost before the meaning of the words had had time to sink in, Koshmar was off her bed, heart beating fiercely, fur rising in prickles, body and mind on full alert.

A kind of savage joy arose in her. Was an enemy tribe invading? Very well. Let them come. She would deal with them. She welcomed their coming. Better to take up arms against enemies than to lie here wrapped up in absurd miserable ruminations.

From her collection of masks she chose the Mask of Nialli, the most ferocious of all. Nialli, so it was said, had been a chieftain with the soul of ten warriors. Her mask was a shining black-and-green thing half again as broad as it was long, with six sharp blood-red spikes jutting upward from it at steep angles on either side. It pressed down with awesome weight against Koshmar's cheeks. Narrow slits provided her with access for vision.

She threw a yellow shawl of office over her shoulders. She seized her spear of chieftainship. She hurried outside into the crossroads in front of the temple tower.

People were running in all directions, wildly, madly.

"Stop!" Koshmar roared. "Everyone still! To me, to me!"

She caught young Weiawala by the wrist as she sped by. The girl seemed half berserk with terror, and Koshmar had to shake her violently to get her even a little under control. From her, finally, Koshmar extracted some fragments of the story. An army of hideous strangers, riding on frightful monstrous animals, had passed through the south gateway of the city, down by the place where the sapphire-eyes mechanicals sat. They had Sachkor with them, as a prisoner. And they were heading this way.

"Where are the warriors?" Koshmar asked.

Konya, someone said, had already gone down toward the gateway. So had Staip and Orbin. Hresh was with them too, and possibly Praheurt. Lakkamai was said to be on his way. Nobody had seen Harruel. Koshmar caught sight of Minbain and cried out to her, "Where is your mate?" But Minbain did not know. Boldirinthe said that she had seen Harruel, looking black-faced and sullen as he often did these days, trudging off alone toward the mountain early that morning.

Koshmar spat. Enemies at the gate, and her strongest warrior was sulking on the mountain! The very one who had made such ceremony over keeping watch day and night against the attack of the Helmet People, and where was he when the Helmet People came?

No matter. If she had to, she told herself, she could get along without Harruel.

She waved her spear aloft. "Women and children into the temple, and lock the sanctuary doors after you! The rest follow me. Salaman! Thhrouk! Moarn!" She looked around, wondering why Torlyri was not here. She had difficulty seeing out of the Mask of Nialli; her side vision was nearly blocked by the sharp-angled projections. But it was a fearsome mask. "Torlyri," she said. "Who has seen Torlyri?" Torlyri could fight as well as any man.

Koshmar remembered that Torlyri had gone off to initiate Hresh in the art of twining. Yes, but Hresh supposedly was down at the gate confronting the invaders. Where was Torlyri, then? And what business did Hresh have risking his irreplaceable life at the gate? Well, there was no more time to lose. Koshmar turned to Threyne, who stood glassy-eyed with fear, clutching her child, and angrily waved her toward the temple. "Go. Hide yourself. If Torlyri's in there, tell her she'll find me at the south gateway. And tell her to bring her spear!"

She hastened down the grand boulevard to the plaza of the gate.

When she was less than halfway there, she caught sight of her warriors standing in a line across the boulevard from one side to the other: Orbin, Konya, Staip, Lakkamai, Praheurt. Old Anijang was with them too, and Hresh. They were facing south, standing still as statues, utterly without movement, scattered so far apart from one another that they would have been all but useless as a defensive force. Koshmar could not understand why they had arranged themselves so ineptly.

Then she came closer to them, and she too halted in her tracks and stared in wonder toward the southern gate.

A fantastic procession was slowly making its way up the boulevard toward them.

The Helmet People had indeed come: thirty, forty, fifty of them, maybe more. And they were riding the most extraordinary animals Koshmar had ever seen, or imagined. Monstrous hulking beasts, they were. Colossal monsters, like walking hills, twice as high as a man, or more, and three times as long as they were high. With every step they took the ground shook as if in an earthquake. The fur of those great animals, thick and shaggy and densely matted, was a brilliant eye-stabbing scarlet. Their high-domed heads were long and narrow, with ears like platters and cavernous nostrils rimmed with black, and fiery golden eyes of startling size. Their four huge legs, which bent oddly at the knee, ended in terrifying curved black claws, rising backward almost to the level of their great protuberant ankles. A pair of towering humps rose on their backs, with a kind of natural saddle between them, big enough for two Helmet Men to ride comfortably on each creature.

If the beasts on which the Helmet People had entered Vengiboneeza were frightful, the Helmet People themselves were the stuff of nightmare.

They all had eerie crimson eyes like the spy that Harruel

and Konya had captured long ago, and fine golden fur. And each of them wore an enormous horrific helmet, and no two helmets were alike. This one was a three-sided tower of metal plates with dark jutting studs emerging everywhere on it, and a pattern of golden flames inlaid in front. This, a domed bowl of black metal with two gigantic mirror-bright metal eyes set at its upper corners. This, a bleak low-brimmed half-mask with three square shield-shaped plaques above it. One warrior wore what looked like a lacquered mountain sprinkled with silver dust; another, a startling red-and-yellow cone with mighty horns; another, a sharp-peaked gold headpiece with a pair of coiling green tails sweeping up and up and up. There was nothing human about those helmets. They seemed to have come from some other world, a dark and terrible one. It was hard to see where the man left off and the helmet began, which made the invaders seem all the more horrendous.

Sachkor rode in the middle of the group, on one of the biggest of the scarlet animals. They had given him a helmet too, smaller than any of theirs but just as strange, with curving iron plates arranged like the petals of an inverted flower, and a golden spike rising above it. His slender form seemed lost atop the vast creature, and he sat quietly, as if dreaming. His face bore no expression.

Surely this tribe is a tribe of monsters riding upon monsters, Koshmar thought. And they are through the gateway; and all is over for us. But we will die bravely before we give up Vengiboneeza to them.

She looked toward Konya, toward Staip, toward Orbin.

"Well?" she cried. "Will you just stand there and let them advance? Attack! Kill as many as you can before they kill us!"

"Attack? How can we attack?" Konya said, speaking very quietly but in a manner that would carry great distances. "Look at the size of the animals they're sitting on. There's no way we can reach that high. Those things would simply trample us as if we were beetles."

"What kind of foolishness is this? Simply thrust at the legs and bellies of those beasts, and bring them down. And then slay their masters." Koshmar brandished her spear. "Forward! Forward!"

"No," Hresh said suddenly. "These are not enemies."

She looked toward him, bewildered. Then she burst into harsh laughter. "Right, Hresh. They're simply guests. Sachkor has brought them to visit us, them and their little pets, and they'll have dinner with us and leave tomorrow. Is that what you believe?"

"They aren't here to do battle," Hresh said. "Put forth your second sight, Koshmar. They come in peace."

"*Peace,*" Koshmar said derisively, and spat.

But there was a look on Hresh's face that was new to her, a look of such strength and insistence that she was shaken by it. It seemed to Koshmar suddenly that it might not be wise to set herself against him in this, for Hresh, she knew, sometimes saw things that no one else was capable of seeing. With an effort she calmed herself, forcing the juices of war to subside within her soul, and sent her second sight toward the advancing horde.

And what Hresh said was true.

She could detect no enmity there, no hatred, no menace.

Yet even now Koshmar could not let herself yield to the boy. Angrily she shook her head. "A trick," she said. "Trust me in this, Hresh. You are wise, but you are young, you know nothing of the world. These people have some way of making it seem as if they pose no threat. But look at the armor they wear. Look at the monsters they ride. They've come to kill us, Hresh, and take Vengiboneeza from us."

"No."

"I say yes! And I say we have to slay them before they slay us!" Koshmar stamped her feet in fury. "Harruel! Where's Harruel? He would understand! He'd be up there among them already, knocking them down from their beasts!" Looking around at them all, from Orbin to Konya, from Konya to Staip, from Staip to Lakkamai, she said, "Well? Who'll come with me? Who will fight by my side? Or must I go out there and die alone?"

"Do you see, Koshmar?" Hresh said, and pointed past her shoulder.

She turned. The thunder of those great black-clawed feet had ceased. The oncoming horde had halted, perhaps a hundred paces down the boulevard, or even less. One by one the huge red animals were beginning to kneel, bending in a bizarre way on those peculiarly constructed knees of theirs, and their helmeted riders were jumping to the ground. Already half a dozen of the invaders, with Sachkor in their midst, were coming up the center of the grand boulevard toward her as though to parley.

"Koshmar?" Sachkor called.

She held her spear in readiness. "What have they done to you? How did they capture you? Have they tortured you, Sachkor?"

"You misunderstand," said Sachkor calmly. "They've done me no harm. Nor did they capture me. I left the city to go in search of them, for I thought they were somewhere nearby, and when finally I found them they received me gladly." His voice was steady. He looked older, wiser, deeper than he had been when he had disappeared earlier that year. "These are the Beng people," he said, "and they have been out of the cocoon longer than we have. They come from a far place on the other side of the great river where we once lived. They are different from us, but they intend us no injury."

Hresh nodded. "He tells the truth, Koshmar."

341

Koshmar still could grasp none of this. She felt as though she were adrift on the breast of a rushing torrent, carried helplessly along. War she could understand, but not this.

"They're lying to you," Koshmar muttered dourly. "This is some trick."

"No. No trick, Koshmar. And no lie."

Sachkor indicated two of the Helmet Men, who stepped forward beside him. One was old and shrewd-eyed, with a dry, wizened look about him that reminded Koshmar somewhat of Thaggoran the chronicler. His fur was a pale yellow, almost white; and he wore a tapering conical helmet that was made of richly embossed bands of different-colored metal, dwindling to a rounded top. Huge black metal ears sprouted from its sides like wings.

"This is Hamok Trei," Sachkor said. "He is their chieftain."

"He? A *man* as chieftain?"

"Yes," said Sachkor. "And this is their wise one, what we would call their chronicler. His name is Noum om Beng." He gestured to a wispy-bearded man nearly as old as Hamok Trei and even more withered, even more wizened. He was of astonishing height, far taller even than Harruel, but so slender and frail that he seemed to be hardly more than a reed. Noum om Beng stood bending forward in a stooping way. His helmet was a stupefying thing of black metal covered with clumps of coarse black hair, from the corners of which rose a pair of long curving purple projections, jointed and jagged, that looked something like the wings of a bat.

Noum om Beng came a step or two closer to Koshmar and made a series of signs in the air before her that might almost have been the signs of the Five, except that they were not. The gestures were different ones and they had no meaning that Koshmar could fathom. Holy signs of some kind they surely were, she thought, but they must be signs sacred to some other set of gods.

How, though, could there be other gods? The thought made no sense. She remembered how Hresh had tried to tell her, that time when they were interrogating the first Helmet Man, that the stranger might speak another language—that is, that he used words different from theirs, though his meanings were the same. Grudgingly Koshmar had accepted that possibility, bewildering though it was. But other gods? Other gods? There were no gods but the Five. These people would not worship unreal gods unless they were crazy. And Koshmar did not think they were that.

To Sachkor she said, "How do you know their names and stations? Are you able to speak with them?"

"A little," Sachkor said. "At first it was impossible for me to understand them at all, or for them to understand me. But I applied myself to the task and a little at a time I was able to learn their speech." He smiled. He seemed to be struggling, but not very hard, to conceal how pleased he was with himself.

"Ask this chieftain to say something to me, then."

"The chieftain rarely speaks. Noum om Beng speaks for him."

"Ask him, then."

Sachkor turned to the wraithlike old man and said something that sounded to Koshmar like the barking of a beast. Noum om Beng frowned and tugged at his thin white beard. Sachkor barked again, and this time the old man nodded and barked something back. With much enthusiasm Sachkor spoke a third time. Whatever he said must have been not quite right, because Noum om Beng looked away discreetly, while the others in the group of Helmet Men burst into harsh laughter. Sachkor seemed abashed; Noum om Beng leaned to one side and whispered with the chieftain Hamok Trei.

Koshmar murmured to Hresh, "What do you think is going on?"

"It is true speech," Hresh replied. "Sachkor understands it, though not well. I can almost understand it myself. The words are like ours, but everything is twisted and broken. With my second sight I can feel the meanings beneath, or at least the shadows of the meanings."

Koshmar nodded. She had more faith now in Hresh's insight into these events, and it was beginning to seem less and less likely to her that the Helmet People had come here on a mission of war. Even their helmets appeared less frightful now that she was getting accustomed to them. They were so massive and so elaborately designed to be terrifying, she thought, that they were actually more comic than anything else, though they certainly were impressive in their ridiculous way. But a residue of suspicion still remained in her. She was helpless here, unable to communicate or even to understand, and for guidance and everything else she was forced to rely on the boy who was her old man, and on this callow youth Sachkor, of all people. That was embarrassing. All in all, she felt profound discomfort.

Noum om Beng, returning his attention now to Koshmar, began to speak, in tones that seemed to Koshmar to be a mixture of barks and howls. She could not easily accommodate herself to the way these Bengs expressed themselves, and several times she was hard put not to grin. But though she comprehended nothing, she could tell that it was a solemn, florid speech, heavy, substantial.

She listened with care, shaking her head in agreement from time to time. Since there apparently was not going to be a battle, at least not immediately, it behooved her to receive these strangers in statesmanlike fashion.

"Can you understand anything?" she whispered to Sachkor, after a time.

"A little. He says that they are here in peace, for trade and friendship. He's telling you that Nakhaba has guided his people to Vengiboneeza, that there was a prophecy that they would come here and find friends."

"Nakhaba?"

"Their chief god," Sachkor said.

"Ah," said Koshmar. Noum om Beng continued to orate.

Behind her, Koshmar heard footsteps and murmurs. Others of the tribe were arriving. She looked around and saw most of the remaining men and even a few of the women—Taniane, Sinistine, Boldirinthe, Minbain.

Torlyri had arrived too. That was good, seeing Torlyri here. She looked unusually tense and weary; but even so, Torlyri's mere presence gave much comfort. She came up to Koshmar and lightly touched her arm.

"They told me enemies had entered the city. Will there be war?"

"It doesn't look that way. They don't seem to be enemies." Koshmar indicated Noum om Beng. "This is their old man. He's making a speech. I think it's going to go on forever."

"And Sachkor? He's all right?"

"He's the one who found them. Went off by himself, tracked them down, led them back to Vengiboneeza." Koshmar put a finger to her lips. "I'm supposed to be listening."

"Your pardon," Torlyri whispered.

Noum om Beng continued another few minutes more; then he ended his speech virtually in mid-howl and stepped back next to Hamok Trei. Koshmar looked inquiringly toward Sachkor.

"What was that all about?"

345

"In truth I couldn't follow very much of it," Sachkor said, with a disarming smile. "But the part right at the end was clear enough. He's inviting us all to a feast tonight. His people will provide the meat and the wine. They've got big herds of meat-animals just outside the city. We have to give them a place to pitch camp, and some wood for their fire. They'll do the rest."

"And do you think I should trust them?"

"I do."

"You, Hresh?"

"They're already within the city, and there are at least as many of them as there are of us, and I think these shaggy red beasts of theirs could be terrible in a battle. Since they claim to be friendly and do in fact seem friendly, we should accept their offer of friendship at face value, until we have reason to think otherwise."

Koshmar smiled. "Crafty Hresh!" To Sachkor she said, "What about the Helmet Man who was here last year? Do they wonder what happened to him?"

"They know he is dead."

"And that he died at our hands?"

Sachkor said, looking edgy now, "I'm not clear about that. I think they believe that he died of some natural cause."

"Let's hope so," Koshmar said.

"In any case," said Hresh, "we didn't kill him. He killed himself, while we were trying to ask him some questions. Once we can speak their language better, we'll be able to explain all that to them. And until then, I think our best tactic is—"

A strange look came into Hresh's eyes, and he fell silent.

"What is it?" Koshmar asked. "Why do you stop like that? Go on, Hresh, go on!"

"Look there," Hresh said quietly. "There's real trouble on the way."

He pointed toward the east, toward the slopes just above them. Harruel, looking baleful and immense, was coming down the road that led from the mountain.

So the invasion he had feared so long had happened at last, and no one had bothered to summon him! And Koshmar had simply opened the city to them—had handed the place away!

The stink of it had risen to Harruel's nostrils as he sat glowering by himself in the forked tree on the sawtooth ridge that was his sentry-post. Dark furies were flickering in his soul, and his eyes were blind with rage. He stared into the dense underbrush of the mountain that loomed over him and he saw nothing at all. But then came that stink, that hideous reek of corruption and decay; and he looked back and saw shaggy red monsters shambling into the city through the southern gate, with Helmet People riding two by two on their backs.

Who would have expected the attack to come from the south? Who would have thought that the three mechanical guardians that the sapphire-eyes had left by the gateway of the pillars would simply step aside, and let these creatures enter?

That is the dung of them I smell, Harruel thought. That is the loathsome scent of their droppings, borne to me by the wind.

He rushed down the mountainside, spear in hand, hungry for war.

The road spiraled down and down, and on each turn of the descent he had a better view of what was happening below. A whole army of the strangers had come in: he could see the helmets glittering in the afternoon sun. And nearly the entire tribe, from the look of things, had gone out to meet them. There was Koshmar, there was Torlyri, there was Hresh. And most of the others, too, gathered in little knots. Koshmar had one of her war-masks on, but there was no war. They were talking.

Talking!

Look, there were two Helmet Men, perhaps the chieftains, standing with Koshmar and Hresh. A parley with the enemy, and the enemy had his war-beasts inside the gate! Was Koshmar surrendering without a blow? That must be it, Harruel realized. Koshmar is giving the city away. She is making no attempt to expel the intruders, but simply handing us over into slavery.

He would have thought better of her. There was the stuff of a warrior in Koshmar. Why this cowardice, then? Why this easy submission? She must be under the influence of Hresh, Harruel decided. He's no fighter, that boy. And he's so sly that he can wrap even Koshmar around his little finger.

With heavy strides Harruel took the last turns of the road and descended into the great boulevard of the gateway. They had all seen him now; they were pointing, muttering. Swiftly he strode into their midst.

"What is this?" he asked. "What are you all doing? How has the enemy managed to enter our city?"

"There is no enemy here," Koshmar said quietly.

"No enemy? No enemy?" Harruel glared at the nearest of the Helmet People, the two old ones standing behind Koshmar. Their hard little red eyes were bleak and shifty. One of them had the look of a king about him—cold, haughty. The other was very tall—gods, was he tall! Harruel realized that for the first time in his life he was looking at someone taller than himself. But the withered, parched old body of the Helmet Man was as slight as a water-strider's. One good breeze would break him in half. Harruel was tempted to strike both of them dead with two quick blows of his spear, the haughty one first, then the frail one. But the voice within him that attempted to keep him from rash deeds spoke to him now, warning him that that was madness, that he must not act without some deeper knowledge of the situation.

He put his face close to those of the two gaunt old Helmet Men, who were studying him with what looked like a mixture of arrogance and curiosity.

"Who are you two?" Harruel bellowed. "What do you want here?"

Koshmar said, "Step back, Harruel. There's no need for this blustering."

"I demand to know—"

"Make no demands on me," Koshmar said. "I rule in this place, and you follow. Give ground, Harruel. These are the Beng folk, and they come in peace."

"So you think," said Harruel.

Rage still gripped him. He was nearly overwhelmed by it. His skin felt hot, his eyes throbbed, his fur thickened with sweat. He could not bear this intrusion by strangers. In anguish he looked toward those who stood nearby, toward Hresh, toward Torlyri, toward Sachkor—

Sachkor?

What was Sachkor doing here? He had vanished an age ago.

"You," Harruel said. "Where have you come from? And why are you in the midst of this parley of leaders, as though you too are someone important now?"

"I brought the Helmet People here," Sachkor declared loftily. There was an insolent glare in his eyes that was altogether new. He seemed like another person, nothing at all like the one Harruel remembered. "I went off to find them, and lived with them, and learned to speak their tongue. And led them to Vengiboneeza to trade with us, and to live in peace with us."

Harruel was so astounded by what Sachkor had said and by the way he had said it that the words of his reply clotted in his throat. He longed to seize Sachkor's grinning head between his hands and crush it like a ripe fruit. But he held himself back. He stood frozen. He made coarse rasping sounds, like a beast, for a moment; and then finally managed to say, "You *led* them here? You helped our enemies enter the city? I knew you were a fool, boy, but I never thought you were so—"

"Sachkor!" a new voice cried, a woman's voice.

Kreun's voice.

She came running up the street, breathless, stumbling now and then on the cracked places in the ancient paving-stones. There was a general stir. The other tribesfolk cleared a path for her, and she ran straight to Sachkor, embracing him with a vigor that nearly sent both of them crashing into Harruel.

Harruel, scowling, stepped back a pace or two. The sweet musk of her assailed his lungs. He had seen little of Kreun since that day when he had encountered her as he descended from the mountain after the night of rain, and he was not pleased to see her now. She could bring only trouble. During these many weeks of Sachkor's absence from the tribe she had lurked like a broken thing in shady corners of the settlement, keeping apart, saying little to anyone, as though Harruel had worked some dark change in her spirit by forcing her that day.

Now she had eyes only for Sachkor. She held tight to him, sobbing, laughing, whispering words of endearment. They were behaving like mates who had been long separated, and not simply two young people who had played a little at coupling.

"They tried to get me to believe you were gone forever," Kreun muttered, pressing her face close against Sachkor's slender chest. "They said you had wandered off somewhere outside the city, or fallen from the mountain, and would never return. But I knew you'd come back, Sachkor! And now here you are."

"Kreun—oh, Kreun, how I missed you!"

She gave him a wide-eyed look, all adoration. Harruel, watching, found it sickening and absurd. "Is it true that you discovered the Helmet People, and brought them here, Sachkor?" she asked.

"I found them, yes. I learned to speak with them. I led them to—"

"This is very touching," Harruel broke in. "But there are matters of the tribe to deal with just now. Move away, girl. All this babbling simply wastes our time."

"You!" Kreun cried, whirling around toward him without relinquishing her hold on Sachkor.

"What's the matter?" asked Sachkor, as the girl began to weep and tremble. "What troubles you this way, Kreun?"

"Harruel—Harruel—" she sobbed.

"What about Harruel?"

She was shivering. Her teeth clacked and her words were thick and indistinct. "He—he—Harruel—on the mountain path—he—he made me—"

"The girl's gone crazy," Harruel shouted, angrily trying to wave Kreun aside.

Koshmar now came close, and Torlyri too, both of them looking perturbed. Harruel felt anger, and beneath it a deep stab of shame. This scene was becoming a disaster. Unbidden, the image of Kreun on that other day rose to his mind, the girl face down on the moist ground, her taut rump upturned and moving wantonly from side to side as she struggled in his grasp, her sensing-organ thrashing about wildly—

Warriors do not force women, Harruel told himself. A warrior should not *need* to force a woman.

I will deny it, he thought.

It was not I who did that thing, it was some demon acting within me.

"What's this all about?" Koshmar demanded furiously.

"Yes, tell us, child," said Torlyri in her softer way. "What are you trying to say? What did Harruel do, on the mountain path?"

"Threw me down," Kreun said, barely more loudly than a whisper. "On the ground. Dropped down on top of me."

"No!" Harruel bellowed. "Lies! Lies!"

They were all staring at him now, even the Helmet Men.

"Held me," Kreun whispered. "Forced me."

She turned away, shuddering, covering her face.

Sachkor bounded forward, glaring up at Harruel, seizing him roughly by the arm, insisting on knowing what had taken place between him and Kreun that day. To Harruel he was like some annoying little yapping animal, or, perhaps, some buzzing insect of the jungle. Casually Harruel swatted him away, as one would a bothersome insect. Sachkor landed hard, in a sprawl, and lay in the dust for a moment. Then he sat up, looking dazed, but seemingly gathering strength for a renewed onslaught. Harruel shook his spear at him, warning Sachkor not to trouble him further.

"Stop this fighting!" Koshmar cried. "Lower your spear, Harruel!"

"I will not. Do you see, he's getting ready to spring again!"

Indeed Sachkor had risen to a half-crouch and knelt there, blinking, muttering. Harruel took a battle stance and waited for him to leap.

Koshmar said angrily, "Hold your temper, Sachkor. And you, Harruel, put down your spear or I'll have it taken from you."

Sachkor remained determined. From his crouch he said, "What is the truth of this, Harruel? Did you indeed force Kreun?"

"I did nothing to her."

"He's lying!" Kreun cried.

Grimly Koshmar said, "Enough of this! We have guests among us. This calls for judgment at another time. Kreun, back to the settlement. Orbin, Konya, take Harruel aside until he's calm. We will hold an inquiry this evening into these matters."

"I will have the truth of this," Sachkor said, "and I will have it now."

Harruel, staring in astonishment, felt the sudden force of Sachkor's second sight trained upon him. That was a surprising thing, a forbidden thing, this shameful probing of his soul. Harruel felt stripped naked, down to the bone and muscle. Desperately he attempted to put up shields across the doorway of his mind to hold Sachkor back, striving to conceal any memory of that time with Kreun. But there was no hiding anything. The more he tried to hide it, the more vividly it all blazed within him: Kreun's firm body squirming beneath him, the feel of her smooth rump against his thighs, the sudden hot delight of the thrust, the pulsing pleasure as he poured his man-fire into her.

Sachkor, roaring, rose up and sprang at Harruel in a wild frenzied lunge.

Koshmar cried out and attempted to step between them, but she was too late. Harruel, still shivering in shock from the invasion of his mind by Sachkor's, acted instinctively, putting out his spear and allowing Sachkor to run right onto it.

Everyone shouted at once. Then there was a dreadful moment of utter quiet. Sachkor looked at the haft of the spear that jutted from his chest as though its presence puzzled him. He made a soft chuttering sound. Harruel let go of the weapon, giving it a slight push as he released it. Tottering, Sachkor glanced around, still amazed, and dropped sideways to the ground. Kreun rushed forward and fell like a discarded cloak beside him. Torlyri, kneeling, attempted to pull her away from Sachkor, but she would not be moved.

The Helmet Men, seemingly astounded by what had taken place, exchanged quiet comments in their strange barking speech, and began to draw back behind the safety of their gigantic animals.

Koshmar went to Sachkor, touched his cheeks and his chest, put her hand to the spear and tried to move it, looked for a long while into his fixed, staring eyes. Then she rose.

"He's dead," she said, as if wonderstruck. "Harruel, what have you done?"

Yes, Harruel thought. What have I done?

To Hresh this day was like a dream that would not end, the kind of terrible dream from which one awoke exhausted, as if one had not slept at all. A dream that began with a journey to the Great World, and then his first twining, and then his dreadful clumsy bunglings with Taniane, and the entry into Vengiboneeza of the Helmet People with their astonishing giant red beasts, and the return of Sachkor, and now this—and now this—

No. No. No. No. It was all too much, much too much.

Sachkor lay on his side, not moving at all, with Harruel's spear running right through him. Harruel stood above him with his arms folded, enormous, icy-faced. Torlyri held the sobbing Kreun. The Helmet Men had withdrawn fifty paces toward the gateway and were staring as though they had begun to think they had marched into a den of rat-wolves.

Koshmar said, "This has never happened before, has it, Hresh? That one tribesman should take the life of another?"

Hresh shook his head. "Never. I have seen nothing in the chronicles concerning such a thing, not ever."

"What have you done, Harruel?" said Koshmar again. "You have killed Sachkor, who was one of us. Who was a part of yourself."

"He ran into the spear," Harruel said numbly. "You saw it. All of you did. He cried out like a madman and ran at me. I put up my spear from habit's sake. I'm a warrior. When I'm attacked, I defend myself. He ran into the spear. You saw it, Koshmar."

"But you provoked him," said Koshmar. "Kreun says that you forced her, that day when Sachkor first went away. They were to be mated. It is against custom to force a woman, Harruel. Surely you would not deny that."

Harruel was silent. Hresh felt wave upon wave of anger, confusion, fear, defiance coming from him. He seemed almost pitiful, Hresh thought. But dangerous nevertheless.

He couldn't have meant to kill Sachkor, Hresh decided. All the same, Sachkor was dead.

"These things must be punished," Koshmar said.

"He ran into the spear himself," said Harruel obstinately. "I simply defended myself."

"And the forcing of Kreun?" asked Koshmar.

"He denies that too!" Kreun cried. "But he lies! Just as he lies when he says he didn't mean to kill Sachkor. He hated Sachkor. He always did. Sachkor told me that, before he went away, and he told me many another thing about Harruel. He said Harruel wants to overthrow Koshmar. Harruel wants to rule the tribe. Harruel says he will be king, which is a kind of man-chieftain. Harruel—"

"Hush," Koshmar said. "Harruel, do you deny the forcing?"

Harruel was silent.

"We have to reach the bottom of this," said Koshmar. "Hresh, fetch the shinestones, and we will do a divination. No, better yet, fetch your Wonderstone instead. We'll examine Harruel with that. We will find out what took place between him and Kreun, if indeed anything did, and we will—"

"No," Harruel said suddenly. "There's no need for this examination. I won't allow it. As for what Kreun says, there was no forcing."

"Liar!" Kreun wailed.

"There was no forcing," Harruel went on, "but I will not deny coupling with her. I was on the mountain, guarding the tribe against its enemies, these enemies who now have come riding right into our midst. I sat there all night in the rain, guarding the tribe. And in the morning I descended, and I encountered Kreun, and Kreun looked pleasing to me, and the scent of her was pleasing in my nostrils, and I reached for her and took her and coupled with her, and that is the truth of it, Koshmar."

"And you did this with her consent?" Koshmar asked.

"No!" cried Kreun. "I gave no consent! I was looking for Sachkor, and asked Harruel if he had seen him, and instead he grabbed hold of me—he was crazy, he called me Thalippa, he thought I was my own mother—he seized me, he threw me down on the ground—"

"I am addressing Harruel," Koshmar said. "Was there consent, Harruel? Did you ask her to couple with you as a man will ask a woman, or a woman will ask a man?"

Harruel was silent again.

"Your silence condemns you," said Koshmar. "Even without examination by the Barak Dayir you stand condemned and accursed, for doing things hitherto unknown to this tribe, for taking Kreun without her consent and for striking down Sach—"

"Her consent wasn't necessary," Harruel said abruptly.

"Not necessary? Not necessary?"

"I took her because I was in need, having spent a hard and lonely night guarding the tribe. And because I desired her, since she seemed beautiful to me. And because it was my right, Koshmar."

"Your *right*? To force her?"

"My right, yes, Koshmar. Because I am king, and may do as I please."

Gods save us, thought Hresh in horror.

Koshmar's eyes widened until it seemed they could widen no more. They were bulging with amazement.

But she appeared to be making an effort to keep tight control over her feelings. To Hresh she said in a strained, rigid tone, "What is this word 'king' that I keep hearing so often these days? Will you tell me that, chronicler?"

Hresh moistened his lips. "It is a title that they had in the time of the Great World," he said hoarsely. "A man-chieftain is what the word means, just as Kreun said a moment ago."

"There are no man-chieftains in our tribe," Koshmar said.

A great wave of strength and strangeness came then from Harruel. Hresh felt it with his second sight and it all but bowled him over; it was like standing in a gale that swept trees from their roots.

"The rule of women is over," Harruel said. "From this day forth I am king."

Calmly Koshmar signaled to Konya and Staip and Orbin.

"Surround him," she said. "Seize him. He has taken leave of his senses and we must protect him against himself."

"Stand back," Harruel said. "No one touches me!"

"You may be king," said Koshmar, "but in this city I am chieftain, and chieftain rules. Surround him!"

Harruel, turning, stared coldly at Konya, who did not move. He looked then at Staip, and at Orbin. They remained still.

Now he faced Koshmar again.

"Be chieftain all you like, Koshmar," he said in a dark, even voice. "The city is yours. Or, rather, it belongs to the Helmet People, now. I will go from it and cease to trouble you any longer."

He looked around. By this time the entire tribe stood gathered. Even those women and children who had locked themselves in the temple when news of the invasion had begun to spread had come forth. Harruel's brooding eyes rested now on this one, now on that. Hresh felt that dark dreadful gaze come to bear on him, and he glanced down, unable to meet it.

Harruel said, "Who will come with me? This city is a sickness, and we must leave it! Who will join me in founding a great kingdom far from here? You, Konya? You, Staip? You? You? You?"

Still no one moved. The silence was terrible.

"Why should we huddle in this dead city any longer? Its fame ended long ago! See, the stinking dung of the enemy's beasts already is piling high in the boulevard. There will be more of it. The city will be buried under it. Stand to this side, those of you who are weary of the rule of women! Stand to this side, those of you who want land, riches, glory! Who will go with Harruel? Who? Who?"

"I'll go with you," Konya said in a rough, ragged voice. "As I promised long ago."

Hresh heard Koshmar gasp.

Konya looked across the circle of tribesfolk toward Galihine, his mate. Her belly was swelling with an unborn. After a moment she crossed the center of the circle and took up her place at Konya's side.

"Who else?" Harruel asked.

"This is insanity," said Koshmar. "You will perish outside the city. Without a chieftain you will suffer the hatred of the gods, and you will be devoured."

"Who else comes with me?" Harruel asked.

"I will," Nittin said. "And Nettin with me."

Nettin looked dumbstruck at that, as though he had hit her with a club. But she crossed obediently beside her man, carrying her babe Tramassilu in her arms.

Harruel nodded.

"I'll go," Salaman said suddenly. Weiawala followed him, and the young warrior Bruikkos, and then, after a moment, the girl Thaloin, who had been pledged a few days earlier to Bruikkos as his mate. Hresh felt a chill invading his soul. He had never expected anyone to choose to follow Harruel; but this was catastrophic. The tribe was breaking in two.

"I am with you also," said Lakkamai.

A soft half-smothered outcry came at once from Torlyri. She bit her lip and moved to one side, looking away, but not before Hresh had seen the stricken look on her face. Koshmar too looked stricken; and Hresh understood that it was a look of fear, for she must be dreading that Torlyri would follow Lakkamai out of the city. But Torlyri remained where she was.

Harruel turned now to his own mate.

"Minbain?"

"Yes," she said quietly. "I will go where you go."

"And you, Hresh?" Harruel said. "Your mother goes, and your little brother, Samnibolon. Will you stay behind?" He walked toward Hresh and stood looming over him. "Your skills will be needed in our new life. You will be our chronicler as you have been chronicler here, and anything you want will be yours, boy. Will you come?"

Hresh could make no reply. Mutely he stared at his mother, at Koshmar, at Torlyri, at Taniane.

"Well?" Harruel asked, more menacingly. "Will you?"

Hresh felt the world whirling about him.

"Well?" said Harruel again.

Hresh looked down. "No," he said, so faintly that he could not be heard.

"What? What did you say? Speak up!"

"No," Hresh said again, more clearly. "I mean to stay here, Harruel." He felt his blood racing fiercely within his body, and it gave him energy and force. "We must all of us leave Vengiboneeza one day soon," Hresh said, "but this is not the time, this is not the way. I will remain. There's work here that I must do."

"Miserable boy!" Harruel cried. "Flea-ridden little cheat!"

His long arm lashed out. Hresh jumped back, nearly but not quite fast enough; Harruel's fingertips struck him across the cheek, and so great was the power even of that glancing blow that it sent him flying through the air and tumbling in a heap. He lay there quivering a moment. Torlyri came to him and lifted him and held him tenderly.

"Who else?" Harruel asked. "Who else follows me? Who else? Who else? Who else?"

12

The Strangeness of Their Absence

That day was known ever after as the Day of the Breaking Apart. Eleven adults had departed, and two children; and for a long time thereafter the strangeness of their absence resounded in the city like a great gong.

It was some weeks before Hresh could bring himself even to enter the event in the chronicles. He knew that he was being remiss in his duty, but still he avoided the task, until one morning he realized that he was not sure whether it was ten adults that had gone, or seven. Then he saw that he must set down an account of what had taken place before he lost a clear sense of it. He owed that to those who would read the chronicles in the times to come. And so he opened the book and pressed his fingerpads against the cool vellum of the first blank page and said what he had to say, which was that Harruel the warrior had rebelled against the authority of the chieftain Koshmar and departed from the city, taking with him the men Konya, Salaman, Nittin, Bruikkos, and Lakkamai, and the women Galihine, Nettin, Weiawala, Thaloin, Minbain—

The hardest thing was entering his mother's name. When he attempted it, it would not come out right, and he put down *Mulbome* and then, erasing it, *Mirbale,* before he was able to make the true name appear on the page. He sat a long time staring at the jagged brown lettering, when he had finally done it, putting his fingers to it again and again to read and reread what he had written.

I will never see my mother again, he told himself. But he could not quite comprehend the meaning of those words, no matter how many times he spoke them in his mind.

Sometimes Hresh wondered whether he should have gone with her. When he had looked at her, at that moment when Harruel was asking him to come, he had seen the silent urging in her eyes. And it had been painful to turn away from her and refuse. The choice had been an agonizing one; but even if it meant parting from his mother, how could he leave the tribe, and everything that was yet undone in Vengiboneeza, and all that he might learn from these Helmet People, and Taniane— yes, and Taniane!—to follow the brute Harruel and his handful of followers into the wilderness? That was not the destiny he saw for himself.

Minbain's was the only loss that stung Hresh deeply. He felt sorry for Torlyri, losing her mate; but Lakkamai had meant very little to him, or Salaman, or Bruikkos, or any of the others who went with Harruel. They were just people, familiar faces, parts of the tribe. He had never been close to them, though, as he had been close to Torlyri, or Taniane, or Orbin, or even Haniman. None of those had gone, or he would have been badly hurt by their going. But Minbain had been a part of himself, and he a part of Minbain, and all that was sundered now. Hresh had seen dark clouds forming ever since Harruel had taken Minbain for his mate. Whatever Harruel touched, he changed, and eventually he absorbed.

How strange it was that Harruel was no longer there. He had occupied a huge place in the tribe—a somber, moody presence, and an increasingly frightening one—and now, suddenly, that place was empty. It was as if the great green mountain that rose above the city had abruptly disappeared. One might not like the mountain, one might think it overwhelming and ominous, but one grew used to seeing it there and if it vanished it would leave a disturbing sense of emptiness behind it.

If it was disturbing to have the tribe so dramatically reduced in size in a single hour, it was more unsettling still to have such a horde of strangers coming to live close at hand.

Within hours after Harruel's secession the entire Beng tribe had entered the city, riding on the great red beasts that they called vermilions. There were more of the helmeted ones than the People had suspected: well over a hundred, including thirty or so who looked to be warriors. They had eighty or ninety vermilions, too, some to ride on and some that carried baggage. Other pack-animals, smaller blue-green ones with odd big-jointed legs, followed along in the train. It took all day for the whole Beng procession to pass through the gates.

Koshmar offered them the Dawinno Galihine district to settle in. It was an attractive part of the city, well preserved, with fountains and plazas and tile-roofed buildings, at a considerable distance from the settlement of the People. Hresh was unhappy about giving them that district, since there were things there that he had not properly explored. But Koshmar chose Dawinno Galihine for the Bengs because it was an isolated sector, connected to the main part of the city only by a narrow avenue bordered closely on both sides by fragile, tottering buildings. She believed that if hostilities were to spring up between the two tribes the People would be able to pin the Bengs down by toppling those flimsy buildings and blocking the road with rubble.

It was Haniman who brought news of that to Hresh, who shook his head. "She's making a big mistake if she thinks that's true," he said. "The Bengs have three times as many warriors as we have. And those monstrous trained beasts. There's no way we could ever blockade them inside Dawinno Galihine."

"But if the old buildings fell, how would they get out?"

Hresh smiled. "They'd use the vermilions to push the debris aside. You think that would be hard for them? And then they'd come rumbling out right into our own settlement and trample everything that was in their way."

Haniman made a string of holy signs in the air. "Yissou protect us, do you think it would come to that?"

With a shrug Hresh said, "They are many and we are few, and we've just lost most of our best warriors. If I were Koshmar, I'd be very amiable in my dealings with the Bengs, and hope for the best."

In fact the Bengs did not seem interested in warfare. As they promised, they invited the People to a feast on the first night, and made generous offerings of meat and fruit and wine. Their meat came from animals Hresh had never seen before, short-legged plump ones that had flat black noses and thick woolly coats of gray striped with red, and the fruits the Bengs had brought with them were strange too, bright yellow, with three swollen nippled lobes that looked like breasts, and a sweet, musky flavor.

There were other feasts after that first one, and general efforts at what seemed like friendliness, though there was not much warmth about it. Often four or five helmeted Bengs came to the settlement of the People and stood about, staring, pointing, trying to make conversation. But what they said in that barking tongue of theirs made no sense to anyone, not even Hresh.

Sometimes Hresh would go with a few companions to return these visits. The Helmet People had settled down in Dawinno Galihine as though they found it perfect for their needs, and had set about clearing away rubble and restoring damaged structures with astonishing vigor and swiftness. They were always bustling around feverishly within their sector, digging, hammering, repairing. The newcomers seemed far more energetic and venturesome to Hresh than his own people did, though he was willing to allow that he had a certain prejudice in favor of the exotic and unfamiliar. One building in particular seemed to be the center of their toil, a narrow black stone spire, gleaming as though it were wet, that was ringed with rows of open galleries along its outer wall. Hresh felt a pang, seeing the Beng workers swarming over that intricate tapering tower, for it was one that he had never managed to explore. When he approached it now, the Bengs eyed him uneasily, and a sharp-faced captain in a ponderous bronze helmet spoke out with brusque jabbing gestures that did not seem like an invitation to enter.

As ever, Hresh was hungry for knowledge of these new people. He wanted to know their history and to learn of all the things they had seen in the course of their journey across the world to Vengi-boneeza. He wondered if they had been able to find out more about the time of the Great World than he had managed to discover. He was eager to hear about their god, Nakhaba, and how he differed from the gods of his own tribe. Fifty other questions bubbled in his mind. He wanted to know everything. Everything, everything, everything!

But where to begin? How?

Since he was still unable to make much sense of the Beng language, Hresh tried pantomime. He drew aside a square-faced, chunkily built Helmet Man who seemed to have an easy, open look about him, and laboriously tried to ask him in gestures where they had lived in their previous days. The Beng responded with barking laughter and wild rollings of his scarlet eyes. But after a little while he appeared to get the drift of Hresh's elaborate miming, and he began to make signs of his own. His arms waved impressively, his gleaming eyes rolled from side to side. Hresh had the impression that he was being told that the Bengs had come from the south and west, near the edge of a great ocean. But he was not entirely sure of that.

The language barrier was a serious problem. Through covert use of his second sight Hresh obtained a feel for the rhythm and weight of Beng speech, and it almost seemed to him that he was comprehending the meanings as well. But seeming to understand meanings was not the same thing as actually understanding them. Whenever he tried to translate a Beng phrase into his own language he faltered and failed.

Koshmar ordered Hresh to devote himself to learning the Beng tongue. "Penetrate the secret of their words," she said, "and do it quickly. Otherwise we're helpless before them."

He went about the job zealously and with confidence. If someone like Sachkor could learn their language, he supposed, then he should have no difficulty with it.

But it proved to be more of a chore than he expected. Noum om Beng was the one to whom he turned, since the frail, dry-bodied old man held the same rank in the Beng tribe that Hresh did in his. He had taken up residence in a labyrinthine building that might have been a palace in the time of the Great World, just across the way from the spiral tower, and here, seated on a black stone bench covered with an ornate many-colored weaving, he held court all day long in the deepest and least accessible chamber of the building, a stark white-walled room without furniture, without ornament.

He seemed willing enough to give instruction, and they spent hours at a time together, Noum om Beng speaking and Hresh listening carefully, trying with more hope than success to seize meanings out of the air.

It was easy enough for Hresh to learn the names of things: all Noum om Beng had to do was point and speak. But when it came to abstract concepts Hresh found the going much harder. He began to think that Sachkor's claim of possessing knowledge of the Beng language had been one part easy words, three parts guesswork, and six parts boastfulness.

The Beng language and theirs were related, Hresh was sure. Phrases were put together in similar ways, and certain Beng words seemed like dreamlike distortions of words in the People's language. Perhaps both languages were descended from a single tongue that everyone had spoken in the world before the coming of the death-stars. But it seemed that during the many thousands of years of isolation when the tribes had taken refuge from the Long Winter in cocoons, each tribe had begun subtly to alter the way that it spoke, until one little alteration and another and another had produced, in time, entirely different vocabularies and grammatical forms.

Hresh felt agonies of despair over his slow progress. He had abandoned nearly all of his other research so that he could devote his full time to the study of Beng. But after many weeks he understood very little. Speaking with Noum om Beng was like trying to see when you had a thick black cloth wrapped around your head. It was like trying to hear the sound of the wind when you were buried in a dark pit far underground.

He knew fifty or sixty simple words, but that was not speaking their language. He still had no way of putting those few words together usefully to transmit information, or to gain it. And the rest of the language was so much smoke and dust to him. Noum om Beng's dry whispery voice went on and on and on, and for all Hresh knew he was speaking of things of the highest importance, but Hresh was unable to grasp more than one word in a thousand. The old man was courteous and patient. But he seemed unaware of how little Hresh actually understood.

"You might try twining with him," Haniman suggested one day.

Hresh was thunderstruck. "But I don't even know whether they twine at all!"

"They have sensing-organs, don't they?"

"Well, yes, but suppose they use them only for second sight? Suppose twining is considered an abomination among them?"

The whole topic of twining was a sensitive one for Hresh. The memory of his disastrous attempt to twine with Taniane still burned in his soul. Since that day he had not been able to speak more than a few hasty words with her, or to look her in the eye, or to think of twining with anyone else. Nor did Hresh see how he could possibly find the audacity to offer to twine with old Noum om Beng. It was such an intimate thing, such a private thing! Maybe three or four years ago he might have tried to suggest such a crazy scheme; but he had less appetite for the outrageous now that he was older.

"You ought to try it," Haniman insisted. "Who knows? It might give you the way into their language that you're looking for."

The prospect of lying down in the embrace of gaunt and withered Noum om Beng, of feeling his stale dry breath against his cheek, of making sense-organ contact with him, did not fill Hresh with joy. If that was what he needed to do in order to gain the key to the mysteries of the language of the Bengs, though—

But Hresh could not bring himself to make the bizarre request directly. It seemed too embarrassing, too blatant. Instead, fumbling with his little stock of Beng words, he tried to explain that he wished he could find some quicker and more direct way to learn to speak the language. And he looked toward Noum om Beng's sensing-organ, and then toward his own. But the old Helmet Man seemed not to notice the broad hint.

Perhaps there was some other way. Second sight? Now and then Hresh had tried a cautious little probe of some Helmet Man's mind, never pushing very deeply. But he had never dared to probe Noum om Beng at all. Hresh remembered all too well how that first Beng scout long ago had taken his own life when Hresh had tried to use second sight on him. Noum om Beng was too shrewd for Hresh to think he could probe him unawares, and he had no way of knowing how the old man would react to a mental intrusion.

That left the Barak Dayir. His talisman, his magic key to everything. Very possibly that was his one real hope of attaining any significant knowledge of the Beng language.

The next time Hresh went to pay a call on Noum om Beng, the Wonderstone went with him, snug in its worn old velvet pouch.

He sat at Noum om Beng's feet for an hour or more, listening to the old man's incomprehensible monologue. The few words that he understood floated maddeningly by, like bright bubbles in a dark cloud of gas, and as usual he could make no sense out of anything Noum om Beng said. Finally the emaciated old

Helmet Man halted and looked toward Hresh as if expecting him to make an equally long speech in return.

Instead Hresh drew forth the Barak Dayir and let it tumble from its pouch into the palm of his hand. Golden light and faint warmth came from it. He murmured the names of the Five and made the signs with his other hand and held the tapered piece of polished stone out where Noum om Beng could see it.

The old man's reaction was immediate and dramatic, as if thirty or forty years had been stripped from his age in a moment. His red eyes glowed with sudden scarlet brilliance and blazing vigor. He made a harsh coughing sound and rose from his chair, and dropped down on his knees before Hresh's outstretched hand so suddenly that the long purple wings of his helmet came close to striking Hresh in the face.

Noum om Beng looked awed and astounded. A stream of babbling words poured from his lips, of which Hresh was able to understand only one, which Noum om Beng repeated many times.

"Nakhaba! Nakhaba!"

Great God! Great God!

Often in those strange early weeks after the departure of Harruel from the tribe Taniane found herself wishing that she had gone with him.

She surely would have, if Hresh had chosen to go. In that moment when Harruel, glaring so fiercely, had ordered Hresh to choose between his tribe and his mother, Taniane had held her breath, knowing that her own fate was being decided. But Hresh had refused to go; and Taniane, letting her breath out slowly, had wiped from her mind the declaration that she would have made a moment later, the one renouncing her people and her life in Vengiboneeza.

So she was still here. But why? To what purpose?

If she had gone, a new and difficult life would have unfolded for her. She already knew about the hardships of the world outside the city. She could imagine what new hardships the reign of King Harruel would bring.

He was rough, crude, cruel, dangerous. He was cold of soul and hot of temper. Perhaps he had not always been that way, but she had watched him change since the Time of Going Forth, more and more becoming a law unto himself. Growling and scowling, objecting to all of Koshmar's decisions, setting out into the hill country on solitary journeys whenever he pleased, organizing his own little army of defense without even asking Koshmar's permission, finally challenging the chieftain outright—and forcing Kreun, that too, simply throwing her down and using her against her will—

Well, that was the way Harruel was. Probably now out there in the wilderness he was coupling with all the women who had gone, not just his mate Minbain but Thaloin too, and Weiawala, and Galihine, and Nittin. He was king now. He could do as he pleased. He would be coupling with me, Taniane thought, if I had gone. But you could do worse than couple with a king.

She wondered why Kreun had refused him. Probably because her head was so full of Sachkor, that was why. Forcing someone was not right, but ordinarily no one needed to be forced. One needed only to be asked in a courteous way. Taniane would have coupled with Harruel in the settlement, if he had asked. But he had never asked. He had always kept to himself, forever muttering and glowering. It struck her that perhaps he had thought she was too young, though she was not much younger than Kreun, and Kreun had caught his fancy. Kreun is very beautiful, Taniane thought; but they say I am beautiful too.

The idea of coupling with Harruel excited her. To feel all that strength, all that dark force of his, between her legs! To hear him grunt in pleasure! To have him dig his fingers deep into the flesh of her arms!

Yes, but Harruel was out there in the wilderness now, and she was still in Vengiboneeza, waiting to grow older, waiting for her time to come. It might never come. Koshmar was full of vigor. There was no longer a limit-age. Taniane had dreamed of becoming chieftain someday; now she saw the realization of that dream receding farther and farther into the future.

"And would you become chieftain if you were with Harruel now?" Haniman asked, giving her a skeptical look. Haniman was her main friend these days, and her coupling-partner. He wanted to twine with her too, but Taniane had never granted him that. "Harruel is chieftain himself. That's what 'king' means. And he has a mate, besides. There'd be no place for you."

"Minbain is getting old. Life in the wild country is harsh. She might die in another year or two."

"And Harruel would choose you? Well, he might. Or take Weiawala away from Salaman, or Thaloin from Bruikkos. Harruel is king. He does as he pleases."

"I think he would choose me."

Haniman smiled. "So you would be the mate of the king. Would that give you any power? Has it given Minbain any power?"

"I am not like Minbain."

"That is indeed so. You think you'd be able to wangle a share in Harruel's authority, is that it?"

"I might be able to do that," said Taniane.

"As Hresh would say, you might also be able to learn how to fly by flapping your arms, if you worked at it long enough. But that's not wonderfully likely."

"Not flying, no. But I could have found my way around Harruel." Taniane grinned slyly. "And Harruel won't live forever. It's dangerous in the wild country. Do you remember the rat-wolves? The bloodbirds? If something happened to Harruel, would Konya become king, do you think? Or would the ones who had left the city prefer the old custom and choose a woman to be chieftain, perhaps?"

Haniman laughed, a sharp snorting kind of laugh. "How marvelous you are, Taniane. Out of nothing at all, you conjure up a role for yourself as Harruel's mate in place of Minbain, and as Harruel's master when you are his mate, and then as Harruel's successor after he dies. But meanwhile you are here and he is somewhere far from here, and getting farther every day."

"I know," she said, looking away.

Haniman's hand came to rest suddenly on her knee, and moved a short way up her thigh toward the meeting-place of her legs. Taniane let it remain there.

Her thoughts turned darker. She was here, and Harruel was there, and, as Haniman had pointed out, she was conjuring great things for herself out of nothing at all. She had made her choice; now she had to live with it.

If only Hresh were not such a fool!

She still winced at his stupidity, that day that he had come rushing up to her idiotically begging her to twine with him. Of course she had wanted to twine with him! But she had felt compelled to say no to him. If she had given in to him so readily, right then and there, she would have had no hope of gaining him in the way she wanted him. He would twine with her, yes, and then he would go off, caught up in the frenzy that comes over one in one's first twining days, and twine perhaps with Bonlai or Sinistine or Thaloin—or with Haniman, for all anybody knew—and eventually the frenzy would pass and he would settle into some sort of a regular twining partnership with someone. With anyone. Not necessarily her. What she had wanted, when she refused him, was for him to go off and gain some twining experience and return to her in a more seemly way, wanting her all the more. And she would have accepted him gladly. But he hadn't done that. Instead he had barely spoken to her ever since; he had kept his distance from her as though it would burn him just to look at her.

The fool! Wisest one in the tribe, and a fool all the same!

Haniman's hand moved farther up Taniane's thigh. The other one began to caress her shoulder. It glided toward her breast.

"Couple with me?" he asked.

She nodded, still thinking of Hresh, how she might have become twining-partner with the sharpest mind of the tribe and gained all manner of wisdom that way: how she might even have mated with him, if custom now allowed the old man to mate. Custom had changed enough to allow the offering-woman to mate with Lakkamai, hadn't it? Though a lot of good that had done Torlyri when Harruel had split the tribe apart. If I were Hresh's mate, Taniane thought, then I would hold power just below that of Koshmar, and if Koshmar died—

"And twine with me afterward?" Haniman asked.

"No," Taniane said. "I don't want to twine with you."

"Not now, or not ever?"

"Not now. Maybe not ever."

"Ah," he said. "Too bad. But you'll couple with me?"

"Of course."

"What if I asked you to be my mate, too?"

Taniane gave him a long steady look.

"Let me think about that one," she said. "Meanwhile let's just couple, all right?"

For Torlyri it was a dark and anguished time. She felt that the light had gone out of her soul, that she had turned to a lump of black ash.

All that pain over a man!

How quickly, how deeply, she had become dependent on Lakkamai! How vulnerable she had left herself to his leaving her! She barely recognized herself in this strange shattered woman who could not awaken in the morning without reaching toward the empty place where Lakkamai had slept beside her, and without hearing in her mind his echoing voice, calmly telling Harruel that he too would join the party that was going from Vengiboneeza.

Torlyri had lived satisfactorily enough for thirty years and some without any great need of men. Her love for Koshmar and her responsibilities as offering-woman had made a sufficient life for her. But then had come the New Springtime, then had come the Going Forth, and everything had changed. Suddenly everyone was coupling, suddenly everyone was mating, suddenly new children were being brought into the world in unprecedented numbers. In that great flowering of the tribe Torlyri had felt herself blossoming, opening, ripening. Changing. She too yearned now for coupling, even for mating. So she had given herself to Lakkamai; and now Lakkamai had gone off with Harruel; and Torlyri found herself desolate, although she tried to tell herself that she was no worse off than before she had become entangled with Lakkamai.

"Come to me," Koshmar said. "Twine with me."

"Yes," Torlyri said. "Gladly!"

Koshmar was a great comfort to her in these difficult days. They twined often, far more often than they had for years, and at each twining Torlyri could feel Koshmar pouring strength, warmth, love into her soul.

Torlyri knew that Koshmar had been deeply hurt by her infatuation with Lakkamai. Koshmar had never said it in so many words, but there was no way for her to hide her true feelings from Torlyri, in twining or outside of it, after all their years together. Still, Koshmar had stood aside, allowing Torlyri to do as she wished. And now that it was over, now that Lakkamai had casually allowed Torlyri to fall from his grasp, Koshmar offered no recriminations, no smugness, no cruelty: only love, warmth, strength.

That could not be easy for her. Yet she did it.

And did it, Torlyri knew, at a time when she herself was undergoing great stress. The secession of Harruel had been a powerful blow to her. Koshmar had never had to face such mockery before. No chieftain had. To be scorned in front of her entire tribe, to be reviled, to be rejected—for eleven of her own people to turn their backs on her—what humiliation, what a lessening of her! And then to have this great horde of Helmet People swarming into the city, with all their bustle and energy, their colossal smelly beasts, their strange costumes, their alien ways. Once upon a time the cocoon had been an entire world, and Koshmar had been supreme ruler of that world; but now the People had come forth into a much bigger world and she was nothing more than the chieftain of a small splintered tribe occupying one small corner of a large city, with a much larger tribe nearby, pressing close, impinging, encroaching.

These things threatened to eclipse the bright sun of Koshmar's power. They struck at her prestige, at her confidence, at her spirit itself. But Koshmar in her extraordinary resilience had withstood all these blows. And had strength left over to share with her beloved Torlyri, for which Torlyri was powerfully grateful.

As they lay together Koshmar's fingers dug lovingly into Torlyri's dense black fur. The familiar warmth of her close at hand was comforting. Torlyri felt Koshmar trembling, and smiled at her.

"You," Koshmar whispered. "My dearest friend. My only love."

Their sensing-organs touched. Their souls slipped into communion.

Torlyri asked herself then how she could ever have wanted Lakkamai more than she did Koshmar.

Afterward, though, when she lay back in the calmness that comes after twining, she knew that that was an idle question. The thing she had received from Lakkamai was altogether different from the love she shared with Koshmar. From Lakkamai had come passion, turbulence, mystery. There had been a communion with him, which she had mistaken for communion of the soul, but she realized now that it had been only a communion of the body· strong, yes, intensely strong, but not a lasting thing. A true thing, but not a lasting one. He had wanted her, and she had wanted him, and for a time they had eased those wants in each other. And then he had ceased to want her, or had wanted something else more keenly, and when Harruel had called for companions to join him in the conquest of the wild country Lakkamai had stepped forward without a glance in her direction, without a thought for her. Nor had he asked her to go with him. Perhaps he had thought she would not—that she would inevitably remain loyal to her duties as offering-woman here. Or perhaps he had not cared. Perhaps he simply had had whatever it was that he had wanted from Torlyri, and was done with her now, and was ready for a new adventure.

Torlyri wondered whether she would have gone, giving up tribe and duties and Koshmar and all, if Lakkamai had asked her.

She could not bring herself to answer that question. She was glad that it had not been asked.

Harruel walked ahead of the others when they were on the march, going by himself, surrounding himself in a mantle of kingly isolation. It was a way of emphasizing his power and his separateness. And it gave him a chance to think.

He knew that he had no real plan, except to march onward and onward until the gods showed him the destiny they had in mind for him. Vengiboneeza, for all the comfort and ease that it provided, had not been that destiny. Vengiboneeza was a dead place and it had belonged to other peoples. All it was was a place to hide and wait: but wait for what? For nothing, he thought. For the whitened ruins to tumble and choke them in clouds of powder? And even if Vengiboneeza could be brought back to life of some sort, the buildings repaired, the machines somehow made to run again, it would not be *their* life. He detested the idea of living in someone else's old abandoned city. It was like sleeping in someone else's dirty bedclothes. No, Vengiboneeza was no place for him.

He was unsure where the place for him was. He meant to keep moving until he discovered it.

But they had gone as far as they could go this day. Night was near. They had entered a cheerful terrain of gentle undulating valleys, rich with dense carpets of new grass both green and red. Just ahead the land dropped away sharply, and what lay before them down there struck Harruel as being strangely beautiful, and beautifully strange.

At the heart of the broad meadow below them was an enormous circular basin, broad and shallow, with a clearly demarcated rim around it. Its center was thickly wooded, a dark grove of mysteries, which promised an abundance of game.

The basin looked too symmetrical to be natural. Harruel wondered about it. Who could possibly have built so huge a thing? And why? If it was some city or ceremonial center out of the Great World, how was it that he could see no trace of ruined buildings? All that was apparent from above was a vast shallow depression, nearly as big across as Vengibonceza itself, perfectly circular, surrounded by a rim and heavily overgrown with shrubs. Well, whatever it was, it was preferable to where they had just been.

For close to a week now they had been tramping through a grim zone of disheartening forests where the branches were knotted tightly together overhead by tangled black glossy vines so that the sun could never get through. The forest floor was dry and barren, covered with powdery duff. The only thing that would grow there was a large pale dome-shaped plant, fleshy and somber, which sprouted without warning in a matter of moments, erupting from the ground with incredible speed. It was sticky, and if you touched it it burned your hand. Yet eerie long-legged blue-furred little animals went loping through the forest at nightfall in search of these squat solemn things, and when they found one they would burrow right into its center to devour it from the inside out. The creatures were hard to catch unless you came upon them while they were feeding, when they were utterly lost in the heat of their gluttony and you could seize them by their legs. But then they gave no joy in the eating, for their flavor when roasted was even less palatable than when you ate them raw. Harruel was glad to be leaving that place behind.

He turned and looked back along the broad ridge that he had just crossed, peering into the late-afternoon darkness that was descending upon them from the east. The sky was almost black, except where a single shaft of golden light struck a towering wall of fiery-edged clouds. He saw Konya and Lakkamai not far behind him and the rest of his people straggling, stretched out at wide intervals halfway back to the forest.

Cupping his hand, Harruel shouted back to Konya, "We'll camp here. Pass it on!"

A warm wind was blowing out of the south. It carried the promise of rain. Large gawky gray-plumaged birds with bright silvery necks that were long and coiling and scaly, like serpents, came fluttering out of the treetops and took off in a great flock, heading northeast. They were disagreeable-looking, but they sang like a chorus of gods as they flew away. A week or two ago, on the other side of the forest, Harruel had seen flocks of small delicate birds with green-and-blue wings that glittered like a handful of jewels when they flew, and they had screeched like devils. He wondered why such mismatches of voice and beauty existed.

If Hresh were here, Harruel would have asked him that. But Hresh was not here.

He stood with his arms folded until Konya and Lakkamai came up to him. "There's good water here," Harruel said. "And plenty of fruit on those bushes. And I think we'll find lots of game down there tomorrow." He pointed toward the basin below. "Look there, down ahead. What do you make of that?"

Konya walked to the edge of the ridge, where the land dropped away. He stared outward into the misty green declivity.

"Strange," he said after a moment. "Like a big round bowl. I never saw such a thing."

"No, nor I," Harruel said.

"Bound to have a world of game living in it. You see there, where the edges rise like a curving barrier? The animals can get in, but they won't find it easy to leave. So they'll stay and thrive."

"A city," Lakkamai said, peering solemnly. "That must have been a city in the old times."

"I'm not so sure about that. I think this is something the gods made. But we'll see tomorrow."

The others were coming up now. Harruel moved to one side while they went about the business of pitching camp.

That would have been another thing to ask Hresh about, that huge shallow basin down in the valley. Why it was there, how it had been formed. You could always depend on Hresh to give you some sort of answer. Sometimes he was just guessing, but more often than not he could provide you with real truths. His books told him almost everything, and he had witch-powers besides, or maybe god-powers, to allow him to see beyond ordinary sight and even beyond second sight.

Though Harruel had no liking for Hresh, though the boy had always seemed to him troublesome, sneaky, even dangerous, still there was no denying the power of Hresh's strange mind, and the depth of the knowledge that he had gleaned from the casket of the chronicles. As it had turned out, Hresh did not choose to come. Harruel had thought for an instant of compelling him, that day when the tribe was splitting up; but he had decided that that was unwise, and perhaps impossible. Koshmar might have intervened. Or Hresh himself might have worked some mischief of his own to keep from coming. Nobody had ever been able to make Hresh do anything he didn't want to do, not even Koshmar.

But Harruel had marched on all the same, choosing a route without benefit of Hresh's wisdom. They were going south and west, following the sun all day long and until it set. There was no sense in going the other way, for that was the way they had come, and there was nothing back there but empty plains, rusted mechanicals, and wandering armies of hjjk-men. This way had the promise of the unknown. And it was a green and fertile land that seemed to be throbbing and bursting with the vitality of the New Springtime.

Each day he had set the pace and the others had made shift to keep up with him. He walked quickly, though not as quickly as he would have if he had been traveling by himself. Minbain and Nettin had babes in arms to deal with, after all. Harruel meant to be a strong king but not a foolish one. The strong king, he believed, demands more of his people than they are likely to give without being asked, but he does not demand more than they are capable of giving.

Harruel knew that they feared him. His size and strength and the somber nature of his soul assured that. He wanted them also to love him, or at least to revere him. That might not be easy; he suspected that most of them thought of him as a wild, brutish creature. Probably the forcing of Kreun was responsible for that. Well, that had been a moment of madness, and he was not proud of himself for having done it; but what was done was done. He thought better of himself than they did, because he knew himself better. They could not see his inner complexities, only his hard, savage exterior. But they would come to know him, Harruel thought. They would see that in his way he was remarkable, a strong and shrewd leader, a man of destiny, a fitting king. Not a beast, not a monster: strong, but also wise.

For an hour, until it was too dark to see, the men hunted and the women gathered small hard azure berries and round prickle-skinned red nuts. Then they settled by the campfire to eat. Nittin, who had never had a warrior's training but who was turning out to be surprisingly quick with his hands, had caught a creature by the stream that crossed the ridge, a sleek agile fish-hunting beast with a long slender purple body and a thick mane of stiff yellow hair along its neck. Its hands, on pudgy little arms, seemed almost human, and its eyes were bright with intelligence. There was just enough meat on it to feed them all, and not a scrap went to waste.

Afterward it was the coupling-time.

Things were different now from the old days, the cocoon days, when people had coupled with whomever they pleased, though usually only the mated people, the breeding pairs, had any interest in it as a frequent activity. That had changed in Vengiboneeza, where nearly everyone had begun to mate and breed. There a new custom had sprung up in which the mated people normally coupled only with their mates. Harruel himself had abided by that until the day of his encounter with Kreun when he came down from the mountain.

But here on the trek Lakkamai had no mate, for he had not brought Torlyri the offering-woman along with him from Vengiboneeza. That did not seem to trouble him particularly, to be unmated here when everyone else was. But Lakkamai rarely complained about anything. He was a silent man. All the same, Harruel doubted that Lakkamai would be content to go the rest of his life without coupling, and there was no one here for him to couple with except other men's mates and the infant Tramassilu, who would not reach the lawful age of coupling for many years.

It was also the case that Harruel, now that he had discovered a keen appetite for coupling himself, did not care to confine himself merely to Minbain to the end of his days. As she aged, she was losing what remained of her beauty, and the effort of nursing the child Samnibolon was a drain on her vigor. Whereas Konya's Galihine was still in the prime of her womanhood, and the maidens Thaloin and Weiawala had the heat of youth about them, and even Nettin had some juice in her. So one night early in the trek Harruel had announced the new custom, and he had taken Thaloin that night to couple with.

If Minbain had any objections, she kept them to herself, as did Thaloin's mate, Bruikkos.

"We will couple as we please," Harruel declared. "All of us, not only the king!" He had learned from the Kreun experience that he must be careful in taking special privileges for himself: he could go so far, but no farther, and then they might rise up and overthrow him, or fall upon him in his sleep.

He was not delighted when Lakkamai and Minbain went off to couple a few nights later. But it was the rule, and he could hardly speak against it. Harruel swallowed his displeasure. In time he grew used to the other men coupling with Minbain; and he himself coupled as he wished.

By now no one gave the matter of coupling a second thought. At coupling-time this night Harruel selected Weiawala. Her fur was soft and glossy, her breath was warm and sweet. If she had a fault, it was only that she was too passionate, throwing herself against him again and again, until he had to push her aside in order to get a little rest.

Far-off animals chattered and boomed and sang shrilly in the night. Then the rain arrived, warm and torrential, putting out their fire. They all huddled morosely together, getting drenched. Harruel heard someone mutter on the far side of the heap that at least in Vengiboneeza they had had roofs over their heads. He wondered who that was: a potential troublemaker, maybe. But Weiawala, clinging to him, distracted him. Harruel forgot about the muttering. After a time the downpour slackened and he slipped into sleep.

In the morning they broke camp and descended the ridge, stumbling and sliding on a trail made slick by the rain. Those who had paid little attention to the great basin in the meadow the night before now studied it with interest as they approached it. Salaman in particular seemed fascinated by it, pausing more than once to stare.

When they were not far above it, so near to it that they could no longer make out the entire bowl-shape but could only see the curve of the closest section of the rim, Salaman said suddenly, "I know what it is."

"Do you, now?" said Harruel.

"It must be a place where a death-star struck the earth."

Harruel laughed harshly. "O far-seeing one! O keeper of wisdom!"

"Mock me if you like," said Salaman. "I think it's the truth, all the same. Here, look at this."

There was a low place in the path before them that had held the rain, and now was little more than a pool of soft gray mud. Salaman scooped up a rock so heavy he could scarcely lift it, and tossed it forward with all his strength on a high arc, so that it landed with a great plop in the middle of the pool. Splashes of mud were flung up far and wide, landing on Nittin and Galihine and Bruikkos.

Salaman ignored their angry protests. He ran forward and pointed to the place where the rock had fallen. It lay half buried in the soft ground, and everywhere about it the mud had been displaced in an equal way to form a circular crater with a distinct rim clearly outlined.

"Do you see?" he said. "The death-star lands in the middle of the meadow. The ground is flung up around it on all sides. And this is what results."

Harruel looked at him, astounded.

He had no way of knowing whether what Salaman had said was true or not. Who could tell what had actually happened here hundreds of thousands of years ago? What amazed and troubled him was the keenness of Salaman's reasoning. To have thought everything through like that, to visualize the crater, to guess how it might have been formed, to realize that he could create the same effect by heaving a rock into the mud—why, that was the sort of thing Hresh might have done. But no one else. Salaman had never shown signs of such sharpness of intellect before. He had been just one more quiet young warrior, obediently going about his tasks.

Harruel told himself it would be wise to keep closer watch on Salaman. He could be very valuable. He could also be a problem.

Konya said, "We can see the rock lying in the mud. Why can't we see the death-star still there in front of us? There's nothing in the center of this thing but greenery."

"It's been many years," said Salaman. "Perhaps the death-star disappeared long ago."

"While the crater itself remained?"

Shrugging, Salaman said, "Death-stars might have been made of some material that doesn't last long. They could have been huge balls of ice, perhaps. Or solid masses of fire. How would I know? Hresh might know such a thing, but not I. All I tell you is that I think that is how the bowl in front of us was formed. You may agree with me or not, as you wish, Konya."

They went closer. When they were near the rim Harruel saw that it was not a tenth as sharply outlined as it had seemed from above. It was worn and rounded, and barely apparent in some places. From the ridge it had stood out because of its contrast to the meadow around it, but down here he could see how the storms of time had smoothed and eroded it. That gave Harruel all the more respect for Salaman's theory, and for Salaman.

Konya said, "If a death-star really did land here, we should not enter."

Harruel, standing on the rim looking down into the dense shrubbery beyond, where he could already see plump animals moving about, glanced back at him.

"Why not?"

"It is a place cursed by the gods. It is a place of death."

"It looks pretty lively to me," said Harruel.

"The death-stars were sent as a sign of the anger of the gods. Should we go near the place where one lies buried? The breath of the gods is on this place. There is fire here. There is doom here."

Harruel considered that a moment.

"Let's go around it," Konya said.

"No," said Harruel finally. "This is a place of life. Whatever anger the gods may have had, it was intended for the Great World, not for us. Else why would the gods have seen us through the Long Winter? The gods meant to take the world from those who used to live upon it and give it to us. If a death-star struck here, this is a holy place."

He was impressed with his own cunning reasoning, and his surprising burst of eloquence, which had made his head throb from the effort. And he knew that he could not let Konya's caution rule him here. The thing to do was to go forward, always to go forward. That was what kings did.

Konya said, "Harruel, I still think we should—"

"No!" cried Harruel. He scrambled up the side of the crater's rim and over the edge, down into the green basin below. The animals that were grazing there gazed calmly at him, unafraid. Possibly they had never seen human beings before, or enemies of any kind. This was a sheltered place. "Follow me!" Harruel called. "There's meat for the taking here!" And he plunged forward, with all the rest, even Konya, losing no time in coming after him.

There was rage burning in Koshmar's breast all the time now; but she kept it hidden, for the tribe's sake, and Torlyri's, and her own.

There was no hour when she did not relive the Day of the Breaking Apart. It obsessed her by day and it came back to haunt her by night. "The rule of women is over," she heard Harruel saying, again and again. "From this day forth I am king." *King!* Nonsensical word! Man-chieftain! Man-chieftains were for creatures like the Bengs, not for the People! "Who will come with me?" Harruel asked. His harsh voice echoed and echoed and echoed within her. "This city is a sickness, and we must leave it! Who will join me in founding a great kingdom far from here? Who will go with Harruel? Who? Who?"

Konya. Salaman. Bruikkos. Nittin. Lakkamai.

"Who will go with Harruel? Who? Who? Be chieftain all you like, Koshmar. The city is yours. I will go from it and cease to trouble you any longer."

Minbain. Galihine. Weiawala. Thaloin. Nettin.

One by one going to Harruel's side, while she stood like a woman of stone, letting them go, knowing there was nothing she could do to stop them.

The names of those who had gone were a burning rebuke

to her. She had thought of asking Hresh not to enter them, or any of this, in the chronicles. And then she had realized that it must be entered, all of it, the splitting of the tribe, the defeat of the chieftain. For that was what it was, a defeat, the worst defeat any chieftain of the tribe had ever suffered. The chronicles must not be only a record of triumph. Koshmar told herself sternly that they must hold the truth, the totality of the truth, if they were to have any value for those who will read them in ages yet unborn.

One adult out of every six had chosen to turn away from her rule. Now the tribe was strangely and sadly shrunken, some of its boldest warriors gone, and promising young women, and two babes, the hope of the future. Hope? What hope could there be now? "The city is yours," Harruel had said, but then he had gone on to say, "Or rather, it belongs to the Helmet People, now." Yes. That was the truth. They swarmed in Vengiboneeza. They were everywhere. It was truly their city now. When they encountered members of the People in some outlying district there were angry glares, sometimes, and harsh words, as though the Bengs resented such an intrusion on their domain. Only occasionally now did Hresh and his Seekers go out to roam the ruins in search of the treasures of the Great World, though Hresh still seemed to go fairly often into the Beng sector for his meetings with their old man. That relationship appeared to have an existence of its own, wholly outside the tensions that were building up between the two peoples. But otherwise the tribe had pulled back, staying close to its settlement, licking the wounds that the Day of the Breaking Apart had inflicted.

Koshmar wondered now and then whether the thing to do was to get out of Vengiboneeza altogether, to return to the open country and begin all over again. But whenever the thought arose in her she choked it back. In this city they were supposed to find their destiny: that was what the Book of the Way said. And what kind of destiny was it to go slinking away like beasts, relinquishing the city to another tribe? The People had come here for a purpose, and that purpose was not yet fulfilled. Therefore we must stay, Koshmar thought.

If ever I see Harruel again, she told herself, I will kill him with my own hands. Whether he is awake or asleep when I find him, I will kill him.

"Are you in pain?" Torlyri asked her one afternoon.

"Pain? What pain?"

"You had the side of your mouth pulled in in a strange way. As though something was hurting you, and you were struggling with it."

Koshmar laughed. "A piece of food, stuck between my teeth. Nothing more than that, Torlyri."

She allowed no one to see the torment within her. She went about the settlement with her head held high and her shoulders squared, as though nothing had happened. When she twined with Torlyri—and they twined often now, for Torlyri had been badly hurt by the defection of Lakkamai, and was in great need of Koshmar's love and support—she worked hard to conceal the troubles of her spirit. When she went among tribesfolk, she radiated cheer, optimism, goodwill. She had to. They were all shaken by the Breaking Apart and by the coming of the Helmet People. A delayed reaction had set in, and it affected almost everyone. These people who throughout all their time in the cocoon had been the only people in their world now had strangers virtually in their midst, and that was not easy to swallow. They felt the pressure of the Helmet People's souls nearby, pushing against their own spirits like the close, dense air that weighs heavy before a summer storm. And the loss of the Eleven—the ripping apart of the fabric of the tribe, the breaking of friendships and family ties that had endured all their lives, the sheer impact of *change* on such a scale—oh, that was hard too, that was very hard.

With such pain on all sides Koshmar could not permit her own to weaken her. But she went often to her little chapel, and knelt and spoke with the spirit of Thekmur and with those of other former chieftains, and took what comfort she could from the wisdom they offered her. She had found a certain aromatic herb that grew in the crevices of the walls of the city, and when she burned it in her altar-fire it made her dizzy, and then she could hear the voices of Thekmur and Nialli and Sismoil and the others who had gone before her. They showed no disdain for her, gods be thanked! They were merciful and kind, even though she had failed as chieftain. Even though she had failed.

The essential thing now was to learn to live with the Helmet People. To resist their encroachments by any means short of war. To work out a division of the city that would not be a humiliating quarantine: their sector, our sector, the shared sector.

But it seemed that the Bengs had other ideas.

"They don't want us going here any more," Orbin reported, pulling out a tattered copy of the map Hresh had made, and indicating a quadrant of the city far to the northeast, against the bulwark of the mountain. "They've got a cord stretched across the entrance to the whole district, and when Praheurt went near it yesterday they shouted at him and waved him away." Haniman had a similar story to tell. "Here," he said. "Along the water's edge. They're putting up some kind of idols made of wood covered with mats of fur, and they look annoyed if we come too close."

"Count them," said Koshmar. "I want to know exactly how many Bengs there are. Make a list, write every one down by the shape of his helmet." She paused. "You know how to write?"

"Hresh has taught me a little of the art," Haniman said.

"All right. Take a count. If we have to fight them, we need to know what we're actually up against."

"You would fight them, Koshmar?" said Haniman.

"Can we let them tell us where we can go and where we may not go?"

"There are so many, though! And Harruel and Konya are no longer with us!"

Koshmar glared. "Those names are never to be mentioned, boy. Were they our only warriors? We can handle ourselves in any sort of struggle. Go and count the Bengs. Go and count them."

Haniman and Orbin reported, after a few days, that there were a hundred and seventeen of them, including the women and children, but possibly not some of the infants inside the houses. At least forty appeared to be warriors. Koshmar contemplated those numbers uneasily. The People had eleven warriors left, not all of them in prime fighting shape. Forty was a weighty presence indeed.

And the Bengs' beasts, their vermilions, rambling and snuffling around at will—they were weighty too, in another way. They went wherever they pleased in Vengiboneeza, and frequently strayed right into the People's own settlement, damaging small buildings, scattering and breaking things that had been left out in the sun to dry, terrorizing the children. In any battle, Koshmar knew, her warriors would face Beng warriors mounted on those monsters. Such combat would be absurd.

There is no way we can fight these people, she thought.

They will take Vengiboneeza from us without raising a finger.

We should leave this place at once, regardless of the prophecy in the Book of the Way.

No. No. No.

"You must teach the Beng language to us all," Koshmar told Hresh. If they were indeed to be the People's enemies—and that was far from certain; in many ways they were still taking pains to be courteous and even friendly—then it was necessary to be able to spy on them and understand what they were saying. Hresh had found a way to master it, as she had known he would. But he said he was not yet ready to teach it to others. He needed a deeper grounding in it first, and more time to analyze and classify his knowledge of it, before he could impart what he knew to the tribe.

It was clear to her that Hresh was lying: that he was simply concealing from her and from Torlyri how fluent he was in the Beng language. He had always been like that, enhancing his own prestige and power by keeping special knowledge to himself. But now it was proper for him to share what he knew with the others, and she let him see that she was on to his game.

"Just another few sessions with Noum om Beng," he promised. "And then I'll hold classes, Koshmar. I'll teach it to everyone."

"Will we be able to learn it?"

"Oh, yes, yes. There's nothing really difficult about it, once you grasp the basic principles."

"For you, perhaps, Hresh."

"We will all speak Beng like Bengs," he said. "Just give me a little more time to grow familiar with it, and then I'll share what I know with everyone. I promise you that."

Koshmar smiled and embraced him. Splendid Hresh! Indispensable Hresh! No one else could have carried them through these difficult times. What a calamity it would have been if Hresh had followed his mother Minbain and gone off with Harruel! But Koshmar knew that she would never have let him go. There she would have drawn the line; there she would have fought, even if it had meant her death, the deaths of them all. Without Hresh the tribe was lost. She knew that.

They spoke for a while of the Beng encroachment, of the barriers that had gone up here and there around the city. It was Hresh's opinion that the Bengs were marking certain places off for purely religious reasons, rather than to protect their claim to any Great World machines they might contain. But he was far from certain of that, he said, and eager to return to his own explorations as soon as conditions in the city became more stable again, lest the Bengs find things that could be of value to the People.

They fell silent. But there was another thing Koshmar meant to discuss with him.

"Tell me," she said after a time. "There's trouble between you and Taniane, isn't there, Hresh?"

"Trouble?" he said, not meeting her eyes. "What kind of trouble do you mean?"

"You want to twine with her."

"Perhaps." His voice was very low.

"Have you asked her?"

"Once. I went about it badly."

"You should ask her again."

Hresh looked intensely uncomfortable. "She couples with Haniman."

"Coupling and twining have nothing to do with one another."

"She's going to mate with Haniman, isn't she?"

"Neither one has said anything about that to me."

"They will. Everyone mates nowadays. Even—"

He cut himself short.

"Go on, Hresh."

"Even Torlyri mated for a while," he said, looking miserable. "I'm sorry, Koshmar. I didn't mean to—"

"You don't need to be so apologetic. Do you think I didn't know about Torlyri and Lakkamai? But that's my point exactly. Even if Taniane does mate with Haniman, and I'm not saying that she will, mating has nothing to do with twining, any more than coupling does. She can still be your twining-partner, if that's what you want. But you have to ask. She won't ask you, you know."

"I told you, I asked her once. It didn't go well."

"Ask her again, Hresh."

"It won't go well the second time either. If she's willing to twine with me, why doesn't she let me know it somehow?"

"She's afraid of you," Koshmar said.

He looked up at her, his huge eyes bright with surprise. "Afraid?"

"Don't you know how extraordinary you are? Don't you think that your mind frightens people? And twining—a meeting of the minds—"

"Taniane has a strong mind herself," said Hresh. "She has nothing to fear from twining with me."

"Yes, she's strong." Strong enough to be a chieftain someday, Koshmar said to herself. Though not as soon as she'd like to be. "But she doesn't know she could match you in a twining. I think she'd be willing to chance it, if you asked again."

"You think so, Koshmar?"

"I think so, yes. But she's never going to come to you first. You have to be the one who does the asking."

He nodded. She could see the thoughts running wildly around behind his eyes.

"I will, then! And I thank you, Koshmar! I *will* twine with her! I will!"

He started swiftly away from her, glowing, impatient.

"Hresh?"

"Yes?" he said, halting.

"Ask her, but not today, you understand? Not while the idea's still bubbling like this in your mind. Stop and think about it first. Stop and think."

Hresh smiled. "Yes," he said. "You're a shrewd one, Koshmar. You understand these things so much better than I do." He took her hands in his and squeezed them. Then he went running away across the plaza.

Koshmar watched him go. He is so wise, she thought. And yet still so young, still practically a boy, so earnest, so foolish. But everything will work out well for him.

It is so easy, she thought, to help others in these matters.

She caught sight of Torlyri standing near the corner of the temple. A Helmet Man had appeared from somewhere and was trying to talk to her, the two of them conducting an animated pantomime, with much laughter and, so it seemed, very little communication. Torlyri appeared to be enjoying herself, at any rate. She was beginning now, Koshmar saw, to come out of the deep depression that had engulfed her after Lakkamai's departure. Her duties as offering-woman must be a great consolation to her, not only the ritual things but the giving of comfort to others, the easing of the fears and confusions that the Breaking Apart and the coming of the Helmet People had caused.

"Look at them!" Koshmar said to Boldirinthe, who had come by just then, and gestured toward Torlyri and the Helmet Man. "I haven't seen her look that lively in months."

"Can she speak their language now?" Boldirinthe asked.

Koshmar chuckled. "I don't think either one has the slightest idea of what the other one's trying to say. But that doesn't matter. She's enjoying herself, isn't she? I like that. I like to see Torlyri happy."

"Helping others lifts you out of yourself," said Boldirinthe. "It takes your mind from your own pain."

"Yes," said Koshmar. "It does that."

The Helmet Man was one she had not noticed before, a lean and sturdy one something like that first one, the scout, of long ago. Perhaps this was his brother. There was a long bare place on his right shoulder going around to his neck, as though he had had some terrible wound when he was much younger. His helmet was less frightful than most, no horns on it, no jutting blades, no glaring monsters, only a simple high-crowned bowl of gilded metal covered by thin red plates in the form of rounded leaves.

Koshmar watched them for a little while. Then she turned away.

Harruel's voice spoke within her, as it so often did when she least wanted to hear it, saying, "*The rule of women is over. From this day forth I am king. Who will join with me in founding a great kingdom far from here? Who will go with Harruel? Who? Who?*"

I think I will go to my chapel now, Koshmar thought. I think I will light the fire and breathe the aromatic fumes, and speak now with Thekmur or Nialli.

It was the Barak Dayir that had opened the way between Hresh and Noum om Beng.

Obviously he had known what it was from the first moment he had seen it. That blaze of excitement, the only excitement Hresh had ever seen Noum om Beng display, was evidence of that. To

the old Helmet Man the Wonderstone was a gift of the gods—
was, in a way, a thing that was divine in itself. He knelt before it
a long while; and then at last he turned to Hresh with a long cool
inquiring look that said, as if in words, *Do you know how to make
use of this thing?*

By way of answer Hresh pantomimed taking hold of the
Wonderstone with his sensing-organ. With gestures he mimicked
a sudden eruption of energy and perception in the air around his
head. Noum om Beng indicated that he should do that now; and
Hresh, after a moment's hesitation, enfolded the Barak Dayir in
the curling tip of his sensing-organ and felt its revelatory power
immediately possess and expand his spirit.

An instant later Noum om Beng put his own sensing-organ
close to Hresh's—not touching it, but so close that there was
barely a flicker of light visible in the open space between—and a
joining of their minds took place.

It was not like the joining that comes of second sight, nor that
of twining, nor even like anything Hresh had previously known
in his experiments with the Wonderstone. Noum om Beng's mind
did not lie open to his. But he was able to look within it, the way
one may look within a treasure-chamber from the outside. Hresh
saw what seemed to his mind to be compartments inside, and
what seemed to be sealed parcels meticulously arrayed within
the compartments. He knew that these were not actual compartments, not actual parcels, only mind-images, mind-equivalents.

A bleak chill wind blew from the entrance to Noum om Beng's
mind. It was an icy place, as cold as the dark ancient caverns
below the old tribal cocoon where Hresh had occasionally wandered when he was a child.

"This is for you," said Noum om Beng. And gravely he handed
Hresh one of the smallest of the neatly wrapped packages from

one of the uppermost compartments. "Open it," Noum om Beng said. "Go on. Open it! Open it!" Hresh's trembling fingers plucked at the wrapping. Finally he managed to pull the package apart. Within lay a box carved from a single gleaming translucent green jewel. Noum om Beng gestured brusquely. Hresh lifted the lid of the box.

Jewel and wrapping and treasure-chamber and all else vanished at once. Hresh found himself squatting alone in darkness, blinking, confused. The Barak Dayir was tightly clutched in his sensing-organ. After a time he became aware of Noum om Beng sitting quietly on the far side of the room, watching him.

"Release the amplifier," Noum om Beng said. "It will injure you if you continue to hold it."

"The—amplifier?"

"What you call the Barak Dayir. Let go of it! Unwind your stupid tail from it, boy!"

Noum om Beng's voice, thin and sharp and reedy, crackled and snapped like a whip. Hresh obeyed at once, uncurling his sensing-organ and letting the Wonderstone go skittering to the floor.

"Pick it up, boy! Put it back in its pouch!"

He realized that Noum om Beng was speaking in the Beng tongue, and that he was able to understand what Noum om Beng was saying, even without making use of the Barak Dayir.

He knew the meaning of the words and he knew how each word the old man uttered was related to the words about it.

Somehow Noum om Beng had sent the Helmet People's language all at once into Hresh's head. With trembling hands Hresh put the stone away. The old man continued to stare. His strange red eyes were cold, dispassionate, severe. There is no love anywhere in him, Hresh thought. Not for me, not for anyone. Not even for himself.

"You called it an amplifier?" Hresh said, using Beng words that came readily to his lips as he summoned them. "I have never heard that word before. What does it mean? And what is it, our Wonderstone? Where did it come from? What is it meant to *do*?"

"You will call me Father."

"How can I do that? I am the son of Samnibolon."

"So you are. But you will call me Father. Hresh-of-the-answers, that is what you call yourself, eh? But you have few answers in your head, boy, and many questions."

"Hresh-full-of-questions is what they called me when I was younger."

"And so you still are. Come here. Closer. Closer."

Hresh crouched at the old man's feet. Noum om Beng studied him a long while in silence. Then, suddenly, astonishingly, his clawlike hand lashed out and struck Hresh across the cheek, just as Harruel had done that time on the Day of the Breaking Apart. The blow was totally unexpected, and it had unexpected force behind it. Hresh's head snapped back sharply. Tears came to his eyes, and anger just after the tears, so that it was all he could do to keep himself from instantly returning the blow. He clenched his fists, he tightened his jaws, he clamped his knees together, until the spasm of rage had passed.

I must never strike him, whatever the provocation, Hresh told himself. I would kill him if I struck him the way he struck me. I would snap his neck like a dry twig.

And then he thought, No, that would not happen. For I would be dead before my hand reached his face.

"Why did you hit me?" Hresh asked in wonder.

For answer, Noum om Beng hit him again on the other side of his face. This blow was as hard as the first, but it came as less of a surprise, and Hresh rode with it, lessening the impact.

Hresh stared.

"Have I displeased you?" he asked.

"I have just struck you a third time," said Noum om Beng, though his hand had not moved at all.

The calm flat statement left Hresh mystified for a moment. But only for a moment; and then he realized what his error must have been.

"I am sorry to have given offense, Father," he said quietly.

"Better. Better."

"From now on I will show respect," said Hresh. "Forgive me, Father."

"I will strike you many times," Noum om Beng said.

He was true to his word, as Hresh found him to be in all other things. Scarcely a meeting between them went by when Noum om Beng did not lift his hand to Hresh, sometimes lightly and almost mockingly, sometimes with astonishing power, and always when Hresh least expected it. It was stern and bewildering discipline, and often Hresh's lip would swell or his eye would throb or his jaw would ache for days afterward. But he never struck back, and after a while he came to see the blows as an essential part of Noum om Beng's method of discourse, a kind of punctuation or emphasis, to be accepted naturally and without demur. Though Hresh rarely understood at the moment what it was that he had said to merit a blow, he would usually comprehend later, perhaps half an hour afterward, perhaps not for several days. It was always some stupidity of his that was being called violently to his attention in this way, some error of reasoning, some shortsightedness, some failure of intellectual etiquette.

Eventually Hresh was bothered less by the blows themselves than by the awareness of inadequacy that they conveyed. What Noum om Beng showed him, as the months passed, was that he was clever but that the powers of his mind, in which he had always taken such great pride, had their limitations. It was a painful revelation. And so he sat tense and stiff through each of his meetings with the old man of the Helmet People, waiting gloomily for the next sudden proof that he had failed to come up to whatever mark it was that Noum om Beng had set for him.

"But what do you discuss with him?" Taniane asked, for now he and Taniane had begun to speak with each other again, though cautiously and without ever once referring to the ill-starred invitation he had offered her.

"He does most of the talking. Nearly all, in fact. And most of it is philosophy."

"I don't know that word."

"Ideas about ideas. Very remote, very cloudy. I don't understand a tenth of what he tells me." Noum om Beng, he said, set all the themes and would not be led in any path that he had not chosen himself. Hresh longed to ask him about the origin and history of the Helmet People, about the downfall of the Great World, about conditions elsewhere in the world at this time, and many other things. Now and then Noum om Beng gave him tantalizing hints, but little more. "He's let me know that the Helmet People have been out in the world much longer than we have," Hresh told Taniane. "That there are many other tribes out there too, and that much of the world is ruled by the hjjk-men. But I get these things from him in a cloudy way, by listening for the answers behind the answers." Indeed most of Hresh's questions simply went unanswered; a few earned him blows, presumably for impertinence, though Hresh was never able to see a pattern in the things he said that led Noum om Beng to strike him. An inquiry into the nature of the gods might get him a slap one day, and a trivial and innocent question about the habits of vermilions might draw one

402

the next. Perhaps it was that Noum om Beng preferred never to be questioned about anything; or perhaps he simply wanted to keep Hresh off balance. Certainly he succeeded in doing that.

"He *hits* you?" Taniane asked in amazement.

"It's part of the instruction. There's nothing personal in it."

"But it's such an insult. To have someone actually strike you with his hand—"

"It's just a kind of philosophical statement," said Hresh.

"You and your philosophy!" But she said it kindly, and her smile was a warm one. Then she added, "This is changing you, Hresh. These talks with that old man."

"Changing me?"

"You keep to yourself so much. You hardly speak to me, or anyone else in the tribe, any more. When you aren't with Noum om Beng you're off alone in your room, or, I suppose, wandering around in the back streets of Vengiboneeza. And you don't go out with the Seekers any more."

"Koshmar doesn't want us going out until we understand what the Bengs are up to."

"But you do go out. I know you do. You go alone, though, and you don't seem to be looking for anything. You're wandering without purpose."

"How would you know that?"

"Because once or twice I've followed you," said Taniane, and gave him a shameless grin.

He shrugged and would not ask her why, and the conversation trickled toward a halt. But he couldn't deny the truth of what she had said. There were changes going on within his soul that he felt he was unable to share with anyone, for he hardly understood them himself. They had to do with the revelation of the Tree of Life, which had so conclusively shown Hresh that the People had no claim to calling themselves human, and with the coming of the Bengs, and the departure of Harruel, and with the whole situation that the tribe found itself in in Vengiboneeza, and with many other things, not the least of them his own relationship, or lack of one, with Taniane. But these were too many things to grapple with all at once. As Torlyri once had told him, nobody can deal with more than one enormous thing at a time.

Now he was approaching the chambers of Noum om Beng once more, and he felt a band of uneasiness across the chest, a squirming in his stomach. These visits were becoming increasingly tense for him.

It had not been that way at the beginning, many months before. Noum om Beng had seemed just a strange-looking shriveled old man then, frail and remote and alien. To Hresh he had been nothing but a repository of new knowledge, a kind of casket of chronicles waiting to be opened and read. But now that they were able to speak one another's language and Hresh was coming to have some truer understanding of Noum om Beng's nature, he saw the depth and power of the man, and the chilly austerity of him, and he could not help a feeling of dismay at the thought of baring his mind to him. Not since Thaggoran had been alive had Hresh known anyone remotely like Noum om Beng; and Thaggoran had been too familiar a figure, and Hresh had been too young, for there to have been anything frightening about their conversations. It was different with Noum om Beng. He opened incomprehensible worlds to Hresh, and that was terrifying.

"You look troubled today," Noum om Beng said, as Hresh entered his chambers on this dry, hot midsummer day. The offhand statement was almost as unexpected as one of the blows Noum om Beng dispensed so freely. Rarely did Noum om Beng show much awareness of Hresh's state of mind, nor interest in it.

Taking his seat before the old man's stone bench, Hresh said, "Koshmar has asked me once again to teach the Beng language to our people, Father."

"Teach it, then! Why have you hesitated so long?"

Hresh felt his face growing warm. "The knowledge is my special possession. I feel jealous of it, Father."

Noum om Beng laughed. It was a laugh much like a cough.

"Do you think you can keep it all to yourself? Teach it, boy, teach it! The day will come when all the world speaks in the Beng way: prepare your people, let them be ready for that."

Hresh moistened his lips. "Do you mean to say that all the world will be Beng, Father?"

"All that is not hjjk."

Hresh thought of Harruel, building his little kingdom in the wilderness, and wondered how he would fit into such a scheme of things. Or Koshmar, for that matter. But he said none of this to Noum om Beng.

"Then you believe that when the gods destroyed the Great World, it was to clear a way for the supremacy of the Bengs?"

"Who knows," said Noum om Beng, "the purposes of the gods? The gods are harsh. All striving is repaid in the end with a hail of death-stars. So it has happened again and again, and so it will happen yet again in times to come. We can never comprehend the reasons for this; all we can do is strive ever onward, struggling in the face of everything, to survive and then to grow and then to conquer. In the end we perish. To comprehend this is unimportant. To survive and grow and conquer is all there is."

Never before had Noum om Beng made so explicit a statement

of his philosophy. Hresh, taking it in as though it had been a rain of blows, sat trembling, struggling to come to terms with what he had just heard.

"Will the death-stars come again to destroy us?" he asked finally.

"Not for a very long time. We are safe from them now, and for so much time to come that it is impossible to comprehend it. But they will come, when you and I have been long forgotten. It is the way of the gods, to send the death-stars to the world time after time. It has been that way since the beginning."

"Am I to understand from what you say that the death-stars that destroyed the Great World were not the first that came to the world?"

"That is so. Millions of years go by between each visit of the death-star swarms. This I know, boy. This knowledge comes to me from the ancient ones. The death-stars fell upon the Great World, and they fell upon the world that existed before the Great World ever was. And upon the world before that."

Hresh stared and could not say a word.

Noum om Beng said, "We know nothing of those older worlds. The past is always lost and forgotten, no matter how hard we strive to save it. It survives only in shadows and dreams and faint images. But the Great World people knew how to read those images, and so did the humans before them."

"The humans—before them—"

"Of course. The humans were old when the Great World was born. But the death-stars are older still. There were no humans when the death-stars fell, the time before the last time; or if the humans did exist, they were only little simple creatures such as we are now, with everything still ahead for them, and they lived through that time of death-stars just as we have lived through this one."

Hresh could not even blink as Noum om Beng uttered these words, which fell upon him like the final strokes of the ax that cuts through the mightiest of trees.

"Once very long ago the humans had their time of greatness and ruled the world," Noum om Beng went on, "and I think that they remembered the death-stars that had fallen when they were young, or else they rediscovered the memory of them, I cannot tell you which. And the time of greatness of the humans, long though it was, ran its whole course in the time between the swarms. The humans' greatness came and went in that time. And then the Great World arose and flourished, and it was upon the Great World that the most recent death-stars fell. Now the world is ours and we will build something great in it, as the humans did and the Great World peoples did after them; and one day, millions of years from now, the death-stars will come again. This is truth. This is the way of the world, as it has been since the beginning."

Hresh sat quietly, struggling with the horror of what he had just heard, trembling under the weight of the unimaginable past, which rose above him like one tower piled upon another all the way to the stars.

After a very long time he said, "If that is so, Father, then it makes no difference, does it, what we do? We may grow and flourish and build something greater than the Great World; and when the wheel turns 'round again, whatever we have built will be destroyed as the Great World was. Nor should we think that when the destruction comes it is coming for punishment's sake, to destroy a wicked civilization. Whether we are good or evil, whether we keep the ways of the gods or spurn them, the death-stars will come all the same. They come and come and come, when the appointed time arrives, and they fall upon the wicked and the virtuous alike, on the lazy and the industrious alike, on the cruel and the gentle alike. We might just as well not build at all, for whatever we build will be destroyed. That is the world the gods have devised for us. It seems terribly harsh to us; but the gods are beyond our comprehension. Is this what you say, Father?"

"This is what I know to be true."

"No," Hresh said. "It is too cruel a belief. It says that there is a flaw in the universe, that things are fundamentally wrong at the heart."

Noum om Beng sat quietly, nodding. Something almost like a smile passed across his wizened face.

"We die, do we not?" he asked.

"At the end of our days, yes."

"Is it as punishment?"

"It is because we have come to our end. The wicked sometimes live long, the good die young: so death is not punishment, except that we are all punished the same way."

"Precisely, boy. There is no sense to it; so how can we hope to understand it? The gods have decreed death for us, each of us as a single mortal being. They decreed death also for the Great World; they have decreed death also for the world of hjjk-folk who rule now, and for the Beng world that will follow after. If you call this a flaw in the universe you are wrong. It is the way of the universe. The universe is perfect; it is we who are flawed. The gods know what they are doing. We never will. But that does not mean that there can be an end to our striving."

Hresh shook his head. "If there's no point to anything, if death comes for each of us and death-stars come for our civilizations, then we might as well live like beasts. But we don't. We *do* keep striving. We plan, we dream, we build." Caught up in his own fervor, he cried, "I mean to know why. I will devote my life to finding out why."

He realized that he was speaking very loudly. He realized too that it was some time since he had remembered to call Noum om Beng "Father," as the old Helmet Man insisted. Yet he had not been struck. Truly this was an unusual day.

Noum om Beng stood up, unfolding and unfolding and unfolding to his full great height, and filling the room in his fragile way like some papery-bodied water-strider that had taken on another form. From far above he looked down at Hresh, and it was impossible to fathom the thoughts that were crossing his face, though Hresh knew they must be powerful ones.

At last Noum om Beng said, "Yes. Devote your life to finding out why. And then come to me, and tell me your answer. If I am still alive, I will very much want to know." Noum om Beng laughed. "When I was your age I was troubled by the same question, and I too sought the answer. You see that I failed. Perhaps it will be otherwise for you. Perhaps, boy. Perhaps."

13

Twinings

What had been the crater of the death-star—for they were certain by this time that that was what the circular basin must be—had now become the capital city of Harruel's kingdom. The territory of one was identical to the territory of the other, and the rim of the crater was the boundary of both. Harruel had named his kingdom Yissou, and the city City of Yissou.

They were both absurd names, so far as Salaman was concerned. "One should not name kingdoms after gods," he said to Weiawala, in the cabin they shared. "Better to have named the kingdom for himself, which is probably what he would have done if he dared, and the city the same. At least that would be honest."

"But giving Yissou's name to the kingdom places it under Yissou's special protection," Weiawala protested mildly.

"As though Yissou were not the protector of all who love him, with or without such little favors from us." Salaman smiled. "Well, Harruel has become very devout in these later days. Talk to him, and it's Yissou this and Yissou that, and Emakkis be our guide and counsel, and Friit preserve us, every other word out of him! All this piety sits very poorly on the tongue of a murderous brute like Harruel, I must say."

"Salaman!"

"I say it to you. Only to you." And he made mock gestures of submission in the air, as though Harruel had just come into their cabin. "Good day, your majesty! Yissou's fragrance upon you, your majesty! What a fine day in the City of Yissou this is, your majesty!"

"*Salaman!*"

He laughed and caught her from behind, his hands over her breasts, and kissed the soft furry nape of her neck.

City of Yissou, indeed! Foolish name devised by a foolish king!

It was not much of a kingdom yet, nor much of a city. At the green heart of the crater, that thickly wooded place where— so Salaman had argued—the death-star had come crashing down long ago, there now were seven crude, lopsided wooden shacks, laced together with vines. That was the City of Yissou. Each of the five mated couples had a rickety shack, and Lak- kamai, the lone singleton, had a place of his own. The seventh building, no finer than the others, was the royal palace and house of government. Here Harruel sat in state for an hour or two every day, though there was little for him to do in the way of royal functions. Disputes requiring adjudication were rare in a commonwealth of eleven adults and a handful of chil- dren, and there had not yet been any ambassadors from far-off realms in need of formal welcome. But there he sat, playing at being king, at the center of this collection of shacks that played at being a city.

Not much of a king or a kingdom, no. And not much of a city. And yet, Salaman thought, they had done well enough for themselves in a short while. The City of Yissou was a little less than two years old now. They had cleared much of the underbrush, and built houses of sorts, and they had rounded up meat-animals that dwelled now in a large enclosure, where they could be caught and butchered as needed. A palisade fashioned from tall treetrunks was more than half complete, running around the entire rim of the ancient crater. Harruel said it was to guard against the attack of enemies or wild beasts, and perhaps that was all it meant to him. Certainly it would be useful if enemies ever came. But Salaman saw it also as a statement of sovereignty, an announcement of the extent of Harruel's royal power.

And Salaman dreamed of the day when under his own sovereignty that wooden palisade would be replaced by one of stone. That day was far off, though. The tribe was still too small for such grand projects. Five men were not enough for building great stone walls. And Harruel was still king. For Harruel, a palisade of wood was a sufficiently impressive thing.

"Come," Salaman said, beckoning to Weiawala. "The air in here is stale. Let's go to the hill."

There was a high place beyond the meadow, south of the crater wall, where Salaman often went to think. From there he could see the entire city, and the forest on the far side through which they had come in their trek from Vengiboneeza, and when he turned the other way he was able to glimpse the dark line of the far-off western sea against the horizon. Usually he went there alone, but now and then he took Weiawala with him. Sometimes they would couple there, or even twine. In that high place fresh breezes blew and he felt more keenly alive than anywhere else.

412

Together, without speaking, they made their way through the little city and past the animal enclosure to the twisting path that led up the southern rim of the crater.

"What are you thinking?" Weiawala asked, after a time.

"About the future."

"How can you think about the future? The future hasn't happened yet, so what is there to think about?"

He smiled gently and said nothing.

"Salaman," she said a little while later, as they climbed, "will you tell me something?"

"What is it, love?"

"Are you ever sorry that you left Vengiboneeza?"

"Sorry? No, not for a minute."

"Even though we have to put up with Harruel?"

"Harruel's all right. He's the king we needed." Halting on the trail, Salaman turned and glanced back at the few pitiful scruffy shacks that were the city, and at the half-finished palisade along the rim. His hands rested lightly on Weiawala's shoulders, stroking the rich fur. She moved backward a step and wriggled against him.

After a moment she said, "But Harruel's so vain, and he's so rough. You scorn him, Salaman. I know you do. You think he's crude and pretentious."

He nodded. What she said was true, of course. Harruel was violent and coarse and something of a blockhead, yes. But he had been the perfect man for the moment, the absolutely correct figure at this juncture of history. His soul was strong and he had shrewdness and determination and ambition, and much pride. But for him, the City of Yissou would never have come into being under any name, and they would all still be back there living the easy life among the ruined palaces of Vengiboneeza—an aimless people, waiting endlessly for the great things that destiny had in store for them to fall into their hands.

At least Harruel had had the courage to make a break with that purposeless, self-deluding existence. He had pulled free of Koshmar's grasp and given existence to something new and vital and necessary here.

"Harruel's all right," Salaman said again. "Let him be king! Let him call things by whatever names he likes! He's earned the privilege."

He tugged Weiawala's hand, and they resumed the climb.

Harruel would not be king forever, Salaman knew.

Sooner or later the gods would summon him to his rest, perhaps sooner rather than later. That coarseness of his, that violence, that blockheadedness, eventually must do him in. And then, thought Salaman, it would be Salaman's turn to be the king here, if Salaman had anything to say about it. Salaman and the sons of Salaman, for ever and ever after. If Salaman had anything to say about it!

They reached the rim and went scrambling over the rounded edge. The palisade had not yet reached this part of the crater wall. Looking back, he could barely make out the City of Yissou now at the heart of the bowl below. Its few little buildings were lost in the ever-encroaching greenery.

But the city, Salaman was certain, was not destined to remain for long a mere collection of ramshackle wooden huts. One day there would indeed be a great city down there: a city as grand as Vengiboneeza, perhaps. But it would not be a hand-me-down city like Vengiboneeza, that had been built by long-gone sapphire-eyes and taken over in its ruination by an opportunistic pack of latter-day squatters. No, he told himself, it would be the proud product of the toil and sweat and foresight of its own people, who would make themselves masters of all the region about it, and then of the provinces beyond, and one day, gods willing, of the entire world. The City of Yissou would be the capital of an empire. And the sons of the sons of Salaman would be the lords of that empire.

Now that he was outside the crater he forged rapidly on toward his private high place. After a time Weiawala called, "Wait, Salaman, I can't go that fast!" He realized that he had left her far behind, and he paused, letting her catch up. Sometimes he forgot how much stamina he had, and how eagerly and swiftly he moved when he was on this trail.

"You're always in such a hurry," she said.

"Yes. I suppose I am."

He tucked his arm around her and swept her along up the hill.

This was Salaman's time of coming into his own. He was seventeen, nearly eighteen, a strong young warrior in his prime.

In the cocoon during his boyhood he had been simply one of many, playing idly at kick-wrestling and cavern-soaring and wondering whether coupling could be as pleasurable as the older ones hinted it was. Though his mind was keen, and he saw things clearly and brightly, he had no incentive to demonstrate his intelligence to others, and more than a little to keep it hidden. So he passed the time unexceptionally through his boyhood, seeking nothing, expecting nothing. He had thought life would be like that until the end of his time, a long placid round of identical days.

Then had come the Time of Going Forth, and the long trek across the plains. In that year Salaman had passed from boyhood to manhood and attained his full strength; for though he was short of stature he was thick through the shoulders and robust in the arms, and he had great energy and endurance. Perhaps only Konya was stronger, among all the warriors, and of course Harruel. In the strange new world beyond the cocoon, Salaman underwent a flowering of his spirit. He began to look forward to a time when he would be a man of significance in the tribe. Yet he went unnoticed, because he was so quiet.

Some men were quiet, Salaman thought, because they had nothing to say. Konya was like that, and Lakkamai. Salaman's reticence sprang from a different cause. It would be dangerous, he had always suspected, to reveal his capabilities too early, considering the general flux and violence of events these days.

The example of Sachkor was much on his mind. Sachkor had been intelligent too; and Sachkor was dead now. Intelligence was not enough—one must have wisdom too—and Sachkor, going off by himself and hunting up the Helmet People, then bringing them back and trying to set himself up as the go-between for the two tribes, had not displayed a great deal of wisdom.

Sachkor had moved too far too soon. He had shown himself to be too clever, too ambitious. His cleverness made him a direct threat to Harruel. Hresh was clever also, cleverer by far than anyone, but he was no warrior, and kept to himself, doing things that were of interest only to Hresh; no one had to fear that Hresh might one day reach for supreme power. But Sachkor was a warrior, and once he had brought the Helmet People back he had placed himself in direct opposition to Harruel. Moreover Sachkor had not had wit enough to hold back from challenging Harruel over the Kreun business. No one who went charging wildly into fights with Harruel was likely to live long enough to see his fur turn white.

In Vengiboneeza, therefore, Salaman had preferred to leave

cleverness to Hresh and heroics to Sachkor. He had quietly made himself useful to Harruel, and when Harruel had made his break with Koshmar he had moved quickly to Harruel's side. By now Harruel had come to rely on him to do most of his thinking for him. In a sense Salaman now was the old man of this new tribe that Harruel had founded. Yet Salaman took care never to seem like a rival to Harruel, only a loyal lieutenant. Salaman knew very little of history—that had been Hresh's private field of study—but he had an idea that when sudden shifts of power happened, it was the loyal lieutenants who very often found themselves moving into the highest positions.

These thoughts were not ones that Salaman shared with anyone else. He had said nothing even to Weiawala about his hopes for the years to come, although perhaps she had picked up something of the truth in their twinings. Even there he attempted to mask his plans from her. Caution was his watchword.

They were at the high place now. Weiawala stood nestling against him as he stared off toward the sea. She seemed to have coupling on her mind.

The sun was high and bright, the air clear, almost shimmering in its clarity. The sky was a piercing blue. The breeze was from the south, strong and sweet, a warm dry wind. Perhaps it would gather intensity later and parch the land, but just now it was a loving wind, tender and kind.

All the world lay before him today.

Salaman imagined he could see everything, the ruined cities of the Great World, the pockmarks of death-star craters, the bare plains where the ice-rivers had flowed, the dreadful hives where the hjjk-folk lived. And then the young new world superimposed upon it, the world of the New Springtime, *his* world, his people's world. He had a vision of it in its full complexity, everything growing, thriving, bursting with life. A wondrous recovery from the terrible time of the death-stars was under way. And he would be at the heart of it, he and his sons and the sons of his sons, the lords of the future empire of Yissou.

Weiawala said suddenly, "Nettin will have another child, do you know?"

Her words broke his reverie as a bird-screech at dawn punctures deep serene sleep. He felt a surge of anger. For a moment Salaman regretted having brought her with him to this place today; and then he calmed himself and managed a smile and a nod. Weiawala was his beloved; Weiawala was his mate; he must accept her as she was, he told himself. Even when she interrupted and distracted him.

"I hadn't heard. It's good news."

"Yes. The tribe is growing fast now, Salaman!"

Indeed that was so. Already Weiawala had brought forth a boy that they had named Chham, and Galihine had borne a girl called Therista, and Thaloin had given the tribe another, Ahurimin. Now Nettin's belly was swelling once more.

Only Minbain, to Harruel's open displeasure, had failed to conceive since they had come to the City of Yissou. Perhaps she was too old, Salaman thought. Sometimes when Harruel had had too much velvetberry wine to drink, he could be heard loudly berating her, demanding another son from her. But one does not make sons by shouting at one's mate, as Salaman had pointed out more than once to Weiawala.

Salaman thought it was shortsighted of Harruel to be insisting on another son, anyway. What the city needed at this stage in its growth was more women. One man all by himself could engender a whole tribe of children in a single week, if he set himself to the task. It was only the work of a moment for a man to pump a child into a woman, after all. But each woman could produce at best only one child a year. Thus the annual increase of the tribe was limited by the number of women; therefore we must beget girls, Salaman thought, so that we will have many more wombs in the next generation.

But perhaps that was too complicated a concept for Harruel. Or else he simply wanted more sons to help him guard his throne. Probably that was it. Already Harruel's little boy, Samnibolon, was showing early promise of unusual strength: a future warrior, no doubt of it. And Harruel, perhaps growing uneasy about his old age, must be eager for a few more just like that one to see him through his declining years.

Weiawala slipped her arm through his. Salaman felt the warmth of her thigh pressing close. Then her sensing-organ lightly brushed against him.

It isn't coupling she wants, he thought. It's twining.

Salaman was not pleased by that. But he would not refuse her, all the same.

Up till now the twining had been the weakest link in their bond. Weiawala was a fine mate but a poor twining-partner, so simple was her soul. There was no fullness to her, no richness. If he had stayed in Vengiboneeza he would still have mated with her, in all likelihood, but for his twining he would have gone to someone like Taniane. She had fire; she had depth. But there was no Taniane here, and Harruel discouraged people from forming twining partnerships of the old kind in the City of Yissou, for the population was so small that such unions, which traditionally cut across mating lines, might lead to ill feelings and strife. Now and then Salaman had twined with Galihine, who had something of

419

the spark he craved; but those times were rare. When he twined at all, it was usually with Weiawala, though without strong enthusiasm. He touched her now, sensing-organ to sensing-organ, to acknowledge the invitation.

But as he came in contact with her Salaman felt something strange, something disturbing, something utterly unfamiliar, reaching his awakened senses from a great distance.

"Did you feel that?" he asked, pulling away from her.

"What?"

"A sound. Like thunder. When our sensing-organs touched."

"I felt nothing but you near me, Salaman."

"A booming in the sky. Or in the ground, I wasn't sure which. And a feeling of menace, of danger."

"I felt nothing, Salaman."

He reached for her sensing-organ again with his.

"Well? Do you—"

"Shhh, Weiawala!"

"Pardon me!"

"Please. Just let me hear."

She nodded curtly, looking injured. In the silence that followed he listened again, drawing on the energies of her sensing-organ to enhance the range and sensitivity of his own.

Thunder in the southern hills? But the day was clear and fine. Drumbeats?

Hooves against the ground? A vast herd of beasts on the march?

Everything was too faint, too indistinct. There was only the barest hint, a subtle vibration, a feeling of wrongness. Perhaps by second sight he could detect more. But Weiawala was losing patience. Her sensing-organ slid up and down along his, blanketing his perceptions in a torrent of desire. Perhaps it was just his imagination, he thought. Perhaps all he was picking up was the sound of ants moving in an underground tunnel nearby. He put the matter out of his mind.

Right at that moment, with Weiawala hot and trembling against him, it was impossible to worry about distant thunder on a clear day, or the imaginary sound of far-off hoofbeats. Twining, any twining, even a tepid twining with mild-souled Weiawala, was an irresistible thing. He turned to her. Together they sank to the ground. His arms enfolded her and their sensing-organs met and their minds came flooding into union.

Torlyri found Hresh in his room at the temple, poring over the books of the chronicles. She made an appropriate sound as she entered—one did not take the chronicler unawares while he had the holy books out of their casket—and he looked about at her strangely, almost guiltily, jamming the book out of sight with curious haste. As though I would presume to spy on the chronicler's secrets! Torlyri thought.

"What is it?" he asked, sounding edgy.

"Am I disturbing you? I can come back another time."

"Only entering some minor historical details," Hresh said. "Nothing of any concern." His tone was airy, elaborately casual. "Is there something I can do for you, Torlyri?"

"Yes. Yes." She took a few steps closer to him. "Teach me the words that the Helmet People use. Show me how to speak with the Bengs."

His eyes widened. "Ah. Of course."

"Will you do that?"

"Yes," he said. "Yes, Torlyri, I will. Certainly. Only let me have another few weeks more—"

"Now," she said.

"Ah," he said again, as though she had struck him below the heart, and gave her such a startled look that it made her smile.

Torlyri was not in the habit of issuing orders, and plainly her brisk tone had caught him off guard. She stood watching him steadily, sternly, yielding none of the sudden advantage that she had won. Hresh, looking uncomfortable, seemed to be considering his response with unusual care, rejecting this possibility and that one. She continued to study him with uncharacteristic sternness, standing very close to him so that he could feel the size and strength of her.

Finally he said, looking a little downcast, "All right. I think I know enough of the language by now. Maybe I'll be able to transmit it to you in a way that will make sense. Yes. Yes, I'm sure I can."

"Now?"

"Right this minute, you mean?"

"Yes," she said. "Unless you have urgent duties just now."

He considered that too. "No," he said after another long pause. "We can do it now, Torlyri."

"I'm very grateful. Will it take long?"

"Not long, no."

"Very good. Shall we do it in here?"

"No," Hresh said. "In your twining-chamber."

"What?"

"By twining, that's how we'll do it. It'll be the quickest way. And the best, wouldn't you say?"

It was Torlyri's turn to be startled now. But as offering-woman she had twined with Hresh before; she had twined with everyone in the tribe; it was not a difficult thing for her. So she took him to her twining-chamber and once again they lay down together and embraced, and their sensing-organs interwove and their souls became one. On their other twining, his twining-day, she had felt

great strangeness in him, and the intricacy of his mind, and a loneliness within him that perhaps even he did not acknowledge; and
now she felt these things once again, but intensified, as if he were
in pain. Forgetting her own needs, she wanted to enfold Hresh in
love and warmth, and ease his sorrow. But that was not something
he meant to allow. They had other purposes this day. Quickly he
slammed down a barrier to screen his own feelings—Torlyri had
not known it was possible to do such a thing, to cut your own self
off so fully from your twining-partner; but of course Hresh was
unlike anyone else—and then, hidden behind that impenetrable
wall, he reached out to her and, using the twining communion as
a bridge, began in a businesslike way to instruct her in the language of the Bengs.

Afterward, when the spell had ended and their souls were
separate again, he spoke to her in Beng and she understood, and
replied to him in the same language.

"There you are," he said. "Now you have the language too."

Sly Hresh! Of course he had known the Beng tongue perfectly
for a long while. That was obvious to her now. Koshmar was
right: Hresh had merely been holding back, feigning the need
for further study of it, so that he would be the only one in possession of the secret. Torlyri had seen him cling to little secrets
like that before. Perhaps it was in the nature of chroniclers to
make mysteries out of the things they knew, she thought, so
that the tribe would depend all the more upon them for special
wisdom.

But he had not refused to teach her. And now she had achieved
what she had come to him to achieve. Now she had equipped herself to do the one thing she dreaded most, which was to go to the
Beng with the scarred shoulder and tell him of her need for him,
of—was it real, she wondered? Could it be?—her love for him.

*   *   *

When he was done with Torlyri Hresh returned to his own room
and sat quietly for a time, scarcely even thinking, simply letting his spirit recover from the drain on its energies to which he
had subjected it. Then he rose and went outside. The plaza was
empty and the late afternoon sun, still high in the west on this
summer day, seemed swollen and sluggish as it dipped slowly
toward the sea.

Without any goal in mind he began to walk quickly away from
the settlement, to the north.

Long gone were the days when he bothered to ask Koshmar's
permission before going out into Vengiboneeza, or took the
trouble to ask a warrior to accompany him. He went by himself,
whenever he pleased, wherever he pleased. But it was unusual for
him to leave the settlement this late in the day. He had never while
alone spent a night away. Today, though, as he walked on and
on and the shadows began to lengthen, he realized gradually that
night was coming and he was still heading outward. That did not
seem to be important. He kept walking.

Even now, after all the years Hresh had lived amidst these
ruins, he had scarcely explored the whole of Vengiboneeza. The
district where he was walking now—Friit Praheurt, he guessed,
or perhaps it was Friit Thaggoran—was one that was almost
entirely unfamiliar to him. The buildings were in poor repair,
earthquake-battered and tumbled, with fallen facades and foundations awry, and he had to pick his way over heaps of chalky
rubble, upturned building slabs, shapeless clumps of statuary.
Now and again he saw the signs of Beng presence here: bits of
colored ribbon to mark a trail, the star-shaped splotch of bright
yellow paint that they put on the sides of buildings which they

regarded as shrines, occasional odorous heaps of vermilion dung. But of Bengs themselves he saw none at all.

Nightfall found him squatting atop a towering pyramid-shaped mound of broken alabaster columns, which once perhaps had stood on the portico of the shattered temple with wide, sweeping wings that lay opposite him. Small furry skittering creatures with long narrow bodies and short frantic legs ran back and forth near him, altogether unafraid. They seemed harmless. One ran up onto his knee and sat there a long moment, cocking its head, peering wisely this way and that but otherwise motionless. When Hresh tried to stroke it, it ran.

The darkness deepened. He made no move to leave. He wondered what it would be like to spend the night in this place.

Koshmar will be furious with me, he thought.

Torlyri will be deeply worried. Perhaps Taniane will be, too.

He shrugged. Koshmar's anger no longer mattered to him. If Torlyri felt any distress over his disappearance, well, it would be forgotten when he returned. As for Taniane—Taniane would probably not even notice that he wasn't in the settlement this evening, he thought. He put them all from his mind. He put everything and everyone from his mind: the People, the Bengs, the Great World, the humans, the death-stars. He sat quietly, watching the stars begin to appear. He grew calm. It was almost a trance.

Just as true darkness fell he saw a glimmer of motion out of the corner of his eye, and at once he snapped to attention, heart pounding, breath coming in short bursts.

He rose and looked around. Yes, something was definitely moving: there across the way, near the foundation of the ruined temple. At first he thought it was a small round animal that had come out to sniff for prey, but then by the white gleam of starlight he saw the metallic sheen, the jointed legs. What was this? A mechanical of some sort? But the mechanicals were all dead! And this looked nothing like the Great World mechanicals that he had seen in his visions, or like the dead and rusting ones on that hillside during the long trek westward. Those had been huge, awesome beings. There was something almost comical about this, a small bustling thing perhaps half as tall as he was, spherical, moving earnestly and solemnly about on curious little metal rods.

He saw another, now. And another. There were half a dozen of them roving the rubble-strewn street. Quietly Hresh approached them. They paid no heed to him. Little globes that emitted bright beams of light were mounted on their upper surfaces, and they flashed these about as though looking for something. Now and then they paused, probing the ruins with metal arms that sprang like whips from their bodies. Sometimes they reached between two fallen slabs, as if making an adjustment to something hidden underneath them. Or making repairs.

Hresh caught his breath. He had long since observed evidence all over Vengiboneeza that repair work was somehow going on— that the city, ruined as it was, nevertheless was under the care of invisible powers, ghosts of some sort, Great World forces that worked behind the scenes in a foolhardy attempt to put the place back together. It stood to reason, he thought. Much of the city was in sad shape, but not so dreadfully ruinous as one would expect it to be after the passage of such a great span of time, and some districts seemed hardly damaged at all. He could easily believe that beings of some kind moved through the city trying to patch it. But there was no real proof that such beings existed. No one had ever seen one, and few among the People cared even to speculate about them, for if they were there they might well be spirits, and therefore terrifying.

Yet here they were. Little round machines, poking in the rubble!

They paid no more heed to him than the short-legged furry animals had. He came up behind them and studied them as they worked. Yes, they were definitely trying to tidy things: sucking up the clouds of stone dust, shoving great girders and slabs into orderly heaps, bolstering arches and doorframes. Then, as Hresh watched, one of them touched a metal extension to a door of red stone set at an angle in the ground and the door slid back as if on a greased track. Light came bursting from within. Hresh peered past the little mechanical and saw an underground room, brilliantly lit, in which all manner of shining machines stood in rows, seemingly in good working order. It was an exciting, tantalizing sight: another Great World treasure-trove, one that he had not known of! He leaned forward, staring intently.

A hand touched him from behind, making him leap with fear and astonishment, and he felt himself gripped and caught.

A harsh Beng voice barked, "Who are you? What are you doing here?"

Squirming about, Hresh beheld a burly warrior of the Helmet Men, flat-faced, scowling, nearly as awesome a presence as Harruel himself. He wore a monstrous bronze cone of a helmet from which great fanciful metal antlers sprang, rising and rising to a terrifying height. His scarlet eyes were grim and fearsome, his lips were angrily clamped. Behind him was the enormous bulk of a vermilion.

"I am Hresh of Koshmar's People," Hresh said in the strongest voice he could muster, though in his own ears it did not sound very strong at all.

"You have no business here," was the cold reply.

"This is the shrine of the god Dawinno, to which I have made a holy pilgrimage. I ask you to turn back, and leave me to my prayers."

"There is no god Dawinno. Your kind may not enter here."

"By whose command?"

"By order of Hamok Trei, king of Bengs. I have followed you across half the city this evening, but you will trespass no more. Your life is forfeit."

Forfeit?

The Beng carried a spear, and there was a short wide blade in a sheath dangling from his sash. Hresh stared, fighting back his distress. The Beng was twice his size; any sort of combat was out of the question, even if he were carrying a weapon, and he was not. Turning to flee seemed equally foolish. Perhaps he could dazzle this warrior with second sight, but even that was risky and uncertain. Still, to die here, alone, at the hands of a stranger, merely for having gone someplace where Hamok Trei didn't want him to go—

Hresh lifted his sensing-organ and made ready to bring it into play. His eyes met the hard scarlet ones of the Helmet Man squarely. The Beng raised his spear.

If he touches me, Hresh thought, I'll hit him with all the power I have. I don't care whether it kills him or not.

But there was no need for that. With a quick brusque movement the Beng pointed to Hresh with his spear, and then pointed over his shoulder, vaguely in the direction of the settlement of the Helmet People. He intended simply to bring Hresh before Hamok Trei. "You will ride with me," he said, indicating the vermilion. As easily as though Hresh had been made of air the Beng scooped him up with one hand and deposited him between the great creature's ponderous humps. Then the Helmet Man leaped up beside him and touched his sensing-organ to the back of the vermilion's head. With a slow, agonizing, lurching motion that made Hresh dizzy to the point of nausea almost at once, the huge red beast set off toward the Beng settlement.

But it was Noum om Beng and not Hamok Trei who emerged to dispense justice that night. The withered old man, summoned from his chambers by Hresh's captor, came tottering forth, looking puzzled. But he began laughing when the situation was explained to him.

"You must not go into places where you should not go, boy," the Beng chronicler said, and slapped Hresh lightly on the cheek. "You saw the signs?"

Hresh made no reply. He would not recognize the Beng markings as having authority over his movements through the city.

Noum om Beng slapped him again, even more lightly, a feather-blow. Then he turned away. To the warrior who had captured Hresh he said brusquely, "Take this boy back to his people."

The chilly light of the midnight moon was glistening when Hresh returned to his own settlement. Everyone was asleep but Moarn, who was on sentry duty. He looked at Hresh without interest as the Beng warrior rode away.

Sleep was a long time coming, and when it did Hresh dreamed of glossy little mechanical creatures rolling in silent armies through endless ruined streets, and of gleaming mysterious objects hidden in the depths of the earth.

In the morning he expected the full wrath of Koshmar to descend upon him. But to his relief and also somewhat to his chagrin, no one seemed even to have noticed that he had been missing.

Torlyri had rehearsed the words a hundred times. Yet as she approached the settlement of the Helmet People they all seemed to fly from her head, and she felt completely adrift, lost in turmoil and confusions, unable to speak even her own language properly, let alone that of the Bengs.

Three days had passed since her twining with Hresh. She had not been able to find the courage to make this journey until now. The morning was hot and humid, and an obstinate sultry wind was blowing, raising gray clouds of dust in the dry streets and sending it swirling irritatingly all about her. Again and again she thought of turning back. This visit seemed utter madness to her. She would never be able to make herself understood. And even if she did, even if she managed to find the man she had come here to see, what was the use? It would bring her nothing but pain, she was certain, and she had already had pain enough.

Tense, tight-faced, Torlyri forced herself to keep going onward, down the long narrow avenue of ruined white-fronted buildings that led into the district known as Dawinno Galihine. At the entrance to the Beng settlement a helmeted sentry appeared and gave her a questioning look.

"You are expected?" he asked. "What is your business? Who are you here to see?"

He spoke in the sharp, barking Beng language. The words should have been gibberish to her. And yet she had no difficulty making out their meaning. So it had worked! True to his word, Hresh had actually taught her to comprehend their speech!

But could she speak it herself now?

No words came to her. They were trapped deep in her mind and would not rise to her lips. *I have come to see the man with the scarred shoulder,* that was what she meant to say. But there was no way she could bring herself to tell this sentry such a thing. She was shy as a girl today; and the man's tone of voice seemed cold and hostile to her, and his words a rebuff and a dismissal, though probably they were meant only as a routine interrogation. Fear assailed her. The resolve that had brought her here had never been strong, and now it fled altogether. She was not here to see anyone; this was all a mistake; she had no business here. Without replying she turned to leave.

"Wait," the Beng said. "Where are you going?"

She halted, struggling with herself, still unable to speak.

Finally she managed to say only: "Please—please—"

She realized that she had spoken in Beng. How strange that felt, using those alien words! Go on, she thought. Say the rest of it. *I have come here to see the man with the scarred shoulder.* No, she still couldn't say it, not to this grim-faced stranger, not to anyone. She could barely say it even to herself.

"You are the offering-woman?"

Torlyri stared. "You know me?"

"Everyone knows you, yes. You wait here. This place, right here, offering-woman. You understand me?" He pointed to the ground. "Here. Stay."

Torlyri nodded.

I am speaking their language, she thought in wonder. I understand what he says to me. And then I open my mouth and their words come out.

The sentry swung brusquely about and disappeared into the Beng settlement.

Torlyri stood trembling. He wants me to wait, she said to herself. Wait for what? Wait for whom? What shall I do?

Wait, a voice deep within her said.

Very well. I will wait.

The minutes slipped by, and the sentry did not return. The hot dust-laden wind blew through the canyon of empty ancient buildings with such force that she had to shield her face from

it. Once again she thought of going, quickly, quietly, before anyone came. But she hesitated. She wanted neither to stay nor to
go. Her own indecisiveness began to amuse her. At your age!
she told herself. These fears, this ridiculous shyness. Like a girl.
Like a very young girl.

"Offering-woman! Here he is, offering-woman!"

The sentry had returned. And *he* was with him. She had not
needed to ask; the sentry had known. How embarrassing that
was! And yet how much simpler for her.

The sentry stepped aside and the other came forward. Torlyri saw his scarred shoulder, his beautiful searching red eyes, his
high, rounded golden helmet. She began to tremble, and angrily
ordered herself to stop. No one had forced this moment upon her.
She had chosen it. All this was something she had brought about
herself.

In another moment she knew she'd be crying. Yet she could
not bring herself under control. Her fear was too great. Her soul
was at risk here. So long as neither of them had been able to speak
the other's language, her little flirtation had been perfectly safe,
an innocent game, a playful pastime. She could always pretend
that nothing was going on between them, that nothing had been
pledged, nothing had been ventured, nothing had been committed. Indeed, nothing had.

But now that she understood Beng—

Now that she could say what was in her mind—

The wind came hotter and harder, so that the heavy burden of
dust it bore darkened the sky over Dawinno Galihine. It seemed
to Torlyri that if it grew any stronger it would blow down these
tottering buildings which had withstood the storms and earthquakes of seven hundred thousand years.

The man of the scarred shoulder was staring at her strangely, as though astounded that she had come, though she had visited the Beng settlement many times before. For a long while he did not speak, nor did she.

Then at last he said, "Offering-woman—?"

"Torlyri is my name."

"Torlyri. It is a very beautiful name. You understand what I say to you?"

"If you speak slowly. And you? Do you understand me?"

"You say our words very beautifully. Very beautifully. Your voice is so soft." He smiled and put both his hands to the sides of his helmet, letting them rest there a moment, as though in indecision. Then swiftly he undid the helmet's throat-strap and took it off. She had never seen him without it, indeed had never seen any of the male Bengs bareheaded. The transformation was an unsettling one. His head seemed oddly small this way and his stature diminished, although but for the strange color of his fur and eyes he was identical now to any man of her own tribe.

The sentry, who had remained hovering in the background, coughed ostentatiously and turned away. Torlyri realized that this removing of the helmet must be some kind of invitation to intimacy, or perhaps some even more heavily charged act of commitment. Her trembling, which somehow had halted without her noticing, began again.

He said, "My name is Trei Husathirn. Will you come to my house?"

She started to say that she would, and gladly. But she checked herself. She knew the Beng language, yes, or such a smattering of it as Hresh had been able to learn and to teach her, yet how could she know the meanings within the meanings? What did "Will you come to my house?" mean? Was it an invitation to couple? To twine? To mate, even? Yissou help me, then, she thought, if he thinks I am pledging myself to be his mate, when I know nothing more of him than his name! Or was it simply an acknowledgment that they were standing in a hot, dusty, windswept street when they could be drinking wine and eating cakes in some more comfortable place?

She stood there, searching his face, praying for guidance.

Into her silence he said—sounding hurt, she thought, although the cadence of Beng speech was so fierce that it was hard to tell— "You do not wish to come, then?"

"I didn't say that."

"Then let us go."

"You must understand—I can't stay long—"

"Of course. Just a short while."

He made as though to go; but she remained where she was.

"Torlyri?" he said, reaching toward her, not quite touching her.

He looked strangely vulnerable without his helmet. She wished he would put it back on. It was the helmet that had drawn her to him in the first place, that simple shining golden dome lightly bedecked with leaves, so different from the eerie nightmarish helmets that most of his tribefellows preferred: his helmet, yes, and something about his eyes, and the way he smiled, and the way he held himself. Of the man behind the eyes she still knew nothing.

"Torlyri?" he said again, almost plaintively.

"All right. A short visit."

"You will come! Nakhaba!" His eerie red eyes glowed like fiery suns in his delight. "A short visit, yes! Come. Come. I have something for you, Torlyri, a gift, a precious thing especially for you. Come!"

Quickly he strode past the sentry, not even looking back to see if she was following him. The sentry made a gesture that she did not understand, but that seemed friendly: perhaps a holy sign, perhaps just a bawdy one. Torlyri made the sign of Yissou at him and went rushing after Trei Husathirn.

His house, as he called it, was a single room. It was situated on the ground floor of some rambling palace of the sapphire-eyes, a structure built of a white stone with a cool yellow fire mysteriously burning within the building-blocks. Trei Husathirn's house was a sparse place, with a pile of furs to serve as a bed, a simple upright altar of some sort in a niche, a few spears and throwing-sticks leaning against the wall, and two or three small wickerwork baskets that might contain clothing or other personal belongings.

Torlyri saw no sign of a woman's presence anywhere about the room's furnishings. She felt a great rush of relief at that; and then she felt abashed at feeling such relief.

Trei Husathirn knelt at his altar and whispered some words she did not hear, and laid his helmet within the altar niche with obvious reverence. Then he rose and came to her side and they stood facing each other, neither of them speaking.

She thought of all that she had planned to say to him, once they were finally alone and now that she was able to communicate properly with him, and she saw now the absurdity of the little speech she had constructed. To speak of love? How? By what right? They were strangers. In their occasional meetings when people of one tribe were visiting the other they had enjoyed eyeing one another, and winking and grinning, and pointing and laughing at things that had suddenly seemed funny to them, the gods only knew why. But nothing had ever passed between them. Nothing. She had not even known his name until a few minutes ago. All that he had known of her was that she was the offering-woman of her tribe, and even that might have had no real meaning to him. And now they were face to face, silent, neither of them with the slightest idea of what to do or say next.

435

To her horror she found herself reaching her hand to his right shoulder, lightly touching the long narrow scar that ran from the fleshy part of his forearm to the side of his neck. The fur was gone there and smooth silver-pink skin showed, very odd to the touch, like ancient parchment. When she realized what she was doing she pulled back from him as though she had put her hand in a bonfire.

"Hjjk-men," he said. "When I was a boy. The beak they have, very bad. Three of them died for this."

"I'm so sorry."

"It was long ago. I never think of it."

The trembling began again. Torlyri steadied herself. His eyes rested unwaveringly on hers, and she made herself meet his gaze. He and she were almost the same height; but she was tall, for a woman. There was great strength to him. Plainly he was a warrior, and surely a valiant one.

It was his turn now to touch her. Lightly he drew his fingers over the spiral of brilliant white fur that ran from her right shoulder over her breast to her hip, and then he ran his hand down the matching stripe on her left side.

"Very beautiful," he said. "The white. I have never seen anything like it."

"It's—not common among us."

"You have a child, Torlyri? With the same white?"

"I have no children, no."

"A man? You have a man?"

She saw the tension on his face.

The easiest thing would be to tell him what was, after all, the truth: No, I have no man. But that was only part of the truth, and she needed to have him know more. "I had a man for a while," she said. "He went away."

436

"Ah."

"He went far away. I will never see him again."

"I am very sorry, Torlyri."

She managed a flickering smile. "Are you, really?"

"Sorry that you have been hurt, yes. Not sorry that he has gone away, no, I could not say that."

"Ah," she said.

They were silent again, but it was a different sort of silence from the hard, awkward one of before.

Then she said, "In my tribe it was never the custom for the offering-woman to take a mate, but then things changed for us when we left the cocoon and new customs came. And I realized that I too wanted a mate like all the others, and I took one. So I had my man only for a little while, and it was very recently. You understand what I am saying, Trei Husathirn? Most of my life I was without a man, and that was all right. Then I had one, and I think I was happy with him; and then he left me and it hurt very much. There are times when I think I would have been better off never having had a man at all than to have had one and lost him in that way."

"No," he said. "How can you say that? You knew love, did you not? The man goes away, but the knowledge of the love that you had can never go away. Would you rather never have had love at all in your life?"

"I have had love, other than the love I had with him. The love of Koshmar, my—" She faltered, realizing she knew no Beng word for twining-partner. "My friend," she said lamely. "And the love of all my tribe. I know I am much loved, and I love them."

"It is not the same kind of love."

"Perhaps. Perhaps." She took a deep breath. "And you? Do you have a woman, Trei Husathirn?"

"I had one."

"Ah."

"She is dead. The hjjk-men—"

"At the same time as *that*?" she said, pointing at the scar.

"A later battle. Much later."

"You have had many battles with the hjjk-men?"

Trei Husathirn shrugged. "They are everywhere. They made us suffer, and we made them suffer, I think. Although they seem not to feel pain of any kind, pain of the body, pain of the soul." He shook his head and grimaced, as though talk of hjjk-men were nauseating to him. "I said I had a gift for you, Torlyri."

"Yes. There is no need—"

"Please," he said. He dug about in one of his wicker baskets and drew forth a helmet, not one of the ferocious kind but a smaller one of the sort that she had seen some Beng women wearing. It was fashioned of a shining red metal, highly polished and very bright, almost like a mirror, but it was graceful and delicate of design, a tapering cone with two rounded summits and complex patterns of interlacing lines cut into it by some master's hand. Timidly he handed it to her. She stared at it without taking it.

"It's wonderful," she said. "But I couldn't."

"You will, please."

"It's too valuable."

"It is very valuable. That is why I give it to you."

"What does it mean," Torlyri said after a moment, "when a woman takes a helmet from a man?"

Trei Husathirn looked uncomfortable. "That they are friends."

"Ah," she said. She had spoken of Koshmar as her *friend*. "And friendship between man and woman? What does that mean?"

He looked even more uncomfortable. "It means—you must

understand—it—means—oh, Torlyri, must I say, must I say? You know! You do!"

"I gave myself in friendship to a man and he hurt me."

"It happens. But not all the time."

"We are of different tribes—there is no precedent—"

"You speak our language. You will know our ways." He proffered the shining helmet again. "There is something between us. You know that. You knew it from the first. Even when we could not speak with each other, there was something. The helmet is for you, Torlyri. Many years have I kept it in this box, but now I give it to you. Please. Please."

Now he was trembling. She could not have that. Gently she took the helmet from him, and held it above her head as though trying it on, and then, without putting it on, she pressed it against her bosom and carefully laid it to one side.

"Thank you," she whispered. "I will treasure it all my life."

She touched his scar again, lightly, lovingly. His hand went to the white stripe that began at her left shoulder, and traveled down her body as far as her breast, and paused there. She moved toward him. Then he embraced her and drew her down toward the pile of furs.

Under the hot cutting wind out of the south Taniane felt her soul stirring with yearnings both of the body and the spirit.

There was a throbbing all along her belly and thighs and inward to her sexual parts that was easy enough to understand. It would be good to couple today. Haniman was probably around somewhere, or else Orbin would do. Orbin was never unwilling.

Then, too, she felt a tension in her forehead and at the base of her neck and downward through her spine that appeared to argue in favor of a twining. She had not twined in a long time. Indeed, it was something she rarely did, for lack of a partner who touched her spirit. But today the need seemed urgent. Perhaps, she thought, she was only confusing it with coupling-need, and that other pressure would go away once she had found the pleasure her body craved.

But there was something else troubling her that was neither coupling-need nor twining-need: a restlessness, a deep sense of impatience and uneasiness, that sprang from no specific cause. She felt it in her teeth, behind her eyes, in the pit of her stomach; but she knew that those were mere outward manifestations of some ache of the soul. That was not an unfamiliar sensation for her, but it was more intense today, as if fanned to kindling-heat by the unceasing maddening gusts of the dry wind. It had something to do with the departure of Harruel and his followers—Taniane by now had come to believe that they must be undergoing the most marvelous adventures in dazzling far-off lands, while she remained trapped here pointlessly in dusty crumbling Vengiboneeza—and it had something to do also with the expanding presence of the Bengs. The Bengs pretended friendship, but it was friendship of a strange kind. In their friendly way they had slowly but steadily taken full possession of nearly every quarter of the city as though they were the masters of the place and Koshmar's tribe a mere raggle-taggle band of amiably tolerated intruders. Taniane was bothered, too, by Koshmar's passivity in the face of this displacement. She had not tried to deal with the Bengs at all. She had done nothing to limit the spread of their power. She simply shrugged and let them do as they pleased.

Koshmar barely seemed to be Koshmar any longer. It seemed to Taniane that the secession of Harruel must have broken her. And there were problems of some sort between Koshmar and Torlyri, evidently; Torlyri was hardly ever to be found in the settlement now, but spent most of her time off among the Bengs. The rumor was that Torlyri had taken a Beng lover. Why did Koshmar tolerate that? What was *wrong* with Koshmar? If she lacked the strength to be chieftain any longer, why didn't she step down, and let someone with a little vigor take over? Koshmar was past the old limit-age now. If the tribe still lived in the cocoon, Taniane thought, Koshmar would have gone outside to her death, and very likely I would be chieftain now. But there was no longer a limit-age and Koshmar refused to relinquish power.

Taniane had no desire to overthrow Koshmar by force, nor did she think the People would support her if she attempted it, even though she was the only woman of the tribe who was of the proper age and the proper spirit to be chieftain. But something had to be done. New leadership is what we need, she thought, and soon. And the new leader, Taniane told herself, must find some way of halting the encroachments of the Bengs.

She crossed the plaza and entered the storehouse where the Great World artifacts were kept. She hoped to find Haniman there, and deal with the simplest of the needs that were assailing her this morning.

But instead of Haniman she found Hresh, morosely prowling among the mysterious ancient devices that he and his Seekers had collected, which had largely been neglected since the coming of the Bengs. He looked up at her but did not speak.

"Am I disturbing you?" she asked.

"Not especially. Is there something you want?"

"I was looking for—well, it doesn't matter. You look unhappy, Hresh."

"So do you."

"It's this filthy wind. Will it ever stop blowing, do you think?"

He shrugged. "It'll stop when it stops. There's rain in the north and this dry air is rushing to meet it."

"You understand so much, Hresh."

Looking away, he said, "I understand hardly anything at all."

"You really *are* unhappy about something."

She moved closer to him. He stood with shoulders slumped, saying nothing, idly toying with some intricate silvery device whose function no one had ever been able to determine. How thin he is, she thought. How slight. Suddenly her heart surged with love for him. She saw that he might actually be afraid of her, he whose great wisdom and mysterious skills of the mind had been so frightening to her. She wanted to put her arm around him as Torlyri might do, and comfort him, and draw him into a warm embrace. But he was hidden away behind a curtain of distress.

She said, "Tell me what troubles you."

"Did I say that anything did?"

"I can see it on your face."

He shook his head irritably. "Let me be, Taniane. Are you looking for Haniman? I don't know where he is. Possibly he and Orbin went down to the lakefront to catch some fish, or else—"

"I didn't come here looking for Haniman," she said. And then to her own great surprise she heard herself saying, "I came here looking for you, Hresh."

"Me? What do you want with me?"

Desperately improvising, she said, "Can you teach me some words of the Beng language, do you think? Just a little of it?"

"You too?"

"Has someone else asked you that?"

"Torlyri. That Beng of hers, the one with the scar that she's always laughing and flirting with—she's in love with him, do you know that? She came to me a few days ago with a funny look in her eye. Teach me Beng, she said. You have to teach me Beng. Teach me right away. She *insisted*. Have you ever heard Torlyri insist on anything before?"

"What did you do?"

"I taught her how to speak Beng."

"You did? I thought you didn't yet know enough of it yourself to teach anyone anything except a few words."

"No," Hresh said in a very small voice. "I was lying. I know Beng like a Beng. I used the Barak Dayir to learn it from the old man of their tribe. I was keeping it all to myself, that was all. But I couldn't refuse Torlyri when she asked like that. So now she knows Beng too."

"And I'll be the next one to learn."

Hresh looked flustered and immensely ill at ease.

"Taniane—please, Taniane—"

"Please what? It's your responsibility to teach me, Hresh. To teach us all. Those people are our enemies. We have to be able to understand them if we're going to cope with them, don't you see?"

"They aren't our enemies," said Hresh.

"So they keep trying to get us to believe. Well, maybe they are and maybe they aren't, but how are we supposed to know what they are if we can't figure out what they're saying? And you are the only one who knows—except Torlyri, now, I guess. What if something happens to you? You *can't* withhold it any longer, Hresh. Now that you've admitted you can teach it. We all need to know Beng, and not just so we can run off and be with Beng lovers, like Torlyri. Our survival depends on it. Or don't you agree?"

"Maybe. I suppose."

"Then teach it to me. I want to start today. If you think I need to get Koshmar's permission, then let's go to Koshmar right now. You ought to be teaching Koshmar, too. And then everybody else that matters in this tribe."

Hresh was silent. He seemed lost in anguish.

"What's wrong?" Taniane asked. "Is it such a terrible thing that I want to learn Beng?"

In a low dismal voice Hresh said, not looking at her, "The way to learn it is by twining."

Taniane's eyes flashed. "So? Where's the difficulty?"

"I asked you once to twine with me, and you refused."

So that was it! She felt a moment of embarrassment; and then, seeing that he was even more embarrassed than she, she smiled and said, as gently as she could, "It was because of the way you asked, Hresh. Simply running right up to me the minute Torlyri had taught you how to do it, and saying to me, 'Let's go, Taniane, let's get right to it this minute.' I was offended by that, didn't you realize that? We spent thirteen years growing up together, both of us waiting for the day when we'd be old enough to twine, and then you spoiled it, Hresh, you spoiled it with your silly clumsy—"

"I know," he said dolefully. "You don't have to tell me all over again."

She gave him a lively flirtatious glance. "But even though I said no that one time, it didn't necessarily mean that I'd refuse you the next time you asked."

Hresh seemed not to have noticed the glance. "That's what Koshmar said too," he replied, in the same leaden tone as before.

"You discussed this with Koshmar?" Taniane said, fighting back her laughter.

"She seemed to know all about it. She said I should ask you again."

"Well, Koshmar was right."

Hresh stared at her. Coldly he said, "You mean, now that you have something special to gain from twining with me you're willing to do it, is that it?"

"You're the most infuriating person I've ever known, Hresh!"

"But I'm right."

"You're utterly wrong. This has nothing to do with your teaching me Beng. I've been waiting ever since that first day for you to show some interest in me again."

"But Haniman—"

"Dawinno take Haniman! He's just someone I couple with! *You're* the twining-partner I want, Hresh! How can you be so stupid? Why must you make me say all these obvious things?"

"You want me for *me*? Not just because I can teach you Beng if we twine?"

"Yes."

"Then why didn't you say so, Taniane?"

She threw up her hands in despair. "Oh! *You!*"

He was silent a long while. There seemed to be no expression on his face at all.

At last he said quietly, "I've been very stupid, haven't I?"

"Very stupid indeed."

"Yes. Yes, so I have." He looked steadily at her for another long silent moment. Then he said, "Couple with me, Taniane."

"Couple? Not twine?"

"Couple, first. I've never coupled with anyone, do you know that?"

"No. I didn't know that."

"Will you, then? Even if I don't do it very well?"

"Of course I will, Hresh. And you'll do it just as well as anybody else."

"And afterward I'd like to twine with you. Yes, Taniane?"

She nodded and smiled. "Yes," she said.

"Not just to teach you Beng. Just to twine for the sake of twining. And later—the next time—I can teach you Beng then, all right?"

"You promise?"

"Yes. Yes. Yes."

"Now?" she said.

"Oh, yes. Yes, now."

In the bright clear morning Salaman went down to his trench to dig. He had long since given up any real hope that the trench was going to yield anything useful, but working in it had the merit of concentrating his thoughts.

He had been digging for no more than five minutes when a long shadow fell across him, and he looked up to see Harruel, hands on hips, peering down at him. The king was wobbling back and forth in a troublesome way, as though about to topple into the open ditch. It seemed very early in the day for Harruel to be this drunk, Salaman thought.

"Still at it, are you?" Harruel asked, and laughed. "By Dawinno, you'd better take care, or you'll dig up an ice-eater down there!"

"Ice-eaters are all gone," Salaman said, without breaking his rhythm. "Too warm for ice-eaters these days. Grab a shovel, Harruel! Come down here and do some digging. The work'll do you good."

"Pah! You think I have nothing better to do?"

Salaman did not reply. Teasing Harruel was always a risky game. He had gone as far as he dared. He bent himself to his task, and after a time he heard the king go lurching slowly away, grunting and wheezing.

Salaman's trench was a long, winding thing that cut back and forth through the center of the City of Yissou like an immense dark serpent, running along the back of the royal palace, then between the house of Konya and Galihine and that of Salaman and Weiawala, and then in an undulating line that went curving around past the place where Lakkamai lived. It was deeper than a man was tall, and about as wide across as a man is through the shoulders.

He had dug most of it himself, with occasional help from Konya and Lakkamai, in his continuing search for some remnant of the death-star that he believed had struck here. Since the first days of the city's existence he had managed to put in an hour or two nearly every day. He would dig for a while, carefully, meditatively, then carry the upturned earth back to fill in at the earlier end of the trench, so that it would not totally obstruct foot traffic in the city. As it was, it made him the butt of much humor and more than a little grumbling. But he went on steadily digging.

Salaman told the others that a piece of an actual death-star would be a holy talisman that could ward off any sort of peril. After a time he came to believe that himself. But his main purpose in digging was to prove to himself that the crater had indeed been formed by the impact of a plummeting star. Theories must have verification, Salaman told himself. One must not rely on guess-work alone. And so he dug on. He dreamed of striking shovel against metal, and finding some great mass of congealed iron lying in the ground just beyond the city's edge, and shouting to the others to come and see, come and see.

He had found nothing so far, however, but stones and the thick roots of trees and occasional scraps of dead animals that some scavenger had buried. Perhaps the death-star lay so deep in the ground that he could not hope to dig down to it in five lifetimes; or perhaps, as he had suspected from the start, the death-stars had been made of some material that did not last, balls of fire or balls of ice, which did their terrible damage but left no remnant behind. The one hypothesis Salaman would not accept, because he was convinced it was false, was that this huge circular crater, so regular in form, so obviously an intrusion on the smoothness of the bland valley, could have been formed by anything other than a death-star. An entire civilization had perished under the impact of those falling stars; Salaman had no doubt that they would have left horrendous scars behind, and that the scars would be in the form of such craters as this one where Harruel had chosen to build the City of Yissou.

But death-stars were not uppermost in Salaman's mind as he dug this morning. Today he was obsessed with that strange message from afar—if a message is what it was—which had come to him while he and Weiawala were touching their sensing-organs together on the high place south of the crater.

That insistent drumbeat throbbing. That pounding, rumbling sound. That frightening undercurrent of menace. His imagination, merely? No. No. The signal had been faint; the distance must be great; but Salaman was certain that he had not dreamed it. It had been subtle but it had been real. There was some movement out there, some stirring in the vastness of the continent. Perhaps there was a threat to the city. Perhaps there were precautions that could be taken.

Fearful, trembling, drenched in his own sweat, he dug like a madman for more than an hour, hacking through the ground as though all answers lay buried there. Bits of muddy sand clung to him everywhere. His fur became gritty with it. He felt it grinding between his teeth, and spat and spat without ridding himself of it. He dug with such lunatic force that the soil went spraying out in a wide arc behind him. He scarcely cared where he flung it. After a time he paused, heart thumping, eyes blurred with fatigue, to lean on his shovel and think.

Hresh would know what to do, he told himself.

Suppose you are discussing this with Hresh. What advice would Hresh give? *I have received a message, but it is indistinct. It may be a message of great import, but I am unable to tell, because I cannot read it clearly. Tell me how you would proceed.*

And Hresh would say, *If a message is indistinct, Salaman, why, hold it to a brighter light!*

Yes. Hresh always had a clever answer.

Salaman threw down his shovel and clambered from his ditch. In amazement he looked back at the ragged work he had done this morning, the wildly uneven cut, the dirt scattered everywhere all around. He shook his head in disapproval. Later he would have to mend it, he thought. Later.

Weary as he was, he forced himself to run. He circled past Lakkamai's house, nearly bowled over an astounded Bruikkos, and sprinted up the trail that led toward the south rim of the crater. A demonic energy guided him. He felt Yissou perched on his right shoulder and Dawinno on his left, pouring their force into him; and there was the healing god Friit running just ahead of him, smiling, beckoning him on. Scrambling, stumbling, gasping, Salaman staggered to the crater's edge, vaulted it, found new wind, went running madly on up the trail to his high place, his private viewing-point.

The earth in all its green majesty lay spread out before him.

He looked toward the sunlit southern hills, and paused a moment to gather his breath and collect his strength. Then he raised his sensing-organ and sent forth his second sight, that special perceptive skill that lay in reserve within all his kind. His sensing-organ became as rigid as a mating-rod. He aimed it toward the bright horizon and poured all the energy he had into it.

Once again he heard the throbbing sound: a low dull booming, resonating through the hills far away.

By second sight Salaman found himself at the edge of an understanding of that sound—but only at the edge. He saw a flash of color, a swatch of brilliant screaming scarlet. What did that mean? And then other colors: yellow, black, yellow, black, yellow, black, pulsing, pounding, alternating and repeating, over and over and over.

With those sensations came a profound feeling of terror that sent him down to the ground, crouching, quivering, digging his fingers deep into the rich loamy soil as if to anchor himself.

Something is coming this way, something frightening. But what? What?

He had held the message to a brighter light, and still the light was not bright enough. But he was aflame with resourcefulness now. Twining alone had not brought him clarity of vision; second sight alone had not, though the perception had been a deeper one. But twining *and* second sight, both at once—

Instantly Salaman was on his feet and running down the slope of the crater back into the city. In his frantic headlong plunge he dislodged all manner of pebbles and even larger rocks, so that a tiny avalanche accompanied him, and more than once he turned an ankle, though he let it slow him only for a moment. He knew that a kind of madness was upon him, that the fire of the gods had entered into him.

"Weiawala!" he called, as he burst into the center of the little city. "Where are you? Weiawala! Weiawala!"

She came out of the house of Bruikkos and Thaloin, frowning, looking around. When she saw him she put a hand over her mouth.

"What has happened to you, Salaman? I've never seen you like this! You're all sweaty—covered with dirt—"

"That doesn't matter." He seized her by the wrist. "Come on! Come with me!"

"Have you gone insane?"

"Come! Up to the high place!"

He started to tug at her. Thaloin now emerged from the house, blinking in the sunlight, staring in bewilderment at the scene before her. The sight of her inspired Salaman to an experiment. If one twining-partner could amplify a mental message from afar, two might yield a far greater depth of perception. With a quick swoop of his hand he caught hold of her too, and began to drag both women toward the trail.

"Let go," Thaloin cried. "What are you—"

"Just come along," Salaman muttered. "Please. Don't argue. It's vital. We're going up the hill—there—"

Grasping Thaloin with one hand and Weiawala with the other, he pulled them along behind him. The noise and furor attracted onlookers—Lakkamai, Minbain, the child Samnibolon—who exchanged mystified glances. As Salaman passed by the royal palace, Harruel came out its back door, brooding and sullen and dark of face, weaving and lurching in the last stages of drunkenness. He pointed to Salaman and laughed raucously.

"*Two*, Salaman? Two at once? Only a king gets two women at once! Here—give me—give me—"

Harruel clutched at Weiawala. Salaman, cursing, butted him in the chest with his shoulder. Harruel's eyes widened. He cried out in amazement and went toppling back, arms flailing, toward the edge of Salaman's trench. Losing his balance then, he tumbled down into it. Salaman did not look back at him. Tightening his grip on Weiawala and Thaloin, he drew them away with him, up, up, up the rough rocky trail to the rim of the crater. He knew he was moving too fast for them: they stumbled and tripped and fell again and again, and he tugged them up, he dragged them onward. Thaloin was much shorter than Weiawala and could barely keep pace, but he paused, and paused again, to help her along. They were offering no resistance. They must have decided that they were in the hands of a madman and the safest thing was to accede to whatever he wanted.

When he reached the high place Salaman threw them down by the overlook point and dropped down beside them. All three lay for a moment, gasping, wheezing, fighting for breath.

"Now we will twine," Salaman said finally.

Weiawala looked astonished. "You—me—Thaloin—?"

"All three."

Thaloin made a whimpering sound. Salaman glared at her.

"All three!" he said again, with the urgency of one who was crazed. "This is important to the security of the city! Twine, and give me your energy, and give me your second sight as well! Twine! Twine!" The two women lay as though paralyzed, trembling faintly. Salaman took Weiawala's sensing-organ and wrapped it around his own, and put Thaloin's atop both. In the softest, most seductive voice he could manage he said, "Please. Do as I say. Give yourselves to the twining."

They were too frightened and exhausted to comply as rapidly as Salaman wished. But he stroked them, he caressed them, he aroused them in their sexual parts as though he meant to couple with them rather than to twine; and after a time he felt the beginning of a communion with Weiawala, and then Thaloin timidly, fearfully joining him also.

Twining with two at once? Had anyone ever dreamed of such a thing? Images flooded in upon him, confusing him at first, leaving him wholly baffled. But Salaman forced himself to sort one from the other and to make his way among them. Gradually the confusion ebbed. A godlike feeling of all-seeing vision spread in him.

"Second sight," he urged. "Use your second sight! Yes, that's the way—"

He saw.

With their help he could send his perceptions into the skies, and beyond, far to the south, the north, the east, the west. It was a dizzying and wondrous sensation. What had been a dull booming was now a terrible thunder, a powerful hammering drumbeat that was like an endless great earthquake. It came not from the southern hills but from the far north, he realized: what he had picked up earlier was only the reverberation of the message as it rebounded from the high land to the south.

He saw the great red animals of the Beng people, the enormous shaggy beasts they called vermilions—an immense herd of them, thousands upon thousands, a teeming scarlet sea of vermilions, an undulating red mass of huge shambling creatures that covered whole mountain ranges and filled valley after valley—on the march, a fearful stampeding multitude of the mighty beasts far away, heading south, heading toward the City of Yissou—

And with them, marching among them, driving the great beasts onward—

Hjjk-folk. A colossal army of them, the yellow-and-black insect-people advancing in uncountable numbers. He could see the glittering faceted globes of their innumerable eyes, he could hear the frightful clacking of their savage beaks.

The hjjk-folk were coming, marching with their vermilions, sweeping everything in their path to destruction. Coming this way.

*　　　*　　　*

It was the strangest twining she had ever had. They had done it right after they had coupled, which perhaps had been a bad idea; for Hresh, though he coupled well enough for someone who claimed never to have done it before, had seemed preoccupied with doing things the right way, and his self-consciousness had eventually become an awkward problem for Taniane. Possibly some of that had carried over into the twining. When she had opened to his spirit he had come forth to her in a breathtaking rush, but almost immediately she could feel him holding something back, setting up barriers, hiding aspects of his soul from her. That was no way to twine. And yet, and yet, despite that mysterious reticence of his it had been an overwhelming communion for her, a powerful, intense, unforgettable thing. She knew that she had experienced only a fraction of him. But that fraction had been far more than anything she had had from anyone else with whom she had ever twined.

When it was over they lay quietly in the twining-chamber, listening to the warm wind gusting through the streets.

She said, after a time, "Can I tell you something, Hresh?"

"Is it something I'll enjoy hearing?"

"I'm not sure of that."

He hesitated a moment. "Say it anyway."

She ran her hand lightly along the soft fur on the inner side of his arm. "You won't misunderstand, will you?"

"How can I say?"

"All right. All right. What I wanted to tell you is that you—well—that you set things loose inside me, Hresh, that are so strong they frighten me. That's all."

"I don't know how I'm supposed to take that."

"In a good way. Really."

"I hope so," he said. He put his hand to her arm, and stroked her in the same way; and for a while they were silent again. Her head was against his breast and she could feel his heart, drum-loud within him.

"Didn't Torlyri teach you that you mustn't hold anything back when you twine?" Taniane asked, after a while.

"Was I holding back?"

"That's how it seemed to me."

"I'm still new at this, Taniane."

"Not much newer than I am. But I know what twining ought to be like, and I know that you were hiding yourself from me, or at least some of yourself, and that hurt me, Hresh, it made me feel as though you didn't trust me, even that you were using me in some way—"

"*No!*"

"I don't mean to upset you. I'm just trying to tell you some of my feelings—so that it'll be better for us the next time—I do want there to be a next time, Hresh, you know I do, a next time and a next and a next—"

"I wasn't holding myself back, Taniane."

"All right. Maybe I didn't understand."

He pulled away, sitting up on one elbow, and looked straight at her. "If I was holding anything back," he said, "it was the things that I've been discovering about the world, about the People, about the Bengs, about the Great World—things that I'm still sifting through, things that have shaken me like an earthquake, Taniane—such gigantic things that I'm only beginning to comprehend them. They're lying right here at the edge of my soul, and maybe I didn't want to pass them along to you when we twined, because—because—I don't know, because I thought it might hurt you to know some of those things, and so I held them back—"

"Tell me," she said.

"I'm not sure I—"

"Tell me."

He studied her. After a moment he said, "That time I used the Barak Dayir to take us into the long building of dark green stone where we saw the Dream-Dreamer ghosts moving around—do you remember that, Taniane?"

"Of course."

"What did you think that building was?"

"A temple," she said. "A Great World temple."

"Whose temple?"

She frowned. "The Dream-Dreamers' temple."

"And who were the Dream-Dreamers?" Hresh asked.

She did not reply at once. "You want to know what I really thought, that day?" she said hesitantly.

"Yes."

"Don't laugh at me when I tell you."

"Absolutely not."

She said, "I thought that the Dream-Dreamers were the humans the chronicles talk about. Not us. That it's just as the sapphire-eyes artificials said, when we first came into Vengiboneeza—that we're wrong to think of ourselves as humans, because all we are is some kind of clever animals. We weren't part of the Great World at all. That's what I've believed ever since we went to that building. But I know that I'm wrong. It can't be true, can it? It's all a lot of crazy nonsense, isn't it, Hresh? The Dream-Dreamers are probably people who came from some other star. And we're human beings, just as we've always believed we were."

"No. We aren't humans."

"We aren't?"

"I've seen the proof. There's no way to hide from it. All over the Great World ruins you see statues of the Six Peoples, and we're not among them. The Dream-Dreamers are. And there was a place in old Vengiboneeza—I've seen it, Taniane, once in a vision that a Great World machine gave me—where they kept all sorts of animals, not civilized beings, just wild creatures. They had one cage with our ancestors in it. Almost like us, they were—and in a cage. On display. Just animals."

"No, Hresh."

"Very intelligent animals. So bright that they built cocoons for us when the Long Winter came—or maybe we built the cocoons ourselves, I'm not sure of that—and left us to wait the winter out. And Dawinno changed us, and made us more intelligent, so intelligent that we misunderstood the chronicles and thought *we* were the humans. We weren't. I know that. The old man of the Bengs knows it too. His people never thought for a moment that they were the same as the humans who lived in Great World times."

"But if the humans are supposed to inherit the earth, as it says in the chronicles, now that the winter's over—"

"No," Hresh said. "The humans are all gone. I suppose they died in the Long Winter, except for Ryyig Dream Dreamer, who may have been the last one. *We're* supposed to inherit the earth. But in order to do that we have to make ourselves human, Taniane."

"I don't follow you. If we aren't human, how can we—"

"By living *like* humans. We almost do, now. We have language, we have writing, we have history. We can build. We can teach our children. Those are human things, not animal things. Animals work by instinct. We work by knowledge. You see? It isn't only the Dream-Dreamers who were human, Taniane! All the Six Peoples of the Great World were! The human humans, and the sapphire-eyes, and the vegetals—"

"The hjjks too? Human?"

Hresh hesitated. "If 'human' means civilized, yes. If it means possessing the ability to learn, and create things, and transform the world. Even the hjjks are human by that standard. A different kind of human, that's all. And we'll be human too. The new humans, the newest humans. If we continue to grow, and build, and think. We have to get ourselves away from Vengiboneeza, first, and create something that's really ours—not just hide here in these ruins. Build a Vengiboneeza of our own, a civilization that isn't just put together out of the rubble of the one that came before. Do you see what I'm saying?"

"Yes. I do. I think I do, Hresh. It's almost the same thing Harruel was saying."

"Yes. Somehow he understood, and he went off to do the thing that we have to do. However crude and rough he is, at least he's begun to build. Which is our task too. We have to touch the past and the future both. That's what humans are—people who continue things, who create links between what was and what is to come. That's why it's important for us to finish exploring these ruins, and find whatever we can from the Great World that still can be used. And take it with us when we leave Vengiboneeza, and put it to our own uses, to build what we need to build." He was smiling now. "We haven't gone looking much since the Bengs came, have we? But I was out by myself, the other night. I found a whole new storehouse of things, far across the city. The Bengs caught me before I could go in—I'm not sure they know what's there themselves, but they want to keep us out anyway. We can't allow that. Let's go back there, you and I. Let's see what's in there. All right? All right, Taniane?"

"Of course," she said. "When?"

"A day, two days. Soon."

"Yes. Soon."

He reached for her, and she thought it was to twine again; but all he wanted was an embrace, and then he jumped to his feet, reaching a hand to her to pull her up too. He had to find Koshmar, he told her. These matters must be discussed. And then there were other important things to do. Always things to discuss, things to do. Off he went, leaving her standing by herself, shaking her head.

Hresh, she thought. How strange you are, Hresh! But how wonderful.

Her mind was spinning. Not human—we must make ourselves human—we must build—we must touch the past and touch the future both—

She wandered into the plaza and stood by herself, trying to make herself calm. Someone came up behind her. Haniman.

"Twine with me," he whispered.

"No."

"You keep saying no."

"Let me alone, Haniman."

"Couple with me, then."

"No!"

"Not even that?"

"Let me be, will you?"

"What's the matter, Taniane? You sound so bothered."

"I am."

"Tell me what's troubling you."

"Go away," she said.

"I'm trying to make you feel better. It's an old human tradition, you know. Woman in distress, man tries to offer comfort."

She glared at him in exasperation. "We aren't humans!" she cried. "What?"

"Hresh says so. He has proof. We're just animals, the way the guardians of the gate said we are. The Dream-Dreamers were the humans, and they're all dead. You're just a monkey with a big brain, Haniman, and so am I. Go ask Hresh, if you don't believe me. Now get away from me, will you? Leave me alone! Leave me alone!"

Haniman stared at her, astounded.

Then he backed away from her. Taniane looked after him, one hand over her mouth.

In the darkness of the chapel, amid the smoke of the smoldering fire, Koshmar saw masked figures moving before her. This, with the terrible warlike beak, was Lirridon. This was Nialli, with the black-and-green mask armed with blood-red spikes. This was Sismoil, featureless, enigmatic. This was Thekmur. This was Yanla. This was Vork.

She gripped the sides of the altar so that she would not lose her balance. A cold sweat had broken out on her, and there was a fiery pain behind her breastbone. Her throat was dry and she knew that an ocean could never quench that thirst.

"Koshmar," Thekmur said. "Poor sad Koshmar."

"Poor pitiful Koshmar," said Lirridon.

"We weep for you, Koshmar," Nialli said.

She stared at the haughty figures stalking about in front of her and shook her head angrily. The last thing she wanted was the pity of her dead predecessors.

"No," she said, and her voice held back within her, a husky hollow rasp. "You must not say these things to me!"

"Come to us, Koshmar," said Yanla, who had been chieftain so many years ago that nothing but her name and her mask remained to keep her memory alive. "Come lie in our arms. You have been chieftain long enough."

"No!"

"Rest with us," said Vork. "Sleep in our bosom and know the joy of unending peace."

"*No!*"

Thekmur, who had been like a mother to her, knelt down beside her and softly said, "We reached our death-days and we went forth into the cold place and lay down to die. Why do you cling so fiercely to your life, Koshmar? You are past the limit-age. You are terribly weary. Rest now, Koshmar."

"The winter is over. There is no longer any cold place. The limit-age is not observed here in the time of the New Springtime."

"The New Springtime?" Sismoil said. "Has it really come, do you think? The New Springtime, really?"

"Yes! Yes!"

"Sleep, Koshmar. Let another woman rule. You have lost half your tribe—"

"Not half! Only a few!"

"The Bengs encroach upon your settlement."

"I will slaughter the Bengs!"

"A younger woman readies herself for power. Give it to her, Koshmar."

"When her time comes and not before."

"Her time has come."

"No. No. No."

"Sleep, Koshmar."

"Not yet. Dawinno take you, I'm still alive, can't you see? I rule! I lead!"

Rising, Koshmar waved her arms furiously about, clearing the fumes that filled the little room. The gesture was costly to her: the pain beneath her breastbone grew startlingly more intense, striking deep into her in a hard stabbing way. But she would not let her discomfort show. Flinging open the chapel's pivoted stone door, she allowed fresh air to come rushing in, and the dim figures of the dead chieftains grew thin, grew transparent, vanished altogether. Coughing, choking, Koshmar staggered out into the daylight. She caught hold of a battered ancient cornice and hung tight to it until the spasms of dizziness passed.

I will never go to this chapel again, she told herself. Let the dead remain dead. I have no need of their wisdom.

Slowly she made her way past the six ruined arches and the five whole ones, across the plaza of pink marble flagstones, up the five flights of megalithic stairs. She went past the stump of the fallen black tower, and south and west through the city in the direction of the settlement. Occasionally Koshmar caught sight of a vermilion of the Bengs wandering by itself, grazing on the weeds that sprouted from the cracked paving-blocks. A pack of monkeys ran past her along the rooftops, screeching derisively and hurling things at her from a safe distance. She gave them a glare of loathing. Twice she saw Helmet Men at some remove, going silently about their unknowable missions; neither of them made any gesture that acknowledged her presence.

She was still some way beyond the settlement in a zone of huge fallen statues and mirror-bright pavilions that had crumbled to silvered shards when she saw the slight figure of Hresh in the distance. He was running toward her, shouting, calling her name.

"What is it?" she asked. "Why have you followed me out here?"

He perched on the shoulder of a fallen marble colossus and looked at her expectantly. "To talk with you, Koshmar."

"Here?"

"I wouldn't want any of the People to overhear us."

Koshmar gave him a dour look. "If this is some fantastic new scheme that you mean to propose, you should know before you begin that you have come upon me at a time when I prefer to be alone, and you find me in a most unreceptive mood. *Most* unreceptive."

"I'll have to risk that, I suppose. I want to talk with you about leaving the city."

"You?" Her eyes flashed in anger. "Running off to Harruel, is that what you plan to do?"

"Not to Harruel, no. And not just me, Koshmar. All of us."

"*All?*" The hot stabbing pain beneath her breastbone returned. She wanted to rub at it. But that would reveal her distress to Hresh. Controlling herself with a severe effort, she said, "What foolishness is this, now? I warned you that I didn't want you to bother me with fantastic new schemes, and—"

"May I speak, Koshmar?"

"Go on."

"I remind you of the day we entered Vengiboneeza, years ago. When the artificial sapphire-eyes jeered at us, and called me 'little monkey,' and told us we were something other than true human beings."

"We made the proper reply, and the guardians of the gate accepted us as human and let us go in."

"Accepted us, yes. But they never agreed that we were humans of the Great World kind. 'You are the humans *now*,' is what they said. Do you remember, Koshmar?"

"This is very tiresome, Hresh."

"What would you say if I told you that I've discovered unanswerable proof that the guardians were speaking the truth? That

463

the Dream-Dreamers were the real humans of the Great World times, and that in the Great World times our kind was little more than animals?"

"Absurd, boy!"

"I have proof."

"Absurd proof. What I said then was that there probably have been many kinds of humans, but we are the only kind that still exists. So the world is rightfully ours. We have no need to discuss this all over again, Hresh. And what does it have to do with our leaving Vengiboneeza, anyway?"

"Because," Hresh said, "if we are human beings, as you say, and if we are the only humans who still exist, then we should go from this place and build a city of our own, as humans do, instead of living as squatters in the ruins of some ancient people."

"This is the argument that Harruel made. It was treason and it broke the tribe apart. If you believe what he believes, then you should go to live with him, wherever he and his followers may be. Is that what you want? Then go. Go, Hresh!"

"I want us all to go. So that we can become human."

"We *are* human!"

"Then we should leave here so that we can live up to our destiny as humans. Don't you see, Koshmar, the difference between humans and animals is that animals simply live from day to day, whereas humans—"

"Enough," said Koshmar in a very quiet voice. "This discussion is over."

"Koshmar, I—"

"Over." She put her hand to her breast and pressed hard, and began to rub. The pain was strong enough to make her want to double over and clutch herself, but she forced herself to sit erect. "I came out here to be alone, and think about things that are of concern to me," she said. "You've intruded on my privacy, though I asked you not to do so, and you've dredged up all sorts of old nonsense that has no relevance to our situation today. We are *not* monkeys. Those gibbering things on the rooftops are monkeys, and they are no kin of ours. And we *will* leave Vengiboneeza, yes, when the gods tell me that our time to leave has come. When the gods tell me, Hresh, not you. Is that understood? Good. Good. Now leave me."

"But—"

"Leave me, Hresh!"

"As you wish," he said, and turned and walked slowly back toward the settlement.

When he was out of sight Koshmar huddled down, shivering, while wave after wave of agony swept through her. After a little while the spasm passed, and she sat up, drenched in sweat, her pounding heart gradually calming.

The boy means well, she thought. He is so serious, so deeply concerned with high matters of destiny and purpose. And very likely he is right that the People should leave this place to seek the fulfillment of their destiny somewhere else. Whether we are humans or monkeys, Koshmar thought—and she had no doubt of which the People were—it can do us no good to remain in Vengiboneeza for many years more. That was clear. Eventually we must go forth, we must make a place of our own.

But not now. To leave now would be giving in to the Bengs. The tribe's departure must not seem to have come about under pressure from them, for that would be a stain on the courage of the People and on her own leadership throughout all the rest of time. Hresh must be made to see that. And anyone else who was impatient to leave. Taniane? She might have put Hresh up to this, Koshmar thought. Taniane was an impatient girl, full of hot ambition. It might even be that she was ready to lead a second secession. Taniane and Hresh were in close league these days. Perhaps, Koshmar speculated, Hresh came here just now with the hidden warning that I must begin to countenance a change in policy, or else a change would be imposed against my will.

Nothing will be imposed against my will, thought Koshmar, in rage. Nothing!

Then she closed her eyes and crouched down again.

I am so very tired, she thought.

She rested, letting her mind go empty, letting her spirit drift in the soothing darkness of the void. After a long while she blinked and sat up once more, and saw that yet another visitor was approaching. The distinctive white-striped figure of Torlyri came into view, walking toward her, waving, smiling.

"There you are," Torlyri called. "Hresh said you had gone this way."

You too? Koshmar thought. Coming to plague me with this business?

"Is there some problem?" she asked.

Torlyri seemed surprised. "A problem? No, nothing at all. The sun shines brightly. All is well. But you've been gone half a day. I missed you, Koshmar. I longed to be with you, to feel you close to me again. To enjoy the pleasure of being near you, which has been the highest joy of my life."

Koshmar could find no delight in Torlyri's words. They had a leaden ring to them, the ring of insincerity, of outright falsehood. It was hard to think of warm good Torlyri as insincere, she who had always been the soul of love and truth; but Koshmar knew that Torlyri spoke now out of guilt and uneasiness, not out of the feelings she once had had for Koshmar. That was ended now. Torlyri had changed. Lakkamai had changed her and her Helmet Man had finished the job.

She said, "I had some heavy thinking to do, Torlyri. I went off alone to do it."

"I was worried. You've seemed so weary lately."

"Have I? I've never felt better."

"Dear Koshmar—"

"Do I look sick? Has my fur lost its sheen? Is the glow gone from my eyes?"

"I said you've seemed weary," Torlyri said. "Not that you were ill."

"Ah. So you did."

"Sit here awhile with me," said Torlyri. She sank down on a smooth slab of rose-pink marble that rose at its far end in the form of a grinning sapphire-eyes face, all jaws and teeth, and beckoned Koshmar down beside her. Her hand rested lightly on Koshmar's wrist, rubbing back and forth.

"Is there something you want to tell me?" Koshmar asked, after a while.

"I want only to be with you. See, what a brilliant day this is! The sun rises higher and higher as we move deeper into the New Springtime."

"It does, yes."

"Kreun is carrying an unborn, the child of Moarn. Bonlai bears Orbin's child now too. The tribe grows."

"Yes. Good."

"Praheurt and Shatalgit will have their second one soon. They have asked Hresh to name it for your mother, Lissiminimar, if it's a girl."

"Ah," Koshmar said. "I'll be glad to hear that name again."

She wondered how it went between Torlyri and her Helmet Man

these days. She never dared ask. Somehow Koshmar had managed to withstand Torlyri's involvement with Lakkamai, even her mating with Lakkamai; but a man like Lakkamai, who hardly ever spoke and seemed to have nothing within him, could not have been any threat to her. It was all bodily pleasure between Torlyri and Lakkamai. But this, with the Helmet Man—the animated look about Torlyri whenever she and he were together, the way she moved, the light in her eyes—and the long hours she spent off at the Beng settlement—no, no, it was different, it was a deeper thing by far.

I have lost her to him, Koshmar thought.

Torlyri said, after another silence, "The Bengs offer us another of their feasts one week from now. I bear the word of that from Hamok Trei this day. They want us all to come; and they'll open their oldest wines, and kill their best meat-animals. It is to celebrate the high day of their god Nakhaba, who I think is the greatest of their gods."

"What do I care what the Bengs call their gods?" Koshmar snapped. "Their gods don't exist. Their gods are fantasies."

"Koshmar—"

"There will be no feasting with the Bengs for us, Torlyri!"

"But—Koshmar—"

She swung around sharply to face the offering-woman. An idea came to her, so suddenly that it made her head spin and her breath go short, and she said, "What would you say if I told you that we're going to leave Vengiboneeza in two or three weeks, a month at most?"

"*What?*"

"And therefore we'll need all the time we have between now and then to get ready for our departure. We can't spare any of it for Beng feasts."

"Leaving—Vengiboneeza—"

"There's nothing but trouble here for us, Torlyri. You know that. I know that. Hresh came to me and said, 'Leave, leave.' I wouldn't hear of it. But then my eyes saw the truth. Then my path became clear. I asked myself what we must do to save ourselves, and the answer came—we must go away from this place. It is death here, Torlyri. Look, do you see the stone sapphire-eyes grinning at us there? The joke's on us. We came here just to dig around and find some useful things of the former world, and we have stayed—how many years is it, now? In a city that never belonged to us. In a city that mocks us in its very stones. And now a city that is full of arrogant strangers who wear absurd costumes and worship imaginary gods."

Alarm flickered in Torlyri's dark eyes. Koshmar saw it and realized miserably that her ruse had succeeded, that she had drawn from Torlyri the truth, that which she had dreaded but which she had desperately needed to know.

"Are you serious?" Torlyri said.

"I'm having the order drawn up, and I'll announce it very shortly. We'll take everything with us that may be of value to us, all the strange devices that Hresh and his Seekers have collected, and off we'll go, into the warm southland, as we should have done years ago. Harruel was right. There is poison in this city. He couldn't get me to see that, and so he left. Well, Harruel is rash, and Harruel is a fool; but in this case he saw more clearly than I. Our time in Vengiboneeza is over, Torlyri."

Torlyri looked stunned.

With rising energy now Koshmar reached for her. A passion that she had not felt for weeks, for months, had begun to burn in her. Hoarsely she said, "Come, now, beloved Torlyri, dear Torlyri! We are alone here. Let us twine—it's been so long, hasn't it, Torlyri?—and then we'll go back to the settlement."

"Koshmar—" Torlyri began, and faltered.

"Shall we twine?"

Torlyri's lips and nostrils were quivering. Tears glistened in the corners of her eyes.

In a low muffled voice Torlyri said, "I will twine with you, yes, if that is what you want."

"Isn't it what *you* want? You said you had gone looking for me so that you could enjoy the pleasure of being near me. Is there any better way of being near me than to twine?"

Torlyri looked toward the ground. "I've already twined once this day," she said. "It was—my duty, you understand—someone came to me in need of the offering-woman's consolation, and I must never refuse that, and—and—"

"And you're too tired to do it again so soon."

"Yes. Precisely."

Koshmar looked at her squarely. Torlyri flinched away.

She will not twine with me, Koshmar thought, because then her soul will be open to me and I will see the depths of her love for the Helmet Man. Is that it?

No. No. For we twined not that long ago, and I have already seen what she feels for the Helmet Man, and she knows that I have seen it. It's something else that she wishes to hide from me, then. Something new, something even more serious. And I think I can guess what it is.

"Very well," Koshmar said. "I can live without a twining this afternoon, I suppose."

She rose, and signaled to Torlyri that she should do the same.

"Koshmar, are we truly going to leave Vengiboneeza in a few weeks?" Torlyri asked.

"A month, perhaps. Six weeks, maybe."

"A moment ago you said a month at most."

"We'll leave when we're ready to leave. If it takes us a month, then we'll leave in a month. If it takes two months, then two months."

"But we will definitely leave?"

"Nothing could alter my resolve in that."

"Ah," Torlyri said, turning away as though Koshmar had struck her. "Then everything is ended."

"What do you mean?"

"Please. Let me be, Koshmar."

Koshmar nodded. She understood everything now. Torlyri would not twine with her because there was one thing Torlyri dared not tell her, which was that if the People were actually to leave Vengiboneeza she would not be leaving with them. She meant to stay behind with her Helmet Man; for she knew that Koshmar certainly would not permit the Helmet Man to come with the tribe, even if he might wish to do such a thing.

Torlyri is lost to me forever, then, Koshmar thought.

Together they walked back to the settlement in silence.

14

The Time of Last Times

This was an ecstatic time for Hresh, bringing the fulfillment of many dreams, and of much that he had never expected to attain. Taniane was his twining-partner and his coupling-partner both. Now that all barriers were down between them, he had come to realize that throughout all their childhood and young adulthood she had looked constantly to him in love and desire. While he, blind to that, lost in his studies of the chronicles and then of ruined Vengiboneeza, had completely failed to perceive the nature of her feelings for him, or even his own feelings for her.

Haniman had been only a diversion for her. He had been a standby lover, to fill her time and perhaps to awaken jealousy in Hresh. Hresh had badly misread the nature of that relationship, to everyone's cost.

But all that was remedied now. All night long, night after night, Taniane and Hresh lay together, breast against breast, sensing-organ touching sensing-organ, in a union of body and mind so intense that he was dazed with wonder at it. As soon as he found the courage, he meant to ask Koshmar to let him take Taniane as his mate. He had not been able to find any precedent in the chronicles for that, the old man of the tribe taking a mate, but there was nothing prohibiting it, either. Torlyri had mated with Lakkamai; and if an offering-woman now could mate, why not a chronicler also?

Hresh knew also of the ambitions that blazed within Taniane: that she saw Koshmar as old, defeated, burned-out, that she yearned to be chieftain in Koshmar's place.

Taniane made no attempt to hide her vision of the tribe's future from him. "We'll rule together, you and I! I'll be the chieftain and you'll be old man; and when our children are born, we'll raise them to govern after us. How could anyone excel a child of ours? A child that would have your wisdom and stubbornness, and my strength and energy? Oh, Hresh, Hresh, how wonderfully everything has worked out for us!"

"Koshmar is still chieftain," he reminded her soberly. "We're not yet even mated. And there's work for us to do in Vengiboneeza."

Though Koshmar had angrily rejected his contention that the tribe must go forth from the city, and had not reopened the discussion, Hresh knew that their departure was inevitable. Sooner or later Koshmar would see that the People were stagnating in Vengiboneeza and that in any case the Bengs were making their position impossible here. And then, without warning—Hresh knew Koshmar well—she would give the order for packing up and clearing out. It was essential, then, for him to ransack the ruins of the city for anything else that might be of value, while he still had time.

For fear of encountering Beng patrols he went exploring now

only by night. When the settlement grew dark and quiet, he and Taniane rose and went out into Vengiboneeza, hand in hand, running on tiptoes. They scarcely ever slept now and their eyes were bright with fatigue. The excitement of the task kept them going.

Three times he tried to reach the underground cache in the place where he had seen the repair-machines at work, but each time he spied Beng sentries nearby, and could not get close. Quietly he cursed his bad luck. He imagined the Bengs prowling around in there, plundering the relics themselves, seizing things of the highest importance, and felt a keen stab of pain that cut through his soul like a blade. But there was no end of other sites to explore. Using the treasure-map of the interlocking circles and the points of red light as their guide, they rushed through corridors, vaults, galleries, buried chambers, and tunnels, moving at a breathless pace until dawn, then sometimes collapsing in each other's arms for an hour or two of sleep before returning to the settlement.

They made many discoveries. But hardly anything seemed to be of immediate or even potential value.

In a great limestone-walled chamber in the part of the city known as Mueri Torlyri they came upon a solitary machine ten times their own height, perfectly preserved, a domed and gleaming thing of pearly-white metal with bands of colored stone set in it, and pulsating ovals of green and red light, and rounded arms that looked ready to move in many directions at the touch of a switch. It seemed almost like some kind of gigantic idol, that machine. But of what use was it?

Another cavern, lined on all sides by inscriptions in a writhing, bewildering script that made the eye ache to follow it, held shining glass cases that contained cubes of dark metal from which waves of shimmering light would burst at the sound of a voice. The cubes were small, no wider across than Hresh's two hands side by side, but when he opened one of the cases and tried to draw a cube out it would not come. The metal of which the cube was made evidently was so dense that it was beyond his strength to lift.

A long noble gallery that had been partly destroyed by the incursion of an underground river still displayed, though it was badly encrusted by mineral deposits, a sort of large metal mirror rising on three sharp-pronged legs. Taniane approached it and let out a cry of amazement and dismay.

"What have you found?" Hresh called.

She pointed. "There's my reflection, in the middle. But on this side—look, that's me when I was a child. And on the right side, that bent and withered old woman—Hresh, is that supposed to be me when I'm old?"

As she spoke, a babbling tumult of sound came from the mirror, which after a moment she recognized, or thought she did, as her own voice distorted and amplified; but she was speaking some unknown tongue, perhaps that of the sapphire-eyes. In another moment the mirror went dull and the sound ceased, and the smell of burning rose to their nostrils. They shrugged and moved on.

Later that night, Hresh came upon a silver globe small enough to fit comfortably in one hand. When he touched a stud on its upper surface it came suddenly to life, emitting a keen piercing sound and steady pulses of cool green light. Boldly he put his eye to the tiny opening from which the light was coming, and a vivid scene out of the time of the Great World sprang to view.

He saw half a dozen sapphire-eyes standing on some bright platform of white stone in a sector of the city that he did not recognize. The sky looked strangely bleak and leaden, and angry spirals of agitated clouds moved through it as though some terrible storm were under way; yet the sapphire-eyes were turning calmly toward one another and ponderously bowing in a sort of tranquil ritual.

The device thus seemed to replicate on a much smaller scale the images of Great World life that the huge device of levers and knobs in the plaza of the thirty-six towers had been showing him. Hresh stowed the little globe in his sash, to be studied more carefully later.

The next night, working in a rubble-filled vault on the opposite side of the city entirely, where it sloped upward toward the foothills of the mountain, it was Taniane's turn to make an extraordinary discovery, in a dank, mildewy cistern five levels down from the surface. She stumbled into it in the most literal way, tripping and sprawling against a stone block that went swinging to one side to reveal a secret chamber.

"Hresh!" she called. "Here! Quickly!"

The hidden room had blossomed into brilliant golden light the moment the door opened. In its center, mounted on a dais of jade, stood a metal tube with a round hooded opening at its top, from which flashes of dazzling color came in flickering bursts. She started toward it, but Hresh seized her sharply by the wrist and held her back.

"Wait," he said. "This thing is dangerous."

"You know what it is?"

"I've seen them in—in visions," he told her. "I watched the sapphire-eyes using them."

"For what?"

"To take their own lives."

Taniane gasped as though he had struck her.

"To take their *lives*? Why would they do that?"

476

"I can't imagine. But I saw them doing it. That glowing opening at the top—it's capable of absorbing anything that comes near it, no matter how big. There's a blackness inside that's some sort of gate to another place, or perhaps to no place at all. They would walk up to it and practically stick their noses inside it, and suddenly it would swoop them up, I don't begin to know how, and they'd be gone. It's an eerie thing, and very seductive. In my vision I walked up to it myself and it would have had me too, except I was only seeing it in a vision. But this is a real one."

He released her wrist and walked slowly toward it.

"Hresh—no, don't—"

He laughed. "I only want to test it."

Picking up a small chunk of broken statuary, he hefted it a couple of times and tossed it underhand toward the glowing hood. It hovered an instant as if suspended in the air just outside the zone of flickering, hissing light; and then it disappeared. Hresh stood expectantly, waiting to hear the thump of the stone fragment falling to the floor. But the thump never came.

"It works! It still works!"

"Try it again."

"Right." He found another piece of stone, a slender one as long as his arm, and in a gingerly way he held it up to the mouth of the device. There was a tingling sensation in his hand and forearm, and abruptly he was holding nothing at all. He stared at his fingers.

He went closer.

What if I poke my hand inside it? he asked himself.

He hovered in place before the metal column, leaning forward on the balls of his feet, frowning, considering it. It was an astonishingly powerful temptation. The thing was insidious. He remembered those immense booming mouth-things, long ago on the great sandy plain, drawing him toward them with their inexorable drumming. This was like that. He could feel it pulling him inward. He was half willing to let it. More than half, perhaps. The thing might offer him . . . answers. It might offer him . . . peace. It might . . .

Taniane must have guessed what was passing through his mind, for she came up to him quickly and caught him by the shoulder, drawing him back.

"What were you thinking just then?" she asked.

Hresh shuddered. "Just being curious. Maybe too curious."

"Let's get out of here, Hresh. One of these days you'll be much too curious for your own good."

"Wait," he said. "Let me check just one more thing."

"It's deadly, Hresh."

"I know that. Wait. Wait."

"Hresh—"

"I'll be more careful this time."

He shuffled forward in a half-crouch, averting his eyes from the zone of brightness at the summit of the column. Bending forward, he slipped his arm around the middle of the metal tube and, as he had somehow expected, lifted it easily from its platform of green stone. It was warm to the touch, and it was hollow; he could probably have crushed it with a light pressure of his arm. Without difficulty he carried it across the room and set it down against the wall. The flickering lights of the hood, which had gone out when he lifted the thing, immediately returned.

"What are you doing, Hresh?"

"It's portable, do you see?" he said. "We can take it with us."

"No! Let it be. Hresh, it frightens me."

"It frightens me, too. But I want to know more about it."

"You *always* want to know more about everything. This one will kill you. Leave it, Hresh."

"Not this. It may be the only one of its kind that remains in all the world. Do you want the Bengs to get it?"

"If it would eat them the way it ate the stone you fed it, that might not be so bad an idea."

"And if they didn't let it harm them, and found some use for it?"

"It has no use except to destroy, Hresh. If you're worried about the Bengs getting it, then drop a heavy rock on it and maybe it'll smash. But let's clear out of here."

He gave her a long searching look.

"I promise you, Taniane, that I'll take care with this thing. But I mean to bring it along."

She sighed.

"Hresh," she said, shaking her head in resignation. "Oh, Hresh! Oh, you!"

Harruel lay dreaming, lost in rapture. The world was carpeted in flowers of a hundred subtle colors, and their soft perfume filled the air like music. He was lying in a smooth stone tub with Weiawala in one arm and Thaloin in the other, and warm sweet golden wine covered all three of them, lapping at his chin. All about him stood the sons of his flesh, a dozen of them, tall splendid warriors identical to him in face and virtue, singing his praises with lusty voices.

"Harruel!" they cried. "Harruel, Harruel, Harruel!"

And then somehow a discordant note crept in, someone singing in a creaky rusty screech of a voice:

"*Harruel! Harruel!*"

"No, not you," he said thickly. "You're spoiling everything. Who are you, anyway? No son of mine, with a voice like that! Get away! Get away!"

"Harruel, wake up!"

"Stop bothering me. I'm the king."

"Harruel!"

There was a hand at his throat, fingers digging in deep. He sat up instantly, roaring in rage, as the dream dissolved in shards about him. Weiawala gone, Thaloin gone, the lusty chorus of tall sons all gone, gone, gone. A gray, gritty film of wine covered his brain and shrouded his spirit. He ached in ten places, and someone had been eating turds with his mouth. Minbain stood above him. She had grasped him not by the throat but by the side of his neck: he could still feel the imprint of her fingers. She looked wild and fluttery with some urgent matter.

Angrily he rumbled, "How dare you disturb me when—"

"Harruel, the city is under attack."

"—I'm trying to rest after—" He caught his breath. "*What?* Attack? Who? Koshmar? I'll kill her! I'll roast her and eat her!" Harruel struggled to his feet, bellowing. "Where is she? Bring me my spear! Call Konya! Salaman!"

"They're already out there," Minbain said, fretfully wringing her hands. "It isn't Koshmar. Here, Harruel. Your spear, your shield. The hjjk-men, Harruel! That's who it is. The hjjk-men!"

He rose and went stumbling toward the door. From without came the sounds of clamor, cutting through the fog that blanketed his perceptions.

Hjjk-men? Here?

Salaman had said something the other day about fearing an attack of an army of hjjk-men. Some vision he had had, some wild dream. Harruel had been able to make little sense of it. But it seemed to him that Salaman had said the invasion was far away, not to come for many months. That will teach him to trust visions, Harruel thought.

His head ached. The situation demanded clarity of mind. Pausing by the door, he scooped up the bowl of wine that always stood there and put it to his lips. It was more than half full, but he drained it in four robust gulps.

Better. Much better.

He stepped outside.

There was chaos out there. For a moment he had difficulty focusing his eyes. Then the wine took hold and he saw that the city was in the greatest peril. A building was on fire. The animals from the enclosure were loose, dashing in all directions, whinnying and baying. He heard shouts, screams, the cries of children. Just beyond the perimeter of the settled area was a swarm of hjjk-men, ten, fifteen, two dozen of them, armed with weapons that were too short to be swords, too long to be knives. Each tall, angular, many-armed hjjk-man held at least two blades, some three or even four, with which they flailed the air in ominous stabbing gestures. They danced 'round and 'round, making the dry chuttering sounds that gave them their name. Harruel saw a dead child lying in a pitiful heap, bloodied animals nearby, tribal possessions scattered everywhere.

"*Harruel!*" he shouted, running into the midst of the fray. "*Harruel! Harruel! Harruel!*"

Salaman, Konya, and Lakkamai already were hard at work, poking and prodding with long spears. Bruikkos had somehow acquired two hjjk blades, one in each hand, and he was right in the midst of the attacking force, leaping and cavorting like a madman, slashing at the orange breathing-tubes that ran beside each hjjk-man's head. Nittin too was fighting, and even the women, furiously swinging poles, brooms, hatchets, anything.

Harruel's sudden presence in the midst of them fired them all onward. He felt a stirring, a warlike frenzy, among the defenders.

He caught sight of his son Samnibolon on the front line. Though hardly more than a child, Samnibolon was wielding a pruning-hook with which he cut without mercy at the hard, many-jointed legs of the hjjk-men. Harruel let out a cry of delight at this proof of the boy's warlike nature, and another when Samnibolon sent one of the enemy tottering. Galihine struck the wounded hjjk-man athwart his back with a knob-ended club, and Bruikkos, turning in an offhand way, delivered the fatal blow with a quick flick of one of his knives.

Pride and wine inflamed Harruel's battle-lust. He laid about him with savage pleasure. As he battled his way toward Salaman's side he used his size and weight to great advantage, kicking and jostling the hjjk-men to throw them off balance and send them scrabbling down on their many knees before he speared them. The best place for that, he discovered, was in the joint where the legs were attached to the hard carapace: the spear went in easily there, and he struck again and again, with great precision of aim and lethal effect.

He reached Salaman's side, and together they advanced toward a group of three hjjks who stood back to back, waving their little swords as though they were stingers.

"Where did they come from?" Harruel asked. "Is this the vision you had?"

"No," Salaman said. "What I saw was a great herd of vermilions—and a vast army of the insect-men—"

"And how many are these?"

"Twenty, perhaps. No more than that. A scouting party for the main force, I think. Lakkamai and Bruikkos blundered upon them by accident in the woods, and they came charging down into the city all at once."

"We'll kill them all," Harruel said.

Already he saw eight or ten of the insect-creatures lying dead, perhaps more.

He sprang forward and jammed his spear into the clustering group of hjjk-men, forcing them to move apart from one another. Salaman at the same time set upon the leftmost one of the three, beating him to the ground with fierce prods of his weapon. Turning, Harruel plunged his spear into the fallen creature's black-and-yellow carapace and felt a satisfying crunching.

Before he could withdraw it, though, the second hjjk-man ran toward him and drew a line of fire along his arm with what Harruel realized was his beak, not his blade. Harruel winced and grunted. He raised his leg in a tremendous kick that shattered the hjjk-man's jaw. Nittin came from somewhere and cut through the hjjk's breathing-tubes. It fell over dead.

"We're getting there," Salaman said, between thrusts of his spear. "Must be no more than six or seven of them left. They're mean, but they don't really know how to fight, do they?"

"They fight in swarms," said Nittin. "Ten to your one, that's how they like to do it, Hresh told me. But they didn't send enough this time. Behind you, Harruel!"

Turning, Harruel saw two hjjks coming at once. He knocked them both down with a sweeping swing of his spear and thrust its butt end into one narrow, fragile, exposed throat. Salaman disposed of the other attacker.

Harruel grinned. He could foresee the end of the battle now, and already he was looking forward to the wine that waited for him in the celebration of victory.

Lakkamai was chasing a frantically scuttling hjjk-man up the trail to the crater's rim. Konya and Galihine had another cornered near Nittin's house. A third had fallen into Salaman's infernal trench and two of the women were jabbing at its claws as it tried to climb out.

Harruel rested on his spear. It is all over, he realized joyously.

But his elation was short-lived. Fatigue and pain overwhelmed him. There was a terrible pounding in his chest, and the fiery wound in his arm was throbbing and streaming blood. The wine that had sustained him through the heat of the battle had burned away now, leaving him grim and weary.

Looking back now at the city, Harruel saw that it was the palace that was burning. The animals had all escaped. He could not tell which child it was that had died; and now he saw one of the women dead too, or badly wounded. So it was not as great a victory as it had seemed.

Bleakness swept in upon him.

This is the punishment of the gods upon me, he thought.

For all my sins. For my forcing of Kreun, and for my other cruelties and rages, and for every unworthy thought, and for my arrogance. For raising my hand to Minbain. And for filling my head with too much wine. The hjjks have come to destroy this city that I have built, which was to have been my monument. We have killed these few, but what of the vast army that Salaman saw in his vision? How will we hold them away? How will we fend off those monstrous vermilions when they come trampling through our streets? How will we survive at all, when the main army comes?

It was another warm night and the air was heavy and close. It was warm all the time nowadays. The cold, harsh time just after the end of the Long Winter was only a dim memory. Yet despite the clinging warmth of the evening Koshmar felt a chill that grew from her bones and spread outward through her whole body, running between her fur and her skin. That chill never left her now.

Restlessly she prowled the settlement. She rarely slept at all any longer, but wandered far into the night, drifting in a lightheaded way from building to building. Sometimes she imagined that she was her own ghost, floating about weightlessly, invisible, silent. But the pain always remained with her to remind her of the burdens of the flesh.

She had said no more to anyone about leaving Vengiboneeza. That had been only a bluff, designed to elicit the truth from Torlyri about whether she would go or stay; and, having had the truth now—for she was sure of it, that Torlyri would never abandon her Helmet Man—Koshmar could not bring herself to issue the order to go. Nor had Hresh said anything to her about it again, or Torlyri. The plan remained in limbo. Is it because my illness has made me too weak to deal with the task of organizing the withdrawal? she wondered. Or is it only that I know our departure would mean the end for me with Torlyri, and I'm unable to face that?

She could not tell which it was. Personal griefs had become hopelessly entangled with public duty. She was weary, weary, weary, profoundly troubled, profoundly confused. All that she could do was wait and hope that time would take care of things. Perhaps this illness would go from her and her strength would return. Or perhaps Torlyri would grow tired of her infatuation with that Beng. Time will solve everything, Koshmar thought. Time is the only ally that I have.

Sudden brightness caught her eye. A single gleam of light came from one of the unused buildings on the far side of the plaza, near the southern edge of the settlement. Then all was dark again, as if a shutter had been hastily closed. Koshmar frowned. No one had any business over there, especially at this hour. All the People were asleep, except only Barnak, who was on sentry duty, and Koshmar had seen him just a little while ago, patrolling the settlement's northern border.

She went to investigate, wondering if a party of Beng spies had slipped in and was hiding right here in the tribe's own territory. What a troublesome folk they were! She had never trusted them, despite their smiles and their feasts. They had taken Torlyri from her. Soon they would have Vengiboneeza too. Dawinno shrivel them!

The building was a five-sided one-story structure of pinkish stone that had the sleekness of metal, or perhaps it was of a metal that had the texture of fine stone. A single triangular window was cut into each of its five faces, and these were covered over by awnings that had the texture of fine gauze but the solidity of wood. Koshmar pushed gently against one. It would not give. She went to another, pushing with more force. It yielded just a crack, enough to let a shaft of yellow light escape. She held her breath and opened it a bit wider, and leaned forward to look inside.

She saw one large room, set deep so that its floor was well below the level of the plaza. The sooty light of animal-fat lamps provided the only illumination. In the center of the room stood a statue carved from white stone, the figure of a tall long-limbed figure, angular and slim, with a high-domed head and no sensing-organ at all: a statue of Ryyig Dream-Dreamer, from the looks of it. About the statue were arranged the leafy boughs of trees, heaps of fruit, a few small animals in wicker cages. Five of the People were crouched beside these offerings, heads bowed, whispering softly. By the dim light Koshmar could make out Haniman,

486

Kreun, Cheysz, and Delim. And that one, with his back to her—was that Preyne? No, Jalmud, she decided. Jalmud, yes.

Koshmar watched the ceremony in mounting dismay that began to grow into shock and horror. It was impossible for her to hear what they were saying, so low were their tones, but they seemed to be muttering some sort of prayers. Now and then one of them would push a bundle of twigs or a clump of fruit closer to the statue of the Dream-Dreamer. Cheysz had her head pressed right against the room's unpaved floor; Kreun too was bowed far down, while Haniman bobbed back and forth in a rocking movement that had an almost hypnotic rhythm. He seemed to be the leader; he spoke and the others repeated.

When she was able to pull herself away, Koshmar turned and ran toward the temple. Heart beating furiously, she hurried to Hresh's chambers and hammered on the door.

"Hresh! Hresh, wake up! It's Koshmar!"

He peered out. "I'm working with the chronicles."

"That can wait. Come with me. There's something that you have to see."

Together they hurried back across the plaza. Barnak, having finally become aware of Koshmar's movements, appeared from somewhere and made a gesture of inquiry, but she waved him fiercely away. The fewer of the People that saw this, the better. Leading Hresh to the five-sided building, she signaled him to silence and pulled him up against the window that she had pushed ajar. He stared in; after a moment his hands gripped the sill with sudden excitement; he drew himself up, thrust his head nearly inside the window frame. When he stepped down again a little while later his eyes were wide with surprise and his breath was coming in tense gusts.

"Well? What do you think they're doing in there?"

"A religious rite is what it looks like to me."

Koshmar nodded vigorously. "Exactly! Exactly! But which god are they worshipping, do you think?"

"No god at all," said Hresh. "That's a statue of a human—of a Dream-Dreamer—"

"A Dream-Dreamer, yes. They're worshipping a Dream-Dreamer, Hresh! What is this? What new kind of worship has sprung up here?"

As though in a daze, Hresh said, "They think the humans are gods—they're praying to the humans—"

"To the Dream-Dreamers. *We* are the humans, Hresh."

Hresh shrugged. "Whatever you say. But those five have a different idea, I think."

"Yes," said Koshmar. "They're willing to turn themselves into monkeys, just as you seem to be. And to kneel down and pray to that ancient chunk of stone." Koshmar turned away suddenly and sat, cradling her head in her arms in despair. "Ah, Hresh, Hresh, how wrong I was not to listen to you! We are losing our humanity in Vengiboneeza. Our very selves, Hresh. We are becoming mere animals. I have no doubt now that you were correct. We have to leave this place at once."

"Koshmar—"

"At once! I'll make the proclamation in the morning. We pack and we go, in two weeks or less. Before this poison spreads any further among us." She rose unsteadily. In the strongest tone she could summon she added, "And say nothing of what you've seen to anyone!"

It was what Hresh had wanted, and his soul should have surged with joy at Koshmar's decision. For the awakening world in all its brightness and wonder lay before him, and he was eager to go forth into it and penetrate its infinite mysteries.

But at the same time he was struck with a powerful sense of loss and sadness. He had not finished his work in Vengiboneeza. Koshmar's decision fell now like a blade across his soul, cutting him off from all in this city that he was yet to unearth and recover. Whatever relics of the Great World they left behind, he knew, would ultimately fall into the hands of the Bengs.

The settlement stirred with frantic bustle. The livestock had to be gathered and made ready for the march; crops must be harvested; all the possessions of the tribe had to be packed. There was scarcely any time for rest, with the departure date only a matter of days away. Now and then Bengs came to call at the settlement, and looked on in perplexity at what was taking place. Koshmar rushed from task to task, so harried and depleted that her condition was a matter of common discussion. Torlyri was rarely seen in this time, and those in need of comfort and calming ways turned instead to Boldirinthe, who offered herself in Torlyri's place. When Torlyri did appear, she, too, had an unaccustomed dark and tense look to her.

Hresh heard people wagering that the departure could not possibly be achieved by Koshmar's deadline, that it would be postponed a week, a month, a season. Yet the frantic work went on and no postponements were announced.

To Taniane he said, "This is our last chance. We have to get the Seekers together and search out as much as we can find and carry away."

"But Koshmar wants us to drop everything else so we can get ready for the march."

Hresh scowled. "Koshmar doesn't understand. Half the time she's still living back in the cocoon, I think."

Though uneasy at the thought of defying Koshmar, Taniane yielded in the end to Hresh's urgency. But reassembling the old team of Seekers proved difficult. Konya had departed with Har-ruel; Shatalgit and Praheurt, burdened with one child and shortly expecting another, had no time for extra work; cautious Sinistine cited Koshmar's orders to halt all present projects to concentrate on the departure, and she could not be shaken from that.

That left only Orbin and Haniman. Haniman brusquely told them that he had no interest in exploring with them, and would not stay for further discussion. Orbin, like Sinistine, said he meant to abide by Koshmar's decree.

"But we need you," Hresh said. "There are places where the walls have fallen in, where heavy slabs block our way. The best artifacts may be in those difficult places. Your strength will be useful to us, Orbin."

Orbin said, shrugging, "The settlement has to be dismantled. My strength will be useful in that, too. And Koshmar says—"

"Yes, I know. But this is more important."

"To you."

"I beg you, Orbin. We were friends once."

"Were we?" said Orbin impassively.

The thrust was a painful one. Childhood playmates, yes, they had been that; but that was years ago, and what had Orbin been to him, or he to Orbin, since that time? They were strangers now, Hresh the wily wise man of the tribe, Orbin simply a warrior, use-ful perhaps for his muscles but not otherwise. Hresh gave up the attempt. He and Taniane would have to do the final exploring alone.

Once more they slipped off under cover of darkness. The place where he had found the repair artificials at work was Hresh's goal once again; and this time he carried the Barak Dayir with him.

"Look there," Taniane cried. "A Beng mark on the wall!"

"Yes. I see it."

"Should we be trespassing here?"

"Trespassing?" he said hotly. "Who was in Vengiboneeza first, we or the Bengs?"

"But we turned back at this point all the other times we saw signs of the Bengs nearby."

"Not this time," said Hresh.

They continued forward. The great pyramidal mound of broken columns came into view. Beng ribbons dangled on the facade of the shattered temple across the way. Two repair artificials wandered past, paying no heed to Hresh and Taniane as they went about their solemn work of poking through the rubble and shoring up the swaying walls.

"Over there, Hresh," said Taniane quietly.

He glanced to his left. By moonlight the terrible shadows of two Beng helmets rose like monstrous stains on the side of a building of white stone. The Bengs themselves, two husky warriors who had been riding a single vermilion, were standing beside their beast, talking calmly.

"They don't see us," Taniane said.

"I know."

"Can we slip around past them somehow?"

Hresh shook his head. "We'll let them see us."

"What?"

"We have to." He drew forth the Wonderstone and let it rest a moment in the palm of his hand. Taniane stared at it with mingled fear and fascination evident on her face. He felt sudden fear himself: not for the sight of the Barak Dayir, but for the risks and complexities of what he was about to do.

He reached down and let his sensing-organ take the talisman. The music of the Wonderstone began to rise in his soul. It calmed him and soothed him some. Beckoning to Taniane to follow him, he stepped into the open, walking toward the Bengs, who looked toward him in surprise and displeasure.

To achieve control, now, without harming them, certainly without taking their lives—

Lightly Hresh touched their souls with his. He felt the two Bengs recoil, felt them angrily struggling to free themselves of his intrusion. Trembling, Hresh kept the contact from breaking. He could not forget that first Helmet Man long ago, who had died rather than let himself be entered this way. Perhaps my touch was too heavy that time, Hresh thought. He must not kill these two. Above all, he must not kill them. But the Barak Dayir guided him now.

The Bengs squirmed and fought, and then they eased and went slack, and stood gaping at him like dumb beasts of the jungle. Hresh let his tightly drawn breath escape. It was working! They were his!

"I have come to explore this place," he told them.

The Bengs' eyes were bright with tension. But they could not break his grip. First one, then the other, nodded to him.

"You will give me any assistance I require," said Hresh. "Is that understood?"

"Yes." A harsh, angry, reluctant whispered assent.

A flood of relief cascaded through him. He held them as though in a harness. But they would not suffer harm.

Taniane glanced at him in wonder. He smiled and touched one finger to his lips.

Then he looked toward one of the repair artificials nearby, and summoned it. Its small mechanical mind responded unhesitatingly, and it swung around and began to move quickly toward the red stone doorway in the pavement that Hresh had seen before. One of its metal arms unreeled and touched the door, which immediately slid back along its track.

"Come," Hresh said to Taniane.

They went down into the brilliantly lit subterranean chamber that lay open to him. A profusion of complex and intricate machines stood before them, gleaming, perfect. A dozen or more of the small repair artificials moved through the rows of devices, evidently performing minor maintenance jobs; and at the far side of the huge room Hresh saw one of the repair machines at work on another of its own that stood motionless. So that was how these things had endured for so many thousands of years! One artificial repairs another, Hresh thought. They could last forever like that.

To the one that had opened the doorway for him Hresh said, "Tell me the functions of these devices."

By way of reply it opened a niche in the wall and drew out a golden-bronze globe small enough for Hresh to hold in his hand. Its metal skin was translucent, and he could see a smaller globe of shining imperishable quicksilver rolling about within it. There was no control stud on it, or any other visible means of operating it. But when he touched it with his mind, amplified as it was by the Barak Dayir, the soul of the little globe opened to him as though swinging back on hinges, and he plunged forward into dizzying realms of knowledge.

"Hresh?" Taniane asked. "Hresh, are you all right?"

He nodded. He felt dazed, awed, astounded. In a swift, intoxicating rush of data the globe told him what uses the things he saw before him had. This device here: it was a wall-builder. This one: it paved streets. This one measured the depth and stability of foundations. This one erected columns. This one cut through rock. This one transported debris. This one—this one—this one—

He had seen devices something like these long before, during his first explorations of the ruins. He remembered how they had run amok when he tried to operate them, wildly building walls and erecting bridges and digging pits and demolishing buildings as if operating by their own whim and fancy alone. He had had to hide those machines away, for they were worse than useless: they were dangerous, they were destructive, they were uncontrollable.

But this little golden globe of quicksilver in his hand—it must be the master control device, Hresh realized, the one that all the others obeyed. With its aid, he could build an entire Vengiboneeza with these machines! A purposeful mind, focused through the globe, could direct this host of city-building machines in anything that needed to be done. No more bridges from nowhere to nowhere, no more walls running in lunatic profusion up the middle of boulevards—but only orderly construction, in accordance with whatever plan he chose. He would be the master, and this globe the foreman, and these other machines the builders.

"What do you have, Hresh? What is all this?"

"Miracles and wonders," he said in a hushed voice. "Miracles and wonders!"

He gestured to the two Bengs, who were looking on from outside the doorway as though stupefied. Though they still strained against his control, they could not break it.

"You!" he called. "In here! Start carrying this stuff out and loading it on your vermilion!"

It took a dozen trips back and forth before everything that seemed to Hresh to be important had been transported to the settlement of the People. Just before dawn Hresh sent the two Helmet Men on their way, with his warmest thanks, and their minds wiped clean of all that they had done that night.

Within the temple Torlyri worked with frantic zeal by fluttering candlelight, packing all the holy things for the journey they would be making. Now and then she paused and stood leaning against the cool stone wall, breathing deeply. Sometimes she began to tremble uncontrollably. Only a few days remained before the departure from Vengiboneeza.

Hresh would take care of the chronicles and everything that was associated with them. The rest, all that the tribe had accumulated in its thousands of years of secluded existence, fell to her responsibility. Little carved amulets, and bowls and statuettes sacred to this god or that, and wands used in the healing of disease, and bright polished pebbles whose origin and purpose had been forgotten but which had been handed down from offering-woman to offering-woman as cherished talismans.

Boldirinthe had helped her with the task the past two nights. But yesterday, while they were working, she had turned to her suddenly and said, "Are you weeping, Torlyri?"

"Am I?"

"I see the tears on your cheeks."

"From weariness, Boldirinthe. Only weariness."

"It makes you sad to think of leaving here, eh, Torlyri? We were happy in Vengiboneeza, weren't we?"

"The gods decree. The gods provide."

"If I could be of any comfort to you—"

"To comfort the comforter? No, Boldirinthe. Please." Torlyri laughed. "You misunderstand what you see. There's no sadness in me. I'm very tired, that's all."

Tonight Torlyri worked by herself. She felt the tears pressing close behind her eyes and knew that they would flow freely at the slightest spur; and she could not bear to be the recipient of Boldirinthe's compassion, or anyone's. If she broke down, she must do it alone.

With trembling fingers she wrapped the sacred things in bits of fur or woven containers and laid them away in the baskets that would be carried with the tribe on the trek. Sometimes she kissed one before she put it away. These were the things that had been the tools of her trade throughout her life, by which Torlyri had ensured the continued kindness of the gods. They were only little objects of stone or bone or wood or metal, but they had godliness in them, and power. And more than that: she had lavished her love upon them. They were as familiar to her as her own hands. Now, one by one, they disappeared into their baskets.

As the shelves emptied she could feel her fate rushing headlong toward her. Time was growing very short.

She heard footsteps outside the sanctuary. She looked up, frowning.

"Torlyri?"

Boldirinthe's voice. She has come anyway, Torlyri thought in irritation. Going to the door, she thrust her head out and said, "I told you, I had to work alone tonight. Some of these talismans only I may behold, Boldirinthe."

"I know," said Boldirinthe gently. "It's not my wish to trouble you at your work, Torlyri. But I bring a message for you, and I thought you would want to have it."

"From whom?"

"Your Helmet Man. He is here and wishes to see you."

"*Here?*"

"Just outside the temple. In the shadows."

"No Beng may enter this building," said Torlyri, growing flustered. "Tell him to wait. I'll come out to him. No, no, I don't want anyone to see us together tonight." She knotted her hands tensely and moistened her lips. "You know where the storehouse is, on the other side of the building, where Hresh keeps the things he's dug up in the city? See if there's anyone in there now, and if it's free, take him there. Then come back and let me know."

Boldirinthe nodded and disappeared.

Torlyri attempted to return to her work, but it was hopeless; she fumbled things, she nearly dropped them, she could not remember the blessings she was supposed to utter as she lifted them from their places. After a few minutes she gave up entirely and knelt at her little altar, elbows forward on its edge, head downward, praying for calmness.

"He's waiting for you," Boldirinthe said softly behind her.

Torlyri closed the cabinet of holies and snuffed the candle. In the darkness she paused to give Boldirinthe a tender embrace and a light kiss, and to whisper her thanks. Then she stepped through the passageway that led to the plaza, and went around the side of the many-angled building to Hresh's storeroom.

It was a warm mild night, with no breeze stirring, and bands of bright-edged clouds lying across the moon. Yet Torlyri shivered. She felt a tightness in her belly.

Trei Husathirn, a single glowberry cluster in his hand to light his way, was pacing like a caged creature in the storeroom when Torlyri entered. He was wearing his helmet, and he seemed bigger than Torlyri remembered. She had not seen him for some days now; there was simply too much work to do at the settlement. He prowled about, poking here and there at the collection of devices that Hresh and his Seekers had assembled. Hearing Torlyri, he whirled and threw up his arms as if to defend himself.

"It's only me," she said, smiling.

They rushed toward each other. His arms encircled her and he pulled her tight, nearly crushing the breath from her. She felt his body quivering. After a moment they parted. His face looked drawn and tense.

"What are these machines?" he asked.

Torlyri said, shrugging, "You'd have to ask Hresh. He uncovered them all over the city. They're Great World things."

"Do they work?"

"How would I know?"

"And will he take them with him when you leave?"

"As many as he can, if I know Hresh." Torlyri wondered if it had been wrong to allow Trei Husathirn to enter here. Perhaps he should not see these things. He was her mate, yes, or something like her mate, but still he was a Beng, and these were secret things of the tribe.

His voice, hard and anxious, troubled her also. He seemed almost frightened.

She reached for his hand and held it.

"Do you know how much I've missed you?" she asked.

"You could have come to me."

"No. No. It was impossible. Everything must be properly packed—there are blessings to say—it's a job that should take weeks and weeks. I don't know how I can ever finish it in time. You shouldn't have come tonight, Trei Husathirn."

"I had to talk to you."

That sounded wrong. He should have said, I had to see you, I wanted to see you, I couldn't stay away from you. But he had to *talk* to her? About what?

She released his hand and drew back, uncertain, uneasy.

"What is it?" she asked.

He was silent a moment. Then he said, "Has there been any change in the day of departure?"

"None."

"So it is just a few more days."

"Yes," Torlyri said.

"What shall we do?"

She wanted to look away, but she kept her eyes steadily on him. "What do you want to do, Trei Husathirn?"

"You know what I want. To come with you."

"How could you?"

"Yes," he said. "How could I? What do I know of your ways, your gods, your language, your anything? All I know of your people is you. I would never fit in."

"In time you might," she said.

"Do you think so?"

Now she did look away.

"No," she told him, barely able to make the single word emerge from her lips.

"So I conclude, after asking myself the question a thousand times. I have no place with Koshmar's tribe. I would always be a stranger. An enemy, even."

"Surely not an enemy!"

"An enemy, to Koshmar, and to others, I think." Suddenly he crushed the glowberry cluster in his hand and threw it to the floor. In the darkness Torlyri felt unexpected fear of him. What did he have in mind? To kill them both, out of thwarted love? But all he did was take her hands in his and draw her close again, and hold her in a tight embrace. Then he said, in a hollow, distant voice, "And also I would have to leave my helmet-brothers, my chieftain, my gods. I would have to leave Nakhaba!" He was shivering. "I would leave everything. I would no longer know myself. I would be lost."

Her hand stroked his ear, his cheek, the bare scarred place along his shoulder. By some strand of fugitive light she saw his face, and a track of tears glistening on it. She thought that the sight would make her own tears flow, but no, no, she had no tears at all any longer.

"What shall we do?" he asked again.

Torlyri caught hold of his hand and pressed it to her breast. "Here. Lie down with me. On the floor, in front of all these preposterous machines. That is what we will do. Lie down. Here, Trei Husathirn. With me. With me."

Morning had come. Hresh looked down lovingly at Taniane, who lay sleeping deeply, exhausted by their night's foraging. Quietly he went from their room into the open. All was still. There was a rich heavy sweetness in the air, as if some night-blooming flower had opened just a little while before.

It had been a night of wonder. The last barriers to the departure from Vengiboneeza had fallen. The little ball of golden-bronze metal ensured that.

Now Hresh held in one hand a different ball, the silvery sphere that they had found some nights earlier. He had not managed to find time before this to examine it properly, but in this misty dawn, after a night without sleep, a night when sleep had been unthinkable, a night of heroic endeavor, the small sphere weighed profoundly upon his soul. It seemed to be calling to him. He looked around, but no one was in sight. The settlement still slept. Hresh hid himself away in a crevice between two mighty alabaster statues of sapphire-eyes who had lost their heads and touched the stud that activated the sphere.

For a moment nothing happened. Had he burned the sphere out, that one time that he had used it? Or perhaps he had not pressed the stud hard enough just now. He cupped it in his palm, wondering. Then there came from it that sharp high sound that it had made before, and pulses of cool green light shot from it again.

Hastily he put his eye to its tiny viewing hole, and the Great World once again was made visible to him.

This time there was music as well as vision. Out of nowhere came a slow, heavy melody, three strands wound one about another, one that was of a dull gray tonality, one that reached his soul in the hue of deep blue, and the third a hard, aggressive orange. The music had the character of a dirge. Hresh understood that it was music fit to signify the last days of the Great World.

Through that tiny hole Hresh found that he had access to a vast and sweeping panorama of the city.

All Vengiboneeza was displayed to him in its final hours. It was a fearful sight.

The sky over the city is black, and terrible black winds sweep through it, creating patterns of turbulence that are black on black. A shroud of dust chokes the air. Feeble beams of sunlight dance erratically through it, falling weakly to the ground rather than striking it. A faint rime of frost is beginning to form on the tips of plants, on the edges of ponds, on windows, on the air itself.

A death-star has lately fallen, Hresh knows. One of the first ones, or even the very first.

With an impact that made all the world shudder, the death-star has plummeted to earth somewhere close by Vengiboneeza—or perhaps not there, perhaps on the other side of the world altogether—and a great black cloud of debris has risen higher than the highest mountains. The air is dense with it. All the sun's warmth is cut off. The only light that breaks through is a pale wintry gleam. The world is beginning to freeze.

This is only the beginning. One by one the death-stars will fall, every fifty years, every five hundred, who knows how often, and each one will bring new calamity over the interminable length of the Long Winter to come.

But for the Great World the first impact will be the fatal one. The sapphire-eyes and the vegetals and the sea-lords and the rest inhabit a world where the air is mild and gentle and winter never comes. Winter is only a faint memory out of prehistoric antiquity, a mere ancestral dream. And now winter returns; and of the Six Peoples only the hjjk-folk and the mechanicals will be capable of surviving it without special protection, though the mechanicals will choose, Hresh cannot understand why, to let themselves perish.

For the Great World it is the time of last times.

A bitter wind blows. A few swirling white flakes dance in the air. Already the new cold has brought frightened beasts sweeping in a wild migration toward the shelter that Vengiboneeza affords. Hresh sees them everywhere, hooves and horns and tendrils and fangs, a horde of shining terrified eyes and gaping mouths and sweat-flecked jaws.

The harsh winds are a mighty drum overhead, beating out the solemn rhythm that commands the animals to seek refuge here. Under the force of that horrific gale they run on and on and on. They swarm in the streets of the city, racing to and fro as if frantic activity by itself will keep them warm enough to live. The wondrous white villas of Vengiboneeza are beset. Wherever the vision lets Hresh look, animals of a thousand kinds climb walls, slither across thresholds, burrow into bedchambers. Great snuffling herds of massive quadrupeds plunge and stampede in the boulevards. The raucous cries of the four-legged invaders cruelly punctuate the serene music that streams from the silvery sphere.

And yet, and yet, and yet—

The sapphire-eyes—

AT WINTER'S END

Hresh sees them going steadily about their business in the midst of the madness. The huge crocodilians are calm, terribly calm. It is as though nothing more serious than a light summer rainstorm has begun to fall.

All about them, fear-maddened creatures of the wilds boil and writhe and leap and prance. And calmly, calmly, never betraying the slightest sense of alarm or dismay, the sapphire-eyes pack away their treasures, dictate instructions for their care, perform their regular obeisances to the gods who even now are sending doom.

Hresh sees them gathering in placid groups to listen to music, to watch the play of colors on giant crystals set in the walls of buildings, to indulge in quiet, reasonable discussions of abstruse issues. In all ways, their normal life continues. A few, but only a few, go to the machines of the hooded lights and are swallowed up; but perhaps this too is normal, and has nothing to do with the advancing catastrophe.

Yet they know that doom is here. They must! They must! They simply do not care.

The cold deepens. The wind becomes more fierce. The sky is starless, moonless, a black beyond black. A chilling rain has begun to fall, and it turns to snow and then to hard particles of ice before it reaches the ground. A deadly shining transparent jacket coats every tree, every building. The world has taken on the glitter of mortality.

The other peoples are responding now to the devastation, each in its own way.

The hjjks are leaving the city. They have arrayed themselves in an endless double file, yellow and black, yellow and black, and are marching out via the southern gate. They are unhurried, perfectly disciplined, totally and monstrously orderly in their evacuation.

The sea-lords are leaving too, and they show no panic either as they go down to the waterfront and slip away from shore. But the lake is beginning to freeze even as they enter it, and there is no doubt that they are going to their deaths. They must know that.

The mechanicals also are departing, by way of the grand avenue that winds through the foothills of the mountain wall and up and over it toward the east. The gleaming dome-headed machines move in a quick, jerky way. Perhaps they are bound for the rendezvous point in the far-off plains where Hresh and his tribe will find them, dead and covered with the rust of millennia, one day in the very distant future.

There is no exodus for the vegetals. They are already dying. They crumple where they stand, poor blasted flowers, slender stems and limbs turning black, withered petals folding over and into themselves. As they topple, mechanicals which have not yet left the city appear and sweep them up. The city will be maintained to the last.

Of all the Six Peoples only the humans cannot be seen. Hresh scans the whole city for the pale, elongated creatures with the somber eyes and the high-vaulted heads, but no, no, there is not a single one to be found. They are gone already, it seems: shrewd anticipators, bound on their journey—where?—to safety? To a quiet death elsewhere, as the sea-lords and mechanicals will have? Hresh cannot say. He is baffled and numbed by the sight of the end of Vengiboneeza. He is mesmerized by those black winds sweeping across the black sky, by the somber death-music, by the migrations of the Great World beings outward and of the wild forest denizens into the city. And by that incomprehensible *acceptance* that the sapphire-eyes unanimously display as the time of last times descends upon them.

He watches until he can bear to watch no more. To the end, the sapphire-eyes show indifference to their doom.

At last he presses the stud with a trembling finger and the vision ceases, the music dies away. He falls to his knees, stunned, overwhelmed.

He knew that he did not understand a thing of what he had seen.

As never before, his soul churned and bubbled with questions; and he had no answers for them, not one, nothing at all.

In the morning when Koshmar tried to rise from her couch a powerful unseen hand pressed itself between her breasts and hurled her back down. She was alone. Torlyri had gone to the temple the night before to continue her task of packing the holy things, and she had never returned. Gone off to her Beng, Koshmar thought. She lay quietly for a moment, panting, wincing, rubbing her breastbone, making no effort to get up. Something was burning within her chest. My heart is on fire, she thought. Or it could be my lungs. I am consumed in fire from within.

Carefully she attempted to sit up again. This time no hand pushed her back, but still it was a slow process, with much shivering and shaking, and several long pauses while she balanced herself on the tips of her fingers and struggled not to slip backward. She felt very cold. She was grateful that Torlyri was not here to see her weakness, her illness, her pain. No one must see; but especially not Torlyri.

By second sight she groped outside her house and became aware of Threyne passing by, with her boy Thaggoran. Shakily Koshmar called to her, and stood in her doorway, grasping the frame, holding her shoulders back, fighting to make it seem that all was well with her.

"You summoned me?" Threyne said.

"Yes." Koshmar's voice sounded husky and quavering in her own ears. "I need to speak with Hresh. Will you find him and send him here to me?"

"Of course, Koshmar."

But Threyne hesitated, not going off to do as Koshmar had bidden her. Her eyes were veiled and troubled. She sees that I am ill, Koshmar thought. But she doesn't dare ask me what the matter is.

Koshmar glanced at young Thaggoran. He was a sturdy boy, long-limbed, bright-eyed, shy. Though he was past seven he stood half-hidden behind his mother, peering uncertainly at the chieftain. Koshmar smiled at him.

"How tall he's grown, Threyne!" she exclaimed, with all the heartiness she could manage to muster. "I recall the day he was born. We were just outside Vengiboneeza, then, near the place of the water-strider, when your time came. And we made a bower for you and Torlyri saw you through your time of delivery, and Hresh came to give the boy his birth-name. You remember that, do you?"

Threyne gave Koshmar a strange look, and Koshmar felt a new stab of pain.

She must think my mind has softened, Koshmar thought, to be asking her if she remembers the day her own firstborn came into the world. With a hand that she struggled desperately to keep from shaking she reached out and stroked the boy lightly along his cheek. He shrank back from her.

"Go," Koshmar said. "Get me Hresh!"

Hresh was a strangely long time in coming. Maybe he is

off rummaging in the ancient ruins one last time, Koshmar thought. Desperately trying to grab whatever he can still find before the tribe leaves Vengiboneeza. Then she reminded herself that Hresh was mated now, or almost so, and perhaps he was simply deep in coupling or twining with Taniane just now and unwilling to be disturbed. It was odd to think of Hresh as being mated, or twining, or doing any of the things that went with those things. For her he would always be that wild boy who had tried to slip out of the cocoon for a look at the river valley one morning long ago.

Finally he came. He had a rough-eyed, ragged look about him, the look of one who has had no sleep at all. But the moment he saw Koshmar he caught his breath and became suddenly alert, as though the sight of her had shocked him into full wakefulness.

"What has happened to you?" he demanded instantly.

"Nothing. Nothing. Come inside."

"Are you ill?"

"No. No!" Koshmar swayed and nearly fell. "Yes," she said, half-whispering it. Hresh seized her by the arm as she tottered, and guided her to a stone bench covered with furs. For a long while she sat there with her head down, while waves of pain and fever went rolling through her. After a time she said, very quietly, "I'm dying."

"It can't be."

"Step inside my spirit for a moment and feel what I feel, and you'll know the truth."

Hresh said, agitated, "Let me go for Torlyri."

"No! Not Torlyri!"

"She knows the healing arts."

"I'm aware of that, boy. I'm not interested in having her practice her arts on me."

Hresh crouched before her and tried to look her in the face, but she would not meet his eyes.

"Koshmar, no! No! You're still strong. You can be healed, if you'll only allow—"

"No."

"Does Torlyri know how sick you are?"

Koshmar shrugged. "How can I say what Torlyri knows or does not know? She's a wise woman. I've never spoken of this with anyone. Certainly not with her."

"How long have you been like this?"

"Some time," said Koshmar. "It has come upon me slowly." Now she did raise her head, and summoned some of the vigor that once had been hers. In a louder voice she said, "But I didn't summon you here to talk about my health."

Angrily Hresh shook his head. "I know some healing arts myself. If you don't want Torlyri to know, fine. Torlyri doesn't have to know a thing. But let me cast the disease from you. Let me invoke Mueri and Friit and do what you need to have done for you."

"No."

"No?"

"My time has come, Hresh. Let it be as it must be. I won't be leaving Vengiboneeza when the tribe departs."

"Of course you will, Koshmar."

"I command you to cease telling me what I will do!"

"But how can we leave you behind?"

"I will be dead," Koshmar said. "Or nearly so. You will say the death-words over me and you will put me in a peaceful place, and then you will all march away. Is that understood, Hresh? It is my last order, that the tribe is to go forth from this city. But I give it knowing that I will not be among you when you leave. You have spent your entire life disobeying me, but perhaps this one time you'll grant me the right to have my own wishes followed. I want no grief and I want no noise made over me. I am at the limit-age; I am at my death-day."

"If only you would tell me what troubles you, so that I could do a healing—"

"What troubles me, Hresh, is being alive. The cure will soon be offered me. One more word from you of this sort and I'll dismiss you from your post, while I'm still chieftain. Will you be quiet now? There are things I must tell you before I lose the strength."

"Go on," Hresh said.

"The journey the tribe will be taking will be a very long one. That I foresee with death-wisdom, that it will carry you to the far places of the world. You can't make such a journey bearing everything on your backs, as we did when we came here from the cocoon. Go to the Bengs, Hresh, and ask them for four or five young vermilions to be beasts of burden for us. If they are our friends, as they claim so loudly to be, then they'll give them. If they won't give them to you, then ask Torlyri to have her Beng lover steal some, and so be it. Be sure that the ones you get are both male and female, so that in times to come we can propagate our own."

Hresh nodded. "That shouldn't be very difficult."

"No, not for you. Next: there must be a new chieftain. You and Torlyri will choose her. You should pick someone fairly young, and strong-willed, and strong-bodied as well. She will have to guide the tribe through many difficult years."

"Is there anyone you would suggest, Koshmar?"

Koshmar contrived a flickering smile. "Ah, Hresh, Hresh, you are sly to the end! With such respect you ask the dying Koshmar to make the choice, when I know already that the choice is made!"

"I asked you in all honor, Koshmar."

"Did you, now? Well, then: I answer you as you ask, and tell you what you already know. There's only one woman of the tribe who is of the proper age and the proper strength of mind. Taniane is to succeed me."

Hresh once again caught his breath, and bit his lip, and looked away.

"Does the choice displease you?"

"No. Not at all. But it makes what's happening more real. It makes me see more clearly than I would like to that you'll no longer be chieftain, that someone else, that Taniane—"

"Everything changes, Hresh. The sapphire-eyes no longer rule the world. Now, a third thing: will you and Taniane be mated?"

"I've been searching in the chronicles for precedent that would allow the old man of the tribe to take a mate."

"No need for further searching. No need for precedent. *You* are the precedent. She is your mate."

"Is she, then?"

"Bring her to me when you return from the Beng settlement, and I will say the words."

"Koshmar, Koshmar—"

"But tell her nothing about the chieftainship. It is not hers yet, not until you and Torlyri bestow it on her. These things must be done properly. There can be no new chieftain while the old one is still alive."

"Let me try to heal you, Koshmar."

"You annoy me. Go to the Bengs and beg some vermilions of them, boy."

"Koshmar—"

"Go!"

"Allow me to do one thing for you, at least." With fumbling fingers

Hresh unfastened some small object that he had around his throat, and pressed it into her hand. "This is an amulet," he said, "that I took from Thaggoran as he lay dead after the rat-wolves attacked us. It is very ancient, and it must have some strong powers, though I have never been able to learn what they are. When I feel that I need Thaggoran beside me, I touch the amulet, and his presence is close. Keep it in your hand, Koshmar. Let Thaggoran come to you and guide you to the next world." He folded her fingers about it. It was hard-edged and warm against her palm. "He had great love and respect for you," Hresh said. "He told me that many times."

Koshmar smiled. "I thank you for this amulet, which I will keep by me until the end. And then it is yours again. You will not be long deprived of it, I think." She gestured impatiently. "Go, now. Go to the Bengs and ask them for a few of their beasts. Go. Go, Hresh." Then, softening, she touched her hand to his cheek. "My old man. My chronicler."

Noum om Beng appeared to have been expecting him. At least, he showed no surprise when Hresh appeared, breathless, sweaty, having come at a trot all the way from his own tribe's settlement to the Beng village at Dawinno Galihine. The old Helmet Man was in his bare stark chamber, sitting facing the entrance as though anticipating the arrival of a visitor.

A remorseless hammering pounded Hresh's skull from within. His soul was aching from too great a buffeting within too small a compass. His mind whirled from all that had happened in these past few frantic days. And now he must come before old Noum om Beng in what would probably be his final opportunity to speak with him, and there was so much yet to learn. The questions kept multiplying; the answers only retreated.

"Sit," Noum om Beng said, pointing to a place beside him on his stone bench. "Rest. Draw breath, boy. Take the air far down into yourself. Take it deep."

"Father—"

"Rest!" said Noum om Beng sharply. Hresh thought he was going to strike him, as he had so often in the early days of his tutelage. But the old man remained perfectly still. Only his eyes moved, compelling Hresh to motionlessness with a steely glare.

Slowly Hresh drew in his breath, held it, released it, breathed again. In a little while the pounding of his heart diminished and the storm in his mind showed signs of dying down. Noum om Beng nodded. Quietly he said, "When do you leave the city, boy?"

"A day or two more."

"Have you learned all you need to know here, then?"

"I have learned nothing," Hresh said. "Nothing at all. I take in information, but the more I know, the less I understand."

"It is the same with me," said Noum om Beng gently.

"How can you say that, Father? You know everything that there is to be known!"

"Do you think so?"

"So it seems to me."

"In truth I know very little, boy. Only what has come down to me in the chronicles of my tribe, and what I have been able to learn by myself, both in my wanderings and in the application of my thoughts. And it is not enough. It is not nearly enough. It can never be enough."

"This is the last time we will meet, Father."

"Yes. I know."

"You have taught me many things. But all of them indirect, all of them the things that lie behind things. Perhaps the meanings of them will burst into life in my head as I grow older, as I reflect on all you have said here. But today I pray we may speak more directly of the great matters that perplex me."

"We have spoken very directly all the time, boy."

"It does not seem that way to me, Father."

In times gone past such a flat contradiction would have brought him a stinging slap. Hresh waited for one now. He would even have welcomed one. But Noum om Beng remained still. After a lengthy silence he said, as though speaking from a distant mountain, "Then tell me, Hresh: what are these things that perplex you?"

Hresh could not recall another time when Noum om Beng had called him by his name.

Out of the myriad questions that came boiling up out of his mind he sought to choose one, the most important one, before the offer should be withdrawn. But it was impossible to choose. Then Hresh saw on the screen of his mind a gray featureless sea that spread to the horizon and beyond it into the stars, a sea that covered all the universe, a sea that gleamed with a pearly light of its own amid utter darkness. There was a sudden bright spark of flame upon the bosom of the waters.

He stared at Noum om Beng.

"Tell me who created us, Father!"

"Why, the Creator did."

"Nakhaba, do you mean?"

Noum om Beng laughed, that strange parched rasping laugh that Hresh had heard only two or three times before. "Nakhaba? No, Nakhaba is not the Creator, any more than you or I, Nakhaba is the Interceder. Have I not made that clear?"

Hresh shook his head. Interceder? What did he mean?

"Nakhaba is the highest god we know," said Noum om Beng. "But he is not the highest god of all. The highest god, the Creator-god, is unknown, and must always be. Only the gods may know that god."

"Ah. Ah," Hresh said. "And Nakhaba? Who is he, then?"

"Nakhaba is the god who stands between our people and the humans, and speaks with them on our behalf when we have failed to meet the demands of our destiny."

Hresh felt himself lost in realms beyond realms.

Despair, disbelief, confusion threatened to overwhelm him.

"A god who stands between us and the humans? Then the humans are higher than the gods?"

"Higher than *our* gods, boy. Higher than Nakhaba, higher than the Five. But not higher than the Creator, who made them as well as us and all else. Do you see the hierarchy?" Noum om Beng drew vast structures in the air with the tip of a finger. The Creator here, at the highest place, the great Sixth of whom Hresh had once speculated; and here the humans, some distance below; and here Nakhaba; and here the Five; and here, lower than all the others though higher than the wild beasts, at least, were the common folk of the world, the cocoon-folk, the furry folk.

Hresh stared. He had asked for revelation, and Noum om Beng had given him revelation unstinting. But he could not absorb it; he could not digest it.

Seeking some familiar corner, he said, "So you accept the Five? They are gods for you as well as for us?"

"Of course they are. We give them other names, but we accept them, for how could we not? There must be a god who protects, and a god who provides, and a god who destroys. And a god who heals, and a god who comforts. And also a god who intercedes."

"A god who intercedes, yes. I suppose."

"That is the one god you came to forget, your people. The

one who stands above the other five and reaches higher yet, and speaks on our behalf with *them*."

"Are the humans gods too, then?"

"No. No, I do not think so," said Noum om Beng. "But who is to say? Only Nakhaba has ever seen a human."

"I think I have," said Hresh.

Noum om Beng chuckled in his rasping way. "Madness, boy."

"No. In our cocoon, during the days of the Long Winter, there was one who always slept, who lay by himself in a cradle in the central chamber. Ryyig Dream-Dreamer is what we called him. He was very long and very pale and pink, without any fur, and his head rose high above his forehead, and his eyes were purple, with a strange glow. It was said that he had always lived with us, that he had come into the cocoon on the first day of the Long Winter, in the time when the death-stars began to fall, and that he would sleep until the day the winter ended; and then he would sit up and open his eyes and prophesy that we must go forth into the world. After that he would die. So it was said, long ago, and written in the books of our chronicles. And all this actually came to pass, Father. I saw him. I was there on the day he awoke."

Noum om Beng was staring at him with a strange fixity of vision, his whole face rigid, his red eyes gleaming. The old Helmet Man's harsh breathing seemed to grow louder and louder, until it sounded like the panting of some approaching beast.

Hresh said, "I think the Dream-Dreamer was a human. That he was sent to live with us, to watch over us, through all the Long Winter. And that when the winter ended his work was done, and he was summoned by his people."

"Yes," Noum om Beng said. He was quivering like a bow-string drawn overtaut. "So it must have been, and why did I not see it? Boy, shall I tell you something? There was a Dream-Dreamer in our cocoon too. We had no idea what sort of creature he was, but we had one just as you did. Long ago, before I was born, if you can imagine a time so long ago. And we had what you call a Barak Dayir also. There are tales of such things in our chronicles. But our Dream-Dreamer awoke early, while ice still held the world. He led us forth and he perished, and our Wonderstone was taken by the hjjks. Nakhaba has guided us well and we have achieved greatness despite our loss, with greater things yet to come: for all the world will be Beng, boy, that much I see clearly. Yet our task has been much heavier because we have not had a Barak Dayir in these later years. Whereas your people—you, boy—having possession of that magical thing—"

Noum om Beng's voice trailed away. He stared at the floor.

"Yes? Yes? What is the destiny of my people?"

"Who knows?" the old Helmet Man said, sounding suddenly very weary. "Not I. Not even Nakhaba, perhaps. Who can read the book of destiny? I see our own: yours is unclear to me." He shook his head. "I never thought that our Dream-Dreamer might have been a human, yet now I see that your guess has much strength, that your guess has virtue. That must be what he was."

"I know that he was, Father."

"How can you know that?"

"By a vision I had, using a machine I found in Vengiboneeza, that showed me the Great World. It showed me sapphire-eyes and vegetals and all the other races. And it showed me humans, too, walking these very streets; and they looked just like our Dream-Dreamer Ryyig."

"If that is so, then I understand many things that were unclear to me before," Noum om Beng said.

That astounded Hresh, that he should be the one to make things known to Noum om Beng, and not the other way around. But still he was baffled. He sat in silence, trembling.

Noum om Beng said, "Guard your stone, boy. Swallow it, if you are endangered. It is an essential thing. We have had to struggle twice as hard for our greatness, or more, because we have been careless of ours."

"And what is the Barak Dayir, then? I had heard it was a thing made in the stars."

"No. It is a human-thing," Noum om Beng said. "That is all I can tell you. Something older even than the Great World. A device that the humans made, so I realize now, and gave to our kind, to use in many ways. But what those ways are, I have never known, and you have only begun to learn."

Hresh reached for the amulet of Thaggoran at his throat, for he felt great tension and fear oppressing him. But then he remembered that he had given the amulet to Koshmar, to see her through her dying hours.

He said, "I wish we were not leaving Vengiboneeza so soon, Father."

"Why? The world is waiting for you."

"I want to stay here with you, and learn all that you can teach me."

Noum om Beng laughed again. Without warning his thin stem of an arm came up and he dealt Hresh an open-handed slap that bruised his lip and numbed his cheek.

"*That* is all I can teach you, boy!"

Hresh licked at a sweet spot of blood on his lower lip. Softly he said, "Shall I go now, then? Is that what you want?"

"Stay as long as you wish."

"But you will answer no more of my questions?"

"You have more questions, do you?"

Hresh nodded, but said nothing.

"Go on. Ask."

"I must be tiring you, Father."

"Ask. Ask. Anything, boy."

Hesitantly Hresh said, "You told me once that the gods repay all our striving by sending death-stars, so that nothing has any meaning. I called this a flaw in the universe, but you said no, no, the universe is perfect, and we are the ones who are flawed. But it still seems like a flaw in the universe to me. And you said also that we must go on striving anyway, though you did not know why. You told me that I must find that out, and when I did I should come and tell you what I had learned. Do you remember, Father?"

"Yes, boy."

"Not long ago I had another vision of the Great World, using a different device from the one that showed me the humans. I had that vision only this night past, Father. What I saw was the last day of the Great World, when the first death-star came and the sky turned black and the air grew cold. The humans were already gone, I could not tell you where, and the hjjks were heading for the hills, and the vegetals were dying and the sea-lords were about to die and the mechanicals were going off to die elsewhere. But the sapphire-eyes, though they knew they were coming to the end of their time, were altogether untroubled by what was happening around them. They showed no fear and they showed no distress. Nor did they do the slightest thing to deflect the falling death-stars from the world, though surely that must have been within their power. I am unable to understand that, Father. If I knew why the sapphire-eyes were able to accept their doom without seeming to care, I might be able to tell you why we must strive ever onward even though the gods will some day destroy all we have built."

Noum om Beng said, "What is the name by which you call your god who is the Destroyer?"

Hresh blinked in surprise. "Dawinno."

"Dawinno. What do you understand of Dawinno, then? Do you think that he is an evil god?"

"How can a god be evil, Father?"

"You have answered your own question, boy."

Hresh did not see that he had. He sat blinking, waiting for some further illumination. But none was forthcoming. Noum om Beng was smiling at him amiably, almost smugly, as if quite certain that he had given Hresh the key to all that troubled him.

Behind his smile the old Helmet Man's face was gray with fatigue; and Hresh himself felt the strength of his mind taxed to its limit. He dared not ask for further explanation. Here I will stop, Hresh thought. Already he had burdened himself with so much that it would take him years, so it seemed to him then, to comprehend it all.

He rose to go. "I should leave now, Father, and let you rest."

"I will not see you again," Noum om Beng said.

"No, I think not."

"We have done good work together, boy. Our minds were well met."

"Yes," Hresh said. There was a strange ring of finality in Noum om Beng's tone that made Hresh wonder how much longer the old Helmet Man could hope to live. From him radiated an awareness of imminent death, and a deep acceptance of it, too, that made him as tranquil as any sapphire-eyes who had watched the sky grow black with the rain of dust that the death-star had flung up. Hresh, who only this morning had heard Koshmar speak so blandly of her oncoming end, felt himself surrounded on all sides by mortality today. How could they be so accepting, these dying folk? How could they shrug their shoulders in the face of oblivion?

Uncertainly Hresh moved toward the door, not really wanting to leave so soon, but knowing he must.

Noum om Beng said, "Was there not another errand for which you came here this morning, other than to speak with me?"

Yissou! The vermilions!

Hresh's face blazed with shame. "There was, yes," he said lamely. "Koshmar asked me—our chieftain—she wondered if—whether we could have—if it would be possible to have—"

"Yes," Noum om Beng said. "We foresaw the need. It is already arranged. Four young vermilions are yours, two males, two females, our parting gift. Trei Husathirn will bring them an hour from now, and he will instruct your people in how to control them, and how they are bred. That was all, was it not, boy?"

"Yes, Father."

"Come here, Hresh."

Hresh went forward and knelt before the old Helmet Man. Noum om Beng raised his hand as though to strike one last blow; but then he smiled, and softened the movement of his arm, and touched his hand lightly to Hresh's cheek in an unmistakable gesture of the deepest affection. With the slightest of nods he indicated that this was the moment for Hresh to take his leave. No other word was said between them; and when Hresh paused at the door to look back and his eyes met the red ones of Noum om Beng it seemed to him that Noum om Beng no longer saw him, that he no longer had any idea who Hresh might be.

It was midday by the time Hresh reached the settlement. The sun hovered in a cloudless sky. Hresh felt the full heat of the day settling upon him like a blanket. The wintertime of frost and cold winds was lost in the infinitely remote past. His fur was dusty and sweaty from his hasty journeys between the settlement and Dawinno Galihine, his head throbbed, his eyes were raw. It seemed to him that he had not slept for a month.

There was furious activity in the plaza, for the dismantling of the settlement was nearing its climax. Parcels were being dragged from the houses, crates were being hammered shut, the wheels of the newly constructed wagons were being oiled. He saw Orbin tottering under three immense bundles, Haniman hammering like a madman, Thrrouk smashing a hole through the wall of a building half as old as time so that some parcel too wide for the door could be shoved through the opening. Though there had been some murmuring against the decision to depart—Haniman seemed to be the chief opponent of the idea, and some of the others whom Hresh had seen that night kneeling to the Dream-Dreamer statue—no one was holding back from the work of making ready for the trek. The People's instincts of cooperation were too deeply engrained.

Taniane stepped out of Koshmar's house and waved to him from the threshold.

"Hresh! Hresh, here!"

He went to her. She was holding herself strangely, as if she had injured her back: her shoulders were pushed up high, her elbows were close to her sides. Her lips were quivering. She was wearing a blood-red sash that he had never seen before.

"What is it?" Hresh said. "What's wrong?"

"Koshmar—"

"Yes, I know. She's very ill."

"She's going to die. If she hasn't died already. Torlyri is with her. She wants you in there too."

"Are you all right, Taniane?"

"This frightens me. It'll pass. Are *you* all right?"

"I've had no sleep. I've been to the Bengs to ask them to give us vermilions. Trei Husathirn will be bringing them in a little while."

"Who?"

"Torlyri's man. Let me go in."

She held him a moment, her hands to the insides of his arms where they bent at the elbow. The embrace, glancing though it was, sent a hot current of energy flowing between them. He felt the strength of her love and it sustained him in his weariness. Then Taniane stepped aside and Hresh entered the chieftain's little cottage.

Torlyri sat beside Koshmar. The offering-woman's head was bowed, and she did not look up as Hresh came up behind her. Koshmar's eyes were closed; her arms were crossed over her breasts; she still held Thaggoran's amulet gripped tightly in her clenched fingers. She appeared to be breathing. Hresh let his hand rest on Torlyri's shoulder.

The offering-woman said, "It is all my fault. I never knew she was this ill."

"I think the disease came upon her very swiftly."

"No. She must have had it a long while. It was eating her from within. And I knew nothing of it until today. How could I have failed to see it, even when we twined? How could I have been so negligent of her?"

"Torlyri, these are not useful questions now."

"In just this past hour she has begun to slip away. She was still conscious this morning."

"I know," Hresh said. "I was here to speak with her, early this morning. She seemed ill then, but nothing like this."

"You should have found me and told me!"

"She said no one was to know, Torlyri. In particular you were not to know."

Torlyri looked up at that, her eyes wild, frenzied, in a way that was almost impossible for Hresh to associate with the calm gentle Torlyri he had known all his life. Angrily she said, "And you did as she ordered you!"

"Should I not obey my chieftain? Especially when it's her dying wish?"

"She is not going to die," Torlyri said firmly. "We'll heal her, you and I. You know the arts. You will add your skill to mine. Go: get the Barak Dayir. There must be some way it can be used too to help us save her."

"She's beyond our help," said Hresh as gently as he could.

"No! Get the Wonderstone!"

"Torlyri—"

She glared fiercely at him. The hardness and determination went suddenly from her then, and she began to sob. Hresh crouched down by her side, putting one arm across her shoulders. Koshmar made a far-off sighing sound. Perhaps it is the last murmur of her life, Hresh thought. He found himself hoping that it was. Koshmar had suffered enough.

Torlyri said, not looking at him, "I came to her this morning and I saw she was ill, and I said that I would do a healing with her, and she denied that anything was troubling her. Too weak to stand, and she said it was nothing, that I should go elsewhere and see if anyone needed my services! I reasoned with her. I argued with her. I told her that this was not her time to die, that she had many years yet to live. But no, no, she would have none of it. She ordered me away. There was no way I could sway her. She is Koshmar, after all: she is an unstoppable force, she will have whatever she must have. Even if what she must have is death." Lifting her head, Torlyri turned tormented eyes on Hresh and said, "Why does she want to die?"

"Perhaps she is very tired," Hresh suggested.

"I could do no healing on her against her will, not while she was conscious. But now she can't resist, and you and I, working together—get the Wonderstone, Hresh, get the Wonderstone!"

Koshmar's clenched hand opened and the amulet of Thaggoran fell from it to the floor.

Hresh shook his head. "You want a miracle, Torlyri."

"She can still be saved!"

"Look at her," he said. "Is she breathing?"

"Very faintly, but yes, yes—"

"No, Torlyri. Look more closely. Or use your second sight."

Torlyri stared. She rested her hand a moment on Koshmar's chest. Then she seized Koshmar by both her shoulders and pressed her cheek where her hand had been, calling the dead chieftain's name over and over. Hresh stepped back, wondering if he should leave but fearing the extent of Torlyri's grief. After a while he came forward again and delicately lifted Torlyri from Koshmar's body, and stood holding her, letting her sob.

The offering-woman grew calm sooner than Hresh expected. Her sobs ceased, her breathing became regular again. She lifted her head and nodded at Hresh, and smiled.

"Is Taniane outside?" she asked.

"She was. I think she's still there."

"Get her," Torlyri said.

Hresh found her waiting on the porch, still standing in that odd huddled way. "It's over," he said.

"Gods!"

"Come in. Torlyri wants you."

They entered the house together. Torlyri stood by the wall

where the masks of the chieftains were hung. She had taken down Koshmar's own mask, made of a shining gray wood with the eye-slits painted dark red, and held it in her left hand. In her right was Koshmar's wand of office.

"We have much to do today," Torlyri said. "We must devise a new rite, for this is the first time in memory that a chieftain has died other than by coming to her limit-age, and we will need words to send her on to the next world. I will attend to that. And also we must invest a new chieftain. Taniane, this wand is yours. Take it, girl! Take it!"

Taniane looked dazed. "Shouldn't there be—an election?"

"You have already been chosen. Koshmar herself accepted you as her successor, and made that known to us. This is your crowning-day. Take Koshmar's mask and put it on. Here, take it! And the wand. And now we must go forth, all three of us, so that everyone will know what has happened, and what will happen next. Come. Now."

Torlyri looked back quickly at Koshmar. Then she slipped one hand into the crook of Taniane's arm and the other into Hresh's, and drew them both from the death-chamber. She moved briskly, with an assurance and a firmness that Hresh had not seen in her for a long while. They stepped outside into the brilliant midday sunlight, and instantly all work stopped, all eyes turned toward them. There was an eerie silence in the plaza.

And then the tribesfolk came running, Threyne and Shatalgit and Orbin, Haniman and Staip, Kreun and Bonlai, Tramassilu, Praheurt, Thhrouk, Threyne and Thaggoran, Delim, Kalide, Cheysz, Hignord, Moarn, Jalmud, Sinistine, Boldirinthe—every-one, the oldest and the youngest, some with tools in their hands, some carrying babes, some clutching their midday meals, and threw themselves down before Taniane, calling her name as she held her wand of office high. Torlyri did not relinquish her hold on Taniane and Hresh. She clung with all her strength, and her grip was a painful one. Hresh wondered if she held this tightly to keep from falling.

But after a little while she released them and pushed Taniane forward to move among the tribe.

Taniane was glowing.

"There will be a ceremony this evening," Torlyri said in a strong, clear voice. "Meanwhile your new chieftain accepts your loyalty, and thanks you for your love. She will speak with you, one by one." To Hresh she said more quietly, "Let us go inside again," and drew him toward her. They reentered the cottage. Koshmar seemed merely asleep. Torlyri bent to scoop up Thaggoran's fallen amulet, and put it in Hresh's hands. It had not been gone from his possession more than a few hours.

"Here," she said. "You'll want this on the trek."

"We should postpone the departure," Hresh said. "Until the rites are done, until Koshmar has been decently laid to rest."

"All that will be dealt with this evening. There should be no postponement." Torlyri paused. "I have been teaching Boldirinthe as much as I can of the offering-woman's duties. Tomorrow I will teach her the highest mysteries, the secret things. And then you must go."

"What are you telling me, Torlyri?"

"That I mean to stay behind, and cast my lot with the Bengs. With Trei Husathirn."

Hresh's mouth opened, but there was nothing he could say.

"I might have gone, if Koshmar had lived. But she is gone and I am released, do you understand? So I will stay. The Helmet Man cannot leave his people, so I will become one of them. But I will still say the morning prayers for you, as though I made the journey with you. Wherever you go, you will know that I am watching over you, Hresh. Over you and all the tribe."

"Torlyri—"

"Don't. Everything is very clear, for me."

"Yes. Yes, I understand. But it will be hard, without you."

"Do you think it will be easy for me, without all of you?" She smiled and beckoned to him, and he stepped into her arms, and they embraced like mother and son, or perhaps even like lover and lover, a long intense embrace. She began to sob again, and then her sobbing ceased, just in time, for in another moment he would have started too.

Releasing him, Torlyri said, "Let me be alone with Koshmar a little while now. And then we must meet, and devise the rites that need to be devised. At the temple, in two hours. Will you be there?"

"At the temple, yes. In two hours."

He left the cottage once again. Taniane, far away across the plaza, was surrounded by fifteen or twenty of the tribe. They were close to her and yet hanging back, as if fearing the flame of her sudden exaltation. Taniane still wore Koshmar's mask. All the plaza now was bathed in fierce noon light that devoured all shadow, and the heat still seemed to be rising. Behind him Koshmar lay dead, and Torlyri beside her bowed in grief. Hresh glanced to his left and saw four immense vermilions plodding down the road into the settlement, with Trei Husathirn riding atop the lead male. Tomorrow we will leave this place, Hresh thought, and I will never see Koshmar again, or Torlyri, or Noum om Beng, or the towers of Vengiboneeza. Somehow it all seemed right to him. He had passed beyond weariness into a place of utter calm.

He went to his room. He drew the Barak Dayir from its pouch and fondled it, and asked it to give him strength. A human-thing,

527

it was. Not a star-thing. So Noum om Beng had said. Older than the Great World, it was.

Hresh studied it, trying to read the signs of its great age in its sheen, in its pattern of intricately carved lines, in the warm glow of the light that dwelled within it. He put his sensing-organ to it and its music rose up like a column around him. It carried his mind easily and smoothly upward and outward, so that he had a view of everything that surrounded Vengiboneeza. He saw here, and he saw there, and at first it was all a marvel and a mystery to him, but then he came to see how to contain his wonder and look upon only a portion of the overwhelming whole; and then he was able to find meaning in what he beheld. He looked to the south, and saw the rim of a perfect circle rising in a meadow, and a little settlement within that circle. He saw Harruel in that settlement, and Minbain his mother, and Samnibolon who was his half brother, and all the others who had gone with Harruel on the Day of the Breaking Apart. This was their settlement, which they called the City of Yissou. Hresh knew all that by seeing with the Barak Dayir. Then Hresh looked the other way, far to the north, toward the place where he knew he must look in order to see what he must see, and he beheld a great herd of vermilions on the march, heading south, making the ground shake as though the gods were pounding it; and with the vermilions were hjjk-folk, a countless army of them, heading south also, taking a route that would bring them inevitably to the City of Yissou. Hresh nodded. Of course, he thought. The gods who rule us have devised things so this will come to pass, and who can hope to understand the gods? The hjjk-men are on the march, and Harruel's settlement lies in their path. Very well. Very well. That was only to be expected.

He descended from the heights and released the Barak Dayir from his sensing-organ, and sat quietly for a time, thinking only that this had been a very long day, and even now it had barely reached its midpoint. Then Hresh closed his eyes, and sleep took him swiftly, like a falling sword.

Salaman had seen the assault on the City of Yissou so many times now in visions that the actual event, as it descended upon the city, seemed overfamiliar to him and roused little emotion at first in his breast. Some weeks had passed since the sudden attack by that small advance troop of hjjk-folk, that ill-fated band of fore-runners; and every day since then Salaman had gone up on the high ridge with Weiawala and Thaloin to twine and cast forth his mind so that he could observe the advance of the oncoming army. Now they were almost here; and now they could be seen without the aid of second sight.

Bruikkos was the first to spy them—for lately Harruel had had sentries watching all day and all night on the rim of the crater.

"Hjjks!" he cried, running pell-mell down the crater trail into the city. "Here they come! Millions of them!"

Salaman nodded. There might have been a cold stone in his breast.

He felt nothing. No fear, no joy of battle, no sense of prophecy fulfilled. Nothing. Nothing. He had lived through this moment too many times already.

Weiawala, trembling against him, said, "What will happen to us? Will we all die, Salaman?"

He shook his head. "No, love. We will each kill ten thousand thousand hjjks, and the city will be saved." He spoke in a flat, unemotional way. "Where is my spear? Give me some wine, sweet Weiawala. Wine makes Harruel fight better; it may be the thing for me also."

"The hjjks!" came the hoarse cry from without. Bruikkos was banging on doors, pounding on walls. "The hjjks are coming now! They're here! They're here!"

Salaman took a deep pull of the dark, cool wine, strapped his sword about his waist, seized hold of his spear. Weiawala too picked up weapons: there was no one who would not fight today, except the small children, who had been put in one place to look after each other. Together Salaman and Weiawala left their little house.

The day was chilly after a long spell of warm, humid weather. A strong breeze came from the north. There was a dry harsh scent riding on that breeze, hjjk-scent, oppressive and insistent, the smell of old wax and rusting metal and dead crackling leaves; and beneath that pungent odor lay another, broad and deep and full, the rich musky scent of vermilions, with which the odor of the hjjks was interwoven as scarlet threads of bright metal might be interwoven in a cloak of heavy wool.

Harruel, fully armed, came limping out of his half-charred palace. Since the day of the first hjjk attack he had gone about everywhere in that lumbering, lopsided way, although so far as Salaman knew the only wound Harruel had received had been in his shoulder. That wound had been bad enough, though Minbain had doctored it with herbs and poultices and by this time it was little more than a ragged red track through Harruel's thick fur.

But Salaman wondered whether perhaps Harruel had had some other wound that day, a deeper one, a wound to the heart, that had crippled him somehow. Certainly he had seemed even darker and more bleak than usual ever since, and he walked in this strange new uneven manner, as though he no longer had the strength of spirit to keep his hips on a level plane.

Now, though, Harruel grinned and waved almost jovially as he caught sight of Salaman. "D'ye smell that stink? By Yissou, we'll clear the air of it by nightfall, Salaman!"

The prospect of war seemed to have brightened Harruel's soul. Salaman nodded an acknowledgment to him and raised his spear in a halfhearted gesture of solidarity.

Harruel must have detected Salaman's indifferent mood. The king clumped over to Salaman and clapped him lustily on the back, a blow of such bone-shivering violence that Salaman's eyes flashed with wrath and he came close to returning it with all his force. But it was meant merely as encouragement. Harruel laughed. His face, looming high above Salaman's own, was flushed with excitement.

"We'll kill them all, lad! Eh? Eh! Dawinno take them, we'll slaughter the bugs by the millions! What d'ye say, Salaman? You saw this coming long ago, eh? Your second sight is true magic! D'ye see victory just ahead for us?" Harruel reared about and signaled to Minbain, who lurked somewhere near the portico of their house. "Wine, woman! Bring me some wine, and make a hurry of it! We'll drink to victory!"

Weiawala, under her breath, said to Salaman, "What does he need more wine for? He's drunk already!"

"I'm not sure that he is. I think he's just intoxicated with the thrill of making war."

"The thrill of dying, you mean," Weiawala said. "How can we survive this day, any of us?"

Salaman gestured wryly. "Then it's dying that excites him, I suppose. But this is a Harruel reborn that we see here today."

Indeed Salaman began then to realize that he too was at last awakening to the thing that was coming upon them this day. His apathy, his torpor, was falling away. He was ready to fight, and to fight well, and if necessary to die bravely. Feeling his soul surging suddenly within him, Salaman understood some of what must be taking place within Harruel.

The first intrusion of the hjjks must have been a hard and bitter disturbance for him. Harruel's kingship, his manhood itself, had been jeopardized. The child Therista had been slain; the woman Galihine had been wounded so gravely that she would have been better dead; the palace had been set ablaze; most of the meat-animals had been set free and it had taken forever to round them up again. Even though the enemy had been turned back in total defeat, everyone knew that a far greater army was on the way and the city could not possibly withstand it. Harruel's little world had been impinged upon from without and soon it would be destroyed.

In these weeks just past the king had been in a somber state indeed. Harruel had steeped himself so deep in drink that the city's stores of wine had been all but depleted by his guzzling alone. Limping and solitary he had roamed the perimeter of the crater night after night, roaring in drunken rage. He had fought a bloody fistfight with Konya, who was his most loyal and dearest follower. He had summoned every woman of the tribe to his couch, sometimes three of them at once, and yet, so the report was, he had not been able to achieve a coupling with any of them. In his more sober moments he had spoken broodingly of the sins that he had committed and of the punishment that he merited, soon to be meted out by the hjjks. Which left Salaman wondering what sins *he* had committed, or Weiawala, or the infant Chham; for everyone would die together when the hjjks overran the City of Yissou, the wicked and the innocent alike.

Still, they had done all they could to prepare for the hopeless struggle that was coming. There had not been time enough to complete the palisade around the crater rim, but they had built a smaller one of sharpened stakes lashed with vines that completely enclosed the city's inhabited zone. Just within it was a wide and deep trench, bridged by planks that could be removed if the invaders came close. A narrow new trail had been cut through the underbrush from the city's southern side to the densest part of the forest that grew on the crater's slope; if all else failed, they could slip away by ones and twos and try to lose themselves in the woods until the hjjk-folk grew bored with the search and moved along.

More than that the defenders could not do. There were only eleven of them, of which five were women and one of those wounded, and a few half-grown children. Salaman expected this to be the last day of his life and it seemed quite clear to him that Harruel's vigor and animation this day stemmed from the same expectation. But though Harruel had plainly grown weary of life, Salaman had not. More than once in these recent days Salaman had thought of taking Weiawala and Chham and slipping away toward Vengiboneeza and safety before the hjjks arrived. But that would be cowardly; and that was probably foredoomed, too, for it was many weeks' march to Vengiboneeza, assuming he could find it at all, and in that great wilderness what chance did a man and a woman and a child stand against the many creatures of the wilds?

Stand and fight; fight and die. It was the only way.

Salaman doubted that the hjjks intended them any particular harm. His one encounter with the insect-folk, that time long ago in the plains just after the tribe had gone forth from the cocoon, had left him with the belief that the hjjks were remote, passionless creatures incapable of such complex irrational feelings as hatred, covetousness, or vengefulness. The ones who had attacked the city had fought in a curiously impersonal, detached way, caring very little about their lives, which had reinforced Salaman's view of them. The hjjks were interested only in maintaining their control. In this case they seemed to be merely on some great migration, and the City of Yissou happened to be in their way, posing unknown but definite danger to their supremacy; so they would eradicate it, as an inconvenience. That was all. The hjjks would probably suffer great losses today. But because there were so many of them, they would prevail.

Harruel's plan was for everyone but the infants and the injured Galihine to wait for the enemy on the rim of the crater. When the invaders came close, the defenders would withdraw to the forested zone just below the rim, and attempt by main force to kill every hjjk that succeeded in clambering over the hastily improvised barricade of brush and thorny vines with which the tribe had surrounded the crater. If too many hjjks got through, they were to retreat closer to the city's inner palisade; and as the situation grew even more perilous they would either hole themselves up within the city and try to withstand the hjjk siege, or else take the southern trail into the woods and hope to remain scattered and hidden until it was safe to emerge.

All of these stratagems seemed absurd to Salaman. But he could think of nothing better himself.

"Everyone to the rim!" cried Harruel in a mighty voice. "Yissou! Yissou! The gods protect us!"

"Come," Salaman said quietly. "To our posts, love."

He had asked for and received the sector of the rim closest to his special place, that high place from which he had first had the vision of the onrushing horde. He felt a deep affinity for that place, and since it seemed certain to him that he would die like all the others in the first hjjk charge, he had chosen that part of the rim to be the place where he would fall. In silence he and Weiawala clambered to it now.

When they reached the rim they halted, for just beyond it was the tangle of thorny stuff that they had so painfully woven there in the past few days to slow down the hjjks' advance. But then a strange burst of curiosity, a sudden overmastering Hreshlike impulse toward the unexpected, came over him, and he vaulted the rim and began cleaving a path for himself through the thorns.

"What are you doing?" Weiawala called. "You aren't supposed to be out there, Salaman!"

"I have to see—one last look—"

She called out something else to him, but her voice was taken by the wind. He was past the barricade now, and running toward his high place. Breathless, stumbling, he scrambled to it.

Everything lay visible to him from here.

To the south were rounded green hills. To the west was the distant sea, a golden streak in the early afternoon sun. And to the north, where a high broad plateau stretched on and on toward the horizon, he saw the invaders. They were still perhaps an hour's march away, maybe two, but there was no question of their direction: they were heading straight for the great meadow in which the crater lay. And they were innumerable. Vermilions and hjjks, hjjks and vermilions, an astonishing parade poured out of the north, a line of them that went beyond Salaman's ability to see. There was a central column of vermilions, packed close together, nose of one up against the tail of the one before it; a wide column of hjjks flanked the beasts on either side; and then two more columns of vermilions made up the outer edges of the advancing force. Both the insect-beings and the giant shaggy beasts moved in rigid formation and at a steady pace.

Salaman raised his sensing-organ and reached out with second sight to enhance his perception of the oncoming force. At once it gave him the full oppressive power of the enemy, the immense weight of the numbers.

But what was this? He sensed something unanticipated, something discordant, cutting across the massive emanations coming from the invading army. He frowned. He looked to his right, into the thick forest that separated this district from the land where Vengiboneeza lay.

Someone was coming from that direction.

He strained to stretch the range of his second sight. Bewildered, astonished, he searched for the source of that unexpected sensation. He reached out—farther—farther—

Touched something radiant and powerful that he knew to be the soul of Hresh-of-the-answers.

Touched Taniane. Touched Orbin. Touched Staip. Touched Haniman. Touched Boldirinthe.

Praheurt. Moarn. Kreun.

Gods! Were they all there? The whole tribe of them, coming from Vengiboneeza this day? Marching onward toward the City of Yissou? He could not detect Torlyri, he could not detect Koshmar, and that puzzled him; but now he felt the others, dozens of them, everyone who had come from the cocoon with him at the Time of Going Forth. All of them here, all of them approaching.

Unbelievable. They are just in time, he thought, to be swept away with us by the hjjks. We all came forth together; and now we will all die together.

Gods! Why had they come? Why *today*?

The day of departure from Vengiboneeza had finally arrived, weeks after the decision to go had been proclaimed, like a thunderclap coming long after a devastating bolt of lightning. After all the weeks of grueling toil, when it had begun to seem that the dismantling of the settlement would go on forever without end, the time of leaving was at last at hand; what was yet undone must now remain forever undone; once again the People would be making a great Going Forth.

Taniane wore the new mask that the craftsman Striinin had made, the Mask of Koshmar: powerful jaw, heavy lips, great out-curving cheeks, dark gleaming surface of burnished black wood, a likeness not of the late chieftain's face but of her indomitable soul, through which the somber, penetrating eyes of Taniane came shining like windows that opened into a vista of windows. In her left hand Taniane held the Wand of Coming Forth, which Boldirinthe had unearthed among the relics of the trek from the cocoon; in her right was Koshmar's obsidian-tipped spear. She turned toward Hresh.

"How much longer until sunrise?"

"Just another few minutes now."

"The instant we see the light, I'll raise the wand. If anyone looks hesitant, send Orbin to give them a prod."

"He's already back there, checking everybody over."

"Where's Haniman?"

"With Orbin," said Hresh.

"Send him to me."

Hresh beckoned down the line toward Orbin, and pointed to Haniman and nodded. The two warriors spoke briefly; then Haniman came jogging up to the front in his strangely heavy-footed way.

"You want me, Hresh?"

"Only for a moment." Hresh's eyes met Haniman's and held there. "I'm aware that you aren't eager to be going with us."

"Hresh, I never—"

537

"No. Please, Haniman. It's no secret to me that you've been grumbling about the Going Forth ever since Koshmar made the proclamation."

Haniman looked uncomfortable. "But have I ever said I didn't plan to go?"

"You haven't said it, no. But what's in your heart hasn't been much of a secret. We don't need any malcontents on this trek, Haniman. I want you to know that if you'd prefer to stay behind, then stay."

"And live among the Bengs?"

"And live among the Bengs, yes."

"Don't be ridiculous, Hresh. Wherever the People go, I'll go too."

"Willingly?"

Haniman hesitated. "Willingly," he said.

Hresh reached out his hand. "We'll need you, you know. You and Orbin and Staip—you're our strong ones, now. And we have plenty of work ahead. We're going to build a world, Haniman."

"Rebuild a world, you mean."

"No. Build one from scratch. Everything's starting over. There's nothing left of the old one except ruins. But for millions of years humans have been building new worlds on the ruins of the old. That's what we'll have to do, if we want to think of ourselves as humans."

"If we want to think of ourselves as *humans*?"

"As humans, yes," said Hresh.

The first red glow of dawnlight appeared suddenly over the crest of the mountain wall.

"Ready to march!" Taniane called. "Shape it up! Hold your places! Everyone ready?"

Haniman trotted back to his place. Taniane and Hresh stood at the front of the line, with the warriors behind them, and then the workers and the children, and to the rear were the heavily laden wagons that the huge docile vermilions would pull. Hresh glanced back at the great mist-shrouded towers of Vengiboneeza to the rear, and the vast shoulder of the mountain behind them. A few Bengs stood near the edge of the settlement, looking on in silence. Torlyri was with them. She wore a helmet, a small graceful one of red metal, gleaming mirror-bright. How strange that was, Torlyri in a helmet! Hresh saw her lift her hand in holy signs: the blessing of Mueri, the blessing of Friit, the blessing of Emakkis. The blessing of Yissou. He waited, and as she made the final blessing, that of Dawinno, their eyes met, and she sent him a warm smile of love. Then he saw tears flood her eyes, and she turned away, moving behind the helmeted Bengs and passing from sight. "Sing!" Taniane cried. "Everyone sing! Here we go. *Sing!*"

That had been weeks ago. Now glorious Vengiboneeza seemed but a fading memory, and Hresh no longer mourned having left its wondrous treasures behind. He had not adapted as well to the heavy double loss of Koshmar and Torlyri. Torlyri's warmth and Koshmar's vigor both had been cut away as if by some dire surgery, and a great open place in the tribe remained where they had been. Hresh still sensed Torlyri's faint presence hovering over the tribe as it moved west and south from Vengiboneeza; but Koshmar was gone, gone, utterly gone, and that was very hard.

No one questioned Taniane's leadership, or his. They marched at the head of the tribe. Taniane gave the orders, but she consulted frequently with Hresh, who chose the line of march each day. It was easy enough for him to find the route, for, even though some four full cycles of the seasons had gone by since Harruel's little band had passed this way, the echoes of their souls still remained in the forest, and Hresh, with only the slightest aid of the Barak Dayir, heard them without difficulty and followed their signal. Now that they were emerging from the forest he had no need of the Wonderstone to guide him to Harruel. The king's dark soul, down there in the meadow, was sending out a strident, inescapable music.

"Only a little while longer," Hresh said. "I feel their presence all around me."

"The hjjks?" Taniane asked. "Or Harruel and his people?"

"Both. The hjjks in infinite numbers, to our north. And Harruel's city straight ahead, and below us, in that circular formation on the meadow. At the center, where it's dark with vegetation."

Taniane stared, as though without seeing. After a time she said, "Can this succeed, Hresh? Or will we all be swallowed up by those million insects?"

"The gods will protect us."

"Ah, and will they?"

Hresh smiled. "I have asked each one individually. Even Nakhaba."

"Nakhaba!"

"I would ask the god of the hjjks to be kind to us too, if I knew his name. The god of the vermilions. The god of the water-striders, Taniane. The gods of the Great World. The unknown and unknowable Creator-god. One can never have too many gods on one's side." He caught her by the fleshy part of the arm, and pulled her close to him, so that she could see the conviction that glowed in his eyes. In a low voice he said, "All the gods will defend us today, for what we do is their bidding. But especially will we be defended by Dawinno, who cleared away an entire world so that we might inherit it."

"You seem so certain of that, Hresh. I wish I could be as certain as you are."

Certain? For one wild moment he felt swept with doubt, and he wondered if he believed any of what he was saying. The reality of what they had chosen to undertake seemed suddenly now to be coming home to him, and his will, which had carried them this far, seemed to be weakening. Perhaps it was the emanations of those numberless far-off hjjks that were battering his soul. Or perhaps it was simply the awareness of the unending work that must be done to create all that which he hoped to create.

He shook his head. They would prevail today, and in all the days that followed. He thought of his mother Minbain down in that meadow, and of Samnibolon his brother by Harruel, who was carrying the name of Hresh's long-dead father into a new era. He would not let them die this day.

"Here we should make camp," he told Taniane. "Then you and I will go on alone, and set up the defensive measures."

"And if some enemy finds us and we perish while we're out there by ourselves, who will lead the tribe then?"

"The tribe had leaders before us. The tribe will find leaders after us. In any case, nothing will harm us while we do what must be done." Hresh took her by the arms, as she had taken him that day of Koshmar's death, and sent strength to her. Taniane's shoulders straightened, her chest rose to her deepened breath. She smiled and nodded. Turning, she gave the signal to halt for the night.

It took an hour to get everything settled down. Then, leaving Boldirinthe and Staip in command, Hresh and Taniane slipped away a little to the west and from there moved to their right, edging around in a northward way toward the shovel-shaped plain that lay between the hjjk-folk and the settlement that Harruel had founded. The shadows were lengthening by the time Hresh came to the place that seemed best, where they could look down into that circular-walled place where Harruel had chosen to dwell. From this distance Hresh saw that that circular formation was a crater of some sort, very likely formed by the impact of something massive falling from a great height. In all probability this was a place where a death-star had landed. Hresh pondered that, wondering if the substance of the death-star might even still be buried there. But he had no time to investigate that now.

They had brought with them a thing of the Great World, Hresh carrying one end and Taniane the other: that hollow tube of metal, hooded at one end, with a region of incomprehensible blackness held captive within that hood, and brilliant light sizzling and hissing at its entrance. Hresh held it by the hooded end, Taniane by the other. The metal was warm to the touch. Hresh wondered what magics were locked within this thing, and how he could ever explore them without being carried away to whatever place it was the tube sent those who approached it.

"Here, do you think?" Hresh asked.

"A little closer to the settlement," said Taniane. "Then if this plan of yours succeeds and the hjjks are cast into confusion we can fall upon them from one side and Harruel and his warriors from the other."

"Good," Hresh said. "We'll go a little closer. And the plan will succeed, Taniane. I know it will."

They went on a short way. Now darkness was coming on. Taniane indicated a place a little higher than the rest, where there was a flat rock on which they could mount the tube, and other rocks around to prop it upright. Hresh guided it into position. The moment it was upright it came alive, crackling with light and mystery. He felt once again the insidious temptation of the thing, its artful pull. But he was ready for it and he shrugged it away. Stepping back, he tested the device by tossing a stone toward its hood. The circlet of lights flashed blue and red and wild purple, and the stone vanished in midair.

Hresh muttered thanks to Dawinno. He was grateful to the god for favors received; but also now he was beginning to grow pleased with himself. This was going well.

"What will bring the hjjks?" Taniane asked.

"Leave that to me," said Hresh.

Harruel could not understand what was going on. All night long he and his tribe had waited on the crater's rim, watching the hjjks come closer and closer, and then halt at sundown, with the obvious intent of marching onward toward the crater when morning came. He had expected that he would die today when the City of Yissou took the full brunt of the hjjk-folk attack, and in truth he was not only willing to die but eager, for the savor of life had gone from him. Now it was dawn-time and the attack had come, more or less. Yet he had thought, and Salaman and Konya also, that the hjjks would attack in a methodical, brutally orderly way, as mere ants might do: for that was all they were, ants of a sort, though much enlarged and with far greater intelligence.

But instead the hjjks seemed to have gone crazy.

Their route of march was leading them straight toward the heart of the crater. But now, as Harruel watched dumbfounded, they were breaking ranks. Their formation was shattering into a wild and formless swarm. He stared, bewildered, as the hjjks ran this way and that on the plain, forming little groups that instantly broke and coalesced again and broke again. All of them were milling aimlessly about one group that seemed to hold its place in the center of the entire heaving mass.

Was it a trick? To what purpose?

And the vermilions appeared to have gone berserk also. At the first light of dawn Salaman had come to him with the puzzling news that he had seen the giant beasts all go thundering off toward the west and disappearing into the rough terrain of ravines and landslides that lay out there. But a little while later it became clear that only about half the vermilions had done that. The rest had broken ranks and were wandering everywhere on the northern plain in twos or threes, or simply by themselves. Complete confusion prevailed. It was still perilous to have so many beasts of that size anywhere near the city. But one thing looked certain: the hjjks would not be able to drive an organized force of the monsters down into the crater as beasts of war. The hjjks had lost control of their vermilions entirely. And, so it seemed, they had lost control of themselves.

Harruel shook his head. "What can be doing this?" he asked Salaman.

"Hresh, I think."

"*Hresh?*"

"He is somewhere nearby."

"Have you gone mad too?" Harruel cried.

"I felt him last night," said Salaman. "As I sat on the high place, where I first had the vision of this army that now thunders all around us. I sent out my second sight and I felt Hresh close by, and others of Koshmar's tribe too, nearly all of them. Except only Koshmar, and Torlyri. They had followed our path through the forest and they were just east of the city."

"You are as crazy as those hjjks," Harruel growled. "Hresh here? The People?"

"Look out there," Salaman said. "Who could have done this to the hjjks and their vermilions? Who but Hresh? My first vision was a true one, Harruel. Trust me on this."

"Hresh," Harruel muttered. "Coming here to fight our war for us? How can this be? How? How?"

He stood staring, trying as the sun rose higher to make some sense out of the incomprehensible thing that was happening to the north. The light that came rolling from the east now brightened half the plateau. There was definitely a center to the melee: the hjjks appeared all to be struggling to reach some place a little higher than the rest, where already a tremendous chaotic mass of the insect-folk had gathered. Harruel sought to find Hresh somewhere about, but of him there was no sign. Salaman must have dreamed him, Harruel thought.

Thaloin came running up from the eastern rim, gesturing in alarm.

"Harruel! Harruel! The hjjks, to our east side! Konya's holding them off, but come! Come!"

"How many?"

"Just a few. No more than a hundred, I think."

Salaman laughed. "A hundred is only a few, is that it?"

"Few enough, compared with what's out there on the plateau." Harruel seized Salaman's shoulder roughly and shook it. "Come, let's go to Konya's aid! Thaloin, send the word around the rim that the hjjks are trying to break through from the east!" Turning, he rushed off toward the battle zone.

Thaloin's estimate, Harruel found, was off by more than a little. Perhaps three hundred hjjks—a party of strays, breaking off from the confused main mass of their people—had come blundering up the side of the crater. They had a few vermilions with them, not many, but enough to trample down the breastworks of brambles that had been placed outside the rim to hold invaders back. Konya, looking immense, casting a long shadow, was ranging up and down along the rim itself, slashing at great-beaked yellow-

and-black soldiers who bobbed up here and there at the edge. Nittin was with him, and, to Harruel's surprise, so was Minbain, and their son Samnibolon. All were thrusting away vigorously at the attackers.

The king drew in his breath sharply and went plunging into the midst of the group, shouting his war-cry: "Harruel! Harruel!"

A hjjk rose up before him, waving his shining jointed limbs. Harruel cut away an arm with one quick stroke of his blade, and brought his spear around to push the hjjk back down the hill. Another appeared in its place, and Harruel cut that one down too. A third fell to Salaman, standing close by him. Harruel looked to his side and saw Samnibolon bravely hacking away. Once more he fought brilliantly for a child, with speed and agility far beyond his years.

"Harruel!" cried the king, in full heat of battle now. "Harruel! Harruel!"

He looked down, past the slope of the crater. There were hjjks straggling about everywhere along the slope, hundreds of them. But they had no plan, and they were moving in a ragged, aimless way. He had no doubt that they could be dealt with, one by one, or if necessary by twos and threes, as in that earlier battle.

The rest of the hjjks, the great preponderant mass of them, still kept converging on that high point in mid-plateau. The site was boiling like an ant-hill now. For an instant the frenzied swarms parted, and Harruel caught sight of something metallic glinting at the midst of everything, and saw a flash of harsh light of many colors; and then the hjjks went piling inward again and whatever lay at the center of the swarm-zone was once more hidden from his view. It seemed to him also that other hjjks, more distant ones, were streaming *away* from the site of battle now—heading back northward, or eastward into the forest, or around the side of the crater and off to the south—anywhere, so long as it was not here, so long as they could get away from this scene of madness that must be so repellent to their orderly spirits.

There was hope, then. If the defenders of the city could only hold the crater against this relative handful of hjjk warriors, they might yet get out of this day alive!

Harruel, grinning, dispatched two more hjjks that appeared like wraiths right in front of him.

Then Salaman tapped his arm. "Do you see there? There, Harruel? At the edge of the forest?"

Turning to the east, Harruel stared in the direction Salaman indicated. At first he saw nothing, for he was looking into the fiery glare of the morning sun. But then he covered his eyes and tried by second sight, and yes, yes—

People there. Familiar ones. Orbin, Thhrouk, Haniman, Staip, Praheurt—warriors all. Hresh. Taniane. The People! Emerging from the forest, coming out onto the crater approach. Fighting their way toward the city, cutting down stray hjjks as they came. Allies! Reinforcements!

A mighty cry escaped Harruel's throat.

The gods had not forsaken him! They had sent his friends to help him in this day of danger! He was forgiven for all his sins, he was redeemed, he was spared!

"Yissou!" he cried. "Dawinno!"

"On your left, Harruel," said Salaman suddenly.

He looked around. Five hjjks, and a vermilion that loomed like a mountain. Harruel hurled himself savagely into the midst of them, laying about him on all sides. Salaman was with him too, and Konya was coming.

Something touched him like fire on the arm that had been wounded. He whirled, saw a hjjk reaching out again to rip open his flesh a second time, and slashed its throat in two. Then he felt a blow against his back. They were all around, sprouting like weeds on the hillside! Salaman called his name and Harruel turned again, striking as he moved. No use. No use. They were everywhere. The vermilion reared and snorted. When its huge feet came down they flattened a hjjk. Harruel laughed. He struck and struck again. Too soon to give up hope. One by one we will kill them all, yes! But then something jagged sliced across his back, and something else just as sharp took him in the thigh. He began to quiver in shock. He heard voices, Salaman's, Konya's, Samni-bolon's. His name, over and over. He swayed, nearly fell, steadied himself, took a few stumbling steps. He swung his blade, fiercely cutting air. He meant to go on fighting until he dropped. All he could do was fight. The city would survive, even if he did not. He was forgiven; he was redeemed. "Dawinno!" he cried. "Yissou! Harruel!" Blood streamed across his forehead. Now he called on Yissou no longer, but on Friit the healer; and then on Mueri who gave comfort. Still he fought on, chopping, hacking. "Mueri," he cried, and then again, "Mueri," more softly. There were too many of them. That was the only problem: there were too many of them. But the gods had forgiven his sins.

Hresh had never felt such confidence as he had in that moment of gathering darkness on the night before the battle, alone in that broad meadow with Taniane. He had taken the Barak Dayir from its pouch—Taniane staring close at it, her eyes glowing with that mixture of fear and keen curiosity that she had shown whenever he had bared the Wonderstone to her—and placed it in the curve of his sensing-organ.

"Be still while I do this," he told her.

AT WINTER'S END

He closed his eyes. Reached out into the army of hjjks— gods, there were myriads upon myriads of them!—and searched patiently among them, picking and sorting through their dry, dis- pleasing spirits until he found what he sought: one pair who had turned aside from the march in order that they might yield to the coupling impulse. In all that multitude there had to be at least a few who would pause to give in to that. And indeed Hresh was able to find more than a few.

One couple in particular were deeply enmeshed in the act, heart and soul, beaks and limbs and abdomens and thoraxes all convulsing as they embraced each other. Hresh shuddered. The female was larger than the male, and she held her mate in a fierce and strange grip, as though she meant not to couple with him but to devour him. From his body small swift organs had emerged and were moving over her lower part with a startling nervous quickness. It was a frightful, alien thing. And yet as he watched Hresh began to find it not so alien. Their forms and limbs and organs were very different from anything he knew, yes, but the impulse that drew them together was not too far from that which made Taniane attractive to him, or he to Taniane. The two of them emitted a potent emanation of desire for union, the hjjk equiva- lent of lust, Hresh thought. And a second emanation that denoted the fulfillment of desire: the hjjk equivalent of passion.

Good. Good. It was what he had hoped to find.

From those two coupling insect-beings Hresh had drawn the essence of their lust-emanation and their passion-emanation, and pulled it by way of the Barak Dayir deep into his own soul. Once he had incorporated it it no longer felt at all alien to him; he understood it, he respected it. He might just as well have been a hjjk-man himself, at that moment.

But he had not kept those essences within himself for long. He

549

spun them forth, he wove them into a column of whirling force that rose to the heavens like a giant tower; and he set that tower in place around the metal tube that he had brought with him from Vengiboneeza.

Then he reached into the camp of the invaders a second time, and found a female vermilion who had come into heat that day. She stood with her back to a lofty tree, uttering horrifying roars and snorts of endearment and stamping her black-clawed feet and flapping her vast ears about like great sheets in the breeze. Three or four gigantic scarlet males jockeyed uneasily about her. Hresh slipped between them and took from her the essence of her heat, and drew that into himself also, and made it fifty times more intense. This he formed into a column too, and set it in place far to the west, where the plateau tumbled off into a broken area of streams and jumbled boulders.

"There," Hresh said to Taniane. "Everything's ready now. I've done all I can. The rest is in the hands of the warriors."

That had been only a few hours ago, in the darkest of the night.

Dawn had come, and with it the battle. And now it was all over.

Hresh walked through the battlefield with Taniane at his side, and Salaman, and Minbain. No one spoke. A mist of death and confusion had settled over everything, and a great silence, and words seemed beside the point.

The hjjks were gone. Hresh could not say how many of them had vanished into the tube of strange light and even stranger darkness, but it must have been thousands of them, perhaps many thousands. In a terrible mad frenzy they had rushed toward the thing and leaped all over it, but it had engulfed them with an insatiable appetite as they came within its range of power, and they had disappeared. The rest of them, those who had not been attracted to the device or who had run from it in fear, were gone also, fled to all the corners of the earth. And those few who had tried to scale the sides of the crater had been killed by Taniane's warriors as they came rushing past, or slain at the top by Harruel's defenders waiting there.

The vermilions too had stampeded off elsewhere. Of all that astounding horde perhaps a dozen were still to be seen, shambling about in a lost purposeless way here and there on the plateau. Good: they could be rounded up, they could be domesticated for the tribe's own uses. Of the others, it seemed that the males without exception had raced into the western hinterlands questing after the impassioned female that they thought to find there, and the females, puzzled or perhaps angered by that lunatic stampede, had gone off on journeys of their own, back to the wilderness from which the hjjks had taken them. In any case there were none hereabouts.

Hresh smiled. It had worked so well! It had worked perfectly!

And the little city—the City of Yissou, that was what they called it—the city was safe.

He looked around. Haniman sat quietly against a pink boulder, dabbing now and then at a cut on his forehead. He was glassy-eyed with fatigue. He had fought like a demon, had Haniman. Hresh had not known there was such strength in him. A little way from him lay Orbin, deep in sleep. He clutched the severed leg of a hjjk in one hand, a grisly trophy. Konya slept too. Staip. It had been a day of terrible conflict.

Hresh turned to Salaman. This quiet warrior whom he had scarcely known in the old days now seemed transformed, enlarged, a man of strength and wisdom and power, a giant.

"Will you be king now?" Hresh asked. "Or call yourself by some other title?"

"King, yes," Salaman said quietly. "Over a tribe that can be numbered on the fingers of two hands. But I will be king, I think. It is a good name, king. We respect kings, in this city. And we will call the city Harruel, in honor of him who was king before me, though Yissou will still, I hope, be its protector."

"He was the only one slain?" said Hresh.

"The only one. He went among the hjjks where they were thickest, and killed them as though he were swatting flies, until there were too many of them for him. There was no way we could get to him in time. But it was a brave death."

"He wanted to die," Minbain said.

Hresh turned to his mother. "You think so?"

"The gods gave him no peace. He was ever in torment."

"He was radiant at the last moment," said Salaman. "I saw his face. There was light coming from it. Whatever torment he was in, it had gone from him in his last moments."

"Mueri ease his soul," Hresh murmured.

Salaman gestured toward the city. "Will you stay with us awhile?"

"I think not," Hresh said. "We will feast with you tonight, and then we'll move on. This is your place. We should not occupy it long. Taniane leads us southward, and we will find a home for ourselves there, until we know where the gods mean to carry us next."

"Taniane is chieftain, then," said Salaman in wonder. "Well, it was what she dreamed. How did Koshmar die?"

"Of sadness, I think. And weariness. But also of knowing that she had completed her task. Koshmar lived nobly and died nobly too. She brought us out of the cocoon to Vengiboneeza, and she sent us onward from there to our next destination, as the gods meant her to do. She served them well, and us."

"And Torlyri? Is she dead too?"

"The gods prevent it!" Hresh said. "She stayed behind of her own will, to live among the Bengs. She is a Beng now, she says. When last I saw her she wore a helmet, do you believe it? Love has transformed her." He laughed. "Her eyes will turn red, I think, like theirs."

Minbain came up to him. "And you, Hresh—what will you do? If you would do what will please me, you will stay behind also. Live here with us. Will you do that? This is a fine place."

"And leave my tribe, Mother?"

"No. All of you, stay! The People reunited!"

Hresh shook his head. "No, Mother. The tribes must not be rejoined. You are all Harruel's people now, with a destiny of your own. What it is, I cannot say. But I will follow Taniane, and we will go to the south. There is a great deal for us to do. All the world is there for us to discover and win. There is much I want to learn, still."

"Ah. Hresh-full-of-questions!"

"Always, Mother. Always."

"Then I will never see you again?"

"We thought we had parted once forever, and look, here we are together. I think I'll see you once more. And my brother Samnibolon, too. But who knows when that will be? Only the gods."

Hresh walked away from them, to be by himself for a time before the feasting began.

This has been a strange day, he thought; but, then, every day has been strange, since that first day of strangeness long ago when I took it into my head to sneak outside the cocoon, and the ice-eaters began to rise under our cavern, and the Dream-Dreamer awoke and cried out. And now Harruel is dead and Koshmar is dead and Torlyri is a Beng and Taniane is a chieftain and Salaman is a king, and I am Hresh-full-of-questions who is also Hresh-of-the-answers, the old man of our tribe. And I will continue my Going Forth, until the ends of the earth, and Dawinno will be my guardian.

The cool wind of this high country blew refreshingly about him. His mind was clear and open and peaceful. A vision arose in it as he stood by himself, a vision of the Great World, achieved now without the aid of any of the machines he had brought with him out of Vengiboneeza. He simply saw it before him, as though he had been transported to it by magic. It was a vision once again of the Great World on its last day, with darkness in the air and black winds blowing and frost overtaking everything; and he was not an observer this time, but a citizen of that lost world, a sapphire-eyes, in fact. He felt the heaviness of his great jaw, and the ponderousness of his immense thighs and tail. And he knew that this was the last day of the Great World, did that sapphire-eyes who was Hresh-full-of-questions. No sapphire-eyes would survive the time that was drawing nigh. The gods had sent a death upon their world.

And Hresh as Hresh understood that it was Dawinno the Destroyer whose day it was that day, while Hresh as sapphire-eyes waited peacefully for his end. The chill that was entering his body would travel inward until it took his life. Dawinno, yes. The god who brought death and change, and also renewal and rebirth. At last Hresh understood what Noum om Beng had been trying to tell him. It would have been a sin against Dawinno to attempt to deflect the death-stars that were heading toward the world. The sapphire-eyes had known that. They abided by the law of the gods. They had not tried to save themselves because they knew that all cycles must run their course, and they must go from the world to make room for those who were to come.

Yes. Yes, of course, Hresh thought. I should have realized that without needing so many slaps from Noum om Beng. I am very clever, he thought, but sometimes also I am very slow. Thaggoran might have explained all these matters to me, if he had lived. But Dawinno had called Thaggoran also to himself; and so I had to learn all this on my own.

He smiled. Another vision was coming alive within his soul: a shining city on a distant hillside, glowing in all the colors of the universe, blazing in light so radiant that it stunned the soul to see it. Not a city of the Great World, this one, but a new city, a city of the world yet to come, the world that he would bring into being. Deep surging music rose from the earth and enveloped him. It seemed to him that Taniane stood beside him.

"See, there," he said. "That great city."

"A sapphire-eyes city, is it?"

"No, a human city. Which we will build, to show that we too are human."

Taniane nodded. "Yes. We are the humans now."

"We will be," Hresh said.

He thought of the golden ball of quicksilver, and the machines it controlled. Miracles, yes. And not *our* miracles. But we will use them in forging a miracle of our own. For us, he thought, it will be an endless Going Forth. Now the task begins, the struggle to prevail, the mastery of ancient skills and new ones, the long upward climb. He would lead the way, and he would say to the others, "Follow me there," and they would follow.

Hresh looked toward the south. In one of the nearest hills there he made out a disturbance on one slope. He saw something huge struggling there, emerging from the earth. It looked almost as though an ice-eater was breaking through from the depths. Could it be? An ice-eater? Yes. That was what it was. An ice-eater, perhaps one of the last to get the word that the New Springtime truly had come. The monstrous creature was breaching the surface now, tossing trees and earth and great slabs of rock to this side and that. Hresh saw its blind face, its black-bristled body. And now it had broken through; and now it lay gasping in the sunlight, dying. Hresh watched, and as he watched the vast bulk of the subterranean creature split apart, and tiny creatures—or at least they seemed tiny at this distance—came from it by the dozens, by the hundreds, little shimmering things, coiling and wriggling busily, an army of small serpents born out of the great dead thing of the former world. Its young, yes. Not hideous like their colossal progenitor, but delicate and strangely beautiful, bright gleaming creatures, blue and glossy green and velvet black, moving in tracks of shining light. Rushing off into the sunlit day to take up the life that was offered them here at winter's end. Renewal and rebirth, yes. Renewal and rebirth everywhere.

So even the ice-eaters would survive, after a fashion, in the new world. The prophecy had said they would die when the long winter ended, but the prophecy had been wrong. They would not die. They would only be transformed. Out of winter's bleak decay new life and beauty could come. Hresh offered them a blessing, the blessing of Dawinno.

How he wished he could tell Thaggoran that!

He laughed, and took Thaggoran's amulet in his hand.

"Oh, Thaggoran, Thaggoran, if I started telling you everything that I have learned since the night the rat-wolves came, it would take me as many years to tell you as it has taken me to live it," he said aloud. "See? The ice-eaters—that's what they become. And the Great World—I've seen it, Thaggoran, and I know why it let itself die in peace. And the Bengs—let me tell you about the Bengs, Thaggoran, and about Vengiboneeza, and—" He clutched the amulet tightly. "I've not done so badly, have I, Thaggoran? I've learned a thing or two, eh? And someday, I promise you, you'll hear it all from me. Someday, yes. But not soon, eh, Thaggoran? We'll sit and talk as we did in the old days. But not soon!"

Hresh turned and began to walk back toward the City of Yissou. It would be time soon for the feast. He would sit with Taniane on his right hand, and Minbain on his left, and if these people of Harruel's had any wine in their city he would drink all he could hold, and then some more, for this was a night of celebration such as had scarcely ever been seen. Indeed. He walked more briskly, and then he began to trot, and then to run.

Behind him, ten thousand thousand newborn ice-eaters, glistening with life, glided away to celebrate their birth into the New Springtime of the world.

ABOUT THE AUTHOR

R obert Silverberg is one of science fiction's most beloved writers, and the author of such contemporary classics as *Dying Inside*, *Downward to the Earth* and *Lord Valentine's Castle*. He is a past president of the Science Fiction and Fantasy Writers of America and the winner of five Nebula Awards and five Hugo Awards. In 2004 the Science Fiction and Fantasy Writers of America presented him with the Grand Master Award. Silverberg is one of twenty-nine writers to have received that distinction.

EBOOKS BY ROBERT SILVERBERG

FROM OPEN ROAD MEDIA

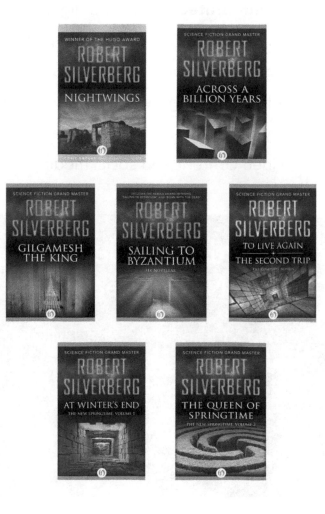

Available wherever ebooks are sold

OPEN ROAD
INTEGRATED MEDIA

Open Road Integrated Media is a digital publisher and multimedia content company. Open Road creates connections between authors and their audiences by marketing its ebooks through a new proprietary online platform, which uses premium video content and social media.

CPSIA information can be obtained
at www.ICGtesting.com
Printed in the USA
LVHW04s2330270818
588360LV00001B/21/P

9 781480 448506